Doug —

Thought you'd enjoy
a mystery in "your own
backyard"!

Happy Birthday

Love,

Eddie and Jeanne

STOLEN IDENTITY

A Suspense
Thriller

Brian Regrut

INTERVARSITY PRESS
DOWNERS GROVE, ILLINOIS 60515

InterVarsity Press® is the book-publishing division of InterVarsity Christian Fellowship®, a student movement active on campus at hundreds of universities, colleges and schools of nursing in the United States of America, and a member movement of the International Fellowship of Evangelical Students. For information about local and regional activities, write Public Relations Dept., InterVarsity Christian Fellowship, 6400 Schroeder Rd., P.O. Box 7895, Madison, WI 53707-7895.

Cover illustration: John Walker

ISBN 0-8308-1371-3

Printed in the United States of America ∞

Library of Congress Cataloging-in-Publication Data

Regrut, Brian, 1946-
    Stolen identity/Brian Regrut.
      p.   cm.
    "A suspense thriller."
    ISBN 0-8308-1371-3
    I. Title.
    PS3568.E47614S76   1993
813'.54—dc20   93-20046
                                        CIP

17	16	15	14	13	12	11	10	9	8	7	6	5	4	3	2	1
07	06	05	04	03	02	01	00	99	98	97	96	95	94	93		

"Greater love has no one than this,
that he lay down his life for his friends."
JOHN 15:12

To Joan and Dad and Mom who encourage me;
to Dean, Amy, Jon, Dale and Kara who inspire me;
to Carrie who helps me better appreciate God's faithfulness;
and to Syd and Lee and Hugh who showed me that good service
begins with a willingness to serve.

1

Encircling the District of Columbia, the way a track encircles a high-school football field, the Capitol Beltway separates the players in the game of national politics from the spectators who live and work beyond the sixty-five-mile ring of concrete and asphalt. It is a ribbon of highway that ties together dozens of the once-sleepy bedroom communities of Virginia and Maryland. But beyond the oaks, poplars, maples and pines that line much of the road, glass and steel boxes look down on the inner and outer loops—endless thoroughfares that teem with traffic day and night.

Even after the morning and evening rush hours, delays are not infrequent, and on this Thursday night in March, hundreds of cars had slowed to a crawl on the northbound, inner loop in Virginia's Fairfax County. An eighteen-wheeler, carrying stainless steel pipes to a distributor in Baltimore, had been traveling in the right lane approaching Gallows Road when a car from an inner lane cut directly in front of it, in an attempt to make the exit. The driver of the truck slammed on his brakes. He swerved left and then right. His load, unable to handle the maneuver, strained against the nylon straps that held the six-inch, thirty-foot-long tubes. One strap snapped, then another. Like pick-up sticks dropped on a table, the pipes spewed across all four lanes while cars—some successfully, some not—dodged to avoid them. The incident and subsequent cleanup extended the evening rush into the night.

Traveling south toward the site of the accident, Virginia State Police Captain Ron Davidson was passing Tysons Corner when he picked up a line of cars traveling over sixty-five miles per hour. Pulling in behind them in the third lane from the shoulder, Davidson was about to begin timing the cars for speeding violations. Neither the speeders nor those they passed realized that the gray Monte Carlo at the back of the line was one of the state's high-performance, unmarked, traffic-control vehicles. Obviously the driver in the far left lane, who was rapidly closing down on the trooper, didn't realize it either.

Checking his rearview mirror, Davidson calculated the car was doing ninety or better. As it passed, Davidson flipped on his siren. His high beams pulsated on and off. Two brilliant blue lights flashed from behind the grill. He wrenched the wheel to the left and floored the accelerator. Brake lights lit up on the first four cars he passed.

The black Porsche 911 that had sped by was widening its lead over the police car, as both passed over the huge U.S. 50 interchange and headed south toward Gallows Road. The Porsche swerved left onto the narrow strip of blacktop that separated the driving lanes from a menacing four-foot-high concrete wall. It swerved back onto the roadway as it passed slower cars.

Davidson gunned the Monte Carlo, pulled onto the smooth blacktop shoulder and prayed that no one would cut in front of him. His flashing lights had the positive effect of persuading drivers to steer their cars to the right and allowed him to keep the Porsche in sight while he called for assistance.

On the inner loop, two miles south, just beyond the clogged overpass, Harold Greer sat at the wheel of his fully loaded propane tanker. He was hoping soon to get out of first gear. For forty-five minutes he had been starting and stopping as the cars in front of him slowly merged into the left lane and crept by the steel-tube pickup crew. Greer liked this straight, flat section of the beltway better than any of the others. This was where traffic usually moved well and where only the lights of a few houses could be seen beyond the leafless trees that for most of the year created the illusion of a rural interstate. Unlike the concrete barrier that separated the inner and outer loops for many miles before and after this section, here the median widened and grass sloped gently down to an intermittent line of hedges that divided the two roadways.

Greer peered past the trucks, buses and cars that spewed noxious fumes into the cold night air. He had just merged to the third lane from the right shoulder, squeezing between a truck laden with drums of phosphorus and a Chevy Lumina. To his right, awaiting a chance to merge, was another tanker weighted down with 8,400 gallons of gasoline. Greer could just make out the accident scene ahead when he saw the flashing lights of an approaching police car far in the distance. Rubbernecking had slowed the southbound traffic at Gallows Road. The driver of the southbound Porsche was distracted by the activity on the roadway and the sea of headlights on the inner loop. During the second he took his eyes from the road to view the incident on his left, his Porsche covered 186 feet. When he looked forward again, he couldn't believe his eyes.

A dark Lincoln Town Car had pulled in front of him and was braking hard. The Porsche's driver wrenched the steering wheel to the left, but not soon enough to avoid clipping the back of the Lincoln with his bumper. The impact sent his car careening across the grass median. He pulled back hard to the right, but his wheels grabbed in the soft dirt and the Porsche rolled sideways through a gap in the hedge toward the immobilized line of cars on the other side. It was still traveling at over sixty miles an hour when it ripped into the front fender of a Camry, flipped into the air and skidded upside down across the sedan's roof. For the horror-filled onlookers who sat trapped in their steel and glass boxes, time stood still as the Porsche showered the contents of its ruptured gas tank on a red Escort just before it ripped a four-foot hole in Harold Greer's tanker.

"Oh, my God, no . . . No . . . No . . ." Captain Davidson was blinded by the ignition of 8,800 gallons of propane. He slammed on his brakes and swerved onto the median. In the seconds it took for the Monte Carlo to slide to a stop in the grass, Davidson's hand dropped from the steering wheel to the microphone's cradle. He didn't see the mushroom cloud rise from the inner loop's roadway. Before the microphone reached his mouth, he felt the pressure of the explosion lift the 3,000-pound police car and flip it over. Defensively, his left hand reached his eyes just as a thousand pebbles of glass ripped into his hands, face and chest.

Blood spilled from a hundred wounds as Davidson pleaded into the radio. "Help me . . ." Then his head dropped onto the radar console to the right of the steering wheel.

*   *   *

As he approached the Braddock Road interchange, heading north on the inner loop, Fairfax County policeman Derek Masters saw the deep blue evening sky explode into daylight. Ahead, to his right, the leafless branches of a hundred oaks and poplars were silhouetted against the glow that seeped through the trees and spilled across the asphalt.

Instead of exiting as he had planned, Masters continued north and called in what he had just seen. Two miles from the scene the fire storm came into view. "This is unbelievable," he breathed. Masters pulled onto the inside shoulder and raced along the concrete barrier. When the barrier ended, he continued to drive along the narrow grass median. Closing in on the inferno, he finally had to brake for cars driving across the median to the safety of the outer loop.

Before Masters could unbuckle his seat belt and open his door, a second explosion momentarily blinded him. He refocused in time to see chunks of flaming steel shower down into the white-hot caldron of molten metal fed by the phosphorus and gasoline from the trucks that had flanked Greer's tanker. A dazed driver emerged from the car in front of Masters, the man's face painted with disbelief and confusion. He looked at the flashing blue lights atop Master's patrol car, glanced back at the gray Escort he had just smashed, turned his eyes back to the policeman and started running. He was quickly swallowed by the headlights of a hundred soon-to-be-abandoned cars.

"I'm leaving my vehicle," Masters said into the radio mike clipped to his shirt. He stepped out onto the concrete less than 200 yards from the inferno.

The stench of seared flesh and burning tires filled Deputy Master's nostrils as he ran toward the disaster unfolding on the roadway before him. Fear and disbelief took turns working on his mind and stomach. Frantic motorists zigzagged toward him, looking like shadow puppets dancing in a grade-school presentation. Masters could see their terror-filled eyes set in blackened, bloodied faces as they passed in front of headlights. Their screams of pain were barely audible above the roar of the fire. Screening his face from the heat, Derek Masters moved forward.

* * *

Mike Downes sat in the warm glow of his richly appointed family room in his house in Richmond's prestigious West End. As he had done nearly every night since his wife's death, he tackled two mounds of paperwork while his CD player shuffled a stack of jazz, classical and contemporary discs. Most of the once-tall pile of papers had been moved and sorted into piles on the larger table to his right. The aroma from a newly poured mug of coffee wafted through the cherry-paneled room. He had no way of knowing that because of the horror unfolding on the Capitol Beltway 100 miles away, he would not soon enjoy another quiet evening at home.

* * *

Far from the conflagration on the beltway, Elizabeth Boget hung up the phone, swept up nine-month-old Kristin and headed out of the bedroom. It was almost 8:45 p.m. and none of her five children had made a move toward getting to bed. She stormed into the rec room and barked at her two boys, "Why aren't you getting ready for bed? Turn off that TV! Jonathan, get in and take your bath. Daniel, is your homework done? Where's Lauren?"

The rising pitch of her voice let the boys know that their plea to finish their program would be futile, but Daniel, the eight-year-old, was never willing to give up without a fight. "But we're watching—"

"Now!" Elizabeth interrupted. With a whining Kristin on her hip, she walked to the television set and punched the on/off switch. The picture faded just as the program was being interrupted with news of the beltway fire. Elizabeth reached down and lifted Daniel off the floor by his shirt collar. Pointing him toward the door, she gave him a firm but gentle push.

"Why do you kids always take advantage of me when I'm on the phone?" she asked the boys who were scurrying out the door. "And where's Lauren?" Her tone now was decidedly unfriendly. And loud.

Thirteen-year-old Lauren put down her book, opened the door to her room and meekly asked, "Are you looking for me?"

"Yes, I'm looking for you," Elizabeth growled, her naturally deep voice dropping an octave. "Don't you see what time it is? Is your report done?"

"Well, almost," her daughter said.

Her mother glared at her. "How much is almost?"

Dropping her chin to her chest, Lauren muttered, " 'Bout half." She knew what her mother was thinking and decided to extricate herself from the situation as quickly as possible. "But I've done the hardest half."

Elizabeth didn't ask what half that was. "You better get to bed now."

Fifteen minutes later, after overseeing the tooth brushing, bathing, clothes picking up and praying, Elizabeth tucked the two youngest into bed. Lauren had changed Kristin's diaper and handed the little girl to her mother as Elizabeth emerged from the boys' room. David, as was his nightly routine, was down in the kitchen making his second sandwich since dinner.

Elizabeth nursed Kristin and dropped her into bed. She said good night to Lauren and headed to the kitchen, where David was just opening his geometry textbook. Looking like a wilted flower, Elizabeth slumped into a chair at the kitchen table. David didn't look up. He was afraid that he might become the object of another tirade. But his mother's fight was gone.

"Here I thought with your father gone, we would get finished with supper early, get homework done, read a book and all get to bed at a decent time." Her tired voice drifted off. "What happened?"

David knew that his mother really didn't want a reply, she just wanted to vent some frustration before going to bed. Elizabeth picked up the evening paper and spread it out on the table. She thumbed through it quickly, not allowing anything to register in her overworked brain, then finally folded it up and dropped it on a chair.

"Good night, David," she said as she stood up. She straightened her 5′9″ frame, not wanting to think about the fact that her figure was being silently and relentlessly rearranged by multiple births, five nursing babies and gravity. She didn't know exactly how forty-one was supposed to feel, but tonight she felt every year of her age.

David's smile helped, but not much. "Good night, Mom," he said.

*   *   *

Two thousand miles away Debbie Steinbaugh was locking the door to the Garden of the Gods branch of Rocky Mountain Savings. As she climbed into her Mustang, she flipped on the radio, just missing the seven o'clock news and the report of the fiery crash in northern Virginia. She was one workday away from the weekend and the start of her Mexican vacation. There were clothes to wash and bags to pack, but those would be jobs for tomorrow night. Now she was on her way to pick up her two girls and take them out for a late dinner.

The thirty-six-year-old divorcée wanted to take her children to Mexico with her, but their father had said no. George Steinbaugh and his new wife, Martha, were not yet sure that the change in Debbie was real or that they could trust her with the girls.

*   *   *

The backup was the worst one since an ice storm in January had paralyzed Washington. But with the rush hour over, it still didn't affect the far side of the beltway, where Sergeant John Milligan, a thirty-year veteran of the Maryland State Police, was cruising with traffic on the outer loop. Noticing a stopped car off the edge of the roadway, he edged over to investigate.

Milligan pulled in close to the front of the car, a Honda Accord. He guessed it was an '89 or '90, but in the dark he couldn't make out its color. Before stepping out of his patrol car, Milligan read off the license number and called it in to the dispatcher. "Looks like I have a deserted car here," he said. After getting confirmation that the car had not been identified with any criminal activity, he picked up his flashlight and stepped from the sedan.

A cold wind penetrated his jacket as he left the warmth of his cruiser. Cars roared by on his right as he walked back to the Honda. To his left, everything was still. A quick sweep of the light revealed that the car was empty. He walked around to the back of the car. Nothing. Then he saw the flat right rear tire, and, in the light of passing headlights, he saw something else. A man wearing khaki slacks, a blue winter jacket, ski gloves and tennis shoes was lying face down on the ground. Smoke was coming from the vicinity of the man's neck. Blood stained the gravel beneath his head. Milligan reached down and rolled the body on its side.

Flames leaped from the man's chest, driving Milligan back, but only for a moment. He kicked a burning highway flare from where the man was lying and rolled him onto his chest to smother the flames. Then he gently turned the man over to get a better look. What he saw made him sick.

From the man's collar to just above his belt, dirt and gravel clung to an oozing chest that revealed a charred sternum. Milligan forced himself to check for a pulse. The man was alive, barely.

Milligan choked back his dinner. He yanked off his jacket and placed it across the body. Then he ran for his radio. In the eight minutes it took for the ambulance to arrive, Milligan stopped the bleeding from the man's head, covered the scorched chest with some sterile gauze and draped the man with a blanket.

Poor fellow, Milligan thought. *I can't believe he's still breathing.*

When the rescue squad arrived, the lead paramedic took one look at the wound and told Milligan to call for a chopper.

"This guy needs special attention," the medic said. "Let's get him to the burn unit at GW."

Because of the anticipated demand for medical facilities for victims of the fire on the west side of Washington, the Med-Evac helicopter was directed to Baltimore Medical Center. As the chopper disappeared into the night sky, Milligan, along with two state troopers who had responded to his call for assistance, surveyed the scene.

In a slow, even voice that still carried a trace of his Irish accent, Milligan said to the others, "Looks like the guy had a flat, pulled over, took out a flare, lit it and then tripped. He struck his head on the side of the car, rolled into the ditch and ended up on the flare, and now . . . now he's about dead." Milligan had trouble mouthing the last phrase. No matter how many times he came face to face with the dead or the dying, Milligan always took the event very personally.

"What I don't understand," he went on, "is why the trunk is locked. Do you suppose he carried that flare in the car?"

Roland Hanks, the youngest of the three law officers, suggested that maybe the man kept a flare in his car to light his cigarettes. Milligan flinched at the trooper's insensitive remark and said, "Let's just get the facts down on paper and get in where it's warm."

The three completed another sweep of the area, working the best they could in the dark and the cold. They concluded that there was no evidence of foul play. They identified the owner of the car from the wallet on the seat and the registration in the glove compartment, and then they climbed into the warmth of the sergeant's car. The radio was filled with chatter about the big explosion and fire in Virginia.

The men listened awhile as sketchy reports indicated that at least two tankers had blown up on the beltway, showering liquid fire on dozens of cars. Fire fighters were battling the subsequent fires. No one knew yet how many cars were involved.

"Wish I was over there where the real action is," said Hanks.

"You ought to get a job in the District if you want real action," Milligan told him.

While the three were talking, the wrecker arrived to tow the Honda to the county auto impoundment. Hanks stepped from Milligan's car to direct the driver of the tow truck. But he wasn't thinking about the abandoned car or the dying man who was being rolled into an emergency room in Baltimore. His mind was on the fire on the opposite side of Washington, and his lost opportunity to be a hero in a front-page story.

*   *   *

Setting her Bible on the nightstand, Elizabeth Boget prayed silently, turned out the light beside her bed and pulled the covers up around her neck. She was exhausted, but she knew she wouldn't sleep well. She never did when Peter was out of town. Not that she had been getting much sleep even when he was home, what with Kristin waking during the night. Still, she missed Peter's warmth, particularly on this cold March evening. She remembered kissing him goodby when he left their suburban Richmond home for his office that morning. Now, she imagined he was watching television in his room at the McLean Hilton, just 120 miles to the north. He wouldn't be calling, she knew. Some women needed the assurance of a daily call from a spouse on the road, but not Elizabeth.

The strength of their relationship and her unfailing love for Peter occupied Elizabeth's thoughts as she lay quietly in bed, yet an alarm was going off in the recesses of her mind. Something wasn't right, but she didn't know what. She raised her head and listened for sounds in the house. She heard David making a midnight raid on the refrigerator. She dismissed the warning signal as nothing more than a need to rein in her son's appetite. She rolled over and once again closed her eyes, not knowing how the events of this night would forever alter the course of her life.

*   *   *

Derek Masters crossed the median and pulled the bloody body of Captain

Davidson from his crushed State Police car moments before tongues of flame set it afire. He helped a family of five, burned and bleeding, scramble through the maze of abandoned cars and then across the median to a waiting ambulance. He grabbed a baby from a car seat and ran to safety after struggling in vain to free the child's mother from beneath the steering column of her wrecked and burning Pontiac. He carried an unconscious woman while guiding her dazed husband to safety. Masters was finally prevented from making another rescue attempt by his fellow officers, who forced him to sit with a paramedic and be treated for his burned hands and face.

Despite the valiant efforts of so many, death hung over the scene. It hung like the dark, oily cloud that blocked the stars and moon from the exhausted workers.

2
_____

Friday, March 16

The following morning the *Washington Post* reported that a sports car pursued by police had been traveling in excess of one hundred miles an hour when it skidded out of control, crossed the grass median and collided with a propane tank truck.

Grisly photos revealed the charred remains of some of the thirteen bodies recovered from the wreckage. Five others were reportedly killed in a chain reaction accident on the outer loop when motorists abandoned cars and ran from the scene. Officials were quoted as believing that more bodies would be found. Other articles contained interviews with survivors who were taken to area hospitals and with families whose homes suffered damage when the explosion blew out windows and rocked walls.

On its editorial page, the *Post* deplored the continued use of the ever-crowded beltway by trucks loaded with dangerous cargoes. On page six of the Maryland Suburban section, a short item was headlined "Norfolk Man Injured in Beltway Mishap."

*   *   *

Though he had watched the news of the disaster on the 11:00 p.m. news, Mike Downes awoke on Friday morning unaware that the events of the previous night were about to take his life in a new direction. The trim telephone-company executive took his morning run through his fashionable neighborhood in Richmond's West End, showered and dressed. While he downed two cups of coffee and finished off a cream-cheese-topped bagel, he reviewed the speech he was to give to the Downtown Rotary at noon.

It wasn't until midmorning that he thought about Peter Boget. He rode the elevator down to the Public Relations office. A cluster of employees was standing at Marge Conners's desk.

"Has anyone heard from Peter this morning?" he asked. The negative responses were not unexpected. "Well, Marge," he said to Peter's secretary, "tell him I want to speak with him when he calls in at noon."

"Yes, sir," Marge replied. She made a shorthand notation on a large pad in front of her and then turned to her computer and entered the message in the electronic file.

"Be sure and have Peter speak to me the moment he calls in," Downes said.

Marge detected an uneasiness along with a hint of urgency in his voice. "Is there something I can help you with?" she asked.

"No . . . Just wondering if he got tied up in that mess last night going to the ad meeting."

"The ad meeting." Her reply was thoughtful, half statement, half question. "I think he was getting ready to go when I left at five. I would guess he got to the Hilton by seven or seven-thirty, unless he stopped for dinner somewhere."

"Probably so," Mike said, though from the look on his face, he was considering more than where Peter might have stopped for dinner.

As Mike turned away, a sense of uneasiness filled the room. Even though the story of the accident was plastered across the front page of the morning's *Times-Dispatch*, Marge hadn't made the connection until Mike stopped by her desk. She watched as he stepped through the door into the hall. Mike Downes was a no-nonsense Virginia Military Institute graduate who, at forty-three, was the company's youngest vice president, but today he was worried about something. And now Marge was too.

Marge Conners opened the top left drawer of her walnut secretarial desk, pulled out the folder containing Peter's itinerary and found the number of the McLean Hilton. When she got the hotel operator, she asked for Peter Boget's room.

After a few minutes, the operator replied. "I'm sorry, we don't have a guest by that name."

"Are you sure?"

"Well, let me check again. That's spelled B-o-g-e-t?"

"That's right."

"No, I'm sorry. Let me connect you with reservations to see what they have."

"Thank you."

A knot tightened in Marge's stomach.

"Reservations, may I help you?" The voice was sweet and Southern.

"I'm checking on a Peter Boget. B-o-g-e-t. He had a guaranteed reservation for last night." She paused. "That confirmation number was CJ 43677." She heard the clatter of a keyboard.

"I'm sorry," said the voice on the line, "our records show that Mr. Boget did not check in last night. We billed his American Express Card, since he had guaranteed late arrival."

Marge mumbled a thank you and slid the handset onto the phone's cradle. She stared at it for a few moments before picking it up and dialing her vice president.

"Mr. Downes," she began, "Peter didn't stay at the Hilton last night. He had a guaranteed reservation, but never checked in." Marge's voice was starting to waver.

"Let's not jump to conclusions," the vice president said in a cool, gentle voice that masked his own concern. "There's probably a good explanation."

"I guess you're right."

"I am a little surprised, but you know Peter." Downes tried to lighten the conversation. "One of the kids probably had a soccer game or something last night, and he drove up early this morning instead."

"And didn't cancel his reservation?"

"It's happened before. I'm sure there is a good explanation. I really don't think there is anything to worry about. When you hear from him, just transfer him to me. Okay?"

"Okay."

It wasn't okay and both Marge and Mike knew it. As soon as he finished talking with Peter's secretary, Downes called the McLean Hilton.

"Please put me through to the communications center at the Mid-Atlantic

Bell meeting in the Grand Ballroom."

"Just one minute, sir."

I don't have one minute, he thought. Then another voice came on the line, a familiar voice. "Communications center," Judy Larkin said.

"Hello, Judy." Mike recognized the voice of the secretary to the advertising vice president. "How are you doing?"

"Fine. Sorry you couldn't make the meeting."

"Thanks. By the way," he said trying to sound casual, "have you seen Peter around?"

"No. His name tag is right here on the table, along with two dozen others," she said matter-of-factly. "He probably got caught in the terrible traffic on the beltway. They've only got two lanes open in either direction this morning, and nothing is moving. In fact, we started an hour late because of it."

Downes considered the possibility. It was the same one that had popped into his mind when he was talking with Marge. Maybe Peter didn't go last night after all. Maybe he went home and got up early and drove to McLean this morning and got caught in traffic and was sitting on the beltway right now.

"Of course. He's probably just stuck in traffic," he said. "When he arrives, ask him to give me a call."

But Mike knew better. Peter had complained that once again the staff in Washington had scheduled a meeting too early in the morning for the people in Richmond. He hated leaving at 5:30 in the morning, fighting the northbound traffic on I-95, but that was the only way to be sure of making a 9:00 a.m. meeting in the Washington area.

Mike hung up the phone, pushed back his chair, put his feet on the edge of his desk, and brought his hands together. He formed a tent with his fingertips and brought the two forefingers to his mouth. For several minutes he stared at the wall. *Should I call Elizabeth just to be sure? No,* he thought, *I don't want to alarm her. Should I mention this to Marge? No, not now.* After a long pause he picked up the phone and dialed directory assistance. After three rings a pleasant voice asked, "City please?"

"Fairfax."

"Go ahead."

"May I have the number for the Fairfax County Police?"

*   *   *

It was midafternoon when a bandaged Derek Masters hitched a ride with a fellow patrolman back to the site of the previous evening's disaster. Masters surveyed the site. It didn't look so bad in the daylight. For the sightseers who crept slowly by the disaster scene, there was little to see: melted highway, scorched earth, burnt shrubs, a crane and two flatbed trucks picking up the last pieces of wreckage. A dozen county policemen and almost as many state police were at the scene, most for traffic control, a few from forensics. The specialists were trying to determine if there were six, seven or eight cars in the mass of melted, twisted steel that extended from the middle of the inner loop into the median. Earlier in the day any hope of identifying passengers in these and several other cars had been abandoned. Now the sleuths were reluctantly agreeing that positive identification of the automobiles was impossible. License plates and vehicle identification tags had melted in the inferno.

*   *   *

Peter Boget never showed up for the advertising meeting. By day's end Mike Downes was beside himself. He called company security and alerted them to Peter's apparent disappearance. Then he pulled open his top desk drawer and dragged his finger down the list of the employees in his department. At "Boget" he ran his finger to the right. He stopped at Peter's home number and dialed. Before he could think about what he was going to say, a young voice said, "Hello?"

"Ah . . . hi. Is your mother home? This is Mr. Downes."

"Just a minute, please." Daniel punched the hold button and yelled, "Mom! It's for you."

Elizabeth whispered loudly from the top of the stairs, "Shhhh. Kristin is sleeping. I'll get it in the bedroom."

Her cheery hello told Mike that Elizabeth was not suspecting anything.

"Elizabeth, has Peter gotten home yet?"

"No. He said he wouldn't be home 'til after dinner."

"Oh, did he call you?" Mike was hoping that this was all a misunderstanding.

"Yes," she said.

He couldn't believe his ears. He couldn't contain his smile.

"He called just before he left the office last night for Washington."

Mike's jaw dropped. "Ask him to give me a ring when he gets in this evening. Thanks."

He hung up the phone too fast.

What was that all about? Elizabeth asked herself. *Mike is usually so cordial.*

Kristin's screaming distracted her. But as she changed the baby's diaper and headed to the kitchen to fix dinner, she replayed the phone call in her mind.

*   *   *

Mark Randolph and Glenn Segal sat facing each other in the third booth of Ying Chen on East 54th Street just off Third Avenue in Manhattan. Randolph, a forty-six-year-old stockbroker, looked dashing in his hand-tailored suit, custom-made, single-stitch broadcloth white shirt and dark paisley tie. His wire-rim glasses and graying temples lent an air of mature authority. The younger Segal, overweight and balding but dressed impeccably, was shifting nervously in his seat. The restaurant had few customers seated for dinner, but a dozen people at the bar provided a noise level that would mask any conversation in the room.

"Where is he?" Randolph asked for the third time.

"I'm telling you, I don't know," Segal replied as he twisted his napkin between his fingers. "Maybe he had car trouble."

Randolph didn't like the answer. If the runner had car trouble they would have been notified. "I think he's either been in an accident or he's been caught."

"Mark, he'll be here."

"I don't think so. Maybe he was involved in that big explosion on the Washington Beltway."

"No way. That's the first thing I checked this morning. He would have been coming around the east side of the city. The explosion was on the west."

The conversation continued as the cashew chicken and the sweet-and-sour pork were served.

"Did you talk to Kennedy?" Randolph pressed, referring to their distributor in Norfolk.

"Twice. She said if we don't get the delivery by Sunday night, she'll investigate."

"What do you mean 'she'll investigate'? We've got commitments! If the stuff doesn't arrive, I want you to begin implementing our contingency plan first thing Monday," Randolph said.

Although Segal and Randolph had worked together at the small investment firm for over ten years, and although they were equal partners in their off-hours business, Mark Randolph always came across as the boss. It had been Segal's idea to use their connections with well-heeled baby boomers to begin a specialty drug business, but it was Randolph who had figured out how to make it work: they sold cocaine at premium prices to the upper-level managers and professionals who worked in midtown.

Their business plan worked flawlessly. Customers would place their orders in advance quarterly. After determining the value of each order, Segal and Randolph would churn the portfolios of these customers to generate commissions equal to about half the agreed-upon price of the cocaine. At the same time, they arranged in-house trades of customer securities held in the name of the investment firm to the account of their supplier in Norfolk. When the supplier needed money, she would simply write checks on her asset-management account or transfer securities to her favorite charities.

Mary Kennedy's account was kept clean and profitable, and to help keep the Feds from looking too close, she always had withholding tax taken from her transactions. This arrangement worked far better than cash and kept law enforcement officials from looking over her shoulder while she maintained all the appearances of a successful architect. Segal and Randolph pocketed the commissions after seeding their own portfolios to protect against a failed delivery.

The system worked so well that the beautiful but tough Irish architect had shut down all her other channels of distribution. She even had begun to cultivate relationships with investment counselors in several cities to identify others who could profit from this type of business.

Neither Segal nor Randolph knew how the cocaine got to Norfolk, nor did they care. They never met the runner and never wanted to. Prior to each delivery Federal Express delivered a key and the name of a parking garage. A U.S. Postal Service Overnight Letter brought the date and description of the car. Segal would then drive to the lot, find the car—usually a white Honda Accord—open the trunk and remove the case. He would transfer its contents to a leather bag, place a coded receipt and the key in the case, and return it to the trunk.

To the two investment counselors, cocaine was a high-stakes adventure, the first game either of them had ever played that brought their lifestyles in line with those of the executives they serviced. Their clients were important businessmen who wanted drugs without the hassle of dealing with street vendors or organized-crime figures. They liked Randolph's plan and used it. In fact, judging from the size of the orders, Segal and Randolph suspected that some of their customers were probably testing the entrepreneurial waters themselves.

An important link in the cocaine distribution chain was a dependable courier to unobtrusively transfer the drugs from Norfolk to New York. Mary Kennedy had the man. Barry Whitehead was a draftsman who had worked for her many years before. But she had fired Whitehead when she discovered the draftsman stealing petty cash to buy drugs. Whitehead had been going through a divorce and was deeply depressed. Above all else, he coveted security and had begged Kennedy not to fire him.

"The only thing I know is drafting," Whitehead had pleaded. "If word gets out, I'll never be able to get another job here in Tidewater."

"Or anywhere else," she reminded him.

After considering her options, Kennedy decided that while she didn't want a druggie in her architectural office, the man might be useful for her other business. She arranged for Whitehead to quietly enter a drug rehabilitation center, and then helped place him in a job at another firm in town.

When she called Whitehead to tell him that he should apply to the engineering firm of Stanley & Heinemann, Whitehead dropped to his knees, thanking Kennedy for her compassion. Kennedy smiled. From that day on, she had owned Barry Whitehead.

*   *   *

At the assistant manager's desk of Rocky Mountain Savings, Debbie Steinbaugh raced through her work. She had switched lock-up duties with her manager so that she could get out at four instead of six. Despite her impending vacation, the attractive blonde had no time to daydream about the beach or romantic escapades. She wasn't thinking about fitting into her new size-ten bathing suit—an impossibility just six months ago—nor about her nights in Cancun. All that mattered now was finishing a few reports, straightening her desk and getting home to pack.

She had made a remarkable turnaround since that weekend two years earlier when Peter Boget had visited her. She had completed her alcoholism rehabilitation program and brought her eating under control. She had returned to church and become involved in a "single again" group in her community. But the focus of her thoughts continued to be her tragic mistake in giving up her children when her husband divorced her. She knew that at the time she'd been an alcoholic, jobless, self-centered individual, but the girls were an important part of her identity and now she wanted them back. She often talked about finding a husband who would be a new father for them—someone like Peter Boget. Someday, somehow, she was going to regain custody of Laura and Jennifer.

*   *   *

Elizabeth Boget asked her son David to turn on the evening news so she could watch as she cleaned up the kitchen. She stopped in her tracks at the first report. "Police today said they are giving up hope of identifying seven to nine people killed in the gasoline tanker explosion on Washington's Beltway last night. Thirty-two people remain in area hospitals, nineteen listed as critical. The official death toll now stands at twenty-eight."

The measured tones of Peter Jennings belied the horror of the footage on the screen. Elizabeth turned off the water in the kitchen sink and walked toward the electronic images that drew her to the family room. She watched the replay of the footage of flaming autos, burned victims and exhausted rescue workers. She was numb. She had not heard from Peter in twenty-four hours. He would have been on the beltway just about the time of the explosion.

The feeling last night at bedtime. The call from Mike. It started to fit. Yet it didn't. She always thought that burning to death would be the worst way to go, worse even than drowning, and her mind could not accept the possibility that it had happened to her own husband. *He will be home any minute,* she told herself. *This is just a coincidence.* A knot was tightening around her dinner, a knot that seemed to be pulling everything within her into a tight ball.

She stepped closer to the television and sat down on the sofa. Reluctantly she picked up the newspaper from the coffee table. She unrolled it slowly. The knot cut off her breathing, and her heart raced. "No," she said aloud, closing her eyes. Then she whispered a prayer and slowly opened her eyes. She didn't need her reading glasses for the words at the top of the page:

Two Richmonders Among 22 Killed in Gas Truck Explosion on Beltway
The headline was instantly etched into her memory, as was the brilliant orange photo showing firefighters and cars silhouetted against the inferno. Elizabeth spread the paper out across the coffee table and began to read. A feeling of weakness spread throughout her body.

Jonathan, her three-year-old, started down the stairs that circled into the family room, but Elizabeth couldn't look at him. *Just a coincidence,* she kept telling herself. The denial she was feeling was strong, but not as strong as the photo in the paper and the images on the screen. Was her Peter in those images? Was he suffering unbearable agony in a hospital somewhere? Was he dead?

"No!" she screamed.

Her shout startled Jonathan, who began to cry. Elizabeth didn't hear her son. Her senses were focused on the man she loved. *He'll be walking in the door in a minute,* she told herself. She stood up and walked to the window to see if Peter was pulling into the driveway. But the tightness in her stomach told her he wouldn't be there.

Midway down the stairs, Jonathan pressed his head between two of the balustrades and, through his own tears, he asked, "Why are you crying, Mom?"

Elizabeth hadn't noticed the tears running down her face. When she did, she ran to the bathroom, closed the door and wept.

*   *   *

In the intensive-care burn unit at Baltimore Medical Center, doctors and nurses were racing in and out of room 323. The unit was a madhouse as interns, residents, nurses and aides tried to care for Whitehead and three other patients flown in from the Beltway blast. At the nurses' station, two doctors were commenting on Barry Whitehead's condition.

"He's lucky. An inch lower and he would have been dead." The doctor shook his head. "Geez, I hate those phosphorus burns. If he survives, he's going to need half a dozen bone grafts."

"At least," the other said. "I can't imagine what would have happened if they hadn't put the flare out before it burned through the sternum."

"I can. We wouldn't be talking about him right now." The doctor shrugged. "Wanna put five down on the next twenty-four hours?"

"You've been up too long when you start betting on life and death. I don't know. He looks strong; he didn't lose much blood, and the burn was contained."

The nurse behind the counter listened with her head down. She disagreed with the doctor's assessment. Whitehead's lungs were damaged from the smoke and he had a scorched larynx. Over 150 square centimeters of his chest were burned away. The thumb and forefinger on his right hand were burned to the bone, and blood continued to ooze from the bandaged lump on his head. Whitehead's blood pressure was 60 over 40, and his heartbeat was slow and irregular.

"Speaking of chances," said one of the doctors, "do you think the Bullets can go all the way?"

"How can you think about basketball at a time like this?"

"If I didn't give my mind a break, I'd go crazy."

"Yeah, I hear you!" He paused, then responded wearily. "I wouldn't put any money on the Bullets. It's going to be the Bulls again—you can bet on it."

His friend laughed and shook his fist in mock anger. "Go back to Chicago, already."

*   *   *

Lauren Boget knocked gently on the bathroom door after Jonathan had told her that their mother was crying. "What's wrong?" Lauren asked quietly through the door. "Did you hurt yourself?"

How could Elizabeth respond? She washed her face, and though the knot in her stomach was as tight as ever, she forced a smile as she stepped out of the bathroom.

Ten eyes were riveted on her as she turned off the light. David and Lauren were standing at the door. Jonathan and Daniel were on the steps just behind them. Kristin was straddling David's right hip.

"You all right, Mom?" Lauren, the bold one, asked.

Elizabeth bit her lip as her eyes met her children's gaze. The fear in her face was telegraphed to the others. Lauren began to cry. Elizabeth's eyes began to water again.

"It's Dad, isn't it?"

The answer was drowned in a flood of tears.

3

Friday, March 16

lizabeth Boget's outstretched arms drew her children like a magnet. They held each other for a long time, and then, pressing a tissue to her watery eyes, Elizabeth headed back into the kitchen and picked up the phone. She pressed a button on the quick-dial pad and waited as the seven tones sang in her ear and a phone began to ring. "Hello." It was an unfamiliar female voice.

"I must have dialed the wrong number," Elizabeth mumbled. "I was calling for Mike Downes."

"Just a minute, Dad's here."

It didn't register in Elizabeth's mind that the call had been electronically forwarded to the house of Downes's daughter. In a moment Mike came on the line. "Hello."

"Mike . . . ?"

Elizabeth didn't have to say any more. "No," he replied quietly to her unasked question. "He never showed up. But the police are searching the area, the hotels, the hospitals." He paused. "Is there anything I can do to help?"

"Just pray, I guess," was her feeble response. "Thanks."

She depressed the switch hook and pressed another button on the phone.

"Hello." The voice on the other end was high-pitched and friendly.

"Joyce." In contrast to the melodic greeting of her best friend, Elizabeth's voice was flat and low and deliberate. "Peter is missing."

"He's what?" Joyce gasped. She was trying to think what else to say. "What do you mean, 'missing'?"

In measured tones Elizabeth continued, "Peter went to a meeting in McLean last night. He never got there."

Joyce was a pessimist and always struggled with bad news. This news paralyzed her tongue. After an anguished pause, Elizabeth continued.

"I think . . . I think . . ." The words wouldn't come. Joyce started to cry. That triggered the tears from Elizabeth, who still hadn't told her best friend her deepest fear.

"Peter," Elizabeth coughed out. "He, he may have been in the crash on the beltway."

The two friends had spent many hours in each other's kitchens. They had played with each other's children and had grown close as sisters in the nine years since they'd met. The Bogets were the first family the McGuires had encountered when they visited Lakeside Community Church. Both lived in Brandermill, a planned community on a beautiful lake southwest of Richmond. At the time, both women had been pregnant, Joyce with her second and Elizabeth with her third. Their husbands, Bill and Peter, loved to play tennis together. As their families grew, so had their friendship. Half a dozen times the Bogets and the McGuires had vacationed together in Nags Head or Myrtle Beach.

A year ago it had been Joyce who called Elizabeth seeking consolation after learning that her mother had died of a heart attack. Now it was Elizabeth making the call, but Joyce didn't know what to say. She repeated, "I'm so, so sorry." Then she added, "I'll be right over."

Joyce only had to say one word to Bill, who by this time was standing next to his ashen-faced wife. "Peter."

Bill knew that Peter had been heading to McLean the previous night. He had watched the 11:00 p.m. news, and he had read all about the crash in the paper.

Softly he said, "Go ahead. I'll put the kids to bed."

*   *   *

At the home of his recently married daughter, Mike Downes said nothing about the conversation with Elizabeth. He read newspapers and watched TV right through dinner. The meal that Anna served him remained untouched except for the coffee. Conversation was nonexistent. Mike placed two calls after he excused himself from the table, one to corporate security, the other to the home of the president. There was no answer to either call. Finally, picking up his coat, he thanked Anna and Martin for dinner and announced that he was going to the office.

"You don't want to tell us?" Anna asked at the door.

"Nothing to tell. I'll call you later." He stepped into the open-air stairwell outside the apartment door. "Feels like rain," he said and disappeared down the stairs.

He drove downtown, pulled into the parking lot under the Virginia Bell building and took the elevator to the twentieth floor. He placed both calls again and this time reached the president, who had just returned from two days in Philadelphia. After relaying the news of Peter's disappearance, he rode the elevator down to the PR department and went to the photo file drawer. He flipped through the hanging folders and pulled out a picture of Peter Boget.

He stared down into the big bright eyes of a man who looked the part of a rugged athlete-turned-businessman. His square chin, thin lips and high cheekbones fit well with his thick, wavy hair. His warm, friendly, expressive eyes spoke of the gentle man behind the photo.

Downes slipped the photo into a file folder, nodded to the janitor who was washing the glass door of the PR office, and headed to the elevator. A few minutes later he was at the exit gate of the parking garage in his company car.

"Were you on last night?" he asked the attendant.

"Yes, sir," said Skip Perkins, the large black man sitting in the booth.

"Do you remember seeing this man leave here last night?" He held up one of the photos.

"Sure. Mr. Boget came through here right at 6:00."

Everyone seemed to know Peter. "Why do you say '6:00'?" Downes asked.

"Well, not too many people come through here after 5:30, so I usually turn on the TV." He thumbed toward the small black-and-white set on the corner of the counter. "The news had just come on, and Mr. Boget waited until the first story ended before he drove off."

Downes did some quick calculations. If Peter had left at 6:00, he'd have been on the beltway at 7:30 and at the Hilton by 8:00 unless he'd stopped.

"Thanks," Downes said to Perkins and pulled onto the quiet city street. Five minutes later he was heading north on Interstate 95. He picked up his cellular phone, called his daughter and apologized. "I'm sorry about dinner tonight. I was distracted."

"We noticed," she said with a hint of sarcasm.

"I didn't say anything, but I should have. Peter Boget—you know Peter— well, he drove to Washington last night and didn't come back."

"Where did he go?"

"I don't know, but the fire on the beltway is a distinct possibility."

"Oh, no," Anna breathed into the mouthpiece.

"I have to check on a few things. I'll probably see you Sunday."

"Okay, Dad."

Downes hung up the phone as his car crossed into Hanover County. As he drove, his thoughts about Peter comingled with others about another person who was no longer part of his life. Two years earlier his wife had gone to the doctor complaining of lower back pain. Within a week she was undergoing surgery for liver cancer. But surgery, chemotherapy, radiation treatments and prayer had not prevented Susie from sliding into eternity three days short of her fortieth birthday.

*   *   *

In a Landover barracks of the Maryland State Police, Sergeant Milligan was reviewing the notes he had written the night before, sipping coffee from a stained mug. He was making sure that all the follow-up work had been taken care of in the Whitehead case. He pulled out a report that had been prepared while he had been home sleeping.

Barry J. Whitehead, 45
Caucasian, 6′0″ 185 lbs
Lives alone in a Norfolk apartment
Divorced. Ex-wife, Jennifer, and 2 children (boy 11, girl 14)
    living in Fort Collins, Colorado
Draftsman with Stanley and Heinemann architects—3 years
Meticulous and quiet. Stays to himself
Drives a 1989 Honda Accord

> Steady worker, usually takes long weekends instead of vacations
> Two weeks ago asked to get off early Thursday, and to take off until next Wednesday to visit friends in New York
> Credit report clean

That was it. Barry Whitehead seemed boring. So boring, in fact, that no one seemed interested in coming for his car, though the owner of the firm had indicated that he would try to get to Baltimore next weekend to visit his employee.

Milligan closed the file. It was time to hit the street.

*   *   *

Glenn Segal was sweating. There was too much heat pouring into the Long Island Railroad commuter train as it slipped through the tunnel beneath the East River on its way out of New York City's midtown business district to the suburban communities to the east. But it wasn't just the heat that caused him to sweat. He had sixty hours to find the cocaine or face the unthinkable. Nearly one million dollars had been laundered through their clients' accounts over the past three months, and now it was payoff time. He knew the cocaine had started on its journey. He had received confirmation that two cases—one more than usual—were in the locked trunk of the Honda and that the runner had left Norfolk on Thursday.

Paying back the money would be far more difficult than Randolph probably knew. He and Randolph had planned for just such a situation. They had always made sure that they had enough liquidity in a jointly held account at the firm to cover a missed shipment. What Segal knew that his partner didn't was that he had secretly pledged the securities against a down payment for the $1.6 million waterfront home he had purchased on Long Island Sound in Glen Cove.

The drug business had proved easier and more lucrative than Segal had ever anticipated. But unfortunately, his appetites and those of his wife, Phyllis, were not easily satisfied. They had found a house she just had to have, and Segal figured the big payoff would cover what he was secretly "borrowing" from the contingency fund he and Randolph were building. He'd never expected a failed delivery.

The train emerged from its underground tube and climbed to an elevated trestle, affording passengers a spectacular, though intermittent, view of the glass and steel towers of Manhattan. Lights burning in a million windows lent a jewel-like quality to the buildings that were silhouetted against an orange-blue backdrop of the fading evening sky. The train raced through Brooklyn and Queens on its way to the bedroom communities of Nassau and Suffolk counties.

But the balding stockbroker wasn't admiring the skyscrapers fading into the distance, and he wasn't noticing the endless variety of neighborhoods through which the train moved on its eastward journey. Segal was thinking about the difficulties that would arise if the police had picked up the courier. Could the courier identify him? Where did he go when he parked the car in the garage? Did he hide and observe Segal making the pickup? Did he follow him to the office?

It wasn't Randolph who handled the merchandise on the pickup, he realized, only himself. And if the courier had been caught, Segal figured it would only be a matter of time before the police would be knocking at his door. Segal was sweating profusely as the "what ifs" swirled through his head.

Still, he kept coming back to one conclusion. He had to get the cocaine. And he had to make sure that the courier, whoever and wherever he was, didn't talk.

*   *   *

Lakeside Community Church's telephone tree was very efficient. Within twenty minutes after Bill McGuire made two calls, most in the seventy-five-family congregation had learned that Peter was missing, and the pastor and his wife were on their way to the Bogets' home. Within minutes, the church's hospitality coordinator was organizing meals for the family.

Joyce McGuire was sitting next to Elizabeth on the sofa when Frank Griffith, the pastor, and his wife, Jennifer, arrived. David sat on the hearth, trying to console his mother and the rest of the family with every reason he could think of that his father might still be alive. Lauren stared at the idle ceiling fan from her perch in the rocking chair. Daniel leaned against his mother saying nothing, while three-year-old Jonathan stood by her knees, asking to play Candyland. Kristin had crawled to the kitchen.

Jennifer opened with a question. "Kids, what would you be doing if your father were here?"

After a long pause, Daniel said, "Getting ready for bed, I suppose."

"I think your dad would like you to do that. David, Lauren, let's take the little ones upstairs and get ready for bed." Jennifer took Jonathan by the hand and motioned to David to pick up Kristin. Daniel followed reluctantly.

The pastor sat down on the loveseat across from Elizabeth and Joyce as Jennifer and the children disappeared up the stairs.

"Let's pray," he said. "Father in heaven, your ways are not our ways. Your timing is not our timing. But your love is our love. Father, pour out your love on this family right now. Comfort them, Lord." After a long pause he continued. "God, I really don't know what to say. Peter is your child. If he is at home with you now, thank you. If he is lying in a hospital bed, reveal him to us, sustain him and bring him home."

Their heads were still bowed when four children, dressed for bed, wound their way back down to the family room. Jennifer settled Kristin in her crib, then returned to the first floor. The children remained quiet, except for Lauren. She asked God to bring her daddy home soon.

While Jennifer camped out in the kitchen to answer the constantly ringing phone, Frank suggested several courses of action, including visiting hospitals in the Washington area. The mere suggestion seemed to lift the family spirits. The pastor warned against being overly optimistic, but all agreed that doing something was better than doing nothing.

"I'm going too," Elizabeth said.

"Me too," David added emphatically.

"Well, I'm not staying home and babysitting," Lauren interjected angrily.

"I'm going too," Daniel piped up.

David shot back, "No you're not, you're too small."

Elizabeth observed the dynamics of her family under stress and backed off her initial declaration. "Maybe I'd better stay."

"I think your family needs you here now, more than ever," the pastor agreed.

"I know. I just feel like I have to do *something.*"

*   *   *

Mike Downes eased off the interstate at the Thornberg exit, thirty-five miles north of Richmond. He slowed his car to a stop at the top of the ramp and then turned left, driving directly to the McDonald's just two hundred yards beyond the southbound entrance ramp. Downes knew Peter Boget's stomach and taste buds. If he had left Richmond at six, he probably would have stopped for a burger along the interstate. He usually did when he drove north. At least, that's how he explained his ridiculously small expense vouchers. His eating patterns were about the only thing predictable about Boget. That and his habit of reading everything he laid his eyes on.

Downes had passed Peter's picture around at a dozen eateries at the Atlee, Ashland and Doswell exits, but got no response. Now he was easing into the McDonald's parking lot. He didn't know employee scheduling patterns, but he figured some of the dinner crew would stay on until closing. Whether anyone would remember a customer from the evening before was questionable.

No one at the counter recognized the face in the photograph. Downes asked for the manager on duty. She did not remember the face either, even though she had worked the counter the night before. "Do you know how many people we serve here each night?"

"A lot."

"Yes, a whole lot," the manager responded. "Sorry."

A teenager in a brown and green uniform was walking through the door as Downes turned to go. The boy had a few plastic trash bags in his hand. Downes pulled out the photo. The young man stared at it intently. "I think he has less hair. You know, when someone is sitting down and you look down on them, you notice their bald spot."

Downes was surprised. "You saw him?"

"Yeah. He asked if we had a newspaper around. I got him one from the back, and he sat over there and read for a while," said the young man, pointing to a corner table.

Downes did some mental calculations, comparing Peter's probable schedule with the time of the beltway disaster. He didn't like the result.

"Thanks," he said and walked out the door. When he got to the car he kicked the rear tire. "Peter, Peter, Peter," he said aloud while he shook his head. "If only you hadn't stopped. If only you didn't read so much."

Moments later, a somber Mike Downes hung a left out of the parking lot, drove past the gas station, turned right onto the entrance ramp and headed south to Richmond.

*   *   *

Elizabeth Boget couldn't sleep. She had made the dreaded call to Peter's sister in California and asked that she, in turn, call his parents in Chicago. She also called her next-door neighbor and her mother, who lived with her brother in Massachusetts. Now she was wide awake, staring through the blackness at a ceiling she couldn't see. Like a videotape on fast-forward, her mind's images of the past twenty years with Peter illuminated the darkness. Ever so often she would slow down the action and relive some of the tender moments, some of the difficult times. She played the births of each of her children in slow motion. She walked through each of the homes she and Peter had lived in as he progressed through the ranks at the phone company. She tried to fast-forward past the usually traumatic moves. Her thoughts were interrupted by a knock at her bedroom door.

"Mom, are you up?"

Lauren said it loud enough that if Elizabeth had been asleep, she wouldn't be now. Before she could answer, Lauren stepped through the door and eased over to the bed. She sat down where her father would ordinarily be lying. "Mom?"

"Yes, Lauren?"

"May I sleep here tonight?" Lauren's voice cracked. She felt the same sense of impending loss—maybe even doom—that her mother felt.

In the darkened room Elizabeth pulled back the covers. "Of course, pumpkin." She used a term that she hadn't uttered since Lauren was a little girl. Lauren was pleased. She slid into the bed and laid her head on her father's pillow. Then she started to cry.

"Mom," she began, sobbing quietly, "I'm scared."

Elizabeth tenderly reached her arm around her daughter, partly to reassure the girl and partly to ward off her own terrifying loneliness.

"You're not afraid, Lauren," she said. "You're just empty. There is nothing to be afraid about. Our friends and family will help us . . . and so will the phone company."

4

Saturday, March 17

Frank Griffith, Josh Sprouse and Rick Wampler met at Shoney's for breakfast early Saturday morning before heading for Washington.

"I still can't believe this is happening," said Sprouse over the first cup of coffee. He was the church's youth leader and a Virginia state trooper. "We've got a lot of ground to cover today. I hope we're more successful than we were last night."

"What happened last night?" Griffith asked.

"We called," Sprouse began, "what would you say, Rick, three dozen hospitals?" Rick Wampler was a partner in a large downtown accounting firm.

"Thirty-two, to be precise."

"Whatever," Sprouse said. "We didn't get a single bite."

The pastor sipped his coffee. "What time did you two get to bed?"

Wampler responded with a sigh. "We didn't. That's why you're driving and we're sleeping. Here's our itinerary, and here's the map. We'll start with Fairfax Hospital, stop at a few others around the beltway and then head into George Washington in the District. We'll stop at these ones in Maryland," he ran his finger down the list in front of Griffith, "and then head to Baltimore."

"Baltimore?" The pastor almost choked on a gulp of coffee.

"Yes, Baltimore," Sprouse answered. "Seems like they Medevaced three or four to the burn unit at Baltimore Medical Center."

"Okay, we better tank up and hit the road." The pastor stood up and headed to the restaurant's well-stocked breakfast bar. "Sounds like it's going to be a long day."

Rick Wampler stood up with him and smiled weakly. "It already has been."

*   *   *

Fifteen-year-old David Boget didn't want to play soccer on Saturday, but he didn't want to stay home either. His team, the Midlothian Stingers, was playing on its home field at the Coalfield Soccer Complex against its archrival, the Charlottesville Chargers. Even though David didn't want to be there, his teammates and coach did, because despite the fact that he was neither a prolific scorer nor a stellar defender, he controlled the mid-field very well and could outrun anyone on the team.

News of his father's disappearance preceded David's arrival and dampened the spirits of parents and players alike. From the moment they took the field, it was apparent that this was not the same team that had won the league championship the previous fall. The blue-shirted players were slow to the ball and passing poorly when they did get it. Jason McGuire, the always steady goalie, was having to make too many stops. Eighteen minutes into the first half, one of the Chargers drove down the right side of the field and crossed to the middle, where a teammate deflected the pass into the corner of the goal. Midlothian managed to hold on and responded with a goal off a penalty kick just before the half. The second period was all Charlottesville. The final 3-1 score belied just how lopsided the game had been.

Afterward, David and Jason McGuire, with Coke cans in their hands, walked slowly across the field. They seemed oblivious to the cold breeze and a sun reluctant to come out from behind a silver-gray cloud. Joyce McGuire caught up with the players and tried to console them. "Hey, boys, it was only the first game of the season. I know you'll do better next week." She didn't say what they were all thinking: the game had been lost on the sideline before the starting whistle ever blew.

"You're right, Ma," Jason said emphatically. "Next week we will do better . . . for David's dad."

David tried to smile, but he was lost in thought. It was the first game his dad had missed in two years. He had missed parts when Lauren's games had overlapped, and David knew that because his father was coaching Jonathan's team this year he would miss some of the Stingers' away games. Still, David had looked in vain for his father along the side of the field several times during the game. Now he paused, turned back toward the vacant sideline and stared at the cold, empty aluminum bleachers as if to will his father back into his life.

*   *   *

The Western Airlines 767 touched down at Cancún Airport. Debbie Steinbaugh was finally on vacation. The closest thing she had had to a vacation since her divorce was the two weeks in the hospital following her breakdown and the four weeks she spent in an alcohol rehab center. She had made a mess of her life and had spent the past three years trying to bring order to the chaos. She realized that the chance encounter with Peter Boget two years before had been anything but chance.

It had been over twenty years since they had spent the summer together. Peter had arrived at the Clarks' rambling, six-bedroom Victorian on the western edge of Colorado Springs near the Garden of Gods. It was just two months after the family had opened their doors to ten-year-old Debbie. Debbie was the daughter of the Clarks' best friends, who had perished in an April fire. Despite Debbie's arrival, the ever-gracious, down-home Clarks had honored their commitment to Peter's parents to let him stay with them for the summer while he worked as a reporter for the Manitou Springs *Gazette.*

Debbie remembered Peter as the brother she'd never had. Like her, he was a visitor, and he seemed to understand Debbie's inability to feel like a real part of the Clark family. Liz Clark tried hard to become a mother to the girl, but with four children of her own she was unable to give Debbie the attention she needed. Rather, it was Peter who had the time—and took the time—to let the young girl talk about her father and mother during those awful weeks after the fire. Often through the years Debbie would say to her foster parents, "I wish your children could be more like Peter."

She never told Peter what she had felt and would only hear about him when the Clarks received an occasional letter. By the time she was fifteen, Debbie no longer cared. She had discovered boys her own age. Before long her grades had plummeted. Soon she had dropped out of school, having the time of her life: she was pregnant at seventeen, married at eighteen, an alcoholic at twenty and divorced at twenty-four. After seven years of eating, drinking, drifting and finally attempting suicide, she had come back to the Clarks, returned to church and sought professional help. A year later, Peter had come back into her life.

He walked into the little church that the Clarks had attended for forty years. Debbie couldn't believe her eyes. He was in Denver on business and had rented a car and driven the seventy miles to Colorado Springs for an overnight visit. He had called and made arrangements to stay with the Clarks, but they had not told anyone. They wanted to surprise Debbie and their children. The surprise was absolute. There was such a happy reunion in the foyer of the country church that Sunday school started nearly fifteen minutes late.

After the service Peter once again became the listener as Debbie poured out her life. He spoke little, offering quiet encouragement and extending love—the love of Jesus, he called it—as only a big brother can. When he returned to Virginia he kept up the relationship. He sent Debbie letters and called with words of encouragement. Her healing process was long and difficult. But slowly, painfully, she successfully threw off the shackles of alcoholism, jealousy, anger, fear and guilt. She also allowed Peter's friendship to become much more than just friendship. With each note of encouragement, each call, she was falling in love with him. She knew he was Elizabeth's husband. And she knew that love was not what Peter had in mind. Debbie soon realized that she was reading into the relationship something that wasn't there. Still, she could not let him go.

Debbie imagined a hundred ways in which their lives would be miraculously and romantically united. She envisioned a wedding; she fantasized about becoming the mother her daughters had never had. She knew this type of thinking was destroying her, and she asked God to do some housecleaning of her heart and her mind. Even though a sense of order was coming to her relationships, she couldn't let go of the secret world she shared with Peter.

Now, as she unbuckled her seat belt, she was ready for this special week. She walked up the runway into the terminal, and there, waiting just beyond the door, was a familiar face. Debbie smiled.

*   *   *

It was early evening when the three men pulled into the parking lot across the street from Baltimore Medical Center. Their stops in Fairfax, Falls Church, Arlington, Bethesda and the District had proved unfruitful. Now they were to visit the burn unit where three victims had been taken following the "Beltway Blast," as it had been dubbed by the news media.

Sprouse's uniform and Griffith's Bible had helped the men get past the normal roadblocks to intensive-care units in the other hospitals. The combination worked again at Baltimore Medical Center.

They took the elevator to the third floor, where they walked out onto an old but shiny tiled floor. The peeling plaster walls said the hospital was behind the times. The nurses' station said it wasn't. A virtual panoply of electronic monitors flashed, clicked and bleeped behind the petite woman who viewed the three men from behind thick lenses set in dark frames. She wore no visible makeup and looked as if she needed some sleep. Her name tag read "Ling Chu, Nursing Supervisor."

"May I help you?"

"I'm Frank Griffith." He pulled the photo from inside the cover of his Bible. "We're from Richmond. Our friend Peter may have been in the . . . ah . . ."

Her demeanor changed, and in a tired but compassionate voice she said, "I know." She took the photo in her hands. It showed a warm, friendly man with dark eyes and thick hair. He looked tall even though he was sitting on the floor. He cradled a baby in his left arm and had a curly-haired toddler sitting on his right knee. In the background were open gift boxes beneath a huge Christmas tree. "Maybe . . ." She seemed lost in thought. "No, it couldn't be."

"Couldn't be what?" Rick Wampler asked.

"Well, none of the people brought in from Virginia has this appearance," she said in a cultured accent, "but he does resemble Mr. Whitehead in 323."

"Mr. Whitehead?" Wampler asked.

The three men looked at each other and back to the nurse.

"Can we see him?" Griffith wondered.

"Only from the window. He's in the trauma unit. We have to be extremely careful to keep patients as free as possible from bacteria that could cause infection. But I have his wallet here. He should have a photo on his driver's license."

Chu disappeared into an office adjacent to the nurses' station and returned with a thin, black leather wallet. She flipped it open and pulled out the Virginia driver's license. She handed it to the three men.

The pastor spoke first. "The eyes are different, but he sure has the same-shaped face and same dark hair."

Sprouse studied the document as if it had been offered to him by a motorist pulled over for speeding. Satisfied, he passed it back to Nurse Chu. "Thank ya, ma'am," he said in a friendly drawl. Their work was done; the three men said their goodbys and turned toward the elevator.

Night had enveloped Baltimore, and sodium vapor lights gave an ashen glow to the faces of the searchers as they crossed the parking lot. The mood of the men matched the night—dark and cold. They had gone to bat and struck out.

*   *   *

At the Boget house, the mood was grim. Frank Griffith had called with the bad news: they had checked every hospital where crash victims had been taken, and Peter was not there. The morgue visits turned up nothing.

Jennifer Griffith was helping to put a donated dinner on the table for the family. But if lunch was any indication, little would be eaten.

Elizabeth hadn't been able to fix the corned beef and cabbage she had planned for dinner. The meal was one of those traditions she and Peter had begun shortly after their marriage. Each St. Patrick's Day they would invite a family in the neighborhood to join them for the traditional holiday fare. She would deck the table with green, have Peter pick up a table arrangement at the florist and pin on her "Kiss me, I'm Irish" button just before the guests arrived. But this year there would be no special dinner. Elizabeth had called the Halls, the new family on the street, and canceled the engagement.

In the kitchen, lots of talking was going on, but only Elizabeth would broach the topic of the explosion. She asked questions for which there were no answers. Mostly whys and what ifs. No one mentioned the hows. No one wanted to think of how Peter died. Did he feel the heat? Was he awake when the fingers of fire reached out to take him? Did he scream when those flames fried his arms? How long was it before he went unconscious? Did his wedding ring melt into the steering wheel?

"His wedding ring!" Elizabeth's shout startled everyone.

She ran upstairs. Jennifer was right behind her.

"What about the wedding ring?" she asked.

Elizabeth raced into the bedroom. "There it is." She reached out to the top of Peter's dresser, picked up the gold band, turned it on its side and tried to read the inscription. Though she couldn't see it without her glasses, she knew what it said: "EMO'M to PSB 6-12-71."

Elizabeth drew the ring to her breast. "At least I have something." She turned to Jennifer. "You know, it's been here all the time. I just didn't see it."

"Why was it here?" Jennifer asked.

"He always takes it off before he splits wood or when he plays basketball. He probably missed it when he got ready for work on Thursday."

Jennifer stared at the dresser. The only things on the polished cherry top were photos of the children. *How could he have missed seeing his wedding ring?* she wondered.

5

I n church on Sunday morning, Mike Downes could not keep his mind
on the sermon. *Of all people, why Peter?* he kept asking himself. Peter
had asked him to go to the ad meeting for him, but Downes didn't
like making that trip any more than Peter did, and anyway he
had been invited to speak at the Rotary. But it wasn't just the guilt that
distracted Downes, it was the paperwork and Peter's work that had him
worried. Not to mention having to deal with Elizabeth. He was a forty-three-
year-old vice president who had worked for twenty years in nine different
cities. Yet he'd never had to face the death of a subordinate. Not even in
Vietnam.

On successive tours, Downes had led men into combat in the Delta
region of the Mekong River and helped defend Saigon during the final
months of American involvement. His philosophy was simple: stay off trails,
move quietly, stay together, avoid the enemy at all costs, but when engaged,
pound them into oblivion. His objective: return home to his wife and children, and make sure that every man under his command got out of the
jungle alive. He had succeeded.

Downes looked past the pastor and the choir to the cross that hung from
the ceiling. Sunlight streamed in from the windows on the left side of the
sanctuary and bathed half the congregation in its warming rays. But no sun
reached the cross. It was illuminated by a light shining from a recess in the

ceiling above. The empty cross, like the empty tomb, reminded him that at least death wasn't final. *But it sure makes living difficult for those left behind.*

Downes knew from others that even though almost everything would be taken care of by the Human Resources department, he would have to get personally involved. That meant more time, time he didn't have—not if he was to stay on track in his quest for the presidency of Virginia Bell. Because Peter's office ran so smoothly, Downes really didn't know what all went on in the Public Relations department. Peter had complained bitterly about reducing his staff when the downsizing order came from Mid-Atlantic Bell's headquarters, but somehow Peter's group was able to stay on top of the work. Downes suspected that everyone was taking a lot of work home on the weekends, but he'd been too embarrassed to ask. Even if he knew, what could he do? With a freeze on salaries and no chance for promotion, Downes's hands were tied. He'd given Peter and his staff the only thing he could: freedom.

As the choir stood for a closing hymn, Downes decided that after the service he would drive to Washington. There was to be a midafternoon memorial service for the victims of the beltway tragedy at the National Cathedral.

His mind told him that he should go to the office and clear his desk for Monday's onslaught of calls. But his heart told him to go to the capital, for the sake of Peter and Elizabeth.

*　　*　　*

Four hundred miles to the north, in his home on Long Island Sound, Glenn Segal hung up the phone. He had not been to bed in over eighty hours, and his concentration and his nerves were shattered. Mary Kennedy had just confirmed for the third and last time that two cases of cocaine had been left in the courier's car on Thursday afternoon.

Something, obviously, had gone wrong—very, very wrong.

The stockbroker's eyes were dull and watery, his face unshaven. "Where the hell is that shipment?" he yelled into the smoke-filled gloom of his opulent study, pounding his fist on his desk. He lit another cigarette. As the smoke encircled his head, he picked up the phone and, for the seventh time in two days, dialed Mark Randolph's house across the Sound in New Haven, Connecticut.

Randolph didn't like being interrupted when he was at his computer, but he took the call anyway. The voice on the other end was quavering.

"Mark, what're we going to do? I just got back from the pick-up point. It still hasn't arrived."

"Look, Glenn, get hold of yourself." Randolph's voice was stern, laced with irritation. "And stop calling me at home. Tomorrow morning get on the phone to customers and see whether they want delivery in two weeks or a refund. It will take awhile, but this is no big deal, is it?"

"But we can't get another delivery before May!"

"May? Explain."

"She says she has to investigate to make sure it's actually lost."

"What do you mean 'actually lost'?"

"She suspects we may have taken the delivery and eliminated the courier."

Segal was agitated, but Randolph remained cool.

"In the morning," Randolph said quietly, "tell her we need another delivery in two weeks, or her account is going to take some heavy losses."

"You don't understand. She said absolutely no delivery until she checks us out and finds the case. We're ruined."

Randolph was getting tired of Segal's dramatics. "Glenn," his voice was firm, "we've got over one million dollars to cover our losses, even if we don't touch her account. Let's just see what happens tomorrow."

Segal didn't want to wait until tomorrow. His life was passing in front of him.

"But, Mark—"

"No buts. Tomorrow."

"But that's a lot of money to—"

The connection went dead before Segal finished his sentence. The panic was setting in. *If only Mark knew that tomorrow would be too late, he'd stop whatever he's doing and get himself over here. Wait until he finds out that the contingency plan isn't going to work.*

Segal inhaled his cigarette smoke deeply, squashed the butt into the glass tray that was littered with tan filters, and slid his chair away from the desk. He stood, supporting his tired body with his hands, and staggered to the bar along the window. He filled a glass with vodka, splashed in a shot of orange juice, returned to the desk and lit another cigarette.

Segal knew his sins were fast catching up with him. The cocaine business had worked so well for so long that he had begun to feel invincible. He'd taken his profits and quickly plowed them into material pleasures—pleasures he had been denied by a wife who spent his money much faster than he could bring it home. He had loathed Phyllis's profligacy. That is, until the cocaine came along and his income finally approached what Phyllis was used to spending. Suddenly he had some buying power of his own, and he'd begun to indulge.

The off-the-rack suits from Penney's had given way to custom-made ones. Arrow shirts had been replaced with tailored creations from the shirtmaker in the lobby of his office building; the monogrammed sleeves made him feel important when he mingled with clients. His three-year-old Dodge Shadow had been replaced with an Acura, which in turn was replaced with a BMW. The three-bedroom starter home in Valley Stream had given way to a six-bedroom house on the water in Glen Cove.

Phyllis loved her husband's newfound wealth, but she never stopped her spending spree to find out where it came from or just how much debt her husband had accumulated. She didn't know that he had over nine thousand dollars in monthly loan payments. And neither she, nor Randolph, nor anyone else knew that Segal had forged the name of his partner on papers pledging their contingency fund against his mortgage. Segal wasn't about to tell her, either. After fifteen years of being reminded by his wife that he wasn't a very good investment counselor ("I can't believe anyone would trust you with their money. You can't even keep me in decent shoes," she would say), he could finally hold up his head when he brought home news, of the new purchases he had made.

He was ruined. Segal realized that as he drained his glass of its warming spirits. Randolph might be in a pretty bad position too. Any way you count it, a million dollars is a lot of change. Now the money was gone. But where? Segal slumped into his chair, instinctively drew the white, smoking cylinder to his mouth and inhaled deeply.

The house was unusually quiet. Phyllis had taken the children into the city for a show. He was alone. Tears of sadness, tears of fear, tears of dread welled up in his eyes and slid down his cheek.

He looked up from his mahogany desk to the paneled walls and ceiling of his study. Lining the bookcases was his collection of eighteenth- and early-nineteenth-century English first editions. He had started the collection while a student at Columbia University and had never stopped buying them. They were valuable, all right, but he knew that he could never sell the books in time to cover the reimbursements. He thought about his cars and laughed. He had bought the BMW and his wife's Volvo station wagon with nothing down.

Phyllis's jewelry? Now there was a thought, but it wouldn't be nearly enough. And anyway, she would divorce him or kill him first.

Option after option was evaluated and then discarded. Like a snake backed into a corner, Glenn Segal was a dangerous man. But unlike a snake, he had no one to strike out against except himself. He slowly turned in his chair, looked through the glass to the inlet and imagined the sound beyond. On this gloomy afternoon with a strong wind blowing from the north, he pictured whitecaps on the sound and waves pounding against the sand, the incessant washing of gray-black water onto the eroding beach. He imagined each wave drawing some of his own life back into the watery deep. His sole identity was his wealth and position, and now the waters of fate were washing both away.

His climb up the stairs and into the master bedroom resembled that of a condemned man climbing the steps to the gallows. He seemed smaller as his shoulders sagged and his chin fell forward to meet his heaving chest. He'd never really cared for the ornate Mediterranean bedroom suite that his wife had purchased, but its dark heaviness matched his mood exactly. He crossed the room and stepped into his long, narrow walk-in closet. Halfway in, he stopped. To his right a pole sagged with the weight of sixteen suits. From the shelf above, Segal retrieved a flecked-blue box that had once contained a pair of size-seven shoes from the "Felipe Montaña Collection." Holding it in trembling hands, he turned and exited the closet. He moved to his wife's dressing table and sat down. Shaking uncontrollably, he uncovered the box and set the lid where Phyllis usually spread the jars and bottles for her twice-daily face-restoration rituals. From inside the box he removed a shiny .38 snub-nosed revolver.

Segal stopped shaking as all emotion drained from his face and determination took over. He set the box on the floor and raised his eyes. The man in the mirror was a stranger. A man whose life had been sapped by a dreadfully boring job and a wife who never could be satisfied. Glenn Segal stared at that man for a long, long time.

"You played the game and you lost," he said to the face in the mirror. Then he raised the revolver to his temple and tightened his finger around the trigger.

*   *   *

The unusually warm March afternoon was cooling off quickly as the sun set on the nation's capital. Thousands of mourners, including many in bandages, filed out of the huge National Cathedral, which overlooked the city of Washington as a lighthouse overlooks the ocean. Their ashen faces stood in stark contrast to the brilliant, sunlit edifice.

Bishop Covington had eulogized those lost on the highway. He had praised those who had risked their lives to save so many, and he had comforted those who had lost so much. Virginia State Police Superintendent Longmont had acknowledged the passing of Trooper Ron Davidson; the chairman of the Fairfax County Board of Supervisors had recounted the heroic deeds of dozens of police officers, including Derek Masters. The mood was solemn. The name of Peter Boget was never mentioned. Bishop Covington had noted that at least six names were omitted. "God alone knows who they are," he had said in the course of his eulogy. "We commit them to his care."

*   *   *

At Baltimore Medical Center, nurse Ling Chu was waiting to be relieved. She was reviewing the duty schedule for the next twenty-four hours when an alarm went off behind her. She spun around. The patient in 323 had just gone into cardiac arrest. She mobilized a team in seconds and sprinted ahead of them down the hall.

The flat, insistent tone of the heart monitor pierced the room. Chu turned off the oxygen flow to Barry Whitehead's mask and waited silently while a young intern placed the fibrillator firmly against Whitehead's rib cage.

"Clear!" the intern said, nodding to the nurse at the cart. She sent a wave of electricity coursing through the paddles.

Whitehead's body stiffened, lifted off the bed and dropped back onto the sheet.

The monitor stayed flat.

"Clear!"

All stood breathlessly, waiting for a heartbeat. The monitor sprang to life. "Beep." Then a pause. "Beep." Then a longer pause. "Beep, beep." It was weak, but it was working. The team let out a collective sigh. One remained at the patient's side as the others left the room.

When nurse Chu returned to her station, the 323 monitor continued to be erratic, but at least there was a signal. She scanned her nurses' station, said a few words to the supervisor who was coming on in relief, and headed home.

*   *   *

Joyce McGuire circled the Lincoln Memorial in her Caravan and headed south across Memorial Bridge. Deep shadows enveloped Arlington National Cemetery on the hill before them, obscuring the grave markers but not the eternal flame atop the grave of John F. Kennedy. Elizabeth Boget, sitting in the front passenger seat, stared at the blackness of the cemetery, but her thoughts were elsewhere.

Four car lengths in front, Bill McGuire was driving the Bogets' Buick station wagon, with Rick Wampler at his side. Five young children were buckled up in the seats behind. "Can you get over to the Bogets' tomorrow night?" Rick asked. "We probably need to help Elizabeth go through some of her papers."

"Yes, but we ought to get in touch with Jim first and have him sort through the legalities," said Bill, referring to one of the lawyers who served on the church's board of deacons.

"I'm afraid this could get sticky," Rick said. "Unless the law has changed recently, I don't think missing people become dead people in the eyes of the law for, I don't know, six or seven years."

McGuire turned onto George Washington Parkway, heading toward Interstate 395. He checked his mirror. His wife was still behind him. "Um . . ." There was a distance in his voice. "What're the chances Peter wasn't in that wreck?"

"Probably better than you think. Lots of people just disappear and then show up months or years later. Don't get me wrong. I don't believe for a minute that Peter would just take off, but people do. You think you know them and then they are gone. Anyway," Rick went on, "the real problem is that there's probably not a judge in Virginia who would declare Peter dead on the evidence we have. If he has an insurance policy, or if anything is in his name alone, it could be years before Elizabeth would benefit from it."

The exit ramp rounded the Pentagon parking lot and brought McGuire's car onto the interstate. He flipped on his turn signal, moved two lanes to the left and set the cruise control.

"I can't believe that," McGuire said.

"Believe what?" David piped up from the back seat.

"Nothing," McGuire sighed. He was relieved to know that David wasn't listening to the conversation. David went back to playing Connect Four with Jason.

*   *   *

Eight miles ahead of them at Springfield, Mike Downes was slowed by traffic congestion at the confluence of I-395, I-95 and the beltway. Perpetual construction had kept the intersection clogged for years. Downes and William Blevins, the director of Regulatory Relations for the phone company, had been sitting quietly, listening to the radio, since leaving the cathedral. Blevins had traveled to the service with several others from Downes's organization. When Downes saw him, he'd invited Blevins to keep him company on the cold, dark drive to Richmond.

Downes broke the silence. "If Peter's dead, what's Elizabeth going to do?"

"Why do you say 'if'?"

"I was just thinking," Downes continued. "This is one huge country, and although circumstances have caused all of us to look at one tiny spot on the map, in the hour and a half after Peter left McDonald's, he could have ended up anywhere in a 1,500-square-mile area. And lots of other things could have happened to him."

"Like what?" Blevins asked.

"I don't know. But given all the pressure he's been under lately, who knows what he might have done or where he might have gone."

Blevins looked at Downes. The red from taillights, white from oncoming headlights and blue-gray from mercury vapor lamps that lit up the intersection gave an eerie glow to the driver's face. "Do you really think he's alive?" he asked tentatively.

Downes stared ahead as traffic slowed to a crawl. "I don't know. I just don't know." He paused. "But the alternative seems too simple."

"And too terrible."

Downes nodded. The two sat quietly for several minutes, waiting for their minds and the traffic to open up.

"What if he is alive?" Blevins asked. "What then?"

Again Downes struggled to get past the I-don't-know stage. "Then I've got to find him."

"That's not your job."

Downes didn't respond.

Blevins sat quietly for a while and then asked, "Where would you start? What if he really is dead?" He tossed out half a dozen questions.

When he was done, Downes looked through the windshield at the sea of cars before him and muttered, "William, I don't know. I just don't know."

*   *   *

The hammer on the revolver slammed against an empty chamber. Glenn Segal pulled the gun away from his head. He looked down at the bullets lying on the bottom of the shoebox. No, he wasn't going to do it. He wasn't going to subject his wife to the shock.

Regaining his composure, he decided he was going after the cocaine and whoever was carrying it. He didn't know where to start, but he had read enough mysteries and watched enough television to give him some ideas. He put the gun back into the box, set it on the shelf and, standing a lot straighter than when he had climbed the stairs thirty minutes earlier, walked down to his study. He pulled out the phone book and looked up the number of US Air.

"This is Ms. Gaines. May I help you?" Segal couldn't believe how friendly and inviting those words were when spoken with a North Carolina accent. He repeated them in his mind, "Thizz iz Mzzz Gaines."

"Yes, Ms. Gaines, I'd like to book a flight to Norfolk." Then he retraced his steps to the bedroom, kicked off his shoes, slid under the comforter that blanketed the bed and succumbed to sleep.

*   *   *

Elizabeth Boget couldn't sleep. She sat silently staring through the windshield. The endless white ribbon of oncoming headlights merged with the equally endless red ribbon of taillights. Both gave way to black as trees closed in on the highway and the sun's final glow gracefully disappeared. Elizabeth's thoughts were far away, yet as near as the cathedral and the bishop's closing prayer.

"The Lord is my shepherd, I shall not want." The words of hope echoed in her ears. "He makes me lie down in green pastures, he leads me beside still waters; he restores my soul." The knot in her stomach was relaxing again. "Though I walk through the valley of the shadow of death I will fear no evil, for thou art with me." She felt that presence with her now. "Surely goodness and mercy will follow me all the days of my life, and I will dwell in the house of the Lord forever." Lost in her thoughts, Elizabeth O'Malley Boget smiled for the first time in forty-eight hours.

6

On Monday morning Virginia Bell's Public Relations office resembled a funeral parlor. Employees spoke in hushed tones as word circulated that Peter Boget had still not returned home. Though the conversation focused on the demise of their director in the Beltway Blast, one employee was quietly suggesting another possibility.

In one of the eight-by-ten cubicles clustered in the middle of the floor, Megan Churchill was sitting at the edge of Lucy Williams's desk, with her elbows propped on a pile of binders. She cupped her hand around her mouth and spoke quietly to the editor of the company newsletter.

"I wouldn't be surprised if he checked out," whispered Megan to Lucy. "I hear that he was in real financial trouble 'cause he broke the bank to build that new house, and then he didn't get any Christmas bonus this year because he got caught doing something. I think he was using cash advances to cover some personal expenses—and the boys in D.C. wanted him canned, and—"

"That's nonsense." Lucy interrupted when Megan paused long enough to catch a breath.

"No, it's not! You were questioned just like I was."

"We're not supposed to talk about that, and you know it." Lucy's voice was rising, but Megan ignored this interruption and kept on talking. "And

Jill told me that when the bonus checks were given out there wasn't one for Peter and that he didn't get a raise and anyway, if I had to go home to a house full of screaming kids, I'd split too."

Lucy hated the way Megan kept the rumor pipeline filled with stories about people in the company. What distressed her more was that the stories she told usually turned out to be accurate.

"I bet the car shows up and they discover Peter's gone to Australia or Brazil." Megan was on a roll. "You know what I think?"

Lucy signaled Megan to leave. "I don't want to hear another word."

But Megan persisted. "You wait. He's probably got a rich girlfriend or something, and they're lying on a beach in Acapulco sipping margaritas."

Disgusted that she'd listened as long as she had, Lucy stood up and walked out of her own cubicle. She left a smiling Megan sitting at the desk.

Lucy was heading for the ladies' room when Marge Conners came around the corner and announced that Mike Downes wanted everyone to come to the conference room for a briefing. The newsletter editor changed directions and headed toward the meeting. Megan Churchill was a few steps behind. They joined four men and six women who were talking quietly as they took seats around the table. Three other men, including Downes, followed them in, as did several women. Peter's secretary was with them.

Mike looked over the group and was surprised to see the entire office staff assembled in one place at one time. He waited until everyone was seated and then began speaking.

"By now you all know that Peter is missing. Some are speculating that he was in the fire on the beltway, but we don't know. The police identified the frame of a car that matches Peter's, but in the intense heat, all means of identification were obliterated. Still, we don't know anything for sure, and for the time being he will just be listed as missing."

Marge was wiping tears from her eyes as Mike continued. "I know that this office runs very smoothly when Peter is away on business or vacation, so I expect it will run smoothly now. I've appointed Janice to act on Peter's behalf." He nodded toward Janice Bland, the News Media Relations manager. "Now, there are two things I want to make clear. If calls come in asking for Peter, we say he's out of the office, period. Refer his calls to the appropriate manager or to Janice. Second, if Peter calls . . . or if anyone calls with information on his whereabouts, call me immediately, day or night."

Mike paused once again and then asked, "Any questions?"

There weren't any. He dismissed the group, and fifteen somber employees filed through the door. Then he called to Megan Churchill. She returned to the room.

"I know you like to talk about people and possibilities," Mike said, trying to be diplomatic. His voice was stern, yet quiet. Megan's face was blank. "But please try to keep your ideas private. We'll have enough trouble putting the pieces together here in the office. We don't need to be dealing with rumors as well. Do you understand?" He waited for a nod from her. "Good." They walked out of the library together.

Megan passed Lucy's cubicle. It was empty. She thought about finding the editor in the ladies' room, a good place to finish their conversation, but remembered that close-minded Lucy had already ended the conversation. *Oh, well,* she thought, *I'll just have to wait until the facts prove me correct.* Megan smiled, turned into her poster-adorned cubicle and sat down at her desk.

*   *   *

As she pulled back the drapes, the soft glow of sunrise enveloped a vibrant Debbie Steinbaugh. She tied the cord that encircled her silky robe at her waist and stepped through the sliding door onto a small balcony. Three floors below, the terra-cotta hotel patio was dotted with umbrella-covered tables and lined with rows of yellow-and-orange striped lounge chairs awaiting the fair-skinned sunseekers from the north. The glass-smooth waters of the huge kidney-shaped swimming pool reflected the deep blue morning sky, which was brightening with each hint that the sun was about to break the plane of the horizon. The white sand beach appeared orange-gray, stretching from the edge of the patio to where it slid beneath the transparent waters of the Caribbean.

"Would you close the drapes, please?" a sleepy voice growled from deep inside the room. "I'm not ready for morning."

Debbie turned and smiled. Jan Stevens pulled the sheet and bedspread over her head and buried her face in a pillow.

"No time for sleeping." Debbie's tone was so bright and melodic that Jan grabbed another pillow and covered her head entirely. "We're on vacation!" But there was no response from Jan.

Debbie quickly dressed, descended the stairs and walked across the still-empty patio. She thought about the interesting set of circumstances that had brought her to the beach at Cancún with an unmarried recovering alcoholic who was ten years her senior. She had told no one whom she was meeting in Mexico, but when her coworkers asked where she was staying, she'd admitted that someone else was making the arrangements. This had sparked speculation in the office, but Debbie had refused to discuss the matter further. She suspected her coworkers were concluding that she was vacationing with a man, but she didn't care. This was one secret she was going to keep.

She didn't want word to get back to her foster parents or to her former husband, since they had few good things to say about Jan Stevens. Liz Clark had disliked the overbearing computer operator the first time she met her—when Jan had been Debbie's roommate at the rehabilitation center in Arizona. Liz didn't like Jan's chain smoking; she didn't like the way Jan had patted Debbie's knee when the two sat next to each other, or the way she draped her arm across Debbie's shoulder. But Debbie loved the attention from Jan that she had rarely gotten from the Clarks. Debbie had latched onto Jan as the two struggled together to overcome their pasts.

After she was released, Debbie, beginning to miss her girls, had headed back to Colorado Springs. Jan Stevens had eventually been released and had returned to her job in Phoenix. The two women had written to each other occasionally, and once Debbie got her own apartment, Jan began calling her. Eventually, she had convinced Debbie to join her for a week's vacation in Cancún. Debbie had offered to pay her own way, but Jan took care of everything. She said it was her way of thanking Debbie for her friendship. Debbie thought the offer was strangely generous.

*   *   *

Mark Randolph was settling into his morning's work. He was hoping that Segal's absence meant his partner was taking care of business. When he picked up the receiver of his ringing phone, he expected to hear Glenn Segal's voice. He didn't expect to hear Segal's first words.

"Mark, I'm at the airport in Norfolk. I rented a car and I—"

"What?" Randolph shouted into the phone. Then he looked at the roomful of brokers and dropped his voice. "You're where? Norfolk? Have you gone crazy? You were supposed to call Kennedy, not visit her. You're going to stir up trouble."

"Mark," Segal said as calmly as he could, "I have to find the merchandise, pick up another shipment or get a refund today, or we'll both be in trouble. Big trouble."

"What are you talking about?" Randolph whispered into the phone. "If we don't get a delivery, we implement the contingency plan, that's all. Look, I want you to stay away from Kennedy until we figure out what happened. You know the rules. No personal visits, no direct calls, no contact outside the boundaries. If you walk into her office, she will crucify you. Let her run her investigation. This is no time to get squirrelly. Now get back on a plane and get in here. Your absence will attract attention. Do you hear me? Talk to Kennedy on the phone one more time. But whatever you do, don't go to her office. This isn't the end of the world."

"It could be."

"What's that supposed to mean?"

"If you would shut up, I'd tell you."

"Not here, not now. Call me back at 11:30. And . . . and please, don't do anything stupid."

"I'm not calling back," Segal said. But Randolph had already dropped the receiver onto the cradle. Segal hung up the phone, picked up his overnight bag and strode out through the airport's automatic doors.

*   *   *

With the older children off to school, Elizabeth Boget sat down for breakfast. She wanted to go back to bed and wake up to discover that this had all been just a bad dream. She knew better.

This can't really be happening, she thought. *Where could Peter be?* Despite having sat through the service at the cathedral, or maybe as a result of it, she began to think of all the other possibilities. Her thoughts were interrupted by the phone.

"Elizabeth, this is Jim." The lawyer's voice was soothing. "I'm terribly sorry to hear about Peter." He didn't wait for a response. "I was calling to see if you would like to get together and go over your papers."

"What sort of papers?" Elizabeth asked.

Jim Parker didn't want to mention the will, life insurance or anything else, but he knew he must. "I just wanted to see if there was anything I could do to help you with any papers you might have to sign concerning Peter's disappearance."

"Oh, I didn't think about that. I'll call you if anything comes up."

"Okay." He didn't want to press the issue.

Elizabeth had answered with a voice that seemed distant to the lawyer. "Thanks for calling."

When she hung up, Kristin's cry brought her back to reality. Ignoring the baby momentarily, she picked up the phone again and dialed.

"Tetterton and Parker," the voice on the other end of the line sang out.

"Jim Parker, please."

"May I tell him who's calling?"

"Elizabeth Boget."

"Oh," the voice turned serious. "Just one moment, please."

"Elizabeth?" It was Jim's voice.

"I'm sorry, I was distracted when you called," said Elizabeth. "We probably should get together."

"I can come by tomorrow evening."

"That will be fine. How about at 8:30 so I can get the kids to bed?"

"Would nine be better?"

"Probably. Thanks."

She hung up the phone and headed to Kristin's room. Jonathan, who had been watching cartoons, followed her up the stairs. He seemed to sense that something was wrong in the house and wanted to stay close to his mother.

*   *   *

Mike Downes's morning was consumed with Peter Boget. As word spread throughout the company, calls were pouring in. Now Charles Piper from Mid-Atlantic Bell's security office was sitting in Downes's office going over the situation. The trim black man with a thin mustache and bright eyes looked up from his notes. "The report from the state police is inconclusive. We'll never know if the car found in the fire was Peter's. And, despite some circumstantial evidence, we doubt he was in the accident. Given all the cars like his on the road, and all the places he could have gone, we have to say that the chance he was killed in the Beltway Blast is very remote."

Downes wasn't too surprised. He'd thought about the probability the night before.

"We think there's a much greater likelihood that he skipped town. In looking over his records, we think there are compelling reason why he might have just left."

Downes looked incredulously at Piper, who kept talking.

"Peter was rated unsatisfactory last year, the first time ever in his career. He was denied his bonus and was not eligible for a pay raise. He has been stigmatized because of the incident, and he may be thinking that his future here is pretty bleak."

"Wait a minute!" Downes exploded out of his seat. "You don't believe that, and I don't believe that. Peter got caught doing something wrong, okay. But your people blew it all out of proportion. He's given half his life to this company, and never, never for a moment has he backed off on his responsibilities. He admitted he was wrong, and he apologized for his action. If you remember, all he did was allow an employee to hang onto a cash advance an extra week or two when she was going through a financial crisis. The total number of dollars involved was—what?—less than two thousand?"

Piper looked straight into Michael Downes's face. "Are you saying that what he did was all right?"

"Of course not."

"Because if you are," Piper said deliberately, "then maybe you need to review the company's policy on personal responsibility."

"Don't be so condescending." Downes was infuriated. "I know Peter Boget, and I know he cares about people and goes out of his way to help them. If you were hitchhiking on the downtown expressway, he'd probably pick you up."

"I doubt it."

"I wouldn't bet against it. Anyway, last year was another story. He went too far. But he's repented and put the incident behind him. I wish you'd do the same."

Backing off just slightly, Piper paused, then said, "We can't rule out any possibility. We just want to get to the bottom of this quickly. I've been working on the case all weekend. We've already asked police in three states and the District to be on the lookout for the car."

Now it was Mike's turn to ease off. "Good, good."

Piper continued, "We would like you to issue a bulletin asking employees to watch out for his car too. You don't have to mention the circumstances or Peter or anything like that, just describe the car."

"That's fair enough," Downes agreed.

"And Mike," Piper said, "I know he's your friend. I know he's a good worker. But how well do you really know him? Be careful what you say. This isn't the same company it was five years ago. Bank on a loser and you might get burned."

Downes was boiling within, but he knew Piper was telling the truth. The two men continued talking about financial issues related to Boget. Piper painted a bleak picture.

"Without the body, dead or alive, everything in his name remains within the company. We may be able to get one more paycheck released into his bank account so his wife has some cash, but that's it for now. He's considered absent without leave, and that means his compensation is terminated. If he was carrying a higher rating, we might be able to get some concessions, but we'll be lucky if we can get Personnel to agree to the paycheck. At least he has direct deposit."

Downes didn't like what he heard. He thought about what this information would mean to Elizabeth and her kids. And he thought about how difficult it would be for him to tell her about it. Downes resigned himself to the inevitable. "What do I have to do?"

"Nothing now, except talk to his wife." Piper began to show some feelings. "I'm really sorry this has to be so hard."

Hard? Hard? thought Downes. You don't know hard. To you security people, everyone is guilty until proven innocent. Since that scandal in New Jersey, everybody and everything seems to be under your watchful eyes. What Piper had said about the company changing was right.

"I'm sorry too." Downes offered, ending the conversation. "Please keep me posted."

Piper stood, shook his hand and left.

Downes swiveled his chair around and peered through the miniblinds on the window. From his corner office he could look out past the imposing Federal Reserve building to the James River as it churned through downtown Richmond on its way to the Chesapeake Bay. His thoughts drifted back to that day in January when he'd had to inform Peter of the action the company was taking as a result of the "incident." That had been the blackest day in his career. Somehow, though, he felt his meeting with Elizabeth might be worse. It had been hard to tell his best employee and his friend that his rating was being changed from outstanding to unsatisfactory, knowing what that would mean financially. It had been even harder to explain how he and the company president had had to fight the people in Washington, who thought Peter should be fired on the spot.

Now he was going to have to tell Peter's wife—or was it widow?—that she couldn't expect any more money from Virginia Bell until Peter or his body was found. He was going to have to explain how she would have to purchase medical and dental insurance on her own. Given the loss of this year's bonus and the expense of the new house, Mike knew Elizabeth would be facing hard times. Hadn't Peter just recently talked about how they were looking at starting up a part-time sales business to help make ends meet?

Downes propped his elbows on his desk and buried his head in his hands. *Why me?* he thought. *Why now?* Then he picked up his phone and dialed Elizabeth.

*   *   *

In the shadow of Old Dominion University's campus, the architectural firm of Kennedy and Associates occupied a sprawling brownstone overlooking the Lafayette River. The location, on a tree-lined street on the west side of Norfolk, was away from the commercial hub of the city. Mary Kennedy liked it that way.

Glenn Segal drove by slowly, looking for the address Kennedy had given him on the phone. When he spotted the building, he pulled to the curb and parked beneath a huge red oak. He crossed the street, walked up five steps to the rambling front porch and pushed open the heavy wood-and-glass front door.

Once inside, Segal's eyes were greeted by Oriental carpets and renderings of what looked like brick and stone homes of the rich and famous. His ears were greeted with hushed sounds of serious office work, totally unlike the very busy noises of his own investment firm. The petite receptionist peered over her half-frame glasses and in a husky whisper asked, "May I help you?"

Segal looked from the name plate on the desk to the receptionist's warm brown eyes.

"Yes, Miss Westfield, I'm Aaron Fishbinder. I've got an appointment with Ms. Kennedy."

"Glad to meet you," she whispered back. "I'll call her."

When she hung up the phone, the receptionist asked Segal to have a seat. "Ms. Kennedy will be with you in a minute." Segal didn't expect "a minute" to mean just that, but in less than sixty seconds a sharp clicking of heels on wood signaled the arrival of Mary Kennedy. She was a handsome woman with close-cropped red hair, high cheekbones and a pleasant smile. She walked down the curved staircase into the foyer. Segal rose to his feet. He'd remembered the freckles and penetrating blue eyes. He hadn't remembered the sleek body, which now was accentuated by an exquisite, tailored black suit. He also hadn't remembered that she was taller than he. But then, the only other time they had met was at a bar and she had been seated, wearing baggy slacks and an oversized sweater.

"Mr. Fishbinder," she said, exaggerating her greeting as she extended a hand. "How good to see you again." Segal knew she was lying. "Come with me to my office."

Once upstairs, they passed into a large, well-appointed office dominated by a glass desk supported by marble pedestals. Beyond the desk, French doors opened onto a balcony that offered a pleasant view of the river. Kennedy closed the office door and motioned to an overstuffed sofa. As Segal sat down, Kennedy pulled up a wing chair and seated herself. Looking down on the overweight, balding stockbroker, Kennedy's countenance changed from that of a gracious host to that of a tyrannical monarch. Her speech was steady and slow.

"How dare you come here unannounced! You know the rules. I don't see you, you don't see me, neither of us sees the courier. If there is a problem, you call. I run a legitimate business that you could jeopardize by your very presence."

Segal cowered. He knew he would not be able to deliver Randolph's message about replacing the goods.

"We had an agreement," Kennedy went on. "I am the seller, you are the buyer. Once a shipment leaves Norfolk, it is no longer my responsibility—though I have someone looking for the courier. You were to insure yourself; that's why I keep my prices so low." Kennedy resembled a cat that had just killed a mouse and was playing with the dead body. "There are forty-eight kilos in two cases in the trunk of a white Honda. You know the license plate, and you have the key. If you want it, find it. But if I get an inkling that you've been made, you will be dead before the cops get one word out of you. Do you understand?"

Segal recovered enough to ask, "His name? What's his name?"

"No one around here has a name. Now, Mr. Segal," Kennedy's words were like a stiletto at his neck, "leave—and don't ever come back."

Kennedy became the gracious hostess as she escorted Segal to the front door. "Goodby, Mr. Fishbinder. Thank you for coming."

Segal shook her hand limply and nodded to the receptionist. He then retraced his steps to the car and drove off.

Kennedy returned to her office and placed a call.

"This is Mary. Did you pick up the print?"

Responding to the coded message, Patrick O'Hearn peered through his windshield at Segal's car as it turned east on International Terminal Boulevard. "I've got it with me now."

"Good."

7

Tuesday, March 20

Rick Wampler, Frank Griffith, Joyce McGuire and Mike Downes were sitting at the kitchen table with Elizabeth Boget. Mike had asked the pastor to be present when he explained the financial situation to Elizabeth. Frank in turn had called Rick, the accountant, and Joyce. Now they were sipping coffee where lately only six had been gathering for dinner, though the children insisted on setting a place for their father. Elizabeth was dressed smartly and wore a gracious smile, but she could not hide the sadness in her eyes or the tension in her face.

Mike reviewed Virginia Bell's policy for compensation.

"So, Elizabeth, that's basically the situation," he said, finishing up. "I'm sorry, truly sorry." He couldn't look her in the eye.

Elizabeth couldn't or wouldn't comprehend what she had just been told. Anger burned within her. She squeezed the tissue that she was holding between her folded hands, then dropped it into her lap. She rested her hands on the table.

"My husband worked for Virginia Bell for twenty years," she began. Her words, carefully selected and cautiously spoken, cut deep into the men at the table. "Now he is gone." She paused for emphasis, then spoke a series of sentences with the volume, tempo and pitch of her voice rising with each one. "He may have been burned alive while driving to a company meeting in Washington. He may have been in a terrible accident and is now lying near death in a hospital somewhere. He may have been kidnapped or God knows what, and you are telling me that his family is being abandoned, that the company is even going to cut us off from his savings and insurance?"

Her verbal assault continued as she punctuated each sentence with a long, icy pause.

"I've got five mouths to feed. Would you like to explain the company policy to them?" Her rising voice was a cold steel knife ripping through Mike's gut. "I've got a bank that will be wanting a $1,600 mortgage payment on the tenth. Do you want to explain the company policy to them?" The knife dragged horizontally. "I've got a $2,000 orthodontia bill that I expected our insurance to cover. Do you want to explain your policy to Dr. Madden?" The knife turned again. "How can there be nothing?"

Tears of rage streamed down Elizabeth's face. "Mike, I thought you were Peter's friend. I thought you were *my* friend. Why won't you do something?"

The three men sat speechless. Joyce put her arm around Elizabeth's shoulder and tried to fight back tears of her own. Mike wanted to reach out and touch Elizabeth, but he didn't dare.

Finally, the pastor spoke. "Elizabeth, Mike is doing more than you think. For the second time in three months he has put himself on the line for Peter—and you. But what happened with Peter has had a profound effect on the people implementing the company policy. Where there might have been some latitude before, there isn't now. But that doesn't mean you have been abandoned." He paused. "We're going to do what we can to help you while you sort everything out."

Rick and Mike nodded assent. Mike reached across the table and placed his hands over those of Elizabeth. He raised his eyes to meet her stare and quietly but deliberately stated: "If Peter's dead, we're going to prove it. If he's alive, we're going to find him."

These words seemed to lift Elizabeth's spirits. She was glad to hear someone talk in terms of a living Peter.

Before the meeting broke up, Frank led the group in prayer.

"Heavenly Father, you alone know where Peter is. Lord, we ask that you reveal his whereabouts to us. If he's dead, I pray you'll comfort Elizabeth and the children, and help us all accept the loss of a friend. If he's injured, bless the hands that are caring for him. And Lord, if for some reason he has chosen to walk away"—Frank had trouble finding the right words—

"stir in his heart a desire to return to his family and to you. Now I pray your special grace and protection on Elizabeth and her children during these difficult times. We pray this all in Jesus' name. Amen."

The others at the table joined in an audible "Amen." And as they lifted their bowed heads, Mike's and Elizabeth's hands parted. For a moment the weight of the conversation was lifted. A tear ran down Elizabeth's cheek and dripped into her coffee cup. The splash and collective chuckle broke the tension. "I guess I'm really messing up your day." She held the crumpled tissue to her nose as she spoke. "When Peter gets back, I'm going to remind him of how much he upset your productivity!"

Amidst the forced laughter, Elizabeth escorted her visitors to the door. She was glad that her neighbor had come earlier and picked up the two little ones, but now she wasn't anxious to face an empty house with so much on her mind. Elizabeth asked Joyce to stay awhile, and the two returned to the kitchen.

*   *   *

"What are you thinking about?"

Debbie Steinbaugh continued to stare into the vast blue-green ocean as she said, "I don't know."

"It's your daughters, isn't it? You miss them."

"Yes . . . and no. It's hard to say."

The two women were reclining in lounge chairs on the hotel patio at the edge of the beach. Their lotion-covered bodies were soaking up the rays of *el sol* as it crossed the equator on its annual migration north.

"I guess I have been working so hard to put the pieces of my life back together," Debbie continued, "I haven't had time to think about where I am going. I want a new life for Laura and Jennifer, but I also want a new life for me. I've had it with men who treat me like some kind of doll to be played with and then tossed in the corner. And I've had it with well-meaning people who want to dictate the terms of my recovery. Of people who won't accept me until I demonstrate sainthood or something."

Jan reached over and placed her hand on top of Debbie's. "I know what you're going through. I've been there. I'm still there. Ever since the alcohol, no one trusts me. No one believes I can be different. You're the only one who really accepts me, and I love you for that."

Debbie turned to Jan. "Thanks." The word was bland. She genuinely appreciated Jan's sentiment, but she was frustrated with the verbal lasso Jan often tossed around her.

"The only problem is that in a few days you'll be heading home to Colorado Springs, where I dare not show my face, and I'll be going back to Phoenix. You'll have your family and friends, I'll just have my job."

"But you have friends. What you need to do is find a church and—"

Jan didn't wait for Debbie to finish.

"I thought you just said you're sick of people wanting you to be a saint."

"I did, but that's not everyone. I've found some very special people at my church who have been helping me."

"With my luck," Jan shot back, "the only help I'd get in church would be from a bunch of rule-setting hypocrites who'd discover my past and assign me to twenty years of penance."

"Come on, Jan, I'm serious. There really is more to life than just living."

"Time out. Let's knock off this church crap. If you want to go, that's fine. I don't. If I want to be miserable, I will. The fact is, church is a crutch. It keeps you from facing reality. Where was the church when you were in the pits? Nowhere. Who helped you out? It wasn't them, was it? No, it was me. Did you forget?"

Debbie felt the lasso tightening. "Why are you always so angry when I mention church?"

"Because you're not content to keep it to yourself. You're forever trying to get me converted."

"Wait a minute, I didn't start this, you did."

"I asked you what you were thinking about. I didn't expect a sermon."

"This is not a sermon!"

"Look, maybe this church stuff worked for you. Maybe your friend Peter helped you discover a—what do you call it?—a relationship with Jesus Christ, but I'm not buying." Jan's tone became sarcastic. "After all, what has this 'relationship' gotten you? You don't have your daughters, and you didn't get Peter."

"I didn't want Peter," Debbie shot back, wishing the conversation hadn't taken this turn. "You know he's like a big brother to me."

"Of course he is," Jan baited her friend. "After he sailed back into your life, he was every other word out of your mouth, and you tossed me onto the back porch. Or have you forgotten that too?"

Debbie remembered. Peter Boget had returned to her life with a life-changing message, but also with a demeanor that swept her off her feet. And yes, his coming had brought someone else into her life, a someone who had in fact pushed Jan out.

Debbie remembered the little things about Peter, like the way he opened the car door for her, something her husband had never done, not even on their honeymoon. And she remembered how he listened—really listened—as she told her life's story. He didn't once condemn her. He just quietly told her about Someone who could help her through her difficult times. She had heard that message a thousand times, but somehow Peter made it come alive. He had pointed her to Jesus, but Debbie had gotten the message mixed up with the messenger. She saw in Peter the kind of man she wished she had married. A man of principle, a man of conviction, a man of compassion.

His message had eventually filtered through, but for weeks after that Sunday-afternoon visit, Peter occupied a large part of her thinking. His letters offering counsel from the Bible and sage advice from a husband and father did more than give her a boost from a big brother. They fanned the flame of passion that Peter had unknowingly ignited.

"So I got a little carried away," Debbie responded to Jan. "But that was then and this is now."

"I know this is now," her friend said. "And if Peter Boget walked into this hotel today, you'd be carried away all over again, and I'd be history."

"No, I wouldn't. I've learned to face reality. Peter was a dream, and I'm over him. Now I see that real peace and contentment come not from any one individual, or one set of ideal circumstances, but from God."

"Oh, no." Jan rolled her eyes. "Another sermon's coming." She leaned forward, spun out of the chaise longue and strode to the edge of the pool. Without turning back, she dived in.

After her swim, she returned to the chair next to Debbie. She adjusted the longue so it was flat, spread out her towel and lay down on her stomach.

"You want me to put on some lotion?" Debbie asked.

"No," Jan said abruptly.

"You'll get burned," cautioned Debbie, fishing through her beach bag.

"I'll be fine."

The two lay quietly for several minutes. Then Jan asked Debbie to put some baby oil on her body.

Reluctantly, but in the spirit of servanthood, Debbie poured some oil on Jan's back and began to spread it out.

Jan relaxed as soft fingers pushed the oil to the edges of her bathing suit. She asked her friend to cover her arms and legs too. "I love the way you do that," she told Debbie.

"I think this is stupid. Now that you're oiled, you are going to end up medium rare."

"Maybe that would attract someone looking for a good meal!"

Debbie didn't respond. Her thoughts were drifting again.

*   *   *

Glenn Segal's thoughts and actions were very directed. Just three calls was all it took to find out who owned a Honda with the license plate number ZDZ965. On the first two calls to the Department of Motor Vehicles, the clerks quoted department policy and refused to give out any information associated with the car Segal was identifying. On the third call, he encountered a man who was more understanding. Segal explained that he had been in a gas station when a white Honda drove out, dropping its gas cap on the ground. Segal thought if the man lived in the neighborhood he'd drop the cap by the man's house and save him the fifteen dollars and the hassle associated with locating a new cap. When he asked the DMV clerk for the address, the clerk not only readily provided the requested information but offered words of commendation for so noble an action.

A twenty-minute drive across the city brought Segal to an apartment complex just inside the Norfolk-Virginia Beach city line. His inquiries yielded nothing of value. Segal decided to head for the Norfolk City Library and start reading Friday's newspapers from cities on the route to New York. He also wanted to get the names and addresses of all the hospitals along that route.

He began with the papers from Hampton, Richmond, Fredricksburg and Washington, D.C. By late afternoon he had reviewed the papers from Baltimore, Philadelphia and New York, all of which had arrived in the mail earlier in the day. In all, six items warranted a closer look, with articles from the *Philadelphia Inquirer, Baltimore Sun* and *Washington Post* seeming to hold the most promise. He realized that dozens, maybe hundreds of incidents would not be reported in the major dailies, and he knew that if the courier had just decided to take off, the trail would be hard to follow. When he realized that the hospital identification task would take many hours, if not days, he decided not to tackle it right away.

Segal headed back to the draftsman's neighborhood before the traffic got too bad and took up residence in a booth at a Texas Sizzlin' steakhouse. The now very hungry stockbroker wanted to eat before he went out to call on neighbors who had not been in earlier. The rib-eye steak was on special, and its photograph at the start of the serving line made a convincing sale. Two would just hit the spot.

He made short work of the steaks, potato and salad and was working on his second cup of coffee when he pulled a stack of photocopies out of his briefcase. He spread the copies of the newspaper articles on the table, pushing his empty plate to the far edge. Then he opened the road atlas he had bought at the airport.

As Segal circled each accident's location, he correlated the time of each with Whitehead's probable route. He found only two good matches. He looked again at the articles from the *Inquirer* and the *Baltimore Sun*. In both, unidentified men were involved in automobile wrecks at approximately the time that Whitehead would have been on I-95 on Thursday night, March 15. Segal read through the *Washington Post* articles about the explosion on the beltway, but a careful review of the map reinforced his belief that Whitehead would have circled the capital to the east.

What was not lying on the table was a copy of the *Washington Post* article about Whitehead. Segal had no way of knowing that the edition of the paper delivered to Norfolk did not contain the Maryland Suburban section.

He also had no way of knowing that the man reading a newspaper on the far side of the restaurant was on Mary Kennedy's payroll and that soon their paths would cross again.

Segal gathered up his papers, put them in his briefcase along with the atlas and ordered dessert.

*   *   *

The patient in room 323 at Baltimore Medical Center was being fed by a steady drip from a feeding tube. After five days, his vital signs were weak and unstable. With each breath his lungs screamed with pain, a scream blocked by a scorched larynx and shut off by a sleeping brain.

"Mr. Whitehead's not doing too well today," said Dr. Rajani in a strong Indian accent. He was sitting at the nurses' station reviewing patients' charts. Nurse Chu was standing nearby.

"No, he hasn't shown much in the way of improvement," she said.

"Has anyone come to visit him?"

"No, not yet. But the police have located some friends."

In fact, Barry Whitehead's employer, William Heinemann, had been contacted by police, but with the whole firm working against a deadline on a special project, no one was in a position to drive to Baltimore to see a comatose coworker—not that anyone wanted to. Whitehead was a loner. He did his work well but spoke only when necessary to get the job done. He wasn't particularly pleasant, but then he wasn't particularly anything. The only thing that did seem to perk him up was attractive women, but he would never say much to them.

Heinemann tried to contact the draftsman's former wife and children who had moved to Fort Collins, but he got a recording telling him the number was no longer in service. The only other numbers he could find in Whitehead's Rolodex were for businesses. Not a single name or phone number of a friend was listed anywhere in Whitehead's records.

The owner of the engineering firm got the name of an acquaintance from Whitehead's barber. The friend said he would try to get up to Baltimore to see Whitehead, but wouldn't be able to bring back his car. Heinemann then agreed with Maryland officials that the safest place for the Honda was the police compound, where the car would be kept until its owner was released from the hospital.

Dr. Rajani closed the chart in front of him and turned to the nursing supervisor. "If anyone calls, be sure to tell them that Mr. Whitehead is in no shape for visitors."

The nurse, who had heard that directive from dozens of doctors before, nodded her head. *His next visitors,* she thought, *may very well be the ones at his funeral.*

* * *

The wind blew through Elizabeth Boget's hair as she stood talking with other parents at the edge of the soccer field. Both David and Lauren were practicing with their teams. Kristin was asleep in the stroller, and Daniel and Jonathan were kicking a ball with some other youngsters beyond the end of the field.

"Jeffery is really getting into this soccer," said one mother to the others. "It's not enough that we bought him a new ball, a new jacket and new shoes this season. Now he wants a second pair of shoes that cost seventy dollars!"

"Does he sleep with his ball?" another asked.

"Mine does," a third replied. "And he juggles the ball as he walks through the house. So far we've only lost a lamp, but my mind is the next to go!"

Elizabeth laughed. "You ought to see our back yard, or should I say mud hole. The kids have been playing back there every day this winter, and it's a miracle our windows are still intact."

The stories continued, each mother playing "I can top that" with anecdotes about her kids and soccer.

"I don't know where all this soccer stuff came from," said Carol Jensen. "When I was growing up, soccer was what people from other countries played. We didn't have a soccer team, and I didn't know anyone who played it, at least not till college. In our neighborhood, the boys played real games like football and baseball."

Jean Martin commented, "I don't know if I would call baseball a real game. It has about as much action as watching water boil."

"Yeah, but did you ever know there were so many ways to spit?" said Carol.

"And tug at . . ." Elizabeth didn't finish the sentence; all the mothers knew what she was thinking, and laughed. For a few minutes, Elizabeth's mind was on something besides Peter.

*   *   *

"What are you staring at?" Jan Stevens asked, turning to follow Debbie's gaze.

"No one. I mean, nothing."

Jan turned back to look at her friend, who was sitting across the dinner table on the hotel's veranda. "You look like you've seen a ghost."

"It's nothing."

"Don't tell me it's nothing. What did you see?"

Debbie slid out of her chair before Jan could put down her glass of iced tea and walked quickly toward the hotel lobby. She stopped, scanned the wide expanse of terrazzo and peered through the front door. Jan caught up with her and searched the lobby too, having no idea what she was looking for.

"I think I'm losing my mind," Debbie said, and the two headed back toward the table.

A puzzled Jan peered at Debbie. "All right, who?"

"Who what?"

"Who did you see?"

"I don't know. Forget it."

"Forget it? You jump up out of your chair and run after her, and you tell me to forget . . ." The wheels in Jan's mind were spinning as the two returned to their table. "Him." She looked into Debbie's eyes. "It's not a her. It's a him, isn't it?"

Debbie's face could not conceal her answer.

Jan kept talking. "Which 'him'? Richard? Klaus? Bob?" Debbie's face was impassive. Jan continued. "Peter?" The mere mention of the name turned on a light inside Debbie that shone through the otherwise blank expression.

"You saw Peter!"

Debbie said nothing.

"Oh, wait. It couldn't be. You've learned to face reality. Peter was just a dream. And you're over him."

Debbie's mouth remained motionless, but her eyes were picking up the oratory. "Okay, okay. I'm sorry. Let's change the subject."

In a few minutes, the two were talking about finding a place to go dancing, but they knew that wherever they would go alcohol would be prominent on the menu. And neither wanted to be too near the temptation.

"So what should we do?" Jan asked as she finished dessert.

"How about a walk on the beach?" Debbie replied.

"How 'bout a movie?"

"In Spanish?"

"No," said Jan, "I read in the tourist's guide that there is an English theater around here somewhere."

"No thanks. I don't get to the ocean very often. I'd rather just sit on the beach."

"And dream? Or face reality?" Jan teased. "I'm going up to read. I'll see you when you're done sitting."

Jan left Debbie at the table, where the attractive blonde received more than a few glances from the men in the restaurant. After a while Debbie got up and strolled into the lobby. She was looking for Peter. Nothing could suppress the feelings welling up inside her. Just the thought that he might be here in Cancún stirred an excitement within her. Then she saw him.

He was beyond the front door, standing in the glow of the hotel's lights. His face, his hair, his stance, she could see it all. She ran through the lobby and at the door called his name.

"Peter. Peter Boget!"

As he climbed into a taxi, Barry Whitehead glanced at the woman standing in the hotel entrance, uttered an expletive and turned away.

So that's how you say his name, Whitehead thought as the cab pulled out of the drive. *Boshay, like* Roget's Thesaurus, *and I've been saying "Boggett." What a jerk.*

Debbie watched as the taxi pull away. *He didn't see me,* she thought. *I must have been standing in the shadows. That's it.* She turned to ask the doorman if he knew anything about Peter, but the language barrier prevented meaningful communication.

Confused and exasperated but excited, Debbie walked through the lobby and onto the patio. She strolled past the pool and onto the beach. Jan, looking down from the balcony, saw Debbie and called to her.

"Dream or reality, Debbie?"

Had Jan seen him too? Had she heard her call Peter's name? Did she know something? Probably not, Debbie concluded.

She looked up toward the balcony on which her friend was standing.

"I don't know," she said. "Maybe both."

*   *   *

The catharsis of the afternoon's laughter helped put Elizabeth in a good frame of mind for the evening's activities. Her children were unusually cooperative in cleaning up after dinner. The two little ones got into bed early, and the others headed off to different parts of the house to tackle their homework. Eventually Jim Parker, her attorney, arrived. He and Elizabeth sat down in the living room, where they sipped coffee as he searched for a comfortable way to broach the subject.

"I've been going over the situation, Elizabeth, and I'm afraid I don't have very good news."

"What else is new?" Elizabeth smiled.

"I've reviewed Peter's will and the trust arrangement he set up in the event of his death. Unfortunately, since he isn't dead, or at least since we don't know if he's dead, those papers are irrelevant. Also, without a certificate of death, you won't be receiving any life insurance. What's more, here in Virginia a person has to be missing for seven years before he can be declared dead, and that's assuming that nothing shows up suggesting fraud."

Elizabeth listened intently as the lawyer continued.

"Legally, there is nothing we can do to speed the process, except find proof or strong circumstantial evidence that he is dead or alive."

"What about Peter's savings at the phone company? Isn't there any way to get it if I need it?"

"I've talked with the people who handle the program at Mid-Atlantic Bell," Jim replied. "The savings plan is in Peter's name, which means that it, like everything else, is tied up right now."

"That's what Mike Downes said, but I thought . . ."

"No. Not from a legal standpoint, anyway."

"But Peter told me that he was going to be taking $5,000 out this spring to cover some of our debts."

"He did, or was going to. Mike didn't tell you, but when he went through Peter's desk, he found the application. It had been returned. Peter had used one of the old forms that can't be used anymore. Mike didn't want to raise your hopes falsely, so he didn't tell you about the form. Knowing Peter's intent, Mike even thought about forging his name, but with the scrutiny this case would be getting from security, he thought better of it. Anyway, any check in Peter's name that you cash or deposit in your account could come back to haunt you. That action would constitute fraud."

"Come on!" Elizabeth said incredulously.

"Believe it or not, it's true."

The lawyer pulled out a blank form from his briefcase. "I've brought along a missing persons declaration for the FBI, and a request for a declaration of death. I'd like you to help me fill out the first. I'll leave the other so you will be able to look it over in your spare time. Even though we can't do anything about a declaration of death for seven years, some of the information that the court requires is information about Peter that is fresh on your mind."

Hollow eyes stared at the forms. Elizabeth didn't want to think about what the pieces of paper meant.

Jim kept talking. "I've done some research and have talked over the situation with the company. While we can't get anything declared legally for seven years, we can set up a trust fund for you and the children into which Mid-Atlantic Bell will deposit some of his savings and some of his ESOP money—that's the Employee Stock Ownership Plan."

"I know."

"But that may take awhile, since we will have to go through the courts, and there has to be a strong probability that something catastrophic has happened. If there is even the hint of fraud or that he has run off somewhere, there is no way a judge will authorize a trusteeship. There's even less likelihood that Virginia Bell would help to put it through."

Jim sorted the forms while Elizabeth processed the information. He set the declaration of death form aside, drained his cup of coffee and handed the missing persons form to Elizabeth. It was almost completely filled out, which relieved Elizabeth.

Pointing to the form, he continued. "The security organization at the phone company already sent one of these to the FBI, along with a photo, but we wanted to be sure that an official one signed by you is also filed to set the seven-years timetable in motion."

Elizabeth read over the information on the form. "I think you got it all," she said with stoicism. "Thank you for doing this for me."

"I can't tell you how sorry I am about Peter," the lawyer lamented. "I know you want to believe he is alive. I truly hope he is."

Elizabeth's mock-sarcastic response lightened the conversation. "I hope he's alive so I can kill him for putting me through this!"

They both laughed nervously.

Jim Parker took the cue and stood to leave. "God is in control. Someday we'll know what this was all about."

"I know."

"Let me know what I can do for you." The lawyer put on his raincoat as Elizabeth walked him to the front door.

"You've already done a lot," she said. "Just keep praying."

"We will."

Jim stepped onto the front porch and was saying his goodbys when Elizabeth stopped him. "Jim. Wait a minute, Maybe there *is* something else you can do for me."

"What's that?"

"I've been working on a flier. It's got Peter's picture on it. I'm going to get it printed tomorrow, and then I was going to mail it to as many hospitals and law enforcement officials as I could find. I wondered if you have professional directories for everything from Fredricksburg to Baltimore— at least for a start."

"Actually, I may have something better," Jim said thoughtfully. "We use a private eye who has assembled a database of all kinds of agencies that can help in locating missing persons. I don't know why I didn't think of him sooner. Let me get in touch with him in the morning."

8
_____

Wednesaay, March 21

Debbie was out of bed early. Her excitement and curiosity had kept her awake much of the night. She dressed quickly and slipped quietly out of the room while Jan slept. She walked to the elevator and stared at the numbers above the door. They lighted in sequence: 1, 2, 3. Then the door opened. Debbie stepped into the vacant car and descended to the lobby.

With her blonde hair bouncing on her shoulders and her blue eyes accentuating her newly tanned face, she walked to the registration desk. Though hinting of the ravages of time and a misspent youth, her face looked more like one that would show up on the cover of a children's storybook than on a magazine at the supermarket checkout. Her lips suggested a smile even when they were closed.

The man behind the registration desk was observing her every movement as Debbie approached.

"May I help you?" he asked.

"Yes." Debbie tried to contain her anticipation. "I would like the room number for Mr. Peter Boget. That's B-o-g-e-t."

"Just a moment, please." His fingers clattered on the computer keyboard. Then he looked up. "I'm sorry, we don't have a Mr. Boget registered."

"Would you check again? I saw him here last night." Her insistence, not to mention her charm, and the fact that the lobby was deserted prompted the clerk to swivel the computer screen so Debbie could see it. He began scrolling through the entire list of guests.

"Maybe you can pick his name out."

She studied the screen as the green names crawled to the top.

"Nothing," she muttered to herself. "He doesn't seem to be on the list."

"He may be sharing a room with someone else."

A completely new possibility flashed through Debbie's mind, cutting into her heart. *What if Peter is here with someone else, and that someone else is a woman who isn't his wife? What if he's in bed with that woman right here, right now?* She didn't want to think these thoughts, but she couldn't help herself. She thanked the clerk and walked out to the patio.

At the edge of the pool she turned toward the hotel. She scanned the balconies, which were bathed in the orange glow of morning. She didn't expect to see anyone, but to her surprise, several vacationers were out on their balconies, taking in the sunrise. None of them looked like Peter.

*   *   *

At the Executive Inn on Military Highway in Norfolk, Glenn Segal was waking from a fitful night. Reason clashed with irrationality. He had knocked on several dozen doors in Whitehead's apartment complex, but learned nothing. He knew that by now Mark Randolph had discovered the unavailability of their contingency fund. He also figured that Phyllis would soon suspect something was wrong. And he knew that he dare not cross Mary Kennedy.

I wonder how Whitehead enjoyed serving at the whim of that woman? How much did she pay him? Did he enjoy his runs to New York? Did he know what he was carrying? Was there more than one courier? How much cocaine did Kennedy move each quarter? Or was it each month? How was she supplied? Where did she process the merchandise? Did she send someone after Whitehead? How long will it take her to make good on the delivery?

Segal couldn't fit the pieces together, and he wasn't sure of his options. Too many questions raced through his mind, and each answer seemed to have something to do with money—lots of money. Money he desperately needed.

He picked up the phone beside his bed and dialed the last person in the world he wanted to talk to.

"Good morning, Mr. Fishbinder." Mary Kennedy's melodic voice finally came on the line. "Were you able to complete your business?" Her sweetness suggested that someone was in the office with her.

"Look, I'm sorry to call. But it's about Whitehead. I need more information. Where does he work? Who are his friends? Where do you think he might be?"

"Yes, Mr. Fishbinder, I see. One moment please."

Kennedy nodded to her secretary, who quickly stood and walked out of the office. When she resumed speaking, it was as if she had had both a vocal-chord and a personality transplant. "Segal," she began, "yesterday you visited the Norfolk City Library, you had dinner at Texas Sizzlin' and you made two trips to an apartment complex. You bought a newspaper, a six-pack and chips at 7-11, and then you drove over to Military Highway and checked into the Executive Inn."

"You've been following me?" Segal asked incredulously. "Why?"

"Security," she said in the same deliberate tone. "I'm watching you because I don't trust you. You are a bumbling idiot. You've seen too much TV. You can't just walk out and say, 'I'm looking for a guy who's got forty-eight kilos of cocaine that belong to me.' Now, before you're found floating facedown in the Elizabeth River, I want you to pack your bags, get on a plane to New York and leave the detective work to professionals."

"But how—how do I know that if you find Whitehead and the—the package, you'll make the delivery?" Segal stuttered.

"You don't, Mr. Segal," said Kennedy, not acknowledging his use of Whitehead's name.

"But I'll be ruined."

"Perhaps."

"You don't understand."

Segal was groveling now, and Kennedy loved it. She terminated the conversation with a few icy words. "I understand this," she began. "If you ever again set foot in my office, call me on the phone or mention my name, the consequences will be grave. Make sure that all further contacts are through Mr. Randolph."

The line clicked in Segal's ear.

Segal slammed down the receiver.

He climbed slowly out of bed and headed for the shower. In the glare of the bathroom lights he stared at the man in the mirror.

"You schmuck," he said to the balding, bedraggled figure in front of him. "You had a good job. Vacations in the Catskills and the Bahamas. A nice home on Long Island, decent kids, a sexy wife. So why did you have to get mixed up with drugs? Why couldn't you be satisfied? You thought you wouldn't get caught. You thought you were too smart. Now look at you. You're pathetic. A million dollars in the hole and a contract on your life." He leaned toward the glass and remembered his last conversation with a mirror. "Maybe you should have loaded that gun."

*　　*　　*

Lightly salted ocean air wafted across the warming sands, picking up the scent of tanning oil from scores of sun worshipers. It floated past the browning bikini-clad bodies that ringed a sparkling blue pool and wove its way through oceans of flowers before filling the hotel's veranda with the unmistakable fragrance of paradise.

Jan Stevens wore an oversized T-shirt to cover a neon-green two-piece suit and a red, blistering body. Debbie sat in her blue tank suit covered with an open blouse tied at her waist. In the shade of an umbrella, they were eating fruit and yogurt and enjoying the idyllic scenery.

"Why didn't you warn me that I was getting fried?"

"I did," Debbie reminded her quietly. "You wouldn't let me put on any more lotion after you got out of the pool. Don't you remember?"

"But it was already 2:30!"

"Yeah, and we're a thousand miles closer to the equator. You were the one who warned me about getting burned, remember?"

Jan paused and smiled weakly. "Yes. I remember. But you're the fair-skinned blonde. I'm the sun worshiper from Arizona."

Debbie turned her chair so she could cross her legs and face the ocean. She picked up her glass of iced tea, wiped the condensation with her napkin and lifted the glass to her lips. After a long, slow sip, she moved the glass down into the napkin on her lap. Staring through her sunglasses at the shimmering seascape, she said, "You know, ever since we got here, you . . . you seem different."

"Different?"

"It's just that you've been—how should I say it?—you've been . . ."

"Go on. What have I been?" There was a hint of irritation in Jan's voice.

"Well," Debbie replied in a whisper, "I don't think we're on the same wavelength."

"What do you mean?"

"I don't know. You seem to be jealous."

Debbie was glad she had said it. She continued looking at the line where the light blue sea met the lighter blue sky, and raised the glass of tea to her lips.

"What do you mean by that?"

"I feel like you're wanting to control me in some way. Every time a man has stopped to talk, you've driven him off. Every time I mention the people in my life, like my girls or the Clarks or Peter, you . . . I don't know what you do."

Jan sat impassively as Debbie continued. "I can't explain what I'm feeling, but I came here to kick off my shoes, toss my cares to the wind and escape for a few days."

"Isn't that what we're doing?" Now Jan *was* irritated.

"I guess so. Maybe there's just too much on my mind," said Debbie.

"Like what?"

"Like my job and my daughters."

"And Peter Boget," Jan added contemptuously.

"No, not Peter Boget."

"Come on, Debbie. You should have seen your face last night. And this morning, when I needed you to put Solarcaine on my back, where were you? Looking for Peter?"

"No, I wasn't looking for Peter. I just took a walk on the beach," Debbie lied. She wished she could retrieve the sentence and rephrase her thoughts, but Jan had already detected the untruth.

"I thought we were going to walk together. Why did you go downstairs without me, if not to find your man?" Jan's sarcasm knifed into Debbie.

"See what I mean? You're trying to run my vacation."

"Debbie, quiet down."

Debbie pulled off her sunglasses and glared at Jan. "No, I won't quiet down! Since I walked off the plane you have been telling me where to go, what to do and when to do it."

Jan responded plaintively. "I'm sorry. It's just that I missed you."

Debbie looked deep into her friend's face. "I missed you too, but not like this."

"What do you mean 'not like this'? Not like what?" Jan asked.

"Like this!" Heads turned toward the two women as Debbie shouted. "You're acting like a mother, or worse—a wife!"

In a hush Jan said, "Let's go upstairs and talk this out."

"I don't want to talk this out!"

"Debbie. Please."

"No." Debbie stood up and walked toward the beach. Jan hurriedly signed the check and raced after her, grimacing as her shirt chafed her burned back. She pulled alongside Debbie at the water's edge.

"If we can't talk, would you at least come upstairs long enough to put on some more Solarcaine?"

Debbie stared at the sea and waited as a weak wave splashed a blanket of foam toward their feet. As it encircled her ankles and then raced back to the sea, she turned and faced Jan. "All right. But I'm coming right back down to the pool."

Jan and Debbie walked back toward the hotel, attracting a fair number of stares. Though they shared a similar past, the two looked strangely different. Debbie looked younger than she had in years. Her figure was trim, her features were soft, and her smile was engaging. Jan's short-cropped brown hair, prominent chin and squared shoulders made her look harder, both in appearance and in attitude. Neither spoke until they reached their room and closed the door.

With great delicacy, Debbie lifted the T-shirt off Jan's broiled back. She unbuckled her top and waved an icy spray across the two-toned skin.

Jan bit her lip and fell across the bed. She buried her face in a pillow to hold back the scream of pain that swirled inside her head. Goose bumps ran up her arms, and she shuddered. Debbie set the aerosol can on the table and turned to go.

"Don't leave me, Debbie." Jan had tears in her eyes as she lay helplessly on the bed.

"I'm just going down to the pool," said Debbie, perplexed.

"I mean, don't leave me." She paused as if to be sure that what she was saying wasn't being influenced by the intense discomfort she was experiencing. "I need you. I want you."

Debbie stood looking down at Jan with a quizzical expression on her face.

Jan lifted her head off the pillow and gazed into Debbie's eyes. "I—I just want you to know that I love you."

Debbie glared back. "You've had too much sun." She shook her head and walked to the door.

"Wait!" Jan cried.

Debbie didn't.

*   *   *

At 2:10 p.m., David Boget's return from school was announced by a slammed door, a dropped book bag and the sound of a refrigerator being raided. Elizabeth's nap was over. She lay on the bed counting the minutes it took for David to inhale a sandwich, swallow twelve ounces of milk, drop the plate and glass in the sink, race up the stairs to his room, step out of his school clothes, pull on his soccer shorts, slam the bathroom door going in and out and race back down the stairs. The clock by her bed read 2:17 as the final door slam signaled his departure.

Miraculously, baby Kristin slept through it all.

Elizabeth was exhausted. She breathed a sigh of relief and rolled over. With Jonathan playing next door and Daniel not due till three, she hoped for another forty-five-minute catnap. She didn't figure on Lauren looking in on her baby sister immediately upon arriving from middle school, but she did. At 2:30, Lauren tapped on her mother's door.

"Mom," she whispered. Then, louder, she said, "Mom. I think Kristin is hungry."

Elizabeth raised her head. "Come in."

Lauren walked through the door with a baby who was half asleep. "The way she was sucking on her pacifier," Lauren whispered, "I figured she was hungry."

"She's sound asleep. Put her back in bed." Elizabeth was stern. Lauren complied, but the moment Kristin's cheek hit the pillow, her nap ended in a wail. Elizabeth's ended as well.

The mother of five wanted to bolt out of the bedroom and assail Lauren, but her body wouldn't cooperate. Six days of despair, fear and anger were taking their toll. She had searched for answers in her Bible, but had always come away with more questions. She kept asking God "Why?" when she knew in her heart that "why," or even "what," didn't matter. She had to focus on "who." She knew that the only person who could meet her needs was Jesus, but she struggled to see how that answer was working in her life.

These were dark days. And with each ring of the phone or knock at the door, Elizabeth hoped for a ray of light. She kept looking for Peter during each foray from home. But she didn't see him. She imagined hundreds of scenarios for his disappearance, most of which resulted in his prompt return home with a fantastic tale of intrigue. She would not—could not—give up hope. But day-to-day realities were draining her strength more rapidly than it was being recharged. Her Bible-reading and prayer times were intermittent, much like her sleeping, and as much as she fought against it, her prayers and thoughts were directed inward. It was easy to follow God when times were good. Now in her time of need she wanted to rely on her own resources to solve her problems. The flier she had prepared was one way to prove that she was still capable of taking charge.

But how long could she keep it up? Even now, she wanted to retreat to the bathroom and lock the world out, but Kristin's persistent wail beckoned her.

*   *   *

Glenn Segal sat in a plastic seat near gate 11 at Norfolk International Airport. He wondered who among those sitting in the waiting area worked for Mary Kennedy. He would soon be boarding a plane for New York to face the consequences of his indiscretion.

After pacing in his hotel room throughout the night, he had finally fallen asleep during "Good Morning America," and had been awakened by a knock at the door.

"Housekeeping." The woman was an alto in the choir of an African Methodist Episcopal Church, and she sang the word.

Segal rolled over.

Again the voice said, "Housekeeping."

Segal heard nothing.

The cleaning woman turned her key in the lock, pushed open the door and stepped into the room. "Housekeeping," she sang for the third time.

The TV was on, but the room was otherwise dark.

She heard an "uhhh" from the recesses of the room. "Oh, I'm sorry." She retreated.

Segal opened his eyes. "That's okay. What time is it?"

"Eleven forty-five."

"Thanks. I'll be out in half an hour."

The housekeeper had backed through the door and closed it after her. Segal rolled out of bed and headed to the shower. This time he didn't stop at the mirror. He had made up his mind to go home and face the music. Playing private eye was much more demanding than he thought. Clues don't fall in place the way they do on TV.

After showering, he had reserved a midafternoon flight to LaGuardia, dressed quickly and driven to the airport.

Now he was waiting for the boarding call. Randolph, he knew, would help him sort things out. And, while Phyllis wouldn't understand, what could she do? He concluded that he would be safer in New York among friends than in Norfolk with one of Kennedy's men on his trail.

*　　*　　*

The fresh salt air and warm water helped Debbie think through her relationship with Jan Stevens. For the first time she saw what her foster parents and her former husband had seen: Jan was a woman who had befriended her not for what she could give to Debbie, but what she could get from her. Their separation had increased Jan's desire for her, even as it had diminished Debbie's interest in Jan. The two were going in parallel but separate directions. Both were putting their lives behind them. Both were looking for substitutes for former loves lost. But while Debbie was looking for a Prince Charming to carry her off to his castle, Jan apparently had chosen the safety of women friends. Now Debbie realized that some of her letters might have communicated the wrong messages to Jan, and her eagerness to join Jan in Cancún obviously had been misconstrued. As she walked, Debbie thought about how she could graciously return the relationship to a simple friendship mode, with no strings attached. Yet she knew that strings were already in place, both emotionally and monetarily. Jan insisted on paying the hotel bill, and at the airport, when Debbie had handed Jan a check for the airline tickets, she had refused it.

More than ever Debbie wanted someone to talk to, someone like Peter.

He would know what she should do. Peter. She smiled as she walked along the white sand. Where was Peter? Had she really seen him? Or had her imagination been hard at work? Dream or reality?

The long walk up the beach brought Debbie to the Hyatt Regency. It was a white tower at the north end of the island, gleaming in the afternoon sun. She strolled in from the beach, visited a restroom and was heading back outside when she saw him. Her heart stopped.

Fifty feet from her stood the square-jawed, dark-haired man who had walked into her life twice before. She froze. *It's a mirage,* she said to herself. But it wasn't, was it? The man looked like the Peter Boget with whom she had spent so many hours, yet he looked strangely different. He was walking in bathing trunks toward the door to the pool. He seemed smaller than she remembered, and his walk wasn't right. Debbie ran across the lobby to catch him before he passed through the door. When she got within ten feet she called to him.

"Peter?"

He didn't turn. As he passed through the door, she caught him and tapped him on the shoulder. Through her broad smile she breathlessly gushed his name. "Peter!"

Barry Whitehead turned and looked at Debbie. Her glow evaporated. "Oh," she said, looking into his face. "You're not Peter." Her voice trailed off.

"Not Peter who?" he asked.

"Peter—Peter Boget. A friend of mine," she answered.

"Must be quite a friend," he said, giving her a once-over.

"He is," Debbie replied as the memory of Peter reignited the flame within her and the glow returned. As the two stood staring awkwardly at one another, she asked, "Were you up at the Mayan Holiday last night?"

"Why do you ask?"

"I saw someone who looked just like you getting into a taxi, and I thought it was my friend Peter. I can't believe how much you look like him."

Barry was still surveying Debbie. He liked what he saw. "So, tell me about this Peter." The two walked toward the pool and pulled two lounge chairs together.

Debbie began describing her friend and then interrupted her story. "What's your name?"

"Barry," he replied and forced a smile.

"Oh, hi." She gave an abbreviated wave with her hand. "I'm Debbie." Then she resumed where she left off.

Barry seemed uneasy as Debbie, having found someone besides Jan to talk to, unloaded much more than she should have. Finally she noted the time and said she had to go. When he learned how far Debbie would have to walk back to her hotel, he offered to put her in a cab.

"No, that's okay. I'm not getting into a cab wearing a bathing suit. I'll just walk."

"Wait here," Barry insisted, "I'll be right back."

Five minutes later, he returned and handed Debbie a few bills and a Cancún T-shirt. "Here, you can put this on."

Thanking him for his company, even though he hadn't said a dozen words in two hours, Debbie pulled the shirt over her suit, walked through the hotel entrance and waited for a cab.

After a short drive down the coast, the cab pulled up to the entrance of the Mayan Holiday. As Debbie walked into the hotel, she was surprised to see Jan.

"So," Jan drew out the word, "you found him." After a pause, her voice began to rise. "I've been looking for you everywhere! Where have you been? Why didn't you tell me where you were going? I've been getting worried."

"I'm sorry," Debbie responded. "I figured you'd be sleeping."

"Sleeping? For four hours? No, I didn't want you to have to be alone all afternoon, so I endured the pain of putting my bathing suit on, covering myself with Solarcaine and coming down here. I should have known that you would be out looking for Mr. Right." Jan didn't mask her feelings. "You don't appreciate me," she said, shaking her head slowly. "And after all I have done for you. Look at yourself."

Debbie didn't want to look at herself; she wanted to go someplace where people wouldn't be watching Jan's tirade.

"You were nobody before I met you. You were at the bottom of the pit, and I helped you out of it. I supported you with letters and phone calls. When you really needed a vacation, I brought you down here so we could be together. And you—you leave me in my misery and go chasing a married man."

Debbie was furious. She said nothing as she walked past Jan. Then a hand grabbed her arm.

"Don't you walk away from me," said Jan in a harsh, measured tone.

Debbie shook her arm loose and walked to the elevators. Several people in the lobby who were watching the quarrel turned away.

* * *

It was after seven when Downes locked his desk and headed for his car. He was perplexed about Peter Boget. Did he really not know the man? Could a Christian, a church leader, a hard-working employee, a devoted father and husband just walk away from life? Could he leave a dependent wife and five children? Downes's heart said no. His head said yes.

When he handed his parking ticket to the attendant, the man looked down and said, "I haven't seen Mr. Boget this week. Did you ever find him?"

Downes's expression was vacant. "Maybe. I don't know."

The attendant didn't understand the strange answer and wasn't about to ask for clarification. "Well, good night."

Downes looped the block and headed for the expressway. *If he's dead, I've got to know,* he thought. *If he's alive, I've got to find him.*

* * *

Debbie showered quickly and changed into a floral print dress. She slipped on a pair of sandals and hastily applied some makeup. She stepped out of the bathroom, picked up the T-shirt Barry had loaned her, grabbed her wallet and headed for the door. Jan sat on the edge of the bed glaring at her.

"Where do you think you're going?"

"I'm going to return this shirt to the man who lent it to me," she said.

Jan sat up straight. "What man?"

"It's not Peter, if that's what you are thinking. Just someone I met on the beach. He lent me a shirt and cab fare so I wouldn't have to walk back down the beach."

"I'm coming with you."

"No, you're not!" said Debbie emphatically. "I'll be back in ten minutes. I'm just going to leave it at the desk." Then she walked into the hall.

Jan followed her. "Wait, Debbie."

Debbie turned and in an exasperated voice asked, "What do you want?"

"My back's killing me," Jan whined. "I need help getting ready."

"Look, I'll be back in ten minutes."

"I don't want to wait ten minutes."

Debbie turned toward the elevator. Over her shoulder she called back to Jan, who was standing in the hall with her feet spread apart and her hands planted on her hips. "Ten minutes!"

The cab quickly covered the two miles to the Hyatt Regency. She asked the driver to wait and skipped into the lobby. She slowed to take in the beauty of the atrium, which was filled with Mexican music, tropical flowers and clusters of suntanned guests. The festive aura was accented by the lighted glass elevators that rose and fell through fourteen floors of open space.

At the desk she asked for the assistant manager. "I'd like to leave this for a . . . a . . . all I know is, his first name is Barry."

He scanned the computer. "I'm sorry, we don't have a Barry registered here."

"Of course you do. I spoke with him today. He went up to his room and got this for me," she said, unfolding the white shirt adorned with a golden sun and brightly colored catamarans skimming atop a turquoise sea.

"I'm sorry," he repeated. "I don't see any Barrys."

"May I look at the guest list?" Debbie asked. "Maybe I misunderstood what he said."

"I guess you can, but there are three hundred names here. Why don't you come inside the office and view the computer there?"

Accepting the invitation, Debbie joined the young man in the office, where he brought up the guest list and began scrolling through it. "Stop." Debbie looked at the screen in disbelief. "I think that's him." She touched her fingernail to the screen just below the listing "Boget, Peter 916."

The assistant manager looked at the woman with the golden hair. "That doesn't sound much like Barry."

"I know. Thank you very much."

"Do you want me to put the shirt in his mailbox?" he called to Debbie as she scooted out the door.

"No, I think I'll deliver it personally."

Debbie was totally confused as she left the office, and the impetuousness that had gotten her into trouble so often in the past was once again driving her. She walked across the lobby and entered one of the glass elevators. It afforded a beautiful view as it rose through the atrium, but she was not in the frame of mind to observe the scenery. She pressed 9 and urged the doors closed. When the elevator stopped, she walked briskly to 916, knocked three times and stepped back. Barry Whitehead opened the door. He turned pale when he saw Debbie.

"Mr. Boget," she said, extending the folded article of clothing, "I've come to return your shirt."

He just stood in the doorway. "Did you forget? I'm Barry." He stammered, trying to think of a last name that wouldn't completely expose him. Only one name came to mind, that of his tormentor. "I'm Barry Kennedy."

"Did *you* forget?" she asked sarcastically. "You registered as Peter Boget."

Barry Whitehead knew he was trapped. He couldn't believe it. Another woman was about to ruin his life. His mind flashed back to his mother, who had controlled virtually every aspect of his life. He hated her for hanging his wet bed sheet out the front window every morning for his classmates to see as they walked to school. He thought of his ex-wife, who had criticized everything he'd done, made fun of his lack of sexual prowess and talked openly about her affairs. Then there was Mary Kennedy, who treated him like an indentured servant, calling on him for favors day and night.

And now Debbie, whatever her name was, had caught him in the biggest deception of his life. *Why did she have to find me in Cancún? Three days either way and I would have been on my way to a new life.* Without expression, he invited Debbie in.

"Let me explain."

Barry told how he and Peter had run into each other at the airport in Denver and were struck with their similarity of appearance. He told her they had had a few beers while waiting to change planes and talked about trading places for a few days. "He was coming to a conference here in Cancún, and I was going to one in Orlando." Barry continued, "We wanted to see what it would be like to be someone else for a few days. We're going to exchange notes on our return trip through Stapleton."

Barry scanned Debbie's face for a sign that she was buying the story. It sounded pretty good to him. She laughed and talked about calling Peter and letting his secret out.

"I'll be talking with him on Saturday," said Barry. "I'll tell him I spoke with you. I didn't want to say anything earlier today. I knew he wanted to keep this all a secret. You understand."

"Yes, I guess I do," Debbie said on her way to the door. He followed her. She stepped into the hallway that overlooked the lobby and headed toward the elevators. Then she stopped, turned and spoke to Barry, who was still standing in the doorway. "Just one thing, Mr. Kennedy." Her voice was formal. "Peter Boget is a teetotaler. I don't think he's ever had a beer in his life."

The anger rising through Barry's neck met the fear that was draining color from his face. Debbie looked like the cat that had caught the canary. Then, remembering the taxi that was waiting for her, she abruptly turned and continued down the corridor. Barry Whitehead stood and stared at her as she waited impatiently for the elevator.

9

On Richmond's downtown expressway, Mike Downes slowed to pay the thirty-five-cent toll. He waited until he was under the protective cover of the booth before he toggled the switch on the car door to open the window. The wipers squeaked across the windshield, but Downes wasn't thinking about the rain. He was too busy trying to assemble in his mind one of the most difficult puzzles he had ever encountered.

Pushing the Beltway Blast well down on his list of possible causes of Peter Boget's disappearance, Downes visualized an array of alternative scenarios. He tried to imagine how each would impact Elizabeth and her children and, of course, how each would impact the PR office. The staff members were feeling enormous pressure, trying to pick up the slack in Peter's absence.

While these thoughts were racing through his mind, Downes kept recalling the words of the security investigator: "Don't hook yourself to a loser."

Was Peter a loser? Was he really a bum who masqueraded as a do-gooder? No, thought Mike, *it couldn't be. Or could it?* His mind searched for answers, but none came. He said a silent prayer. Still nothing came. Finally, as if a spotlight had been thrown onto a dark stage, Mike remembered Peter's book, the one he always said he was writing.

For years the public relations director had told people that they or their actions would show up in his book. No one ever saw it, but this phantom book tended to make most people uneasy, and it probably had had some role in protecting Peter when the boom was being lowered.

Now Downes realized that maybe, just maybe, that phantom book really was in his computer. Maybe answers to the questions about his disappearance were sitting in his office. He exited the expressway at Floyd Avenue, made two rights and a left and got back on the toll road heading downtown. The rain continued to make driving difficult, but he didn't notice. His mind was on the computer waiting on Peter's desk and the secrets he was about to unlock.

*   *   *

Dread overwhelmed Debbie Steinbaugh once the brass doors of the Hyatt's elevator isolated her from the man who was posing as Peter Boget. She dared not look out of the glass cylinder as it descended through the hotel's atrium. The confident smile that had telegraphed her "I've got you" message to Barry Kennedy—if that was really his name—was swallowed by the realization of what she had just done. She had told a man whom she didn't know that she had trapped him in a lie, a lie that could only mean one thing: calamity had befallen Peter. She trembled as she asked herself a battery of questions. *Who was the man who had given her his shirt? Why did he register as Peter Boget? What did he know? Who was he hiding from? What would he do now that someone else knew he was not the person he claimed to be?*

When the doors opened, Debbie strode quickly out of the elevator and headed for the door. She turned neither left nor right but walked directly through the lobby, out the front door and into the waiting cab. She didn't notice that nine floors above her Barry Whitehead was entering one of the glass elevators.

As the taxi took off, Debbie leaned forward as if to make the speeding cab move even faster. She had to get to a phone. She had to call Peter. She had to know. Her dread was replaced by fear as she realized that Barry could be a murderer, that Peter could be dead and that Barry might be coming after her and . . .

She tried to put those thoughts out of her mind as the taxi pulled up to the entrance of her hotel. Debbie paid no attention to the cab pulling in behind her as she counted out some pesos and handed them to the driver.

She brushed past the bellman and, with long strides, crossed the hotel lobby toward the elevator. Her heart was racing, and she was breathing heavily. She had only one objective—to get to the safety of her room so she could place a call.

But as Debbie passed the concierge's desk, a hand clamped down on her forearm and spun her around. She was inches away from a face that communicated bitterness and rage. Debbie tried to jerk her arm free, but the hand, like the jaws of a German shepherd, held on.

*   *   *

At the Virginia Bell building in Richmond, Mike Downes eased into his high-backed executive chair, unlocked his desk and pulled out the file drawer. He flipped through the hanging files, reached into one and retrieved a large envelope. He unclasped it and dumped out seventeen small, sealed envelopes. He sorted through them until he came to the one with "Peter Boget" handwritten across the front. He opened the envelope and unfolded the enclosed piece of paper. It listed the password for Peter's private file on his computer.

The security organization had already investigated Peter's computer and had even informed Downes about the encrypted file they couldn't access, but Downes had completely forgotten that Peter had gathered passwords from his staff and had given them to him. This evening, in the car, he had remembered the envelope in his desk.

Downes placed the unopened envelopes back in the larger one, slipped it back into the file, locked the drawer, turned out the lights and headed to the PR office on the tenth floor. In the elevator he unfolded the small piece of paper. He chuckled as he stared at the password: COWABUNGA-DUDE.

*   *   *

"Cowabunga, dude!" Jonathan Boget shouted as he jumped from his bed onto the floor. The three-year-old, clothed in green Teenage Mutant Ninja Turtles pajamas, was racing around his bedroom. His mother was putting Kristin to bed, and Jonathan was taking full advantage of her absence. "Heeee-ya!" he yelled over and over again as he attacked an imaginary foe.

"David," Elizabeth called to her oldest son, "would you help your brother get his teeth brushed, and then get him into bed?"

"Sure, Mom." He paused just outside the door to Kristin's bedroom, where his mother was changing the baby's diaper. "Do you hear him up there?"

"I hear him," Elizabeth smiled through her sigh.

"You're going to have to get rid of that Turtles video, Ma, I don't think they're 'in' anymore."

"Who?"

"The Turtles," he replied. "I mean they're history."

Elizabeth smiled at David, who turned and headed for the bedroom Jonathan shared with Daniel. When she looked back up, David was again standing at the door.

"That was really fun tonight, Mom. We ought to do that more often."

"I thought you didn't like looking at family videos."

"I guess I never thought about how entertaining they are. You know what I mean. I mean trying to get that family photo was great."

"I could tell," she laughed. "I thought you and your sister were going to wear out the tape running it backwards and forwards and all that slow-motion stuff."

The video had been taken in December, while the family posed for a family photo to enclose in Christmas cards. Peter had set the camcorder on a chair to record the event. Besides showing the usual fidgeting kids and the combing and recombing of children's hair, the video captured the passing of baby Kristin from Lauren to her dad after he triggered the ten-second timer on the Nikon. At the moment of transfer, Kristin began depositing her dinner on Peter's arm. In an effort to avoid having his suit soiled, Peter swung the baby away from himself just as the camera flashed. Frozen forever on Kodak film was the memorable scene of a fashionably attired Peter holding six-month-old Kristin by one leg above the heads of three children who were jumping to avoid the white liquid dribbling from the baby's mouth. The fourth child, little Jonathan, seemed to be unaware of the unfolding disaster and stared at the ceiling with a finger up his nose.

David turned more serious. "It was good to remember Dad, too," he said, biting his lip. Then he stepped out of the bedroom and turned toward the noise at the end of the hall. "Okay, Jonathan, it's time to brush your teeth."

The three-year-old didn't hear David. In his room he continued to karate-chop invisible forces, interspersing his "heeeyas" and "hiiiiiyas" with "radical" and "awesome" and "that's cool, dude"—the vocabulary of his favorite heroes.

*   *   *

Standing in the lobby of her hotel, Jan Stevens gripped Debbie's forearm tenaciously. "And where do you think you're going?"

Debbie started to say, "To make a call," but Jan interrupted. "You told me you'd be back for dinner in ten minutes. I've been waiting for thirty-five."

"Not now," said Debbie, trying to shake free. "I've got to make a call."

"Who to? Peter?" Jan asked sarcastically. "Look, I didn't plan this vacation to have you chasing some man all over the beach. Do you understand that?"

"Let me go!"

"No, I'm not going to let you go. You said we were going to dinner, so I say we're going to dinner."

"And I said not yet."

Jan jerked Debbie's arm. "Listen to me, we're going to dinner. You owe that to me."

"I don't owe you anything." Debbie's voice was rising, and again she tried to free herself from Jan's grip. Several people in the lobby turned to look at the arguing women.

"Look, Debbie, you've got to forget Peter and all the rest of the men on this planet. They're nothing but trouble."

"*You're* nothing but trouble!" Debbie exploded. "Let me go." With as much strength as she could muster, she swung her captive arm up and out, lifting Jan's in the process. When the taut, burned flesh on Jan's back stretched with the arm movement, the jolt of pain caused her to release her grip and begin a scream that was punctuated by the impact of Debbie's suddenly free hand slapping against Jan's face.

Two dozen eyes watched as Jan reflexively slapped Debbie across the chin and yelled, "Are you trying to kill me?"

Aware of the spectators, a red-faced Debbie lowered her voice. "No, I'm not trying to kill you. Just leave me alone! I'm going upstairs to make a call. I'm going to find out what happened to Peter, and I'm going now." She turned her back on Jan, who now had tears welling up in her raging eyes.

Jan couldn't conceal her anger, and now she didn't care if everyone in the hotel was watching her. She was shaking, and her jaw hurt so much that she could hardly open her mouth. "You're going to be sorry!" she shrieked at the blonde who was disappearing into the elevator.

Debbie stopped, turned around, pointed her finger at Jan and said icily, "Sorry? I don't think so. You're the one who's going to be sorry." She whispered the rest of the sentence to herself as she backed into the elevator. "Sorry that I'm leaving, that I'm fed up and I never want to see you again."

The doors closed. Jan stood motionless in the lobby for several seconds, then began looking at each of the people who had gathered to watch the fight. One by one they dropped their eyes and walked away. Jan passed through the lobby and walked out toward the beach, while Debbie rode the elevator to the third floor, oblivious to the person standing behind her. She was so angered, embarrassed and confused that when the doors opened on her floor, she didn't realize that the other person in the elevator was stepping out behind her. It wasn't until she turned the key in the door that she became aware of his presence.

A hand reached past her head and pushed the door open. Startled, Debbie glanced back over her shoulder in the direction of the arm. Color drained from her face as she looked into the eyes of Barry Whitehead.

"Can I come in?" He wasn't asking so much as telling. "I've got to talk to you."

*   *   *

Mike Downes walked into his missing friend's office, switched on the desk lamp and sat down in front of Peter's computer. A half-dozen photos of Peter with his family hung on the wall to Mike's left. Twice as many framed awards flanked the door, which was centered on the far wall. To the right was the wall known throughout the company as La Galleria-Bella. The entire wall was covered with corkboard onto which hundreds of pieces of paper had been pinned: newspaper articles, cartoons, posters, ads— anything and everything related to the phone company, politics and the free-enterprise system. Most were humorous, some were merely outrageous. Several times a week new items would appear, even when Peter wasn't around. His employees, his friends, even the company president would drop by now and then to tack up a one-liner or a cartoon.

But Downes hadn't come to admire Peter's gallery; he'd come to read his private electronic files. He knew that security had already reviewed all the files on the computer and all the disks in his office, ostensibly looking for clues to Peter's disappearance. He also knew from Marge that they went through all of the file folders stacked on Peter's desk and on the credenza and window sills behind the desk. He suspected they were more interested in searching for unauthorized entries in the computer, or a company paper clip attached to a personal note, anything to support their theory that the missing director was really a bad apple.

Downes was aware of the security crackdown on the personal use of computers. He supported rigorous enforcement of the company's policy prohibiting the use of computers for nonbusiness activity. It was one of just a few issues on which he and Peter found themselves on opposite sides. Peter had objected to the computer policy and had prepared a report for the Mid-Atlantic Bell executive committee demonstrating how allowing employees to use computers for personal work on noncompany time would improve productivity and morale. He had argued, unsuccessfully, that at a time when salaries were frozen and people were being asked to do more with less, allowing use of computers would be a low-cost way of rewarding employees for their service to the company while giving them an opportunity to polish their computer skills.

Now Downes was going to find out if his subordinate had willingly violated company policy, and if clues to his whereabouts were lurking in the bits and bytes of Peter's computer.

*   *   *

Startled by Barry's presence, Debbie stumbled backward into the hotel room. Barry stepped in after her and allowed the door to swing shut. Debbie sat down on the bed, but immediately wished she hadn't. Barry towered over her. She was scared.

"There was an accident." His first words were cold and emotionless and had the effect of adding shock to the fear Debbie was already experiencing.

Barry had followed the blonde woman to plead with her not to reveal his identity, to let him escape into anonymity. He knew it was going to be another scene like the one he had had with Mary Kennedy when she found out about his drug use, but he had run after Debbie anyway. While every eye in the lobby was riveted on the fight between two women, Barry had slipped into the elevator and waited.

Now he stood over the cowering woman. Dressed in white slacks and a red shirt, Barry looked more in control than Debbie wanted to see. She had no way of knowing that he was trembling with fear on the inside. After letting his first words sink in, he grabbed a chair and sat down in front of her. Their knees were nearly touching, and Debbie was very uncomfortable. Still, she desperately wanted to hear about Peter. She didn't move.

Barry pleaded his case in a voice that resembled a 33 RPM record being played at 45—high and fast. "It was along the interstate at night. I got a flat. This car pulls up and out steps a man who looks like the man I see in the mirror every morning. We laugh, and he asks if I need help. I tell him I can't open my trunk. He goes up to his car—it was in front of mine—gets a flare, lights it and starts back toward me. I fumble with the trunk lock. He comes up along the right side of the car—you know, away from the traffic—steps into a hole, trips and hits his head on the mirror. He's holding the flare and falls into the ditch along the side of the road. He rolls onto the flare and I think he's a goner. I roll him over, but when I do his clothes flame up in my face so I let him go and run to his car to go for help. There's a phone in the car, but I can't figure out how to use it so I drive to the next exit. But then I'm thinking, if I go back with help, the cops will question me and open the trunk and find—"

He stopped abruptly and stared into Debbie's ghost-white face. "Then I think, if I become him and he becomes me and I become dead, then the people who are after me won't be after me anymore and then I can go to Ephrata and live a normal life and I don't have to be a slave and I won't end up in jail—unless someone discovers me." Barry stopped, leaned forward and took Debbie's hands in his own. She tried to pull them out, but he squeezed them tightly. In a low, slow voice he said, "You're that someone. That's why I'm begging you never to breathe a word of this to anyone."

He's crazy, Debbie thought, *weird and crazy.* She was confused and didn't understand what he meant by "I become him and he becomes me and I become dead." She wasn't sure she wanted to know. What she was sure of was that she didn't like being in a hotel room with a strange man who had her in his grip—especially not now, when the news of Peter's death was overwhelming her, choking off her breath.

"Do you understand? I can't have anyone know I'm alive, or they will come and kill me." Barry's words were very understandable, but Debbie couldn't comprehend why this man would come to her hotel room, force his way in and tell her such an unlikely story. Was he planning to kill her? Was he going to kidnap her? And what about Peter?

She began trembling. Her mind tried to fit together the pieces of this complex puzzle. Why was this man begging for anything? Why wasn't he making *her* beg for something? She pulled her hands away. "But how could you leave a man to die on—"

"You don't get it, do you? I just asked you never to say a word about this, or someone will track me down and kill me."

"Who?"

"You don't need to know." Barry's words were direct and forceful, yet they seemed to allow room for further discussion.

"You can't leave a man to die and not expect to have to answer for your actions." Debbie wanted to retrieve her words, but she was too late. Barry's countenance changed suddenly. The anger simmering beneath the surface burst into rage. His eyes were on fire, his body coiled for action. He stood abruptly, flinging the chair against the wall, and pushed Debbie flat onto the bed.

"Promise me you'll never breathe a word of this to anyone," he demanded. "My life is on the line."

With great difficulty, Debbie stopped shaking long enough to say, "I promise."

The next words spoken by Barry were vile, unlike all that had preceded them. To Debbie, it seemed as if an evil spirit had taken control of his tongue, if not his entire mind and body. "No you don't. You're lying, just like every other woman I know. You don't care about me, you only care about this Peter, this dead Peter." His voice was sinister. "And your kids."

He backed away from the bed and picked up the wallet Debbie had dropped when she stumbled into the room, the one she had been holding when she had returned the shirt.

"Gimme that," Debbie said.

Barry pushed her down and opened the wallet. He flipped through the photos and leered. "Nice-looking girls. Your daughters, I'd guess." He closed the wallet and stuffed it in a pocket in his pants.

Debbie propped herself on her elbows. "What are you doing?"

"Insurance."

His twisted smile told Debbie exactly what he meant. She leaped to her feet, but before she could utter a word, Barry grabbed her by both arms and threw her back onto the bed.

"I know people like you. Pretty on the outside, but ugly where no one can see it. The moment I walk out of here, you're going to tell your friend or call the police. But I can't let that happen, can I? So I'm just going to take this wallet," he said as he patted his pocket, "so I know where you live and what your kids look like. Just in case you forget your promise and decide to open your mouth."

"I won't, I won't. Please leave me and my kids alone." She pulled her legs up under her and inched backward on the bed.

"I know you won't, but I want to be sure."

"What are you going to do to me?" A terrified Debbie was sobbing as she tried to pull herself away from Barry, who was now leaning directly over her.

"Let's say I'm settling a score. I'm going to give you something to remember me by," Barry scowled.

"No—please."

"The time has come for women to stop messing with me." In a blur of motion he unfastened his belt, yanked it through the loops of his trousers, swung it into the air and brought it whipping down onto the bedspread next to Debbie's head. "Do you understand now?"

Debbie didn't understand. She didn't know that at that moment she had become the object of Barry Whitehead's seething hatred of women. She was the mother for whom nothing he had done had been good enough. She was the teacher whose false accusation of cheating had cost him his college scholarship. She was the fiancée he had found in bed with his roommate. She was the wife who had ridiculed his every effort to be a husband and father. She was Mary Kennedy, who had reduced him to indentured servitude. And now he was going to symbolically get back at them—each one of them—with one uniquely male act.

He ordered Debbie to strip.

"But I'm not going to say anything," Debbie pleaded. "I promise, I promise." She was crying as she slid back across the bed, hoping to find an opening to run. "Don't do this to me, please don't do this to me."

Dropping his slacks to the floor, Barry crawled onto the bed after her, his belt still in his hand.

"Don't do this to me." Debbie started to scream, but the sound was choked off by a tightening in her chest and throat.

"I said *strip!*" Debbie was weeping, but she wouldn't cooperate.

"Let me help you."

This time her scream came, but it was silenced when Barry forced his belt hard into her mouth. Debbie writhed to escape but was no match for Barry, who was uttering a stream of profanities as he tried to pin her down.

Just then another scream filled the room as Jan Stevens pounced on the back of Debbie's assailant.

Jan's nails tore into Barry's cheek as she grabbed his head and tried to pull him off Debbie, but the surprised man flipped her the other way. As she went sprawling toward the edge of the bed, Jan grabbed for Barry's shoulder, missed and instead ripped open the flesh on Debbie's forehead. As she fell off the bed, Jan's right temple was punctured by the corner of the nightstand.

Barry jumped to his feet, shocked back into reality. Jan's scream had shut down the monster within, leaving him dazed and shaking.

He reached for his slacks, mumbling, "Oh, God . . . what have I done?" Continuing the chant, he took three quick steps to the door, then stopped. He looked back long enough to see Jan's limp body lying on the floor with blood spilling across her face and collecting in a puddle on the floor.

Then he looked at Debbie. Her anguished face was devoid of color, her tangled hair had lost its form. Her blouse was torn and hanging open, her wrinkled skirt was halfway up her thighs, and a trickle of blood ran into her left eyebrow from a gash on her forehead. "I'm sorry. I'm so sorry." His voice was plaintive as he repeated the phrase while backing out of the door. In the corridor he spotted an exit sign, raced to the stairwell and disappeared behind the door.

Deborah Blanton Steinbaugh's nightmare had only just begun.

*   *   *

Mike Downes turned off Peter's computer. He was frustrated. In the private electronic folder he had found three folders, one containing files on each of Peter's subordinates. Another contained a collection of anecdotes about life at the telephone company—great stuff for the book Peter was always referring to, but without a clue to his disappearance.

The third folder was the source of Downes's frustration. It was shielded from prying eyes by another layer of encryption. Labeled "DBS," it contained a series of documents identified only by number. *What or who is DBS?* he thought. *Why are these locked files buried so deep in his private area? Are they personal?* Had Peter deliberately defied company policy? Did the files hold the secrets to Peter's disappearance? Downes began to realize that he probably would never know.

Before he turned out the desk light, Downes stepped up to the family photos on the wall. "Where are you, Peter?" he asked softly, looking at a picture of his smiling friend cradling a newborn in his arms. "And what is DBS?" Downes reached back toward the desk, twisted the switch on the lamp's base and walked out of the office.

*   *   *

For Elizabeth's children, the loss of their father was cushioned by the special attention paid the family by aunts and uncles, grandparents, teachers, neighbors and members of their church. The outpouring of sympathy obscured the questions that continued to arise about Peter's true whereabouts. Because Elizabeth refused to allow those around her to talk in terms of a dead husband and father, some who were prepared to offer a full measure of support held back, waiting for additional revelations. But the support that did come buoyed the family and brought about a new sensitivity among the children to the needs of the household. Almost overnight David and Lauren became more cooperative and the bedtime struggle was eased.

As Elizabeth rocked Kristin to sleep, David helped his brother slide between his "Turtles" sheets, pulled the comforter up to his neck and turned off the light.

"Mom will come by in a few minutes to pray with you. Don't get out of bed."

A giddy Jonathan was twisting and turning under the covers, still fighting bad guys in his mind.

*   *   *

The two Cancún policemen shot questions at the unresponsive blonde woman, who sat on the floor of a hotel room cradling the bloody head of another woman. Debbie Steinbaugh remained motionless, staring at an overturned chair, as one of the men grabbed a towel from the bathroom and pressed it against the wound that was spilling blood into Debbie's lap. The other checked for a pulse while barking orders to the hotel staff to call for an ambulance.

Jan Stevens wasn't dead, but her pulse was hardly detectable and her breathing came in intermittent gasps. The fact that Debbie herself was in a state of shock further concerned the officers. After checking her facial wounds, they decided she was not in any danger. At least, not medically.

Two additional officers arrived with the emergency medical crew and immediately began questioning everyone they could find. The screams, the fight in the lobby and the previous argument in the restaurant were quickly documented. Within an hour after they arrived, the police had scoured the room for evidence and identification. Then, taking Debbie by the arm, they escorted her to a waiting patrol car.

*   *   *

From a phone booth in the lobby of his hotel, Barry Whitehead called home to Ephrata, Pennsylvania. When his father's answering machine completed its message, he said, "Pop, this is Barry. I've decided to come tomorrow instead of Saturday. I'll be arriving in Lancaster at 5:45 p.m. on a commuter plane from Philly. I'll call at noon tomorrow from Miami to see if you can pick me up. Thanks."

*   *   *

Word of Jan's condition reached the police station before Debbie did. When she arrived, she was booked for attempted murder. Still catatonic, Debbie was handcuffed and taken to a small interrogation room.

"What's your name?" asked the principal interrogator in heavily accented English.

Debbie said nothing as she stared blankly at the wall.

"What are you doing in Mexico? Why don't you have identification?

Answer me. You must tell me: why did you try to kill Jan Stevens?"

No response.

"Don't give us a hard time. We just want to know your name."

For two more hours she was questioned intermittently in both Spanish and broken English, but Debbie was unable to reply. She was shaken and slapped, and water was thrown in her face. Through it all she sat listlessly, unaware of her surroundings and her inquisitors.

When police placed an airline ticket bearing the name "D. Feinbaugh" in front of her, she said nothing. In her emotional state, she could not tell them that the ticket, the only piece of identification recovered from the hotel room, had her name misspelled. Finally, recognizing the need for a psychologist, the police ended the questioning and requested that someone talk to the prisoner in the morning.

The single cell in the police station was already occupied by two men who had been brawling in the street, so the police took Debbie to the jail west of the city. After a transfer of papers, a guard escorted her through the commons area, where she received more than a few hoots and whistles from the inmates looking out the barred windows in the doors of the men's cell block. The women's cells were on the other side of the commons area. Her cell was already populated by two recently arrested prostitutes, a teen-ager arrested for heroin possession and a woman who had knifed her lover and his wife just two nights before. By the time she was deposited in the hot, damp concrete cell, Debbie was shaking.

Two of her cellmates rested in hammocks suspended from hooks in the walls. The prostitutes were trying to make do on the concrete floor, using small bundles of clothes for pillows. The cell was devoid of all creature comforts save a bucket for bodily secretions. Oblivious to the stench of human excrement and urine that overpowered the smell of sweating bod-ies, Debbie lay down on her side on the bare concrete floor in a corner of the cell, where several large roaches were running back and forth look-ing for a late-evening snack. She pulled her knees up to her chest and began rocking back and forth.

Shiny brown roaches soon began exploring the newest visitor to their abode. With their antennae waving, the two-inch-long insects crawled onto Debbie's blood-stained skirt and blouse. She began weeping, but made no attempt to remove the filthy creatures. Instead, she wrapped her arms more tightly around her legs and continued rocking.

The hookers took turns getting up from the floor and yelling for their pimp through the bars of the cell door, demanding to be released so they could go back to work, or at least that they be given the hammocks they were sure their pimp had paid for.

"Oye," yelled one of the prostitutes, "tengo tres hijos que debo cuidar!"

"Cállate," said the accused murderer, demanding quiet. And pointing out that they weren't going to be set free soon, she repeated herself. "Estoy tratando de dormir. Cállate!"

The prostitute ignored her and continued to rail. The heroin addict slipped out of her hammock and stepped toward Debbie. She bent over the sobbing woman and brushed some of the insects from her hair, squashing them beneath her shoe. She tried to console the woman, but, unable to elicit a response from the blonde, she soon retreated to her bed.

Seven hours had elapsed since Debbie Steinbaugh had innocently returned the T-shirt to the man posing as Peter Boget. No one at the police station knew of Barry Whitehead, because no one at the hotel remembered seeing him. No one had checked Debbie for evidence of rape, because no one suspected that anyone but Jan Stevens had been in the room with her. The evidence against her was incontrovertible. Even if she could have told them what had happened, Debbie would not have been believed. Mercifully, she escaped into sleep.

10

I f Mike Downes had the power to cause time to stand still, he would have picked a moment soon after dawn. The overnight rain had washed Richmond clean and allowed the fragrance of hyacinths to permeate the cool morning air. A chorus of birdsong floated out from the branches of cherry trees dressed in their dazzling spring fashions. Against a backdrop of the long, slender needles of Southern pines, maple trees ushered in spring with millions of tiny red flowers. Yellow fountains of forsythia gushed from the ground beneath the canopy of oak and elm and gum and hickory trees that had yet to awaken from their winter sleep. On the tips of countless azaleas, swelling buds were preparing to paint the city in a hundred shades of white, red, pink and violet.

Knifing through the trees and streaming onto exquisitely manicured, mulch-lined green carpets, the sun reflected off water droplets that clung to leaves, petals and blades of grass and transformed them into sparkling jewels. The sun seemed to smile on everyone who was out inhaling the aroma of spring.

Downes was one of the many who were soaking in the splendor. As he ran through his neighborhood for the first time in a week, he waved at neighbors picking up their morning papers, smiled at walkers and joggers who passed him in the street, and shouted a few good mornings to passing bikers. He slowed to a walk as he arrived back at his driveway, allowing Goldie, his aging golden retriever, to catch up. He pulled the *Times-Dispatch* from the slot beneath his mailbox and, walking up his tulip-lined driveway, stopped and slowly scanned the yard.

Each bulb that was now bringing forth its unique blend of colors had been planted by Susie, the woman he had married in the springtime of his life and whose death had brought a winter chill to his existence. Each forsythia branch had been pruned by her as well, and now they showed signs of two years of neglect. The holly that had been waist-high when he and Susie moved into the house was now as tall as he was. For a moment Downes was lost in his memories.

The flapping of Goldie's tail against the back of Downes's leg brought him back to the present. He became aware of a ringing telephone. He bounded up the front steps, opened the door and walked to the kitchen.

"Mike Downes speaking."

"Did I wake you up?"

"No. Who's this?"

"Oh, sorry. This is Charles Piper. We found the car."

There was only one car the security supervisor could be talking about: Peter's.

"Where?"

"At the airport, BWI. There was a message on my voice mail this morning. An employee arriving late last night from Atlanta noticed the car in the parking lot and called in with the license number and location. Stan Jefferies, Maryland Bell security up in Baltimore, is on his way to the airport now. I thought you'd like to know."

"This is the best news I've had in a week," exclaimed Downes. "What's this Jefferies going to do when he gets to the car?"

"I don't know. We'll have to wait another hour or so until we can get into the car-pool records and find out the key numbers for the car. Then we'll get a locksmith in Baltimore to duplicate the keys for us and someone will bring the car to our service center in Glen Burnie."

"What about the police?"

"I'll be talking to the FBI this morning, since we filed the missing persons report with them, but unless there is evidence of foul play, neither they nor the police in Maryland will want to be bothered."

"Yeah, right," Downes responded thoughtfully. "I probably should call Elizabeth right away and let her know."

"You really want to do that before we check out the car?" Piper asked. "We don't know what we're dealing with yet."

Downes countered, "If you thought your wife was dead and somebody found evidence that she was alive, wouldn't you want to know as soon as possible?"

"I get your point. Look, let me get into the office and start putting together what I know about the car."

Downes added a few pointers. "The parking ticket should tell us when he got there, and probably someone should begin checking flights out of Baltimore."

Piper was amused. "Mike, we're professional investigators. We've already talked about all that and more."

"Okay, let me run and call Elizabeth. Oh, by the way," Downes said, "I cracked the password and got into the private file on Peter's computer."

"You what?" Piper gasped. "What did you—"

Downes smiled into the phone. "Work on the car. I'll tell you about the computer later." Before Piper could respond, the vice president hung up and dialed Elizabeth.

*　　*　　*

Boarding the Long Island Railroad at the Huntington station, Glenn Segal began his ninety-minute commute to work. Since returning from Norfolk, he spent most of his time worrying about the cocaine. The rest of the time he spent worrying about what Phyllis was going to say when he had to let her in on his terrible secret. So far, he and Mark Randolph had successfully stalled their clients, but they were running out of time and they both knew it.

The early-morning sun slanted in the window over Segal's left shoulder as the train skimmed toward the city. He studied the numbers on the paper in front of him. Each set represented a client and the transactions associated with his account during the previous three months. Segal didn't need a calculator to figure up the numbers; spreadsheet math was one thing he was very, very good at. He was figuring how much and how fast he could move money back into his clients' accounts without the activity tripping the company computer program that tracked unusual trading patterns. What he couldn't figure out was where the money would come from.

He didn't know how or why, but he believed that sooner or later someone would come after him. He tried to think which of his two dozen clients could least afford to lose a large chunk of change. Or maybe the culprit would be Mary Kennedy herself. *Would she turn loose a hit man? What would he look like? How would he do it?* Hour by hour Segal's conversations with himself became more morbid.

*　　*　　*

Heads turned when Mary Kennedy walked into the meeting room at the Omni Hotel for the monthly breakfast meeting of the Architectural Association of Hampton Roads. Her external appearance belied the icy blood that flowed through her veins.

"Morning, Mary." A man holding a cup of coffee nodded to her.

She flashed a smile and maneuvered through the small crowd to the coffee table, where she made herself a cup of tea. She exchanged small talk with several people, but kept moving toward a cluster of people at the far end of the room. She had come to the meeting not to hear the speaker, nor to have a continental breakfast with her peers. Her single motive was to speak to William Heinemann and get him to ask for her help in retrieving Barry Whitehead's car.

Through her intelligence network she had learned of Whitehead's accident and the whereabouts of the Honda. She knew her runner was in Baltimore Medical Center, but she didn't know if the cocaine had been discovered.

"William," she greeted her colleague with a friendly but formal tone. She extended her hand. "How long has it been?"

"Since the Christmas party," he said. "I've been so busy, I've had trouble getting down here to these meetings."

"Me too. So what's keeping you so busy?"

"Two office buildings in Virginia Beach and a hotel down in Nags Head." Heinemann sounded tired.

"Hope they're making you money!"

"I hope so too, but the overtime is killing me. I finally had to bring in some temporary drafting help, with Barry out."

Kennedy's furrowed brow signaled she didn't understand, so Heinemann continued. "Whitehead, Barry Whitehead. Remember, the fellow who used to work for you."

"Whitehead? Oh yes, I remember him."

"Well, he's in bad shape in a hospital up in Maryland."

"I'm so sorry," replied Kennedy in mock sympathy. "What happened?"

Heinemann related the story and then said, "I've been trying to break away to get up and visit him, but with all the work, I can't. With his family in Colorado and no real friends that I know of, I don't know if anyone has been to see him."

"What a shame."

"Well, it wasn't until now. He was in pretty bad shape and couldn't have visitors, but I understand he's out of his coma. The police wondered if we knew someone who could bring his car back to Virginia, but I told them to hang onto it till he gets out."

"Is it still drivable?" Kennedy continued to pretend.

"Sure," Heinemann said. "Why do you ask?"

"Oh, nothing." She shrugged off her reply.

Heinemann probed. "What?"

"I've got an employee flying up to D.C. in the morning and was going to offer to have him bring back the car," Kennedy said offhandedly. "But he's going to be out by the Cap Center, not up in Baltimore."

"No, no," said Heinemann. "Barry's in Baltimore, but the car is in Landover at the county impoundment."

"Quite a coincidence." Mary Kennedy was smiling. "Let me talk to Richard and see if he'd be able pick it up. Where did you say it was?"

"Somewhere in Landover," said Heinemann. "Let me call when I get back to the office, and then I'll give you a ring."

Kennedy flashed her "I'm really glad we talked" smile and added, "Can you also get me Barry's address? I'd like to drop him a card."

"Thanks, Mary."

The red-headed woman, with teacup in hand, turned and walked to a seat to await the start of the program. Inside she was laughing. She had accomplished everything she'd come for. In thirty-six hours she would have her cocaine back, and no one would be the wiser.

*　　*　　*

For a few marvelous minutes after taking Mike Downes's call, Elizabeth Boget seemed to float across the kitchen floor. She hugged and rehugged her children. She declared a holiday and said they could all miss the bus and stay and have a celebration breakfast together.

"He's alive, he's alive," she kept singing to the delight of her children. "Your dad's alive."

But soon pragmatic Lauren asked, "How can we be sure?" breaking the magical spell that had enveloped the house.

"Lauren," Elizabeth grinned. "They found Dad's car. They found his car. He wasn't killed in the explosion. He's alive!"

"Then how come he hasn't called?" Lauren asked.

Trying to keep up the good cheer, Elizabeth told her daughter, "I don't know, but there is probably a perfectly logical explanation. Now, let's get some eggs on, and David," she yelled across the kitchen, "you and Jonathan set the table out on the screened porch. It's a gorgeous day out there, and we're celebrating!"

*　　*　　*

"Don't you think it's strange that nobody's been to see Mr. Whitehead?" nurse Tracy Lang asked her supervisor. "He's been here a week. You'd think that by now his wife or someone would have been here."

Without looking up from the chart she was studying, Ling Chu said matter-of-factly, "He's not married."

"You sure about that?"

"That's what the police told me," said Chu. "Why do you ask?"

"I was just checking his IV and I looked at his left hand. There's been a wedding band on that hand recently. You can't miss it."

"He wasn't wearing one when he came in." Nurse Chu pulled out Whitehead's chart and flipped through some pages. "And given the fact that he's divorced, I wouldn't think he'd have one on."

"Maybe he's someone else."

The nursing supervisor grunted a "maybe" and resumed her work.

Less than two feet from the chair in which Chu was sitting, one of Elizabeth's bright yellow fliers was peeking out from a stack of papers and magazines that had just been delivered to the nurses' station.

As Lang sorted the papers, she stopped at the flier and did a double-take. "Look!" she said excitedly. "Mr. Whitehead *is* someone else." She forced the flier in front of Chu.

"No, he's not," Chu said, glancing briefly at the photo. "Some of Mr. Boget's friends have already been here. Turns out that Mr. Whitehead and Mr. Boget look a lot alike."

"I'll say." Lang studied the photo on the flier, then pitched it into the trash can.

*　　*　　*

At the Boget household, joy was soon tempered by reality. After driving the three older children to school, Elizabeth sat sipping her second cup of coffee. Joyce McGuire was across the table from her, asking questions that Elizabeth didn't want to think about.

"Let's assume he got on a plane," Joyce said, trying to be helpful. "Where would he go? I mean, let's assume he decided to go see someone. Who might that someone be? Maybe we should make a list of names and start calling them."

"Okay," Elizabeth replied, "let's say he did get on a plane. It would have been late, and he knew I was going to sleep early, so he wouldn't have called until he landed."

"*If* he landed." Joyce bit her lip. She wished she hadn't said that.

"What do you mean? Do you think the plane crashed?" Joyce said nothing as Elizabeth spit out a stream of possibilities. "No, we would have gotten a call. Unless he bought the ticket under another name. But he wouldn't do that. He may have gotten sick when he got off the plane, but someone would have called—unless he . . ."

Joyce leaned forward. "Unless he what?"

"Unless he . . . I don't know," Elizabeth finally confessed. "I can't figure it out. I mean, what are the available possibilities? Do you suppose something happened to him after he got there? Wherever 'there' is."

Joyce thought about some other possibilities but remained mute. For a week she had thought about the ring on the dresser, but she had never said anything to her best friend. She couldn't put into words what she wanted to say, and she wasn't too sure that what she wanted to say should be said— at least not now. She turned her response into a joke.

"He probably got picked up by a flying saucer, and he'll walk back in here with the most marvelous tale of flying through space with some little green men."

Elizabeth smiled, but she was thinking about grimmer possibilities. "I guess that would be better than another accident or a kidnapping."

Joyce continued with her fantasy. "Think of all the stories he would tell. Gosh, he would be the center of attention of every party he attended for the rest of his life." Joyce was laughing. "I can see him now standing out there with a bunch of grandkids, pointing his cane up to the sky and saying," she swept her hand out toward the back yard and, in a poor imitation of a weak-voiced old-timer, continued, " 'Yesiree, back before the turn of the century I visited that there star, yep, I did, on one of them flying saucers.' And then the kids will ask him about what the trip was like, and he'll go on and on till they all fall asleep right there in the grass. And you, Elizabeth, you'll be sitting in a rocking chair right here on this porch, shaking your head and telling him to knock it off." Joyce swiped her hand across her neck two times in a "cut it off" gesture and cackled.

Elizabeth laughed too. For the moment, reality was avoided.

*   *   *

The news of the discovery of Peter's car spread through the company in minutes. By 9:00 a.m. the PR office had responded to nearly sixty calls for confirmation of the rumor and for additional information. But there wasn't any information to pass along. At 9:05 Mike Downes took a call from Charles Piper, who was relaying a message from Stan Jefferies that the car was opened and everything looked fine. The only items of interest were that the flares that should have been in the trunk were missing and a portable computer was on the floor of the front seat.

"Seems strange that someone would walk away from a two-thousand-dollar computer," said Piper. "What's even stranger is that the tag has been removed," he added, referring to the company's inventory number tag that was affixed to every asset valued over five hundred dollars.

"Not that strange," Downes replied. "That's probably Peter's personal Powerbook."

"Oh?"

"He didn't want you guys hassling him about using a company computer for personal business," Downes explained.

"I see."

"Have your man send it back down here, so we can give it to Elizabeth."

After exchanging farewells, Downes hung up the phone. It rang a moment later. Glancing down at the name on the phone's LED display, Downes answered. "What did you forget, Charles?"

Piper went straight to the point. "What do you think?"

The meaning of his question dawned on Downes. "Peter's private computer file. It contained files on his employees."

"Anything interesting?"

"Not really." Downes didn't want to mention the "DBS" file and was hoping Piper wouldn't ask.

"Is that all?" said the security supervisor.

"Well, one file in the private folder was still encrypted. I couldn't read it."

"Oh, really." Piper's voice took on a sinister tone. "I'd like to see it."

Downes was biting his tongue. He didn't want security to know about this file, at least not yet. But he couldn't say no, because it wouldn't have mattered. The security organization pretty much had free rein to investigate any real or alleged impropriety.

"Stop by when you're free and I'll take you down to Peter's office."

*   *   *

By the time he reached his building on Madison Avenue, Glenn Segal was perspiring. It wasn't from the walk, though the sun had warmed him more than he had expected on this brisk morning. The sweat was directly related to what was going on in his head.

All seemed normal as he walked through the investment firm's glass doors on the lobby level of the new high-rise. He nodded hellos and strolled to his desk to begin his daily ritual of wiping the handset of his telephone, cleaning the screens on the two computer monitors above his desk and pulling out the folders of accounts he expected to work on during the day. Before he got to the second screen, his phone rang.

"May I see you in the conference room, please, Mr. Segal?"

Segal recognized the voice as that of the branch manager. The voice was cold, formal and ominous. It did not ask a question so much as state a command. The sweat froze on Segal's body. "Yes, sir," he responded slowly.

The thirty steps to the conference room were taken in slow, measured paces, the way a condemned man might walk to the gas chamber. Six eyes greeted Segal when he entered the room. Four, he soon learned, belonged to investigators from the Securities Exchange Commission. One of the blue-suited government men motioned for him to sit down.

"They just want to ask you a few questions," Segal's boss explained as he left the room.

It was well past lunchtime when Glenn Segal emerged from the conference room, but he wasn't hungry. He walked back to his desk and flopped into his chair. For a minute or more he stared at a computer monitor, but not a single number on the screen registered in his brain. Finally he responded to a reminder from within that he had downed three cups of coffee during the interrogation.

Mark Randolph joined Segal in the men's room. After checking to see that the stalls were empty, Randolph stepped up to the urinal next to Segal's and in a harsh whisper asked, "Where have you been?"

"They've got us. They don't know why, but they know we're doing it," sighed Segal.

"What are you talking about?"

"The account. The SEC grilled me for four hours today. They wanted to know about every trade I was involved in."

"And?"

"And, I told them—"

An opening door abruptly ended the conversation.

"Ah, Mark," said the branch manager, stepping into the restroom. "I was looking for you. When you're through here, would you join me in the conference room?"

Segal washed and dried his hands and, without turning back to look at his business associate, walked out to his desk.

*   *   *

"You didn't believe me, did you?" Megan Churchill sat down across from Lucy Williams in the lunchroom, where the company's editor had retreated for a midafternoon break. Having missed lunch trying to get an employee bulletin out the door, Lucy had been looking forward to a few minutes of sanity before returning to finalize the layout for Monday's edition. Now Megan, the office rumormonger and chatterbox, was intruding on Lucy's quiet time.

"But I know men," Megan boasted. "They're all alike. You turn up the heat and they're out looking for another love and another life."

"Just stick it!" Lucy glared at the intruder. "I'm busy!"

"Come on, Lucy, get real. Peter's gone AWOL," Megan chortled. "I told you he couldn't hack it." Putting on an accent of a Hungarian fortuneteller, Megan waved her hands over an invisible crystal ball and continued. "Vait. I see another voman. A bee-oo-tiful voman. And she is holding hands with Peter—yes, with Peter Boget—and they are strolling along a beach, a bee-oo-tiful beach, and . . ."

"And that's enough!" Lucy stood up and started walking away. "Sometimes, Megan, I think you're such a jerk."

Megan smiled back, "We'll see, we'll see." Then, after a pause, she added, "You wouldn't want to bet on this, would you? A buck, maybe, that Peter split with another woman?"

Lucy didn't hear the end of the sentence. She was out the door before Megan could finish.

*   *   *

Throughout the day the phone at the Boget residence was ringing with words of rejoicing and encouragement. But by late afternoon the euphoria of the morning was flagging. With each call, with each retelling of the good news, Elizabeth's excitement was being tempered and her strength was being drained. Now she had gathered her children to tell them the latest word from the phone company.

"Mr. Downes just got off the phone," she began. "They've been checking all the flights that left out of Baltimore-Washington Airport since last Thursday night, and Dad wasn't on any of them. At least, he didn't buy a ticket there or get on an airplane using his name."

"Did he use another name?" David asked.

"Nobody remembers seeing him, selling him a ticket or anything else."

"Maybe he was mugged or something."

"The police checked that too. That night and the next day were all pretty quiet. And we checked the credit card records and nobody has used them.

They are just missing, like your dad." Elizabeth looked into the faces of her sullen children.

"Mom, is Daddy *ever* coming home?" asked Jonathan.

Elizabeth pulled the young boy to her and boosted him onto her lap. "Sometimes we don't know the answers to our questions. That's why we pray. God knows where Dad is and what he is doing. Someday we'll see your daddy again. Maybe soon, maybe not for a while. But always remember how much he loves you, and never forget to ask God to protect him wherever he is."

After giving Jonathan a long, gentle hug, she set him on the floor and stood up. "Now, kids, I want to get ready for supper. And David, Mrs. McGuire will be by in a few minutes to take you to soccer practice. Tonight, some of the church people are coming over, so I want you to get your baths right after supper, and then to bed." She continued to issue orders, but the children were already scattering, all except Jonathan. The three-year-old looked at his mother, and as two big tears ran across red cheeks he asked, "Will he come back and take me fishing? He promised. He promised he'd take me fishing on Easter."

"Well, then," Elizabeth was struggling to keep her composure, "I guess he'll be home by Easter, if he promised you."

Jonathan smiled, turned and headed outside.

11

T
hat's it? Whaddaya mean, that's it?" Downes, sitting at his desk, was
yelling into his phone. "One of my employees is gone, you think he
went to Denver, and you're telling me that the case is closed? What
kind of an investigation is that?"

On the other end of the line, Charles Piper was formulating a response.
"Mike, Peter Boget has voluntarily left his town, his job and his fam—"

"How do you know it was voluntary?"

"I'm trying to tell you," Piper went on. "Four of us spent all night showing
Peter's photo to everybody who worked in this airport last Thursday. At 7:30
this morning we found a stewardess who flew to Denver last Friday morning. She said Peter was on her flight. We went back to the ticket agents and
found that the ticket was purchased with cash by a man who fit Peter's
description who used it at the airport on the night of the fifteenth."

"So why aren't you going after him?"

"We don't have any reason to. Cripes! The name he used to buy the ticket
was—now listen to this—'I. M. Outahere.' What does that tell you? It tells
us that it's not a company matter anymore." Piper paused, waiting for a
reply from Downes, but none came. "Do you want to tell his wife, or do you
want me to?"

Downes was still processing the information Piper had passed along. He
spoke deliberately and clearly. "Peter wouldn't just walk away. There must

be some mistake or some very good reason for what he did. I find it incomprehensible that you would just drop the matter after we have come this far."

Piper was straightforward with his response. "As far as we're concerned, he's absent without leave. We see two or three of these every year, and we have no reason to go after them. When he gets ready, he'll contact someone. Or his family can hire someone to track him down. Unless he uses the company credit card, or we find out he stole company property or something like that, we have no reason to go after him. He has done nothing illegal, so the FBI isn't interested." Piper paused. "I know he was your friend."

Downes interrupted him emphatically. "He *is* my friend, not *was*. And where is Elizabeth supposed to come up with the money to hire someone to track him down? If it weren't for her friends and family, she wouldn't be able to put food on the table this week, much less pay the mortgage next month."

Piper's response reflected his fatigue. "Look, Mike, I'm just doing my job. After leaving Peter's office yesterday I drove up here to Baltimore. I was out at the airport all night. I haven't been to bed in thirty hours."

"I'm sorry."

"You have to come to grips with the fact that no matter what you think about the man, his record over the past year isn't good. I've passed along these findings to Mazzetti."

Downes wasn't happy that Mid-Atlantic Bell's vice president for corporate affairs had been told all this before he was. Francis Mazzetti, who had been brought in to clean up long-standing problems in several of the operating companies, swung a meat cleaver at everyone even suspected of violating a corporate regulation. With the CEO's backing, Mazzetti had quickly and effectively identified offenders, secured resignations from them and then, using the company grapevine, made sure that the remaining sixty-five thousand employees knew why the violators were leaving. Peter Boget was on his hit list for violating corporate policy, and he would have lost his job had not Downes and Virginia Bell's president, Earl Hendrick, successfully intervened. Mazzetti had taken a personal interest in Boget's activities from that time forward, looking for a repeat offense that would allow him to nail Boget and embarrass Downes.

"Oh, there is something else." Piper seemed to be looking for the right words. "Remember 'DBS'?"

"Sure, what of it?"

"In the computer we found in Peter's car I located a DBS file. It's another of the reasons Mazzetti wants us to drop off."

"What are you talking about?"

"The file. It contains letters. Personal letters," Piper took a deep breath, "to a woman in Colorado."

*   *   *

Mary Kennedy spoke graciously to the SEC examiner calling from New York. "Yes, Mr. Beale, I am happily aware of the fact that my account is growing far in excess of industry averages. That speaks very well of Mr. Randolph, doesn't it?"

Martin Beale was used to people trying to duck questions. "Ms. Kennedy, have you ever suspected that there were errors in your account?"

"Yes, but I checked and found everything to be in order." Then she added, "Have you found something I need to be made aware of?"

Beale continued, "How much direction do you give Mr. Randolph on the handling of your account?"

"Quite a bit, actually."

Beale thought he was onto something until Kennedy responded.

"I tell him I want short-term profit and liquidity. I let him know when I want to make charitable contributions, and he does the rest."

"Charitable contributions?" Beale was unprepared for her statement.

"I believe that those of us who have been fortunate enough to have acquired wealth should give away as much as we can to relieve suffering in the world."

Kennedy's friendliness and openness took Beale by surprise. He should have had his antennae up. But it was a warm, sunny Friday. He had been putting in a lot of overtime lately, and frankly, he was more interested in catching an early-afternoon train to New Rochelle than in trying to determine the culpability of the beneficiary of some brilliant securities trades. After several additional routine questions, Beale was ready to call it a day.

"Oh, one last thing," he asked. "Do you keep the receipts you get each time there is a transaction involving your account?"

"Of course." Kennedy didn't miss a beat. "I've got them here in my office. If you need to see them, just drop by anytime."

After hanging up, Kennedy placed four calls in quick succession. She called Patrick O'Hearn on his cellular phone in his room in a Holiday Inn in Maryland and relayed a new set of instructions. She called William Heinemann and left a message with his receptionist that Richard Donovan had become ill and would not be able to pick up Whitehead's car as previously planned. She called the automobile impoundment in Prince George County and, posing as an associate of William Heinemann, alerted them that a Mr. Fishbinder, not Richard Donovan, would be picking up the Whitehead car. Then she placed a call to Ireland that was patched through to Mark Randolph in New York. Kennedy was taking no chances. She wanted to be sure that even the most sophisticated call-tracing equipment would not be able to find her.

"Mr. Randolph, this is Kathleen McIlhinney from the Crystal Gallery in Dublin." Kennedy laid on the accent. "I'm terribly sorry to inform you that the two gifts you ordered were inadvertently routed to another address. We're trying to get the party to forward them to you, but they are insisting on payment for delivery service in advance, and we'll not be able to wire funds until Monday. If you need the gifts this weekend as you indicated, I can only suggest you make arrangements to pick them up. Again, I'm so very sorry. I hope you are not terribly inconvenienced by this error on our part. And we want you to know that there will be absolutely no charge for the items."

Randolph caught on quickly and responded exactly as Kennedy had expected. "Thank you very much. I will dispatch an associate of mine to arrange a pickup. Do you have a phone number where I can get in touch?"

Kennedy's response was effusive. "If you have a fax number, I would be most happy to send you all the information you will need."

Randolph gave her the number of a public fax in the office-supply store in the building's lobby, thanked her profusely and hung up the phone.

The charade was unnecessary. Randolph's phone had not yet been tapped.

After he picked up the fax, Randolph read it, jotted some notes, enclosed the paper in an envelope and dropped it on Glenn Segal's desk. The two said nothing. Moments later, Segal was booking a flight to Washington.

* * *

The unusually warm March afternoon was about to give way to a line of thunderstorms that were moving rapidly toward Richmond from the southwest. The Swift Creek Reservoir and the communities of Brandermill and Woodlake, built along its eighteen-mile shoreline, lay directly in the path of the darkening sky and the rolling thunder. Elizabeth Boget hung up the phone and sent her children into the yard to pick up toys and bring in bicycles as the storm's advance winds swirled through the trees.

The first huge drops of rain slammed onto the deck as Elizabeth and David swooped up Jonathan and his Big Wheel and raced to the shelter of the screened porch. Moments later, the black clouds paused to dump the contents of a small pond in the Bogets' back yard.

With her crossed arms pressed against her chest, Elizabeth looked out across the yard. The torrents beat against the roof of the porch and spilled into growing puddles, creating a cacophony that masked all other sounds. Through the screening, Elizabeth looked past the blooming fruit trees, searching for a place where life transcended time and circumstances.

She had answered the telephone just as the storm blew up and had heard the entire three-sentence message in less time than it took for a clap of thunder to complete its house-rattling roar. Now she had time to digest the brief but ominous words.

"May I stop by?" he had said somberly. "I've got to talk to you about Colorado."

Elizabeth turned and walked back into the house, shutting out the storm just as a bolt of lightning struck dangerously close to the house. The thunder shook the building and sent Daniel and Jonathan scurrying toward their mother. A scream from upstairs notified the family that Kristin was awake.

Lauren raced down the stairs to see what had happened. "Did you hear that?" asked the wide-eyed teenager.

David sarcastically replied, "Hear what?"

"The thunder!"

"Didn't hear nothin'. You hear anything, Mom?"

Elizabeth wasn't in the mood for joining in one of the jokes David loved to play on his sister. "Yes, that was a close one. Lauren, go back upstairs and unplug the TV and VCR in the rec room. David, get the TV down here.

We don't want ours to fry the way the Rognesses' did last summer."

As David pulled the plugs, Elizabeth continued. "Mr. Downes is going to be coming over soon, and I'll need to talk to him. I'm going to get Kristin." She raised her voice so her daughter, who hadn't returned from the second floor, could hear. "Lauren, when you're finished, would you please come down and help David start dinner?"

Jonathan clung to Elizabeth's skirt as she headed up to retrieve Kristin. When another flash lit up the house, he buried his face in her hip and covered his ears to shut out the blast that followed.

Another bolt of lightning startled her momentarily and elicited simultaneous screams from Kristin and Jonathan. Then her thoughts turned to Peter and . . . Colorado. Did Debbie Steinbaugh have something to do with all of this? "Debbie," she whispered. "Please don't let it be Debbie."

*　　*　　*

To enter the commons area of the Cancún prison, visitors must pass through the administration building and then through a small, square concrete room where a guard is posted next to the large door of steel bars that separates the prisoners from their freedom. When María Escobar, the Cancún consular agent, arrived at the door, a guard inside the commons located Debbie Steinbaugh and walked the pale blonde toward the gate. She was wearing red shorts, tennis shoes and an oversized black T-shirt with pink lettering set against a profusion of pastel flowers. The message on the shirt proclaimed, "I had the time of my life in Cancún."

The consular agent, shorter, darker and prettier than the woman approaching her, saw in Debbie's eyes a terror and sorrow she hadn't expected in a murder suspect.

"Miss Feinbaugh," she began, "I'm María Escobar from the United States Consulate. I've come to help you."

Debbie was still in a state of shock from the events of Wednesday evening, as well as from the questioning she had been subjected to and the conditions of the prison. She looked and spoke as if she had spent the night sloshing back and forth in a washing machine. Her first words were a mixture of pleading and declaration. "I didn't kill anybody. I didn't kill anybody." Tears welled up in her bloodshot eyes.

"I am just here to find out if you are okay, and who we should contact.

The police did not find any identification."

"I didn't kill anybody," Debbie repeated.

"What's your name?" queried Escobar, confused by the responses she was receiving.

"Don't let my girls know I'm in jail. Please don't let them think I could do this."

"Is your name Feinbaugh?"

The woman hanging onto the bars dropped her head. "I told them he tried to rape me but they didn't believe me. I told them he knocked Jan to the floor, but they didn't believe me. I told them I didn't kill anybody, but they keep telling me I did." Her sobs gave way to full-scale weeping.

* * *

Ephrata is one of those picturesque towns in Pennsylvania Dutch country in the southeastern part of the state. Famous for its springs, the quiet community centers on a tree-lined, three-block shopping strip on Main Street. Just west, across Cocalico Creek, the buildings of the historic Ephrata Cloister are a reminder of the German religious order that arrived in the early 1700s and established a community of sisters and brothers who lived a disciplined life of prayer, service and celibacy. It was to this cloister, and the compassionate men and women who occupied it, that George Washington had sent his sick and injured troops during the long winter nightmare of Valley Forge.

One block past the hotel, on the front porch of an old brick duplex, Barry Whitehead was pacing the concrete floor. His father sat nearby in a padded rocker and tried to console him: "If it was an accident, then it was an accident. Just forget about it."

George Whitehead had no idea of the gravity of his son's situation. All he knew was that shortly after learning of his mother's death, Barry had phoned and said he was tired of Norfolk, he was in a jam with a friend who was controlling his life, and he needed a place to stay for a little while. The request seemed strange to the senior Whitehead, who had had little contact with Barry for many years, but he offered to let his son come home.

Barry had told his father only half the story; he left out the attack on Debbie Steinbaugh, saying only that he had inadvertently bumped a woman who had then tripped and fallen against the nightstand. He stopped pacing and stared at his father, who continued to rock. "How can I forget about it? For all I know the woman may be dead. They'll come looking for me."

"Who's going to come? You told me that no one knows you're here and you never used your real name in Mexico."

"But that woman, the other one—Debbie whatever-her-name-was—she saw me and spoke to me. She could identify me."

"You worry too much," said the man rocking in the chair. "You always did. Look, you just told me it was an accident. The woman got a bump on her head, and this Debbie probably explained the story to the police and everything is fine."

Barry shook his head and resumed his pacing. "Only for a while," he muttered, "I'll only be safe for a while. Sooner or later, she will come after me."

"This Debbie woman?"

"No—Mary. Mary Kennedy."

"I'm confused. Who's she?"

"The one who controlled my life."

"Oh, I thought she was a man."

Barry stopped pacing again and sat down on the porch's stone railing directly in front of his father. "Women," he said with irritation in his voice. "It's always been women, and it always will be women." His tone was quiet but forthright. "They are the instruments of the devil. They live to destroy men. They want us to care for them, to clothe them, to feed them, to bow down before them, to give them babies—but only when *they* decide they want them. You can never do enough for them. Then when they decide they've milked you dry, they toss you out."

The elder Whitehead sighed. "I know, son. I know."

Barry reached into his pocket and pulled out a wad of money. "For this," he shook the bills in front of his father, "Mary Kennedy will come after me."

His father was flabbergasted with his son's display of cash.

"Where did you get all that money?"

"That's what I'm talking about. I finally got paid for all the work I did for her, but"—his voice dropped to a raspy whisper—"she doesn't know it yet."

"What do you mean?" asked an incredulous father.

"I took it!" Then he dropped his head into the hand filled with bills. Barry Whitehead began to tremble. "Oh my God," he said mournfully. "She'll send her dogs to track me down. She'll come to get it back, and then she'll kill me." Tears filled Barry's eyes as he contemplated his fate.

Perplexed, the elder Whitehead rose from his rocking chair and patted his son on his shoulder.

"You worry too much, Barry. You worry too much." Then he walked inside, leaving his son with his money and his thoughts.

The words were little consolation to a man who remembered the terrified look on the face of the woman he had left shivering on the bed and the lifeless face of the one slumped on the floor of the Cancún hotel.

*   *   *

"Let's go over this one more time," María Escobar said, shifting her weight from one foot to the other. She was holding her pad in her left hand and her pen in her right. "Your name is Debbie Steinbaugh, not Feinbaugh. You live in Colorado Springs, and you're here on vacation."

"That's right," Debbie sniffed. Between her tears and the catcalls of her fellow prisoners, she had retold her bizarre story. Three times she had broken down. By the time she was through, the consular agent didn't know what to make of it.

"Let me make sure I have this right." She began flipping through her notes. "Your friend Peter Bojay was in an accident, but you don't know where, and someone who looks just like him came to Cancún and tried to rape you. In the process he killed Jan Stevens, whom you were fighting with in the hotel."

"Uh-huh."

"And he did this because he found out that you knew he wasn't this Peter Bojay when you took back a shirt to his hotel room while your friend was lying in bed with a bad sunburn?"

Debbie grunted her reply and wiped back her runny nose on the sleeve of her T-shirt. "That's what I told you, isn't it? Don't you believe me?"

Ignoring the question, Escobar continued. "And then he ran away and left you with Jan, and then the police came and took you to jail?"

Debbie raised her head. She looked like a helpless, frightened child whose innocence and beauty had been sucked from her life. "I didn't kill anybody. I didn't! You've got to believe me."

*   *   *

By the time Mike Downes arrived at the Boget residence, dinner was ready. Elizabeth made sure that the children were okay and then excused herself to the living room. She sat down in a wing chair across the coffee table from Mike, who eased into one of the room's two sofas. As he began to speak, he leaned toward Elizabeth to reduce the chance that the children would hear what he had to say.

"Elizabeth," he said, "I'm glad no one else is here, because what I want to talk to you about probably should stay between you and me for the time being."

"What about Debbie Steinbaugh?"

Mike was sure he had never mentioned Debbie's name. But Elizabeth continued, "And where is Peter?"

"We don't know. That's why I'm here. Do you know why Peter might have flown to Denver?"

"He's in Denver? With Debbie?"

"No, that's not it at all," he said calmly, hoping to diffuse her rising anger.

"Then what is it?" She was gritting her teeth. Mike knew there would be no gentle way through this discussion.

"All we know," he said, "is that Peter was seen on a flight to Denver last Friday morning, and a ticket agent thinks she remembers him paying cash. That's all we know so far."

"And?" Elizabeth asked.

"And what?" Mike replied.

"And what else? You're not telling me everything."

"His computer was left in the car at the airport. One of our security people found some letters to—" He paused, and Elizabeth completed the sentence for him: "Debbie Steinbaugh."

"I haven't seen them myself," Mike said, "and wouldn't have looked at them if I had gotten to the computer first, but one of our men thought it was a company computer and scanned it looking for any nonbusiness-related files. That's when they found the letters." Mike paused. "I'm sorry."

"Recent letters?"

"I don't know. Why?"

"I remember the letters from a year ago."

Lauren interrupted the conversation when she peered around the archway. "Mom, Jonathan spilled his milk."

"Would you please take care of it?"

"It's a mess."

"Please, just go back to the table."

Elizabeth turned back to Mike, but she had forgotten what she was talking about.

"The letters," he said to jog her memory. "Debbie's letters. So you know her?"

"Yes, sort of. I've talked with her on the phone. She's got quite a story, and Peter . . . It goes way back."

Elizabeth told the story to Mike. When she was done, she looked into his eyes. "I don't believe there's anything between them, if that's what you're suggesting."

"I'm not suggesting anything. I just thought there may be something to . . . I don't know . . . to the fact that I found a file with her initials on it in his computer at the office the other night, but the file was encrypted and I couldn't read anything. In fact, I didn't know what 'DBS' stood for before today."

Elizabeth pondered the situation. "I guess there is only one way to find out." She stood up and walked out of the room, leaving Mike sitting on the sofa. Before he could react, she was back with a cordless phone and an address book.

"I'll call, if you'd like," he offered.

"No," Elizabeth said. "I don't mind calling, because I'm sure there is no connection."

Liz Clark, Debbie Steinbaugh's foster mother, always came quickly to the point. "Elizabeth? Why on earth are you calling?"

"I was trying to reach Debbie, but there was no answer."

"She's in Mexico."

A lump blocked Elizabeth's throat. "Mexico?"

Mike could tell from her expression that something was wrong.

"Yup," Liz continued, "she flew down last Saturday. In fact, we're just leaving to pick her up."

"She's coming home tonight?"

"Tomorrow, but we're taking Debbie's girls up tonight so they can go swimming at a hotel."

Elizabeth interjected the dreaded question. "Did she go to Mexico with anyone?"

"Nope, went by herself. Least, I think so. You know she never tells us much. But I think she was meetin' up with someone. That's what her girls think. Why'd you want her, anyway?"

Elizabeth's strength flowed out of her the way milk flows out of a spilled glass. "Thanks," she whispered. The phone dropped out of her suddenly limp hand and into her lap. She looked at Mike. "This is only coincidental," she said through trembling lips.

*   *   *

A greatly relieved Mark Randolph began making his coded telephone calls to clients to set pickup schedules. The goods would be late, but only by a week. Between calls, Randolph was calculating how he could rectify the appearance of a trading bias in Mary Kennedy's favor. He would have to talk to her, but knew that she would go along as soon as she realized that to fail to do so would jeopardize their mutually beneficial relationship.

*   *   *

Now that Jennifer Griffith, the pastor's wife, was by Elizabeth's side, Mike Downes redialed Liz Clark. He briefly explained why Elizabeth had called earlier and asked Mrs. Clark where Debbie was staying.

"I don't rightly know," she replied in an accent that reminded Mike of West Virginia. "She just said Mexico."

"Do you know what plane she got on?"

"No. She said she had someone who was gonna drive her to Denver. Like I told Elizabeth, Norwood and I are taking her girls up tonight to a hotel where they have an indoor pool and then we're going to meet her when she arrives."

"Norwood?"

"That's my husband."

"I see. Do you know what flight she's arriving on?"

"Sure. Just a minute." After getting the number, Mike thanked her, slid the switch on the phone to "off" and set it down on the coffee table.

Elizabeth was surrounded by her children, who were waiting for an encouraging word from Mr. Downes.

"Well," he said, standing up, "not a word on your dad, but we should know a lot more by this time tomorrow."

He quickly related the conversation, then turned to go. He stepped through the front door and onto the porch, where he picked up his wet umbrella. The rain had stopped, and a cool mist hugged the ground. "I'll call you tomorrow, Elizabeth. Or sooner, if I learn anything else."

When he hit the walkway at the bottom of the stairs, Elizabeth smiled. "I'm not sure I want you to call me any sooner, thank you."

He smiled back, waved at the children standing with their mother in the doorway and walked to his car.

*   *   *

María Escobar spent most of the evening trying to sort out the story of Debbie Steinbaugh. The police did not believe it, but they promised to investigate for a Peter Bojay. They also showed the airline ticket to María. One told her, "I checked to determine if the airline had any more information, but they didn't. I also told them they didn't need to hold this seat"— he waved Debbie's ticket—"or the seat on the plane to Phoenix for Miss Stevens."

By the time she passed the information on to the consulate in Mérida, the Yucatán state capital two hundred miles to the west, there was only one person available to work on contacting Debbie's family. He said he would get on it right away. With several hours of additional work before she could get away for the evening, a tired María Escobar said good night to her assistant, Juanita Méndez, locked the door, kicked off her shoes and returned to her desk. She placed one more call. "Eduardo? I think I'm going to pass on dinner. It's been a wild day. I've got to finish some reports. Then, I'm heading home to bed."

*   *   *

Despite the fact that it was a Friday night, the drive from National Airport to the Holiday Inn at New Carrollton proceeded smoothly. It was just after seven-thirty when Glenn Segal entered the hotel's lobby, picked up a phone and called for a cab. By nine he was driving Whitehead's Honda Accord back into the hotel parking lot. He quickly transferred the suitcases to the rented car he had driven from the airport. They were much lighter than he'd expected, but he didn't stop to think why. He wanted to get as far away from the Honda as he could—in the shortest possible time.

What seemed to Segal to be a lifetime's worth of worry was lifted from his shoulders. He smiled at the ease with which he was able to sign for the car and gain possession of his merchandise. His spirits were buoyed by the belief that the gods had given him a second chance, a chance to end his involvement in the drug trade. A chance to get out of a business that had solved some of his problems while creating a whole new set of them. As he backed out of the parking space and turned toward the exit, he thought about the long drive back to New York. It would be a joyous drive, a drive that would save him and Randolph from being hung out to dry by the SEC.

But Segal never reached the street. Two cars with flashing lights appeared out of nowhere to block his path. Segal's head spun around to see two more cars pull in close behind him. He tried to calculate the odds of escaping by driving onto the sidewalk and outrunning the police to the road, but that would be worse. In seconds, six Maryland state policemen surrounded the vehicle with their guns drawn.

Segal's front doors were yanked opened, and he found himself inches from the shotguns of two law enforcement officials. "Get out of the car with your hands in front of you," said one. The other backed away and let the ghost-white stockbroker emerge from behind the wheel. "Open the trunk, please," ordered the first officer.

Segal was shaking uncontrollably. Sweat soaked his shirt. Police-car headlights and spotlights lit the scene like a Broadway stage. Pointing to the suitcases, the state trooper ordered them opened. Segal nervously obliged. Each contained numerous plastic bags filled with a white substance.

"Whatcha got there?" asked the policeman nearest Segal.

"I don't know; I was just sent to pick this up."

"Really? Didn't you tell the officer at the impoundment yard that you came to pick up a car and take it to Norfolk? And isn't it strange that you could open the trunk when there's no trunk key on the ring we gave you?"

The officer ordered Segal to the ground, but he began to protest loudly. "I've been set up! You can't do this to me!" A policeman forced him down, but he continued to protest. "Hey, this isn't mine! It belongs to someone else. She sent me here to pick up these suitcases." Handcuffs were clamped onto his wrists, pulled up behind his back. In the glare of the lights, Segal kept yelling, "This isn't mine. It belongs to Mary Kennedy of Nor—"

Segal's last word was drowned out in the deafening roar of his rented car exploding into a thousand pieces. Like rag dolls, the policemen surrounding the car were thrown back by the blast, and brightly illuminated for as long as it took the flying shards of glass and metal to shatter the lights that ringed the scene. The acrid smell of plastic explosive filled the air.

Watching from a darkened room on the hotel's fourth floor, Patrick O'Hearn smiled. He removed his earphones and set them and the receiver into a nylon bag. He placed a remote detonating transmitter next to it and covered everything with a jacket and a pair of binoculars. He slipped a cellular phone into his pocket. Leaving the room key on the desk, he walked out of his room, descended four flights of stairs and walked around the crowd that was gathering to witness the gruesome scene.

At the far end of the parking lot, a car pulled up. O'Hearn opened the door and slipped into the passenger seat. Closing the door, he turned to the driver and said, "Can you believe the coppers would pull such a stunt?"

Richard Donovan, a native of Dublin and a green-card holder on Mary Kennedy's payroll, replied, "Can you believe the bloke would run his mouth like that? I'm glad Mary called us off the pickup."

"I'm glad we came prepared," said O'Hearn. "Let's get back to Norfolk."

12

Mike Downes was too busy placing calls to see or listen to any news during the night. It wasn't until midmorning on Saturday, after four hours' sleep, that he fixed himself some eggs and toast and sat down with coffee and the morning paper. "Two policemen killed in Maryland blast," the banner headline said. He read the story quickly but didn't find it sufficiently interesting to even follow the jump to page three. He skimmed the editorial page and turned to the business section.

Before he finished the lead article, he dropped the paper onto a chair beside the table and pulled out a legal pad filled with notes. He reached for his phone and dialed. After seven rings he heard a tired voice on the other end of the line.

"Charles, this is Mike, Mike Downes. Did I get you out of bed?"

"No, I'm still in it," said the manager of company security.

"I need your help."

"I knew I'd be sorry I didn't stay in Baltimore, where I could have gotten a decent night's sleep. First it was my wife leaving to go shopping with the kids, then it was Mazzetti, now it's you. How can I help?"

"Who do you know in Denver?" Downes waited, but no reply was forthcoming. "I called as many limo services and car rental companies as I could identify last night, but I'm not getting anywhere. I need to find someone who will circulate Peter's photo at Stapleton Airport like you did at BWI. This phone stuff isn't working."

"If you're still looking for Peter, I can't help you," said Piper in an almost sorrowful tone. "That was what Mazzetti's call was all about. He doesn't want us to waste any more time or money on Peter unless he makes a wrong move. He told me to keep my focus on the bottom line. You know, we've got a bunch of toll-fraud cases backing up that he wants us to start tackling Monday morning."

Downes pressed his case. "What if I asked you to help me unofficially?"

"No, Mike, I'm sorry. Now is not the time to jeopardize my job. Mazzetti doesn't call working stiffs like me—at home—on a Saturday just to *suggest* something. I just can't help you right now."

"I understand," said Downes, ending the conversation.

He dialed Earl Hendrick and got a quick reply to his request for a few days off. The company president didn't mince words. "I have supported you every step of your career from the time I hired you. I supported you when you had to put your career on hold to take care of your wife. I backed your support of Peter last year despite pressure from up north. And I support your fervor in tracking him down. In fact, I have asked for special help in locating him, but I have been rebuffed, especially after getting the report on Peter and the woman in Colorado."

Downes was shocked. "What report?"

"Mazzetti has been keeping me posted."

Downes could barely contain his rage. "Posted? Mazzetti?"

"Yes, that is what I am telling you. Peter's disappearance has cast a shadow on the Virginia company and our—your and my—collective judgment in defending him in the past."

"I'm sorry. Until I spoke with Piper a few minutes ago, I didn't realize . . ."

"That is all right," said the president. Then Hendrick added, "Mike, from one friend to another—let it go for a while. You are held in high regard throughout Mid-Atlantic Bell. You are in an excellent position to assume the presidency when I retire, and I expect it will be this year. I do not want to turn over Virginia to a stranger from up north. We have gone through enough trauma with the continual staff cutbacks. But we still have a special spirit that has held our company together."

"Not according to the new employee attitude survey," Downes reminded his boss.

"I know. That is the problem. That is why you need to protect what we have, to keep it intact. If you become preoccupied with Peter, you will lose the opportunity to guide this company, to lead nine thousand employees through the difficult times that lie ahead. And you are still young, Mike. Mid-Atlantic Bell will need a man like you to take the helm."

Downes didn't argue, though that was precisely what he wanted to do. He knew Hendrick was right about the presidency, but he couldn't let Peter go, because that meant letting Elizabeth and the kids go. And that meant going back on his promise—the promise to do whatever it would take to bring Peter home. He wished there was more he could do without jeopardizing the company and the employees he loved. Michael Downes quietly thanked his mentor and set the phone down on the kitchen table.

*   *   *

Segal's violent death rocked Mark Randolph. For the very first time he realized what kind of people he was dealing with. Though he had read, seen and heard mountains of information about the lawlessness of the drug trade, he'd never pictured himself or Glenn or Mary Kennedy as being one of "them." Now he knew better. His friend had been executed, and it was obvious that Kennedy had ordered it.

The attractive, competent architect spoke not one word of remorse when she phoned him during the night. Though she did not acknowledge authorizing the killing of another human being, she spoke only of the necessity of preventing people like Segal from "jeopardizing our lives and our livelihood." She calmly explained how life would now be safer for those still in the business. She even offered to send a partial shipment, with no advance money necessary, as a good-faith gesture.

Randolph was wary. He was playing on someone else's turf, and he realized he could lose the whole game. He knew that with one false move, his next home could be a cinder-block cell or a concrete crypt. For the first time since dealing cocaine he had to face the reality of his choices. He had to assume responsibility for crossing the line from right to wrong. Now that he was well past that line, Mark Randolph was in the grip of doubt and fear.

*   *   *

A call to the Maryland State Police barracks during the wee hours of Saturday morning had netted Mary Kennedy the information she needed to confirm that Barry Whitehead and Mark Randolph were the only remaining threats to her security. The confusion surrounding the explosion left an overworked operator vulnerable to mistakenly transferring a caller he thought was an agent with the Drug Enforcement Agency to Sergeant John Milligan. Milligan in turn detailed the opening of the locked trunk, the hole cut between the trunk and the back seat and the two suitcases containing twenty-four kilos of cocaine.

When O'Hearn and Donovan returned to Norfolk, Kennedy had dispatched them to Whitehead's apartment and quickly learned that it was empty of virtually all personal effects. She instinctively knew he had no intention of returning from New York, if he had planned to go there at all. She was convinced that he must have cut the hole to the trunk, removed the twenty-four kilos and disposed of them sometime between the time he entered the interstate in Norfolk and the time of his accident. The timing would make it seem impossible, but there was no other way of accounting for the missing merchandise—if it really was missing. Kennedy realized that she had not clarified with Sergeant Milligan whether there were twenty-four kilos total or twenty-four in each case. She also didn't know how many had been destroyed in the explosion.

It was close to lunchtime when she awakened O'Hearn. "Patrick, I must see you. There is some unfinished business that we must take care of tonight."

"The usual place?"

"In an hour."

*   *   *

Although it was only noon, Saturday already had become one of the longest days in Elizabeth's life. After her friends left at midnight the night before, she had spent the night sitting on the floor of her bedroom, going through the twenty years' worth of photos and correspondence that she kept in boxes on the closet floor. She had read Peter's love letters and the beautiful cards he had made for her each year for Valentine's Day. She studied each photo of the man who had devoted himself to loving and serving her and his family.

But for the first time in her life, she was reading and studying to find what wasn't said, to see what might not have been evident at first glance. She was looking for signs of betrayal, searching for a reason Peter would leave her and the children.

She had slowly looked through the box containing her husband's photos of his summer in Colorado. She'd cried when she looked into the eyes of the young girl with nearly white hair sitting on the back of a motorcycle, her hands wrapped around Peter's waist. Elizabeth hadn't remembered the picture, but the girl had to be Debbie.

Throughout the night, memories had come flooding back. With each emotional swing a new stream of tears stained her cheeks. Only Kristin's morning wake-up cry had forced Elizabeth to drag herself through the motions of motherhood.

Later that morning, she had packed David off to his cross-town soccer game against the Strikers and taken Lauren to her gymnastic lessons. Her senses dulled by fatigue and distracted by boys fighting in the back of the station wagon, she had driven off the road, struck a mailbox and flattened one hundred dollars' worth of someone's shrubbery before bringing the car to a stop in a bed of tulips.

Though the homeowner had been gracious, Elizabeth couldn't handle the situation. She'd called one of her neighbors to come and retrieve her and the family station wagon—now minus a headlight.

*   *   *

Laura and Jennifer Steinbaugh were growing faster than their mother could keep up with them. At fifteen, Laura was as preoccupied with boys as her mother had been when she was that age. Jennifer's life, on the other hand, revolved around the basketball court, where her height and skill surpassed those of all the boys in her sixth-grade class.

Both girls were also good swimmers, and they liked the idea of Gramps and Gram taking them to a hotel in Denver with a large indoor swimming pool. With money as tight as it was, the girls were surprised but delighted when they were offered a chance to stay overnight in a hotel. They both spent all morning in the pool, and after lunch they drove with Liz and Norwood Clark to the airport to meet their mother's plane.

They passed through the electronic security checkpoint and walked the long corridor to the gate where the plane from Houston was due to arrive.

At 3:45, the first of the passengers from American Airlines flight 1631 walked up the skyway and into the terminal. For five minutes a cluster of greeters diminished in size as each person intercepted a friend or loved one with shouts, hugs and kisses. Soon only the Clarks and their grand-daughters remained looking down the long, empty ramp. "She's probably got a pile of gifts she's trying to carry off the plane," said Jennifer hopefully.

Or she's too drunk to move, thought Laura, remembering the mother she had grown to loathe as a child.

But Debbie never appeared.

"Excuse me," Norwood asked a flight attendant who walked up the ramp. "Is there anyone else on the plane? A woman with blonde hair?"

"Not anyone getting off. I'm sorry."

Liz Clark was more angry than concerned. She was closer to her grand-daughters than to the foster child who had given her so many heartaches through the years. She was disgusted that Debbie would be so unthinking as not to call and let them know that she had missed her plane. Then she realized that Debbie might have called and not known how to reach them. Norwood Clark asked the agent at the counter to check and see if they had been mistaken about Debbie's flight.

After punching some numbers into the computer in front of her, the agent looked up. "I don't show a passenger by that name on this flight."

"But she had a reservation."

"Maybe she changed her schedule. She doesn't show up here. I'm sorry."

Liz knew that Debbie was very independent, but she had begun to see a real change in her foster daughter since her encounter with God. Liz had come to believe that Debbie was really going to make it, and she suspected that the current situation would soon be sorted out.

It was nearly six o'clock, and the next plane from Dallas wasn't due in until 7:10. Liz, her husband and Debbie's daughters decided to get some dinner and wait. No one remembered the call from Elizabeth Boget.

*   *   *

Mark Randolph had been born with a silver spoon in his mouth, but he had spit it out after arriving at Brown University in the sixties. His disdain for authority had led him into the inner circles of the peace movement. Financial realities had brought him out. After college, he cut his shoulder-length hair and landed a job on Wall Street as an assistant research analyst. Before long he was managing other people's money and, with his background in research, proved to be good at it. He also discovered computers and found himself spending evenings in front of a screen discovering new worlds via modem—worlds that offered new ways for him to vent his anti-authority feelings. He learned electronic subversion on clandestine computer boards from hackers with such colorful names as Ms. A. Round, Hack Attack, Big Byte and his own Mark the Shark. Then Randolph learned of Glenn Segal's drug-dealing scheme and, parlaying his computer knowledge, eased into a side business that now had him very worried.

The word of Glenn's death slammed home the reality that the business was not without risk. Now facing the possibility of an SEC probe and having his cocaine dealing exposed deeply troubled him. So did the thought of being taken out by a customer or, more likely, his supplier. Randolph knew that he would have to make a choice, though none of the alternatives were particularly attractive.

He closed a second suitcase and zipped up a bulging garment bag. He carried them all down to the front door and waited for the airport limousine to pull into the driveway. Then he picked up the phone and dialed his parents. He got the Randolphs' answering machine.

"Mother," he said, "I've got to go out of town for a while. Please look after the house."

13

A n impatient Mark Randolph waited to clear customs at Gatwick Airport south of London, while his friends stood just beyond the gate. He wanted to get on with his journey to Brighton. His bleary eyes and rumpled clothes told the story of a long, sleepless flight across the Atlantic. But he knew that soon he would be able to rest.

Britt and Molly Caldwell's modest home was a short walk from the beach, and on warm summer days it took on the aura of a beach house along the Connecticut coast. But it was only March, and Randolph knew that he could expect to be both cold and damp in the attic guest room. Nevertheless, the fact that these longtime friends, whom he hadn't seen in nearly three years, would open their home on a day's notice meant a lot to Randolph. He was particularly gratified that they didn't ask why he needed a place to stay three thousand miles from his home.

*   *   *

On the second Sunday morning since her husband's disappearance, Elizabeth didn't want to go to church. The events of the past seven days had been too traumatic, too exhausting and too embarrassing. But somewhere she found the strength to awaken the children and get them ready, despite the fact that daylight saving's time brought morning an hour earlier than usual. Then she found the courage to take them.

As the children piled out in the church parking lot, Elizabeth stayed behind the wheel, lost in thought. She was startled when the passenger door on the station wagon opened and Joyce McGuire slid in beside her.

"Hard morning?" asked Joyce gently.

Elizabeth continued to stare through the windshield. "Not especially."

"Do you want to talk about it?"

"About what?"

"About why you're sitting here." Joyce's voice reflected the pain she saw in Elizabeth's face. Then her friend turned to her and began to cry.

"They never called," she told her, sobbing. "They said they were going to pick up Debbie at the airport and would call me, but they didn't. And nobody answered the phone at their house all evening. I don't think there is a problem, but I keep running into situations I don't understand."

Joyce tried to console her friend. "Why don't we go inside?"

Looking up through her tears, Elizabeth explained the other reason she wanted to stay in the parking lot, the real reason.

"I can't go in there. I can't face those people who have stood by our family through the years—who looked up to us as the model couple. Everyone thinks I should face up to reality, but I don't believe Peter left me, no matter what they think. The problem is, if I go in there, people are either going to try to make me feel better or they're going to look at me as the woman who failed as a wife and mother."

"Come on," Joyce shot back, "you don't believe that, do you?"

"I don't know what to believe anymore. I already had one call from someone who wanted to know what was going on between Peter and me that would cause him to take off with another woman. She didn't ask it like that, but that's what she was saying." Tearfully, Elizabeth added, "I don't believe Peter has gone off with another woman. I don't care what the circumstances suggest. I believe in Peter . . . I'm just not sure anyone else does."

Joyce reached out and put her arm around Elizabeth's shoulder. She spoke words that she knew were inspired by Someone else. "Elizabeth, it's not you or Peter who is on trial here, it's Satan. His greatest joy is your despair—because that despair will cause you to doubt, and your doubt will lead you away from the Comforter at the very time you need him the most. If you allow the despair to turn you inward, if you allow it to separate you from God, Satan will win a victory. Last week you said that Peter is in God's hands. Do you still believe it?"

"Of course I do, but . . ." Elizabeth paused and looked Joyce in the eye. "But what I need to know is, do you?"

"Of course I believe he's in God's hands."

"Do you also believe he's in someone else's arms?"

After a long pause, Joyce responded, "I don't know."

"That's the problem. That's why I don't want to go in there," she said, motioning to the church building. "If my best friend has doubts, what will everyone else think?"

Joyce sat completely still, staring down at a shiny seatbelt buckle that lay on the seat between them.

Elizabeth suddenly broke into a smile. "You're right," she said, "Peter and I are not on trial here."

She blotted her tears, checked her face in the mirror and, before Joyce could respond, patted her on the thigh and thanked her for being her friend. Then, leaving a bewildered Joyce sitting in the front seat, Elizabeth stepped out of the car and into the sunlight.

*   *   *

Across town, in one of the many large, red-brick, steeple-topped edifices in Richmond's West End, sat Mike Downes. Throughout much of the service, his mind was somewhere else. It was in Mexico, and it was on what Earl Hendrick had told him two days earlier: "If you become preoccupied with Peter, you will lose the opportunity to guide this company—to lead nine thousand employees through the difficult times that lie ahead."

The Scripture reading brought Mike back to the present.

"What do you think," the minister was reading from Matthew's Gospel, "if a man owns a hundred sheep, and one of them wanders away, will he not leave the ninety-nine on the hills and go to look for the one that wandered off?"

The simplicity of the parable and its obvious wisdom struck the vice president as he sat in the pew. But then Hendrick's other words began to crowd out the truth of the verses: "You are still young. Mid-Atlantic Bell will need a man like you to take the helm."

Throughout the sermon, Mike's mind bounced between the competing ideas. Finally, when the organist played the first chords of the closing hymn, Mike leaned toward his daughter, who was sitting beside him, and said, "I've got to go."

Before anyone in the row stood to sing, he got up, shuffled past them to the aisle and walked quickly to the back of the sanctuary. Upon emerging through the church's main door, he dashed to his car. He glanced down at his watch as he wheeled his gray Olds out of the parking lot and headed to River Road.

*   *   *

Although Sunday afternoon is a popular time to visit hospitals, on the Baltimore Medical Center burn unit only smaller groups of people—mostly family members—were allowed in to see loved ones. For the patient's sake, all had to be fitted with paper masks, gowns, head coverings and gloves.

A Maryland state trooper posted to guard Barry Whitehead was similarly clothed, except his gown was slit down the right side to provide ready access to his firearm. The trooper warily eyed the two people who entered the room. He rose quickly from his chair at Whitehead's side and, with his hand on his gun, stepped to meet them.

"Just a minute, please," he said sternly. Then, noting that the men seemed to be quite old, said in a more conciliatory tone, "May I help you?"

"We've come to see Martha," said the one leaning on a cane. His voice was raspy but carried a trace of a foreign accent.

"I believe you've got the wrong room."

"This isn't 325?"

"No, this is 323," said the trooper as he moved toward the men.

The man with the cane turned first, the other helping him as they walked through the door. Before the door closed, the man with the cane stumbled forward and fell to the floor of the corridor. The other man who had tried to keep him from falling knelt beside him. The law officer rushed to the aid of the fallen man, while Patrick O'Hearn, who had been walking up the hall from the opposite direction, slipped into the unguarded room. He completed his assignment in twenty seconds and emerged from the room, passing the trooper who was helping the fallen man into a wheelchair.

Forty-five minutes later, the old men were removing their makeup and changing their clothes in the back of O'Hearn's van as they drove south out of Baltimore.

*   *   *

"Earl, this is Mike." Hendrick was surprised by the call. "I've been trying to reach you all day. I got over to your church before noon, but didn't see you."

"Of course not. I'm in the middle of Chesapeake Bay."

"I know. After I went by your house and didn't find you, I stopped at the club and Paul told me you had gone sailing. I'm sorry to bother you."

The president interposed, "No bother. What seems to be the problem?"

"I want to thank you for what you said to me on Friday," Downes said, but Hendrick knew that wasn't why his vice president would be calling him on his boat on a Sunday afternoon. "I want you to know how much I appreciate the advice and help you have offered me over the past years. And I wanted to tell you that I have decided to go after Peter."

"Would you repeat that?"

"I'm taking a few days off. I'm going to Denver—and Mexico if I must— to find him. I can't stand by and watch what's happening to Elizabeth and her family. And I can't sit around listening to the rumors circulating within the company. I've got to know where he is and why he has done what he has done."

"Mike, don't."

"I'm sorry, I've made up my mind."

"I know you are concerned," Hendrick said, "but think about all the work that needs to be done here. Think about the leadership we need on the PR side. Think about your career. Is Peter worth it?"

"I think he is," Downes answered. "Elizabeth doesn't believe her husband would just walk away, and I guess I don't either."

"Mike, Mike." Hendrick shook his head as he spoke into the phone. "You did not think Peter was capable of violating company rules when you first heard about security's investigation last year. Remember? But he did."

"That was different."

"Do you really think so?" He didn't wait for an answer. "Of course, this is your decision. You have a right to take the time off. But I have to say that I do not approve of your taking it now, during the busiest time of the year—especially with your secretary still out. And I will not be able to defend your actions in Washington."

"I just wanted you to be the first to know my plans. Sharon gets home from her vacation today, and she'll be back in the office on Tuesday. And I'm taking work with me. I'll call you tomorrow."

*   *   *

Elizabeth wasn't treated as a leper, though a few people at church avoided direct contact with her. But for every person who didn't stop by to express concern and offer support, two or three did, completely overwhelming Elizabeth and her family with their love.

Now, as she was fixing dinner for her children, she continued her afternoon-long conversation with Sally Martin, one of her neighbors. With the afternoon slipping quickly into evening, Elizabeth knew she was behind schedule. But with the kids out enjoying the extra hour of light, she knew it didn't matter.

"How much would it take to get a private investigator?" Sally drawled. The Alabama native answered her own question as she mentioned her husband and his security firm. "Howard uses several, and I think he said they range between three hundred and a thousand a day."

"Great," replied Elizabeth dejectedly. "I may not have enough even to cover the mortgage next month . . . I wonder if they take MasterCard?"

The two laughed. Then Sally continued. "I don't know, but Howard may be able to get one to lower his fees for you."

"Jim Parker said that tracking down a missing spouse could cost five to ten thousand—and that would be an easy case," Elizabeth said, mixing pancake batter. "I think I'll get half of Peter's monthly pay on Friday. That will be it until he comes back."

Sally didn't say anything. For nearly three hours the two women had discussed flowers, the grass that needed to be cut, the neighbors and the health of each of their kids. Only now were some of the issues surrounding Peter's disappearance coming out, and Sally thought it best not to pry. She had heard from some of the neighbors and the children about the accident and then the discovery of his car. But except for dropping by with a cake for the family, she had not spoken to Elizabeth since the incident.

Now she studied Elizabeth's methodical meal preparation—the pouring of batter onto the griddle, the browning of the sausages and the perking of a pot of coffee. When the three grapefruits were pulled from the refrigerator, Sally walked over to help section them.

"I don't know what I'm going to do," Elizabeth was saying. "Some of the people at church have offered to handle the investigation themselves, and some have come forward with money to help pay expenses, but this is all too overwhelming for me. Nobody has the time to leave their job to go looking for Peter, and no one is in a position to put up that kind of money for a search." Elizabeth rattled on as she removed the first half-dozen pancakes from the griddle and poured six more. "Peter's boss said he'd help, but he told me last night that the company itself won't do anything else."

Sally interrupted. "You don't mean it. I can't believe it."

"I can," Elizabeth said with more than a hint of bitterness in her voice. "It's a long story."

Sally was cutting the fourth grapefruit half when Elizabeth stopped what she was doing, looked at Sally and started to laugh. "What are we doing? I've got enough food here for an army, and there isn't a kid in sight."

Sally laughed too. "As light as it is, I guess I really didn't think about supper, but I best be getting my own kids gathered up."

"Why don't you bring them all over here?"

"No, you go ahead. Howard will be back from the golf course soon, and we'll probably be going for pizza. Thanks anyway." Sally rinsed her hands and turned to go. "It's going to be all right. You just wait 'n' see."

At the front door, Elizabeth thanked Sally for stopping by.

"What're neighbors for? Let me talk to Howard. Maybe he can work something out. I'll call you."

A ringing phone drew Elizabeth back to the kitchen before she could call her children to the table. She could hear Kristin stirring in her crib, and she was grateful for her daughter's long nap. Debating whether to take the call or go up and get Kristin, Elizabeth let the answering machine take the call and went upstairs.

When she returned to the kitchen, she played the message. "Hello, Elizabeth, this is Mike. Sorry I missed you. I'm at the airport on my way to Denver. I've called the Clarks. There is still no word on Debbie, and they are very worried. I'm going to find Peter and bring him back. I'll call you in the morning." The voice was calm and determined.

It took a few moments for the impact of the message to sink in. *Mike Downes is going to Denver? After what he told me last night?* Cradling her daughter in her arms, Elizabeth said to Kristin, "Maybe it is going to be all right. Maybe it really is."

*   *   *

For the second night in a row, Debbie Steinbaugh was sleeping on a hammock in her cell. The consular agent had purchased the hammock for her for a little more than the price of a good meal in town. It was a far cry from the firm mattress and down pillow she was used to, but it was infinitely more comfortable than the concrete floor. Her eyes were open, but they were not seeing. Her ears were registering sounds, but they were not hearing.

She was lying on top of the extra pair of shorts, two T-shirts and three changes of underwear that María Escobar had asked the guards to give her from her suitcase. Debbie had been warned to guard her clothes closely, lest they disappear.

Though she'd been interrogated by officials each day, she'd never wavered from her convoluted story and her insistence of innocence. She had been told that she'd get an attorney in the morning.

The prostitutes from Wednesday night were gone. Their place in the cell had been taken by a woman arrested for ramming a broken whiskey bottle into the neck of a customer in the bar where she worked.

The hairy-legged, antennae-twitching insects with whom she had spent her first three nights on the concrete floor remained.

14

Monday, March 26

After a short and not-too-restful sleep at an airport motel in Denver, Mike Downes showered, dressed and grabbed a quick breakfast at a fast-food outlet nearby. After eating, he took a cab to the airport.

Just as he had done when he landed the evening before, he walked from counter to counter, showing the photos he had of Peter and asking if anyone had seen him.

"Yes, I know it's not your policy to discuss other customers," he repeated over and over, "but Peter Boget's wife and five children are counting on me to find their father. A flight attendant on a plane from Baltimore said he got off here in Denver around noon on Friday a week ago."

Shortly before ten, Downes struck gold.

"Yep, looks familiar," said the elderly gentleman behind one of the many car-rental counters inside the airport. "Was by here, maybe Saturday morning."

"He was?" After three hours of searching, Downes had begun to expect rejection. "How do you know?"

"I don't know for sure," said the man, carefully eyeing the picture Downes had placed in front of him, "but I think so." Then the man slowly lifted his eyes and struck a thoughtful pose. "Let me tell you why I remember him."

"Please do," said Downes, who wanted to yank the words out of the man.

"Most of our customers are regulars who drop their papers and keys in this box here," he said reaching out and tapping the box on the counter. "But he wanted to pay cash. So I opened the drawer here, and told him I didn't have the right change for his hundred-dollar bill. Said I'd have to go next door." He pointed his thumb in the direction of the next car-rental counter. "Then he says to me: 'Wait, I'm late for my plane, just keep the change.' But I'd never do that—keep the man's change—so I told him I would put his change in an envelope for the next time he came by, but I don't think he was listening 'cause he just took off."

Although the attendant continued his story at a pace more suited to a campfire than to communicating vital information about a missing person, Downes couldn't believe what he was hearing. Someone here had seen Peter—not arriving on Friday, but leaving on Saturday.

"Do you remember renting the car to him?"

"No, he must have come by when I was off. You see, I'm getting up in years, and I only work at the counter here a couple days a week. It gives me something to do and keeps me out of the way of the missus."

Downes was hoping that every question wouldn't be answered with a story, but he had to continue. "Did you get his name?"

"Sure. Got it on the receipt."

"Boget?"

"No, no, that doesn't sound right," he replied, scratching the back of his head.

A customer walking to the counter drew the attendant's attention, and he raised his voice to greet the approaching man. "Mr. Brown. Good morning." He placed a set of keys on the counter and pulled a packet of papers from the rack behind him, opened them and handed a pen to Mr. Brown.

"Good morning to you, Mr. Merrill." The man signed his name with a flourish, picked up his keys and headed for the door.

Looking at his watch, the attendant said to Mr. Brown, "The shuttle will be along in less than two minutes." Then he turned back to Downes. "I'm sorry, where were we?"

"Did you write his name on the envelope with the change in it?" Downes asked quickly.

"Of course I did."

After a long pause, Downes finally asked, "May I see it?"

"No. I don't have it anymore."

"Did he come back and claim it—the money, that is?"

"No. My son didn't think we should leave nearly fifty dollars laying around, so he took the money and said he would see to it that a check was sent to him."

"May I see the receipt?" Downes asked.

"I'm sorry, I can't let you see the man's receipt."

"Of course you can't," said Downes, "but I bet you can show it to the FBI."

"Who's talking about the FBI?"

"I am," Downes said quietly, hoping the threat would shake loose some more hard information and fewer stories. "If I tell them that a missing man may have been kidnapped and that you may have some information, they'll be here asking questions and issuing a subpoena for your records and asking you to testify in court."

"You've got a point there," the man replied. "But those records wouldn't be here, they would be at the office." Reaching for the phone, he said, "Let me call my son."

After a brief exchange on the phone, the man said, "Robert Merrill, the president, said he would talk to you at the office. If you hurry, you may be able to catch the shuttle."

*　　*　　*

At midday, after receiving a message on the intercom, Mary Kennedy picked up her phone. "Hello, William. Seems we've been talking a lot lately."

"Yes," answered the managing partner of Stanley and Heinemann. "I'm just calling to find out about Friday. You didn't send anyone to get Barry's car, did you?"

"No. Didn't you get my message?"

"Yes, I did."

The woman continued, "Richard became ill and never went to Washington. I'm sorry."

"Did you talk about the car with anyone else?"

"No." Kennedy paused. "No, I don't think so. Is something wrong?"

"The FBI came by this morning. Somebody picked up the car and was killed in an explosion in a hotel parking lot Friday night."

"Oh my God, how terrible. What happened?"

"The police didn't say much, but the paper said a bomb went off. The driver and two policemen were killed. I told the FBI that you had offered to send someone to pick up Barry's car, so they'll probably be calling you. I just wanted to be sure it wasn't one of your employees."

"No, Richard is in this morning and feeling much better."

"And there is something else," Heinemann's voice was sad. "Barry Whitehead passed away over the weekend."

"Oh, how terrible."

Whitehead's employer began to castigate himself. "I should have gone to see him. I should have made sure that his family was notified. I can't believe that I could get so engrossed in my work that I would let one of my own employees die and never go to the hospital. Mary, I just didn't realize how bad off he was . . ."

"I'm really terribly sorry. Is there anything I can help you with?"

"Unless you have an extra hundred hours and a draftsman you can give me, I don't think so."

"I'm sorry. We're awfully busy right now ourselves. Has a funeral been planned?"

"The FBI is tracking down his wife and kids right now," said Heinemann. "Nobody else knows if he has any other family. He never talked about his mother and father . . . Then again, he never talked about much of anything."

Kennedy agreed, "I remember."

Heinemann added, "I guess if no one steps forward, I'll take care of it. It's the least I can do. If you'd like to know about the arrangements, I'll call you."

"Thank you. Thank you very much."

*   *   *

Robert Merrill looked more like an automobile mechanic than the president of a car-rental agency. Then he opened his mouth, and Downes knew he was dealing with an executive peer. "Please come in and have a seat in my office," said the man in the blue overalls. "Would you like a cup of coffee?"

"That would be good," Downes nodded.

"Fine. Jill, would you please help Mr.—"

"Downes."

"Right. Mr. Downes, if you'll give me a moment, I'll be right back," Merrill said. He disappeared behind a door on the side of the auto-repair facility that was adjacent to the small, glass-walled office building.

Downes was taken aback when the manager returned. In five minutes Robert Merrill had transformed himself from mechanic to business executive, complete with a red handkerchief protruding from the breast pocket of his black suit. Noticing Downes's surprise, he held up his hands, palms toward his chest, so his clean fingernails were apparent. "Aren't latex gloves wonderful? And coveralls? I don't do much garage work anymore, but one of my mechanics has been out since last Thursday, and we had a big run on cars this morning."

He took his seat behind an imposing mahogany desk that seemed out of place in the chrome-and-glass office. He motioned for Downes to sit down also. "So," he said, "my dad said something about the FBI."

Downes proceeded to tell the same story he had told at the airport and asked for the same information, but this time without the veiled threat of FBI intervention.

"We have a company policy that all customer-related information is confidential. We're not Hertz or Avis. We're a family-owned business—my dad started Executive Autos over forty years ago—and we depend on a regular clientele of businessmen who expect a special level of service and dependability. I wouldn't give away information on any of those customers, any more than I would give your information to anyone else if you rented from us."

Downes took the hint and interrupted the discussion to say, "Speaking of rentals, I'll need a car for a few days."

"Wonderful. Let's take care of that right away." He touched a button on his phone, and moments later Jill, the smartly dressed, dark-haired assistant, stepped through the door. "Mr. Downes here needs a car," said the president. Then, turning back to Downes, he asked, "How 'bout a Thunderbird?"

"Sounds fine."

"If you give Jill your license and a credit card, it'll be ready when we're through." Jill retreated with the documents in hand.

Downes looked at Merrill. "A very pleasant assistant."

Merrill's face lit up. "Thank you. I think so too. We'll be married for twenty years this June."

Returning the conversation to business, Downes asked, "You have access to your rental records, don't you?"

"Of course."

"If I tell you what's on one, would you at least say yes or no?"

"Maybe."

"Do you have a blank one?"

"Sure, right here." Merrill liked Mike Downes. He didn't know if it was because Downes was a no-nonsense, let's-get-to-the-point sort of guy or whether it was the compassion he exhibited for his lost employee, but Merrill decided that he was going to help as much as possible. He pulled out a form and handed it across the desk.

Downes turned the form back toward Merrill and pulled a mechanical pencil from his pocket to use as a pointer. "I think you have a contract dated March 16 that says 'Peter Boget' here." He pointed to the block on the form that was labeled "name" and then slid his pencil down the page, stopping at several of the empty blocks. "It has a credit-card imprint here, and that card would either be an American Express card that has the name of Mid-Atlantic Bell under his name, or it's a MasterCard with this number on it." He pushed a list of Peter's credit-card numbers across the desk. "Down here," he said, pointing to the miles-driven block on the form, "there will be at least 140 miles, and the contract will show that Mr. Boget paid in cash." Downes stopped and looked up. When their eyes met, he asked, "Will you look and see if I'm right?"

"Yes I will."

Merrill disappeared and returned in a few minutes with a yellow sheet in his hand. "You're close," he smiled. "Close enough for me to let you see this." He handed the sheet across the desk.

Downes scanned it quickly, noting in his mind the 148 miles driven and the return to the airport on Saturday morning. In the upper left corner, the form was imprinted with Peter's company credit-card number. The signature looked okay too.

After a few final exchanges, Downes stood to go. "You'll never know how much you have helped a family in need."

"You're going to keep me posted, aren't you?" Merrill handed Downes his business card and escorted him back through the building to a waiting Thunderbird.

Downes stopped. "Robert, may I leave this car here for a while and take your shuttle back to the terminal? I've got some more questions to ask before I head to Colorado Springs."

Sweeping his hand toward the waiting minivan emblazoned with the Executive Autos logo, Robert Merrill said, "Please, be my guest."

*   *   *

Martin Beale was angry. The short, bespectacled Securities Exchange Commission investigator knew he was onto something big. He also knew that with Segal and Randolph gone, his chance for glory was fading. He had asked several people to come to a briefing in the conference room at the midtown branch office of the investment firm of Michaels & Trent.

The conference room that served as an office for Beale and his assistant, the matronly Audrey Dowling, had been returned to its original function for the meeting. Piles of records, reports and computer disks that had been piled on the table were now stacked neatly on the floor along one wall. At 2:10 Carl Trent, the seventy-six-year-old managing partner of the investment firm, entered the room.

Six people were sitting around the table, which held only an overhead projector at the end where Beale was standing and three ashtrays placed up the middle of the table. Only the one nearest Beale had any hint of cigarette usage, though the room smelled from Beale's chain smoking. Seated around the table were Hugh Waters, the branch manager; Melissa Savage, the assistant manager; Singe Madaven, the director of information management systems for Michaels & Trent; Derek Lewis, the head of the company's security department; and Audrey Dowling. All stood to join Beale in welcoming the grandson of the company's founder. After Carl Trent sat down, all followed suit except for Beale, who took his position next to the projector, opposite the deeply tanned corporate patriarch.

Beale, whose pale skin suggested he spent far more hours behind a desk than out of doors, began to speak when he had the attention of everyone present.

"Mr. Trent," he said, peering through his thick glasses at the managing partner, "we were just speculating on the whereabouts of Mark Randolph and Glenn Segal."

Beale wasn't expecting a response, but he got one anyway.

"I wish I knew," said Trent with a distinct edge to his voice.

Beale began to pace the floor, speaking in an agitated voice. "I asked them a few questions on Thursday, they seemed very jumpy on Friday, and now they have both stayed home from work today. Do you think that's strange?"

Trent and his employees nodded their heads. Waters said, "That's very strange!"

"I think so too," intoned Beale. "Look, gentlemen—and ladies—this is not a formal hearing or anything like that, yet. But something funny is going on, and I intend to find out what. I talked to Segal's wife this morning, and she's worried sick. He never came home from work on Friday, something she said has never happened in all their years of marriage. And Randolph can't be reached at his apartment here in Manhattan or his home in Connecticut."

Shifting in his seat, Trent interjected, "I know all that. What I want to know is why you thought it was so important for me to come here. I cut a luncheon meeting short to get up here by two, and I want to know what you've discovered!"

"What I've—that is, what we've—discovered is that your boys, Randolph and Segal, seem to be laundering money."

"What?" The financier was genuinely surprised, as were the others in the room.

"Laundering money, as in taking ill-gotten funds from one place, legitimizing it though your company books and passing it off as clean somewhere else."

"No way," whistled the branch manager. "Not those two."

Beale stared him in the eye and nodded affirmatively. "I'm afraid so." Then he laid out his thesis to a dumbfounded audience.

"In this case, they have taken stock from the accounts of over two dozen clients and transferred it to a woman in Virginia, who has reaped enormous benefits from the acquisition of stock she never paid for. In addition, they have churned these same clients' portfolios to the tune of half a million in commissions just since the first of the year."

The people sitting around the table were listening attentively. Someone let out a low whistle as Beale continued. "What tipped me off was that no one has complained about the way your boys have been unproductively churning their portfolios." Beale smiled sarcastically. "If your company had been more interested in customer service than in racking up commissions, you might have figured this out yourself. A lot sooner."

Trent rose from his chair. "Young man," he said gravely, "nobody, but nobody, speaks like that about this company, do you understand? Keep the editorial comments to yourself. We have one of the best performance records on Wall Street. Now you tell me something we don't already know, or you can pick up your attaché case and leave."

"Okay," said Beale, only slightly humbled by Michaels & Trent's top man. Looking down the mahogany table at Trent, he said, "Your boys were in bed with Mary Kennedy and their clients, executing transfers that never showed up on your records."

"That's impossible!" declared Madaven indignantly. "Our computers would have picked that up."

"*Should* have," Beale shot back. "But they didn't." Then he paused and looked around the room to be sure that all eyes were focused on him. In a steely voice, he added, "They didn't because your boys were smart. They knew the thresholds of detection and operated consistently at five percent under those thresholds. Let me show you."

Beale flipped on the overhead projector and proceeded to show transparencies of a number of transaction records. The members of the firm sat in rapt attention as the investigator explained more of the details. He spoke uninterrupted for eighteen minutes, turned off the machine and asked for questions. No one wanted to go first.

The managing partner's brow communicated to those who chose to look at him that he was greatly displeased. He eyed each of his employees as he slowly spoke. "Michaels & Trent has a peerless reputation that has survived recessions, depressions, bank failures and a fire that destroyed our computer room. I don't want anything—and I mean anything—to leave this room that would endanger that reputation." Turning to Beale, he asked, "What do you intend to do with this information?"

"I don't know yet. I've notified my office, and they have in turn alerted the FBI."

"The FBI?" exploded Trent.

"Yes. We always tip off the FBI to try and determine if any of the people involved might have underworld connections. But that shouldn't affect you until Randolph or Segal are indicted, or we find more problems. The fact that you brought the problem to us, and the fact that the problem seems to be isolated, suggests that there will not be any serious ramifications for Michaels & Trent—unless of course, someone, like a client, steps forward and complains about improper trades. Or Randolph and Segal show up with another story."

Trent seemed relieved to hear that his company would not be front-page news in the *Wall Street Journal.* "Will that be all?" he asked, rising from his chair.

"I think so, for now."

*   *   *

At an American Airlines gate counter, Downes found what he had been looking for. Only two flights left Denver for Mexican beach resorts during the half-hour following the 10:42 p.m. check-in time for Peter's car rental. One was scheduled for 11:15 to Mexico City and Acapulco, the other at 10:55 to Dallas with a connection to Cancún. Downes reasoned that if he had thirty-three minutes to catch a plane, Peter wouldn't leave forty-plus dollars at the ticket counter. But if the plane was leaving in ten minutes, that might be a different story.

With that information in hand, he learned who was collecting tickets for the flight and tracked down the woman at a gate in the airport's west wing. She remembered the man in the picture. "He was the last one on. He was all red from running."

"Was he alone?" Downes queried.

"Oh, yes. He boarded by himself."

*   *   *

Elizabeth resumed vacuuming after listening to Mike's message. She wanted the noise of the motor to numb her mind and drown out the usual interruptions by her children. Now was the time for contemplation.

As she pushed the cleaner into the bedroom, she stopped and studied the ring on her husband's dresser. She had returned it to the place where she had found it after his disappearance. It was a constant reminder of the commitment he had made to her twenty years earlier and that he had reaffirmed regularly.

The ring had been a topic of conversation with Joyce McGuire on more than one occasion, and it had become a symbol to many who knew about it of the power of love that blinds some women from reality. But with each new revelation, with each innuendo, Elizabeth became firmer in her resolve that Peter wouldn't leave her.

After reading Peter's letters to Debbie Steinbaugh in the computer that Charles Piper returned to her, she was convinced that there was no romantic involvement between Debbie and her husband. The letters contained information that he had said he was writing to her, and although they were more eloquent than she thought they needed to be, and though some of the phraseology was similar to that of the romantic letters she had received from Peter when they were courting, Elizabeth could not bring herself to believe that these were anything more than inspirational letters from an older brother to a sister.

She knew that to give in to the rumors would mean facing a world more difficult than she could imagine, so her daily prayer was that God would sustain her for just this one day. Her whole focus changed from one of looking to the future while dwelling on the past, to looking at today and leaving tomorrow to God.

* * *

Interstate 25, connecting Denver with Colorado Springs seventy miles to the south, is the dividing line between the mountains and the prairie. For Mike Downes, the vista was awe-inspiring. To his left, he saw rolling hills interspersed with meadows that hinted at the flat prairie just beyond. The absence of the dense foliage that lines so many of Virginia's highways made the towering rock formations that punctuated the landscape seem more powerful and prominent than any he had seen in the Old Dominion. It also made the grazing cattle appear to be more rugged than their Eastern brethren. For this East Coast executive, it was the quintessential picture of the Wild West. He could imagine stagecoaches, cowboys and Indians riding that range, and he knew that somewhere out there—beyond the hills, beyond the unmarked border with Kansas—was Dodge City and a hundred other towns where law was once defined by a Winchester, a Colt .45 and the U.S. marshal who wielded them.

As the Thunderbird sped south, Pikes Peak appeared, growing in size and majesty with each approaching mile. That mountain reminded Downes of the other world on his right—the foothills of the Rockies. They formed a rock-and-evergreen skirt for the snow-covered front range that rose behind them.

As he neared his destination city, Downes looked to his right and he observed, on the plateau, the glass-and-aluminum chapel of the United States Air Force Academy campus. Soon other academy buildings came into view, and his thoughts drifted back to his alma mater and the discipline that was drilled into him at Virginia Military Institute. That discipline had served him well during his upward climb through Mid-Atlantic Bell. He would need the same discipline and creative thinking to find Peter and bring him home.

*   *   *

"That's a crazy idea, ma'am," Patrick O'Hearn said to his boss, and then wished he hadn't used those words.

"Crazy? I don't think so." She glared at the man seated across from her in the basement coffee room of her architectural firm. It was after business hours, and the two of them sat with freshly poured glasses of imported beer. "Federal agents will be down here within a few days, checking my books to find out where my money comes from and where it goes. Now if someone looks too closely, they are going to want to know about my contributions to charitable organizations in Ireland. If they are real sharp, someone may draw a relationship between my contributions, my work and our cause."

Mary Kennedy always referred to her support of the IRA as "our cause." Born into poverty in the Catholic ghetto in Belfast, she had been the sixth of eleven children, and the only one to attend college. She had learned hatred of the British government as a youngster and translated that hatred into action while attending college in Dublin. She came to America to study architecture at the University of Virginia and was hired by an alumnus who owned the architectural firm of Green, Minor & Company in Norfolk. Her managerial ability exceeded her design skills, and she soon was managing the small firm's day-to-day operations. She'd purchased the company from the owner when he retired in 1985. Though always active in fundraising activities for "the cause" among sympathetic Irish-Americans throughout Hampton Roads, she'd stumbled upon the opportunity to make a substantial contribution to the efforts of the IRA while in Venezuela, overseeing the design and construction of a port facility for a Norfolk-based company.

Now Kennedy knew that she had to shut down the drug business immediately. She also had to deflect any focus on her operation from people investigating the cocaine in Barry Whitehead's car and Glenn Segal's death. She knew that if the investigators from New York began comparing notes with the investigators from Maryland, life would become very difficult. She laid out her plan, but O'Hearn didn't like it.

"What you're asking me to do is crazy," he declared again, trying to say no to the woman who had brought him to America simply to do her dirty work.

But Kennedy was not to be denied. With a smile that could melt the hardest heart, she looked into O'Hearn's rugged, red face and let the words glide from her tongue: "Consider the alternatives."

*   *   *

Dinner at the Clarks' was quiet, yet somewhat festive. Despite the circumstances, Liz Clark had made a huge pot of chili and baked four pans of cornbread, all of which was to be consumed by three families that had joined "Grams" and "Gramps" for a hastily arranged evening meal to discuss Debbie's situation. Mike Downes pulled into the driveway just as the families were gathering in the kitchen. John, the Clarks' forty-four-year-old son, stepped outside and greeted him.

"Mr. Downes?" he asked as the phone-company executive emerged from the Thunderbird.

"Just call me Mike," he said, extending his hand. "And you must be one of the Clarks."

"John," he replied, meeting the extended hand halfway. "Come on in; supper is on the table."

Downes closed the car door and followed the gregarious, wiry man into the kitchen.

Greetings were quickly exchanged, and Downes was given a few minutes to wash before the meal was served. When he returned to the kitchen, he was told about the telephone call that Norwood Clark had received earlier in the day from the U.S. Consulate in Mexico—a conversation that was bereft of details either because the man didn't have them or because Mr. Clark was unable to recall them.

Then, with the children eagerly eyeing the supper set before them, Norwood led the family in prayer. He folded his bony hands and set them on the edge of the table. All around the table bowed their heads.

"Our dear Heavenly Father," he began, "thou knowest that our hearts are heavy, Lord, as we think on the news that Debbie is in jail. Thou knowest her heart and her circumstances, and that her history with thee was not good at one time, but is getting better. Watch over her and protect her. And, Father, if there be anything thou wouldst have us do, please reveal it to us in this our hour of need. Now bless these thy gifts we are about to receive. We pray this in the blessed name of our Savior. Amen." Norwood raised his balding head slowly and, after a thoughtful pause, spoke above the chatter and activity that immediately followed his "amen." "I believe that one of us has to go down and be with Debbie."

Around the table, each person looked at the others. In the silence Downes could sense their reservations. He could read the unwillingness on their faces.

Eventually John Clark responded. Addressing Downes, he said, "I guess you can tell that we haven't been all that close to Debbie. She never really adjusted to her parents' dying, and I suppose we never really adjusted to the idea of having a new sister."

He continued speaking as the chili and cornbread slowly disappeared from the table. Finally, he said, "While we're shocked to hear that she's in a Mexican jail, we can understand how it could happen to someone like Debbie. And I guess that right now, flying to Mexico is probably not high on the agenda of anyone sitting around this table—even if we could afford it, which, truthfully, would be hard to do right now. But I do agree with my father: one of us needs to go. Mom would probably be the best, if she were up to it."

"I'm up to it."

The family matriarch was not about to admit that her erratic heart all but disqualified her for such a strenuous journey, but her son was genuinely concerned for her welfare.

"That's okay, Mom," John said. "I'll go."

Before anyone else could contribute to the discussion, Downes interjected, "I've already got a flight booked for tomorrow afternoon. I'm looking for Peter, not Debbie. But I figure that if I find one, I might find the other. I'd be happy to meet her and give you a report, so you could decide who should go down."

"That's a great idea," said Betty, John's wife, who knew the family's finances.

Downes nodded and then pursued an earlier line of questioning about any recent interaction between Peter and Debbie.

"That girl's always been very independent," Liz sighed. " 'Bout the only time we'd hear from her was when she was in trouble and needed some money or needed someone to drive five hundred miles to pick her up somewhere."

John continued. "She's been back at church, and has really changed, but in a lot of ways Debbie's still Debbie. She's made new friends outside the family, and we don't see that much of her, except on Sundays. Then she goes her way and we go ours, and . . ."

"And we're experiencing a relationship that was out of whack for so long, we don't know how to fix it," Betty interrupted. "Even after she came back to the church, even after Peter's visit, it was hard to renew a relationship with her." Betty turned to the youngest of the Clarks' four children. "Wouldn't you say so, Shirley?"

"I guess so. Even though we graduated from high school together and have been doing some things with her and her girls over the past year, it's been slow. She never seemed to trust us with details of her life. Not that I blame her; we all rode her pretty hard for years when she was throwing her life away."

"And none of us really wanted to admit that we were related to someone whose mood swings were so . . . so moody," said another brother, moving his hand in a wave motion above the table. "We've seen her so upset that she'd crawl into a chair for hours on end—staring at nothing, saying nothing, just sitting and rocking."

"But never violent," Liz added. "I just can't believe she can be in jail for murder. There must be some kinda mistake." Digging in her apron pocket, she pulled out a small piece of paper and said, "This María Es-co-bar"—

she sounded out the word one syllable at a time—"she's in Cancún and she's talked with Debbie, and she's gonna call tonight." She put the paper back in her pocket and continued, "Hopefully she'll know more, but I wantcha to hear me when I tell you that for the life of me I can't figure out what Debbie was doing with that Stevens woman."

"Stevens woman?" Downes queried.

"Jan Stevens, the one she's s'post've killed."

"Oh, right."

"Now, there's been a couple times I'da liked to kill that woman myself." Everyone around the table laughed knowingly.

Downes probed again, looking at Norwood at the head of the table. "Did the man from the consulate say anything about Peter?"

"Nope," he said through a mouthful of dinner. "Not a word."

The discussion of Jan and Debbie continued. Downes sat quietly and took in the many comments that came forth from members of the family. Finally he asked, "Did Debbie ever talk about Peter?"

Liz Clark laughed out loud. "Talk? Talk about Peter? There musta been two months last year when that was all she talked about when she saw us. You'da thought he'd brought her a million dollars the way she went on 'bout him. She'd talk all 'bout his letters . . ."

"Letters?"

"Sure." It sounded more like "shore."

"Lots of letters?"

"I don't rightly know. I don't think she ever said."

"Have you read any?"

"Course not," Liz replied indignantly. "But she read some of them to me. He's a writer, ya know, and he can say some things beautifully."

"I'm sorry, I didn't mean to suggest—"

"That I read them?" She grinned and the others sitting around smiled. "That's okay, I probably would've if I could've."

Downes continued the questioning. "Has anyone been in her house since she left?"

"Oh, yes," Shirley chimed in, "every day. To collect her mail, feed her cat and things like that. And it's just an apartment, not a house."

"I see," Downes said scratching his head. "I wondered if there was any-thing there that might tell us more about her current relationship with

Peter, or that might help us find them."

Norwood looked at his watch and said, "It isn't too far from here. Would you like to see it?"

"Actually, I'd like to wait for the call," Downes answered. "But standing around doing nothing doesn't suit me. Let's go."

Shirley suggested that she go with the two men because she knew her way around the apartment. "I'll take the kids home," her husband said.

John, who lived with his wife and three teenagers in Woodland Park, high in the mountains northwest of the Springs, agreed to stay and wait with his mother for the call.

"Make sure you get a phone number, so we can ring her back if we need to," Norwood said, pushing Downes out the door.

*   *   *

"Here we go." Shirley Blankenship looked up from the small kitchen table in Debbie Steinbaugh's one-bedroom apartment. She held aloft a newspaper clipping. Downes reached across the table and, taking the four-by-six-inch piece of paper in his hand, saw that it was an ad, probably cut from the Sunday paper's travel section. It read:

CANCÚN
SAVE $80 PER COUPLE
6 NIGHTS — $569 per person

ClubMex! OLÉ! The best values ever on a luxury vacation
to Mexico's most beautiful beach resort.
You'll stay in a deluxe beachfront hotel along the white sand
beaches of the sparkling Caribbean.

CLUBMEX VACATIONS INCLUDE:
Roundtrip Air Travel from Phoenix
Hotel Accommodations
Airport/Hotel Transfers
Baggage Handling, Hotel Taxes and Gratuities
Friendly, Knowledgeable Destination Representatives

CALL YOUR TRAVEL AGENT TODAY

When Downes finished reading it, he handed it to Norwood Clark. "Did you say Jan Stevens was from Phoenix?"

"Yes, why?"

"This is probably out of a Phoenix paper," he said, pointing to the city name in the ad.

Downes looked to Shirley, whose short, dark hair and large glasses gave her the appearance of a no-nonsense businesswoman. "You've been through everything?"

"Just about."

"And no other letters from Peter?"

"Just the ones I showed you."

* * *

Liz Clark was first to the phone when it rang. The pleasantly accented voice of the consular agent floated across the line.

"Mrs. Clark, this is María Escobar. I am the Cancún consular agent. You were expecting my call?"

"Yes, we were," she said as John Clark ran up the stairs to join the conversation from the extension phone in the Clarks' bedroom.

"I have been to see Debbie today. This morning a lawyer stopped in to talk with her. I'm afraid there is no chance of bail." Explaining the situation, Escobar said, "She will have to remain in jail until she goes to trial. Six months, maybe more."

John whistled loud enough to be heard by both women.

Liz said, "Even if she didn't do it?"

"Even if she didn't do it."

* * *

Downes gazed thoughtfully on the documents stacked in front of him. Some were letters, most were bills. The bills were all current; the letters were all old. Peter's letters were the same ones he already knew about from Peter's laptop computer. All were in envelopes postmarked one year ago. "There has to be more," he said, "somewhere." He handed back the stack of phone receipts that had yielded information on only three calls to the East Coast during the previous fourteen months. The only one to Peter's home phone number lasted all of two minutes. "There's got to be more letters."

"Why?" Shirley asked.

"Because there's a big file in his computer, and it's got the initials *DBS* on it, the same initials that are on the file with the other letters, these letters," he put his hand on the pile of papers in front of him. "But we can't read the letters, because they're encrypted—the contents are hidden from view."

"And you think they are letters to Debbie?" asked Mr. Clark, mulling over Mike's words.

"What else could they be?"

"But they're not here."

"So it seems."

Shirley returned the pile of bills, fliers and newspaper clippings back to a large basket that had been sitting on a corner of the kitchen counter. "What now?" she asked.

"Back to see if the call has come in yet."

*   *   *

Liz and John were still on the phone when the three walked into the kitchen. They listened to Liz's side of the conversation for ten minutes. When the conversation ended, they sat down around the table and heard the detailed explanation.

Liz animatedly began telling the story in no particular order, confusing those trying to understand what had happened. When she got to the part where she said, "He apparently tried to rape her and killed Jan," with no explanation of who "he" was, Mike interrupted. "That's not possible—not Peter!"

John took over the conversation. When he got to the incident with White-head, John explained, "She said Debbie said that someone who looks like Peter tried to rape her and that Jan tried to stop him. He knocked her down and she hit her head on a nightstand."

"And they don't believe her?" Mike asked.

"No, because she and Jan fought in public, and Debbie supposedly said in front of twenty witnesses that she was going to kill Jan."

"Has anyone seen Peter or this man who looks like Peter since?"

"I don't know, she didn't say."

"Do you have the consul's number?" Downes asked. "I'd like to talk to her and see what else she knows about Peter. Do you mind?"

Norwood motioned to the phone, "No, please do."

After ten rings, Downes hung up the phone. "No answer."

"It's after nine. She's probably gone," said Shirley.

"I'm about gone myself," said Downes. "I think I need to find a motel for the night. Then in the morning I'd like to go to the bank where she worked—see what some of her coworkers know, and figure out if the bank has any plans to do anything for her. But it's getting late . . ." He stood up.

"You can stay with us," Liz and Norwood offered.

"That's okay. I can get a place."

"No, no, no," Norwood Clark broke in on Downes's last words. "I insist you stay with us. We have plenty of room."

Too tired to argue, Downes agreed to spend the night.

*   *   *

Jonathan's crying awakened Elizabeth. Her eyes were too blurry to view the clock by her bed, but she knew it was well past midnight. Before she could get to the bedroom door, she heard the crying interrupted by the unmistakable sound of a child throwing up. When she opened the door, she could see in the glow of the hall nightlight the young boy retching on the hardwood floor two steps away from the bathroom door.

"Peter, come quick," she said. Then she flipped on the bedroom light and looked back at the vacant bed.

She shook her head, remembering that there was no Peter to jump to her aid. There would be no one to clean up the mess on the floor. There would be no one to help change the sheets that she guessed were also soiled. She was alone.

"Peter," she whispered as she ushered a closed-eyed, weeping Jonathan around the mess in the hall and into the bathroom. "I need you. *We* need you. Please, please come home."

15

A strong wind drove the icy rain against the windowpane of Mark Randolph's room. He shivered, even under the two blankets his hosts had provided him. He could smell the coffee brewing two floors below and imagined his friends preparing to leave for work. He hoped the quiet house would afford him the environment to sort out his current circumstances. He didn't want to talk to anyone, watch TV or read anything. He just wanted to think. But for now, he decided more sleep was in order. He pulled the covers around his head and closed his eyes.

Unfortunately, though the blackness of his cotton-and-wool sanctuary helped him escape the cold damp air of the attic room, he could not escape the fear of knowing that federal investigators were probably already going through his books and would find him guilty of gross negligence at the very least. He could not escape the fear of knowing that no matter how reasonable and friendly and well-off his clients, none would sustain a loss of tens of thousands of dollars without taking remedial action.

And he could not escape the fear of knowing that if Mary Kennedy would sanction the murder of her best customer to keep him from talking, she soon would be after him as well.

*   *   *

Elizabeth dragged herself out of bed at 6:30, slipped on a robe and headed to the kitchen. As often as possible, she or Peter would share breakfast with the two older children before school. The kids had to catch their respective school buses—David to Clover Hill High and Lauren to Swift Creek Middle—before seven, so breakfast was usually a hurried affair. But while the two ate, one of the parents would read aloud from a book of devotionals. Elizabeth had been equal to the task each morning since Peter's disappearance.

Walking into the kitchen, she was surprised to see David already holding the open book in his left hand. He and Lauren looked up when their mother stepped through the doorway.

"Hi, Mom. I wasn't sure you'd be getting up this morning," said David.

Lauren quickly added, "We smelled what happened last night. Yuck. Who was it?"

"Jonathan."

"Anyway," David said, "we figured you'd be too tired to get up this morning, so we thought we'd go ahead without you."

The initiative shown by the children overwhelmed Elizabeth. She told David to continue while she began lunch preparation for Daniel. When her first-born finished speaking, she felt a rush of admiration pump strength throughout her weary body. The young man seemed to have gained two years of maturity in less than two weeks. "Thank you, David."

David's face broke into a big grin.

"Maybe today, Mom," he smiled. "Maybe today's the day he'll be coming home."

"I hope so," she smiled back.

"I hope so, too," Lauren said jokingly. "You need some sleep—or something. You look awful!"

"Thanks, thanks a lot." Glancing at the clock, Elizabeth switched to her mother-as-sergeant routine. "Now, get your teeth brushed, make sure you've got all your homework. Are your lunches made?" They were, and the two were soon bounding out the front door. Within an hour, eight-year-old Daniel was off to second grade. And with Jonathan and Kristin miraculously still asleep, Elizabeth headed back to bed.

*　　*　　*

Barry Whitehead's beard was beginning to fill in. It was considerably darker than his recently dyed, sandy-colored hair. Five days without shaving and a bottle of Clairol for Men were transforming his appearance. He had not been out in public since his father picked him up at the airport.

The years of disciplined work with pen and ink at a drafting table that had allowed him to master Peter Boget's signature during the flight to Denver were again paying off in a set of forged documents. These were helping him to create a new identity. He was particularly grateful for Debbie Steinbaugh's driver's license and bank ID card, which he used as models for the documents he was creating.

When the doorbell rang, Barry quickly retreated from the kitchen and went to the second floor while his father responded to the bell.

The elder Whitehead opened the front door to find two men dressed in suits and raincoats standing on the concrete porch that overlooked Ephrata's Main Street.

"Mr. George Whitehead?" the taller of the two asked. Upon receiving a nod, both men produced wallets containing badges and identification cards. "I'm Neil Jackson. This is Cliff Williamson. We're from the FBI. May we come in?"

George froze. His shoulder and left foot prevented the door from swinging open, but the real barrier to the agents' passage was the doubt and fear etched into the lines of the man's face.

"We don't mean to frighten you. We just need to talk to you about your son."

"What about my son?" he sputtered. "Are you talking about Barry? What do you want with him? What has he done?"

"Please relax. We've come to tell you something very important, and to ask for your help," Jackson said calmly. "May we come in?"

"I don't know. I mean, I guess so." The man was stumbling over his words. "Come in. Come in." He backed away from the door and stepped quickly to the sofa, where he picked up the morning newspaper and motioned for the two agents to sit. He folded the paper and deposited it in the dining room. Then he scurried back. "Can I get you some coffee?"

"No, thanks," the men replied in unison.

"Good." George Whitehead forced a smile. "I don't have any made."

* * *

The sky was brightening, but the sun had not yet appeared above the mesa that stood between the Clark house and downtown Colorado Springs. Mike Downes swung out of bed and let his feet touch the cold linoleum floor. He was drawn by the view from the second-story window, which looked west toward massive rock formations that he knew from his map were the Garden of the Gods.

Downes donned a jogging suit, laced up his Nikes and, with all the stealth he could employ in the creaky house, tiptoed down the stairs and out the kitchen door—the only exit used with any regularity by the Clarks.

He quickly located the entrance to one of the most spectacular natural wonders he had ever seen. For over an hour he alternately ran and walked among the towering red rock formations that dotted the landscape to create the appearance of an enormous rock garden cultivated by God himself. Downes wished he had brought gloves to keep his fingers warm, but he wasn't about to leave the majesty and serenity of this unusual city park just because the temperature was twenty degrees lower than he had anticipated. For a man who never seemed to find enough time to commune with God, this experience was exhilarating. Away from the distractions of his all-consuming job, and doing something he believed he was called to do, he was finding a new vitality sweeping through his soul.

Among the sandstone formations he felt a godly presence that nudged him into prayer—prayer for Peter and Elizabeth and Debbie and himself as he continued his search. As he ran, he praised God and listened for his direction. When he finally returned to the Clarks', Liz was brewing coffee, frying bacon and scrambling eggs. The bag of flour, the can of baking powder and the container of buttermilk sitting on the kitchen counter confirmed what his nose had already detected—the best part of the breakfast was in the oven.

"You've got five minutes to shower and get down here," Liz barked when Downes walked through the door.

Norwood was setting the table for four, but Downes didn't stop to ask why. With a "Yes, ma'am," he bolted up the stairs, grabbed some clothes and raced to the shower.

* * *

As they stood to leave, the two FBI agents thanked George Whitehead for his time and reiterated their request. Pointing to the card that White-head held in his trembling hand, Neil Jackson said, "Please contact us the moment anyone calls you or shows up here looking for your son. Night or day, dial this 800 number and give the person who answers this file number. Like we told you, we are dealing with very dangerous people who may not be satisfied with what they have already done. If your son knew others, and they think you may know who those others are, they will come."

Cliff Williamson added, "And as soon as you would like to make the visit, call us and we will arrange it."

"I'm truly sorry if we have frightened you," Jackson added. "Please accept our apologies."

The lawmen walked to the door and let themselves out, leaving White-head to ponder their words.

*   *   *

Downes arrived at the breakfast table in jeans and a sweater and little else. His short, wet hair fell roughly into place, and his face was darkened by the stubble of twenty-four hours of growth.

"Very good, Mike," said Norwood looking at his watch. "Five minutes on the nose. We're going to be joined shortly by Debbie's boss, who we invited to breakfast. We thought she might be able to provide some background that would be helpful, and we wanted her to hear about last night's call before you went over there this morning."

Downes thought about his appearance and said, "I guess I should have gotten back from my run a little sooner."

Setting a basket of biscuits on the table, Liz gave her overnight guest a once-over. "Probably," she said with her usual lack of diplomacy. All three laughed.

Just then a knock at the kitchen door drew their attention. The multi-paned window on the top half of the door was trimmed with green-checked curtains that framed the round face of a short woman.

"That's Maggie Hardaway," said Liz, striding to the door.

Once inside, and following Liz's introductions, the plump woman removed her coat and sat down at the table.

"You said drop by for a cup of coffee, not a breakfast of champions," the banker smiled. "Wouldn't my husband like to be sitting down at this table!"

While they ate, Downes asked Hardaway a dozen questions about Debbie, but learned little new information. "She received a call on Friday afternoon," Hardaway said. "It was from someone who left a message that 'all was on for the morning.' "

"What did that mean?"

"I don't know. One of the tellers took the message while Debbie was with a customer. She smiled when she got the message, but never said anything else."

"What about the voice? Did anyone recognize it?"

"I wouldn't know," the branch manager said. "Maybe the woman who took the call would know. Come on by; maybe she or one of the others heard something I didn't."

"When do you open?"

Hardaway looked at Mike's tousled hair, unshaven face and sweater hanging loosely over a shirtless chest. She smiled as she said, "Before you can get there."

*　　*　　*

As expected, FBI agents arrived at the offices of Kennedy and Associates shortly before ten in the morning. They spoke with the owner and questioned Richard Donovan for fifteen minutes. Satisfied with their responses, they departed.

Mary Kennedy had just walked back up the elegant staircase after escorting the agents to the front door when one of the agents stepped back inside and approached the receptionist. "Miss Westfield," he said, "is Mr. Fishbinder available?"

"We don't have a Mr. Fishbinder working here," she answered in her deep whisper.

Standing out of view at the top of the steps, Kennedy held her breath.

"Oh, I must have gotten confused," said the agent, turning to go. "I'm sorry."

Kennedy waited until the men departed before descending the stairs. She walked to the receptionist's desk and, in a hushed voice, thanked her. Kennedy had spent thirty minutes drilling Jean Westfield on handling responses to the FBI, and she was pleased that the woman had recognized their ploy to gain additional information.

"It could happen again," Kennedy warned her. "Stay aware. Be particularly alert for phone calls late in the day—toward the close of business. Client confidentially is of the utmost importance."

*   *   *

After questioning each of the employees in the bank branch, Downes realized that there was nothing more he could learn in Colorado Springs about Peter's whereabouts. The woman who had taken the Friday afternoon call was unable to shed any light on the call, except to say that the connection was bad.

Maggie Hardaway graciously allowed Mike to use her office to place some calls. First he called María Escobar. He pressed for details, but none were forthcoming.

"I'll be in Cancún at six," he told her. "Can I meet you in the morning?"

"We open at nine tomorrow morning, but I'll be here until about seven tonight. Stop by if you get in on time."

Downes followed his call to Cancún with a succession of unfruitful calls to Virginia—including an unanswered one to the Boget residence. When he finished, he thanked the branch manager for the loan of her office and headed out to his rented car.

He looked west to gaze high on the snow-covered slopes that were dazzling against an iridescent sky. He imagined the sun playing on the red rock monuments in the Garden of the Gods at the base of the mountains. The majesty of the setting brought to mind the immense task before him. He had been in Colorado for a day and a half, and instead of being closer to solving the puzzle, he felt the solution seemed farther away than ever.

*   *   *

David Boget had suited up for soccer practice shortly after he had come home from school. He consumed his usual snack and was in the driveway working on his dribbling before his mother drove him to the field. When the ball rolled under the family station wagon, he got down on his hands and knees to get it. That was when he noticed a black, oily puddle under the front of the car. He went in to get his mother, who was folding laundry.

"I think we have a problem." David said. The two went outside. The phone rang while Elizabeth was kneeling in the driveway to inspect the problem, but neither she nor David heard it.

"I hope it's nothing serious," said Elizabeth pessimistically. "You better call and see if you can get a ride to practice with someone else."

*   *   *

Near the airport in Denver, Downes stopped at Robert Merrill's office after returning the rented Thunderbird. The entrepreneur greeted Downes with a smile. "Did you find him?"

"Not really. But I've found out who he's not with."

A quizzical expression crossed Merrill's face. "Is that good?"

"I think so. Time will tell." Looking at his watch, he added, "Speaking of time, I've got a plane to catch in thirty minutes. Again, thanks for your help."

"Thank you for letting us serve you." Merrill wanted to know more but didn't let on. "Tell your friends about us—and please come again."

Toting his one piece of carry-on luggage, the athletic Downes offered a casual salute to Merrill and then jumped into the waiting shuttle for the short ride to the airport. With ticket in hand, he headed for his gate. After checking in, he called Earl Hendrick.

"You are going *where?*" the surprised president barked after Downes mentioned Cancún. "I surely hope you are not using the company credit card."

Downes laughed, but Hendrick was serious. "Remember, you are on vacation, not business. And even though I realize it is your vacation, Mike, I want to warn you that this escapade is going to hurt you with some of the boys in Washington. They are going to question your judgment."

Thoughtfully and carefully, Downes asked, "Do you question my judgment?"

Earl Hendrick was worried that his prodigy was about to throw away his career, a career into which Hendrick had poured countless hours and not a little of his own power and prestige. Just as a father likes to believe that his child will attain a higher station in life than he had been able to attain, the Virginia Bell president wanted to see Michael Downes assuming the top spot at Mid-Atlantic Bell. Now, in light of Mike's actions—no matter how noble—he had to respond to his friend's question directly and honestly: "Yes, I am beginning to question your judgment."

*   *   *

Fueled by information leaks and speculation, Mike Downes's adventure took on a larger-than-life dimension within the Public Relations department at Virginia Bell's headquarters. Some saw the vice president's personal involvement as proof that the situation was serious and that Peter had to be rescued. Others suggested that his involvement had something to do with Megan Churchill's persistent stories of Peter being fired for wrongdoing but being saved by Mike's personal intervention. Marge Conners, while taking a call from Mike, had said "Cancún" loud enough to be heard by a passerby, who quickly resurrected the rumor that the director of communications had abandoned his family for another woman.

But one person, Lucy Williams, the editor of the company newsletter, didn't believe the rumors. She, alone among the staff members, knew how much time and energy Peter Boget had poured into her career, helping her overcome family difficulties and then showcasing her talent so she could land her present job. She knew that he had violated company policy, because she was the beneficiary of his actions.

Megan dropped by Lucy's cubicle.

"If you've come to talk about Peter, I don't want to hear it," Lucy told her.

"My, you're touchy today."

"Yes, I am. I wish you'd get back to work on what's important around here and leave the detective work to the experts."

Megan laughed mockingly. "Experts? You mean experts like Mike Downes? Get real! You think that because that engineer can find typos in your newsletter that qualifies him as a detective?"

"What I'm talking about is Peter. He is one of the kindest, most compassionate men in this company, and he deserves more respect from you."

"Is that your sermon? I think you and Marge are the only two members of his fan club. In fact, that worries me." Megan leaned forward and whispered, "Is he more than a boss to you?"

Lucy's patience was evaporating rapidly. "Get out of here," she said. "One more comment like that, and I'll do my best to see that you're cleaning out your desk by the end of the week."

Megan pulled back in genuine surprise. "You're serious, aren't you?"

"Try me."

*   *   *

Barry Whitehead was sitting with his father at the kitchen table in the back of the small, narrow house. He had just finished his third piece of pizza and was downing his second can of beer. When he set the can on the table, he said, "So what do you think we should do?"

"About what?" his father answered through a mouthful of pizza.

"About Boget," came the indignant reply, "what do you think?"

"I think you have a helluva nerve coming here and not telling me that you nearly killed one man, and that you were driving around with a million dollars' worth of cocaine in your car," George Whitehead said, glaring at his son. "What I should do is call the police and have you tell them your story. What's going to happen to me when they discover I've got a cocaine dealer and a murderer right here in my house?" He didn't wait for an answer. "They're going to send me to jail, that's what."

Barry recoiled. "Look, I didn't kill anybody. That man stopped to help me and went back to his car to get a flare. It was dark, he tripped and fell." Barry stood up, walked to the stove and, leaning against it, continued explaining his story to a disbelieving father. "Hey, I wasn't even close to him when he fell. I ran around to the car, turned him over, and his clothes burst into flames. What was I supposed to do?"

The senior Whitehead studied the man standing by the stove. "Barry, I don't know you anymore. I wonder if I ever did."

"Look, I had no idea the cocaine was worth that much. I can tell you that I didn't get anywhere near that for the six I took. I thought I was doing well to get ten thousand a bag. And I'm telling you, someone else got their hands on that shipment before I did, because when I took the six, I made sure that there were twenty-one packs left in each bag."

"Great," his father gestured in an uncomplimentary fashion. "I have a son standing in my kitchen who I haven't seen for five years, who tells me he's been screwing around with drugs, that he ripped off a hot-shot dealer, but that he's not to blame, that some crooked cop really got the loot." Before he let Barry respond, he softened his tone. "What I don't get is why you went to all this trouble stealing this man's identity. Why didn't you just take off? You planned to come up here anyway—at least that's what you told me. So why didn't you?"

Barry walked back to the table and picked up a piece of pizza.

"When this Boget guy stopped, he offered to call for a tow truck from his cellular phone and bring me a flare. When he fell, I didn't know what to do, so I ran to his car to call for help. But I didn't know how to make his phone work, so I took off for the next exit. By the time I called for help and doubled back, a cop was already on the scene. Was I supposed to stop and try to explain a dead man next to my car? And cocaine in my trunk? They'd lock me up and throw away the key."

"Not if you're just a driver," his father interrupted.

Barry's response was quick and sharp. "Drivers don't carry sixty thousand dollars in cash stuffed in their shirts. What was I supposed to do? Wait around and get arrested?"

"But why take his wallet?"

"I didn't; it was on the front seat of his car, and mine was back on the dashboard of my car. As I drove by the scene it all clicked. If they find my car and someone who looks like the photo on my driver's license lying dead next to it, Barry Whitehead is dead—officially and totally." He paced the old kitchen. "I was scared, and it all seemed so logical at the time."

George Whitehead did not respond. He sat looking at a nervous, confused man whom he remembered as his handsome, confident son preparing to take on the world. Shaking his head slowly, he waited for more.

"I didn't plan on a flat tire. I mean, I was just going to go to New York, make my delivery and fly to Colorado to see the kids. That's all. And then—"

"Did you?" George interrupted. "Did you see the kids?"

"No. One of their neighbors said she took off with them."

"So you went on to Mexico?"

"Yeah, just like I planned."

"And you pretended to be this Boget guy?"

"Seemed like a great cover to me. His license, credit cards, business cards and company ID were better than the fake stuff I made. I figured what the heck?"

"What the heck?" The plumber looked at his son in disbelief. "You leave a man to die alongside the highway and steal his wallet, and all you can say about it is 'What the heck?' "

Barry shrugged.

His father stared up at him. "What am I supposed to do now?" The older man answered his own question. "Well, for one thing, I better go see this

Boget guy, or the FBI is going to think I don't give a damn about my own son. Which I'm telling you right now, I don't."

Walking back to the table in the small, simple kitchen, Barry sat down and stared thoughtfully at the half-empty box of pizza. He took another swallow of beer and said, "I don't like it. If Mary Kennedy tried to kill me once, she'll try again if she learns I'm still alive. She could be staking out the hospital right now. When they find out who you are, they'll use you to get to me."

"The agents said they have moved him to a safe place. If I don't go, someone will think something is funny. Maybe the FBI, who already knows who I am, will come back and find you." George Whitehead paused and looked at his son, whose washed-out face accentuated the fear in his eyes. "I'll call tomorrow and tell them I can go on Sunday."

*   *   *

Although the plane from Dallas didn't get off the ground until 5:30 p.m. local time, the two-hour flight landed at 6:30 in Cancún. At 6:55 Mike Downes was walking into the reception area of a modest office on the third floor of a contemporary building in downtown Cancún.

He was greeted by Juanita Méndez, assistant to María Escobar, and offered a seat next to a portly gentleman dressed in a khaki suit, with whom he struck up a conversation. "Are you waiting to see Miss Escobar?" Downes asked.

"No, just making a telephone call. How about you?"

"I just flew in. I'm looking for a friend, but I don't know if he's here."

The heavy-set man wiped the beads of perspiration from his forehead. "This is no place to try to find someone. There must be a quarter million people who live here and another hundred thousand who come and go each week."

"Well," Downes said, "I know where one of them is. Jail."

"Really? Good luck. This isn't the place to get yourself in jail. Do you speak Spanish?"

Downes shook his head. The man raised his eyebrows. "Ha, are you going to have fun."

"What do you mean?"

"I speak Spanish and I have a lot of patience, but I want to tell you, I still am having trouble navigating the legal system around here. If you don't speak Spanish, you can almost forget it. For over three months I have been trying to get a hotel here in town to pay me for updates I've made to its computers. Even with a local lawyer, I'm getting nowhere. And jail—that's bad news. Around here they lock you up and forget about you. They tell me you're guilty until proven innocent. I never want to find out if that's the truth!"

The salesman rattled on, barely taking a breath. While he was speaking, Escobar stepped through a doorway and approached Downes. She was young, dark and beautiful.

"You must be Mr. Downes," she said, extending her hand. "I'm María Escobar," she beamed, pronouncing her first name as if there were a *d* in the middle.

Downes stood quickly, his six-foot frame snapping to attention. "I'm Michael Downes," he said, shaking her hand. "Everyone calls me Mike."

"And everyone calls me Señorita Escobar. Please come with me." She returned to her office with Downes close behind.

*   *   *

"I knew he wouldn't leave me for another woman! I knew it," said Elizabeth into the phone. She was jubilantly telling Joyce McGuire what she had heard from Mike Downes—the story about Debbie Steinbaugh, the other man, the attempted rape and the murder.

"Are you okay?" Joyce asked.

"Yes," she paused. "Yes. I surely am. I feel it deep inside—Peter is waiting for me somewhere. Somehow, he'll be home soon. I know he'll be home soon!"

*   *   *

Soon Joyce was on the phone with their pastor. "I'm really concerned. I think Elizabeth is losing it."

"Why do you say that?"

"She just got word about the woman we thought Peter may be with, and she's in a Mexican jail suspected of murder."

"Of Peter?" he asked with trepidation.

"No, of a woman she was with in a hotel in Cancún."

"What?"

"It's a long story, and I don't know if I got it all straight. The main thing is that I think Elizabeth needs help. I'm heading over there now."

"I'll call her."

After Frank Griffith hung up the phone, he dialed Elizabeth, heard the story of Debbie Steinbaugh and was more confused than when Joyce had tried to relay it.

"Elizabeth, I'll come by in the morning to go over everything, okay?"

"Sure!"

The response was bright and sunny and not in keeping with the gravity of the story the woman had just told. Registering his concern, Frank said, "I'll see you at nine."

The pastor placed one more call, this one to Edith Mercer, a trained counselor. He briefed her on the situation. "The main thing I'm concerned about is the tremendous stress she is under. One more piece of news, good or bad, and I think she'll have a breakdown."

"I can understand that," the counselor responded.

"Would you be available in the morning to visit her? I'd like another person to evaluate her situation."

"I'll make myself available."

16

I 'd rather not talk about it," said Elizabeth Boget, responding to Edith Mercer's suggestion that she discuss her insights into Peter's whereabouts. "I've got enough problems. I don't need to be psychoanalyzed too."

"We haven't come to psychoanalyze you, we've come to help you," Pastor Frank Griffith said gently. "You are under a lot of stress, and sometimes stress prevents us from seeing things clearly."

Elizabeth was a strong woman. Despite her bouts of crying over her situation, she had an inner resolve that was so strong at times that she resisted help from others. Now she had to decide if she needed help and if she wanted it. She knew Edith well enough to know that she was a well-respected counselor. Should she open up and let others see inside her? And was she brave enough to look inside herself—to look below the first level of disappointment and weariness to the deeper and darker level of her heart, where fear and anger dwelled?

Frank spoke again. "Why don't we spend some time in prayer?" The women agreed.

*   *   *

"This girl better be saying her prayers," exclaimed Martin Beale to his assistant when he finished outlining his discovery. "Because we're going to put her in a concrete cell." He slapped the pile of reports on the table in front of him and added a long and loud "Yeah!"

The short man with the big mouth and even bigger ego got out of his chair, walked the two steps to the telephone on the credenza in the conference room and dialed his boss. While he waited, he washed down the pastry he was eating with a big gulp of lukewarm coffee. "I'm so freakin' tired of this short cord on this telephone! Can't we get a cord long enough that I can sit at the table and talk?" The assistant disappeared out the door as Beale began talking to his boss at the main office.

"I've checked all the accounts of every one of Segal and Randolph's clients, and guess what I found?" He didn't wait for an answer. "These guys are pretty good. All their clients—every one of them—enjoyed consistent and not unexpected levels of gains. All, that is, except those clients whose investments ended up in Mary Kennedy's portfolio. Those clients—about two dozen of them—had accounts that hemorrhaged cash. Their stocks and bonds ended up in Kennedy's portfolio without passing through the company's trading system."

"So what's new there? You told me that yesterday."

"Yeah," Beale replied, "but this couldn't have happened before computers, because it's just too obvious." Then he added wryly, "People set up computers to analyze data and they think those machines are magic. It still takes people like me to see the big picture."

"So tell me already, what's this big picture?"

"I don't know. Drugs, arms, high-tech trading, illegal gambling," said Beale smugly as he set his wire-rim glasses on the credenza and lit a cigarette. "Give me another week and I'll find out. But let me tell you, Kennedy's got something going in Ireland." He inhaled again and then ground the cigarette into the ashtray, which was already filled with half-smoked butts. "In the past twelve months she's transferred over two million in stocks and bonds into the accounts of orphanages and missionary organizations over there."

"So?"

"So who gives away that kind of money anymore? You think she's a Rockefeller?"

"No, but she *is* a Kennedy!" His boss laughed, redirecting the conversation. "How about the trades? You haven't figured out how they were made?"

"Not yet, but I will, despite the fact that Madaven, their computer guru, says it couldn't have gone undetected. But shoot, kids can get into computers and reprogram the trajectories of our nuclear missiles. It's a cinch someone could change an account code on a stock trade!"

His boss laughed, "I know. Let me send someone over tomorrow who really knows computers to see what she can do at Segal's or Randolph's terminal. By the way, have you figured out where those two went?"

"Not a clue."

*　　*　　*

Mark Randolph's day was not going well. Sitting at a small table in the parlor of his friends' home in Brighton, England, he had placed long-distance calls to all his cocaine clients to alert them that the deal had fallen through and to warn them about probable investigations. He'd reached all but two. He'd told each one that he would be away for a while, but when the excitement died down he would make sure that each would be repaid. He had also advised them to unload every gram of evidence that could be used against them if the police became involved. The clients hadn't liked what they heard. They'd informed him that they already had been contacted by the Securities Exchange Commission. One had been more than just unhappy.

"Randolph," said Murray Ross, "you screwed me. I wiped out my life savings to make this purchase, and I've got buy commitments from sixty-three customers. You owe me $105,000, and I'm going to get it if I have to sell my story to the *Wall Street Journal*. Now I want fifty thousand in cash by the end of the week, or I'll make sure that you never get to spend another dime."

"I can't get hold of that kind of money right now," Randolph explained. "I've got federal investigators swarming over my books and probably searching my house by now. The stocks you traded are gone. I've got reserves, but I have to wait till things cool off before I can get at them. You've got to understand," he pleaded.

"I do understand, but I've probably lost half my clients. I've already lost my job because I failed a surprise drug screening. I lost my family to a messy divorce last year, and if I don't get cash in hand by the end of the month, I'll lose my house." He paused to let it sink in. "Then again, except for the house, I really don't have much else to lose, and this would make one helluva story." Ross could imagine Randolph sweating on the other end of the line. "I can see the headlines now: 'Cocaine dealing shocks Wall Street,' 'Randolph charged with money laundering.' "

Randolph knew the man wasn't joking. This was what he feared. One squeaky wheel and the whole cart would fall apart.

"How much do you need right now?" Randolph reluctantly asked.

"Ten thousand."

"I'll try to get you five. The usual place?"

"I guess so."

"Friday at nine?"

"Tomorrow at eight—in the morning."

The stock broker quickly calculated the time differential. "That may be tough, but I'll see what I can do."

"And I need half a kilo."

"Can't do it."

"You better try. When I missed a Saturday delivery, one customer who paid in advance said he'd get me. I offered him his money back, but he demanded the coke. I want you to try very hard."

"I'll see what I can do."

"Don't see. Do. And no funny stuff. I've got a friend holding the whole story for me. If I don't show up with the cash and the coke, the press and the cops have the story tomorrow afternoon."

After Randolph ended the conversation, he placed a call to Norfolk, Virginia.

*   *   *

With Kristin on her shoulder, Elizabeth walked with Frank and Edith to the driveway. "I'm sorry about how I greeted you today. There is a lot on my mind, and I am frustrated, but believe me when I tell you that I am at peace over Peter's disappearance. You can call it what you will, but I honestly believe that Peter is not in Mexico. He isn't chasing another woman. God has his hand on that man."

Standing by the car, Frank placed his arm around Elizabeth and gave her a gentle hug. "I know." He brought his hand up and ruffled Kristin's hair. The baby smiled. Frank continued, "Elizabeth, we love you."

Edith agreed. "We're here to support you, whatever it takes."

*   *   *

"Cancún, Mexico, is really two cities focused on one industry, American tourism." Mike Downes was reading a reprint of an article while he waited for María Escobar in the consular agent's office.

The Cancún of the travel brochures is a Caribbean beach resort seven hundred miles south of Florida's panhandle. It's fourteen miles of opulent resorts and stunning hotels that grew up overnight on an unspoiled barrier island near the northeastern tip of the Yucatán Peninsula. In the 1960s the stretch of beach was selected by government computer to be the site of a resort that would attract U.S. dollars to Mexico. Its outstanding beaches, coupled with its proximity to the wonders of the Mayan culture that dot the Yucatán landscape and its accessibility from America's East Coast and Midwest cities, made it a logical choice.

Cancún had no infrastructure and lacked a work force to build a resort, so when the building boom hit in the seventies, engineers, managers, tradespeople and laborers descended on the community and quickly overran it. In the process, they drove out the less-educated native Indian population and created Cancún's second city, the boom town of 200,000 that is made up of merchants, managers and professionals along with low-paid hotel workers, cab drivers, civil servants and unemployed displaced persons. This second city is a combination of a beautiful, modern urban community and the slums that ring the central marketplace. It is a city of broad, tree-lined boulevards that boasts one of the best public transportation systems in the country. It is the marketplace where locals sell their wares in the street and where shops and restaurants vie for the dollars of the tourists who leave the beaches and the pools and the tennis courts of the seaside resorts to take hair-raising taxi rides downtown to experience the "real" Mexico.

The two cities, separated by a causeway and a twelve-mile-long lagoon, share a common bond formed by American dollars, the "Yanquis" who brought them, and an underpaid police force. That force tries to minimize crime by being very visible—brandishing shotguns and rifles while patroling in old cars and pickup trucks—and by exacting on-the-spot payment in lieu of fines from transgressors of the law.

Downes set the article aside. These were the two cities he had toured by cab between six and nine in the morning. Sitting in the cramped reception area, Downes observed a family of three waiting nervously to speak with the consular agent and listened to the repeated ringing of the telephones. Shortly, Escobar emerged from her office, gave some instructions to her assistant and, motioning for Downes to follow, walked out the door.

A taxi was waiting in the parking lot below. "La cárcel, por favor," Escobar said as she climbed in.

From the moment they pulled out into traffic, Downes was treated to a running commentary on what he was seeing as they sped west out of town toward the jail.

"This may take awhile," Escobar explained as they neared their destination. "Judicial speed is not a hallmark of Mexico."

"And it is in America?" Downes said.

*. * *

After reviewing his itinerary, Mary Kennedy was giving Patrick O'Hearn a few final words of advice. "Don't drive drunk. We cannot afford to have you stopped by the police. If someone gets nosy, we'll be in big trouble."

"Ma'am," O'Hearn said in an I've-heard-it-all-before voice, "I understand. You don't have to worry about me getting picked up." He took the map and directions from the lunchroom table and slipped them into his jacket pocket. Then he nodded to his employer and benefactor and walked toward the door that led to the garden behind Kennedy and Associates' building.

Kennedy's eyes followed him. As he stepped outside, she had the last word. "Be careful."

* * *

For twenty-five minutes Downes and Escobar waited in the jail's administrative offices for clearance to enter the commons area. It never came. Instead, they were told they could speak to Debbie Steinbaugh through the door of bars. They waited some more for Debbie to be brought to the barrier.

While they waited, Downes reviewed what he knew about Debbie and again showed Escobar the photographs of the pretty mother of two taken at Christmas. They also discussed Peter Boget and the strange circumstances that had brought Downes to Cancún to find his friend. Escobar outlined an action plan to help Downes trace Peter. While they talked, a prison guard escorted the object of their visit to the very unquiet, unprivate steel-barred door.

As she approached, the only thought that ran through Downes's mind was that if Peter ever left Elizabeth for this woman, he was crazy. Walking toward him, past the men playing volleyball and the clusters of standing prisoners, was someone who did not resemble the woman he had just viewed in the photos. The prisoner was a gaunt, drawn figure with sallow skin and limp, yellowish hair streaked with dirt. She was wearing the same outfit she had had on the first day Escobar had come to the prison.

When Debbie reached the steel bars, there was a vacancy in her eyes and a strong body odor that caused Escobar and Downes to back away.

"Debbie," the consular agent began, "this is Mike Downes, a friend of Peter Boget's."

More than a glimmer of life shone through Debbie's deadened eyes. But when she opened her mouth to speak, only sobs came through.

"Debbie," Downes began, "I've just come from Colorado Springs. Everyone is fine, but they are very worried about you. Señorita Escobar has told me all about what happened, and I'm here to help you."

Smiling through the sobs, Debbie began to speak. "How are my girls?"

"They are worried about you, but they are all right."

The words began to transform the woman standing at the fence. "Thank you for coming." After a long pause, she turned back toward the other prisoners clustered in the open area behind her, and spoke again. "This place is a living hell. I've got to get out of here. I've told everyone that I didn't do anything, but nobody believes me."

"What don't they believe?" Downes asked softly.

"They don't believe I was attacked by a man who looks like Peter. They don't believe that the man tried to rape me. They don't believe he knocked Jan onto the floor and hurt her."

Talking through iron bars while surrounded by dozens of people coming and going made Downes uncomfortable, but he decided to find out as much as possible about the incident. First, he asked the most pressing question on his mind. "Have you seen Peter?"

"No," she said emphatically. Then she explained, "Barry, whatever his name is, said he'd been in an accident." Her voice trembled as she spoke.

"Can you tell me where?"

"I don't know," she answered, shrugging her shoulders.

Downes offered her a reassuring smile of understanding and support. Then after glancing toward Escobar and the guard, who was less than three feet away, as if to say, "I hope you don't mind if we take some more time here," he spoke to Debbie in a gentle voice. "Why don't you start at the beginning?"

*   *   *

"Mrs. Boget, this is Wayne at Midlo Transmissions. I'm afraid I've got some bad news."

That wasn't what Elizabeth wanted to hear from the shop where her car had been towed earlier in the morning.

"This *month* has been bad news," she said stoically. "What's the bottom line?"

"About fifteen hundred dollars."

"Fifteen hundred dollars to fix a transmission?" she gasped.

"I'm sorry, it needs to be replaced."

*   *   *

At the steel door in the Cancún jail, Mike listened intently. Escobar held his microcassette dictation machine as close to Debbie's mouth as the guard would allow, while he scribbled notes as fast as Debbie told her story. Both listeners interrupted her frequently and asked that she clarify her points. Within thirty minutes the story was out.

"Do you believe me?" The sad eyes begged for a yes.

"It's a bizarre story," Downes answered, "that's for sure. But everything you've told me sounds plausible. How about if I begin checking and come back tomorrow?"

The suggestion that help had arrived triggered tears again. "Thank you so much."

"I've given a photo of Laura and Jennifer to the guards. They'll give it to you back in your cell."

The glimmer of life in her eyes brightened perceptibly.

Downes added, "Let me start looking. I'll be back tomorrow."

Escobar interrupted. "He might not be back tomorrow, but I will try to see if he can come in here to visit you." Turning to Downes, she explained, "Visiting is permitted only on Sundays. For a fee, they may let you in."

"I didn't know," said Downes.

"Things are pretty primitive here," Escobar added. Turning to the prisoner, she asked, "Do you need more clothes?"

"No, I have enough."

"Have you been able to take a shower?" she asked diplomatically.

"I'll get one this afternoon."

After saying goodby, Debbie turned and walked back into the commons area, where hundreds of prisoners were milling around.

"Debbie!" yelled Mike Downes.

She walked back to the steel bars that separated her from freedom. From his portfolio, Downes pulled the photo of Boget that he had been showing to people everywhere he went. He had wanted her to look at the photo and tell him what was different about the man who had attacked her. He had become so engrossed in her story that he had forgotten to show it earlier. When she got close, he held up the photo and asked, "Is this what the man who attacked you looked like?"

No one was prepared for what followed.

Terror filled Debbie's sunken eyes. She jerked her right hand into the air and pulled it past her ear as if clutching a knife. In a wail that stopped the volleyball game behind her and brought the guards running, she yelled, "Murderer!" and brought the imaginary knife down through the bars toward the photo. Downes instinctively jumped backward. Escobar stood in stunned silence. The guard sitting next to the door jumped to his feet. Then as quickly as the episode began, it ended in tears.

"I'm sorry," she sobbed. "The picture . . . I know that's Peter's picture, but it scared me. The last time . . . the last time I saw that face it was—it was . . ." Her sobs turned to a steady, wrenching cry. "He, he was on top of me, ordering me to take my clothes . . . I still have terrible nightmares." She lifted her hands to show Downes and Escobar that they were shaking. The quivering was just as obvious on her lips and in her eyelids.

A second guard arrived at entrance to the commons to see what the problem was. After a short exchange with Escobar, the other guard escorted the weeping woman back to the women's building. As they walked away, Escobar, with her hands behind her back, her head forward and her eyes staring at the ground, asked, "What do you suppose that was all about?"

"I think she's telling the truth," Downes answered, nodding his head. "I'd like to have had that on a videotape for review by a psychiatrist, but I don't think that was an act. That photo opened a door to a part of her mind that she's closed off. I'm going to come back tomorrow and try to find out what else is in there."

* * *

Earl Hendrick listened in disbelief to the tale that Mike Downes was spinning. "You are telling me that Peter is seen on a flight to Denver, is seen on a flight to Cancún, checks into a hotel under his own name, ends up in bed with a woman to whom he writes love letters, kills another woman who is coming on to his girlfriend and then disappears, and leaves a woman in jail who covers for him by saying he was somebody else?"

"No, no, no. You aren't listening. I'm telling you that Debbie says the man isn't Peter."

"Who else could he be?"

"Somewhere along the line, the two traded places. If the story is true, then Peter may be dead or in a hospital somewhere."

"Mike, are you smoking something?" Hendrick asked very seriously. "Do you know what you sound like? You sound like a fool. My version of the story is better than yours, Mike, because there is a lot more reality in a woman covering for a lover than in a cockamamie story about a look-alike who ends up attempting rape. You know what I am saying? Your credibility is heading south with each new revelation."

Downes went on the defensive. "I know the story is bizarre, but I believe there may be a mystery man."

"Mike, wake up! This is not some fairy tale where the good prince finds the princess and they live happily ever after. This is real life. This story is so bizarre, you could not sell it to the *National Enquirer* or 'A Current Affair.'"

"But Earl, listen. What if Peter was in an accident?" Downes could sense that his boss was shaking his head. "What if the story is true, and we abandoned him to some unknown cemetery or, worse, some convalescent home, and his wife had to sell her house and end up on welfare? Could you live with that?" When he received no audible response, he submitted his own answer: "I can't."

"Mike, stop and think. Do you know this stranger's name?"

"I'm not sure."

"Do you know where he is from? Do you know where he went?"

"No and no. But I have been able to track him this far."

An exasperated Hendrick pointed out another problem. "Okay, so you tracked him to Cancún. But that is because you were looking for Peter. Do you really believe he will hide behind Peter's identity again, now that he knows he might be implicated in a rape and murder? Do you really think he will continue to pretend to be Peter Boget when he must know police will be looking for Peter? Even if your story has the slightest possibility of being true—which I do not think it has—I am telling you that the chance of finding this man is so remote as not to warrant your further involvement."

As Downes listened to his mentor, his mind told him the man was right. But his heart . . .

"Look, Mike, take a day or two down at the beach. Go swimming or fishing or lie out in the sun, and get your mind off this thing. Then come back and let us get on with life. If Peter was in a hospital, his family would have been notified. You know, they do check fingerprints to identify people. If he is on the run, then sooner or later he will be picked up for something stupid, and we will hear about it. Either way, your chasing him is noble and honorable, but it is not in the best interest of your career, your reputation or the company."

"You really think I'm all wet?"

"Have you heard a word I have said? I think you ought to cut your losses and come home. No one is going to believe this story, and as along as you pursue it, your credibility is," he paused, "is going straight out the window. What you told me will stay with me. I advise you to keep it that way too. If the boys in Washington get drift of it . . ."

"I'm sorry, Earl, but credibility is not the only issue here. If Peter's in trouble, someone has got to find him. If Washington doesn't like it, I'm sorry. And if security won't do their job, I guess I'll have to do it for them."

*   *   *

At Ryan's Irish Pub in the strip shopping center adjacent to the Landover State Police barracks, five troopers were sitting around a large table, eating overflowing plates of food and drinking from tall glasses of beer. The watering hole, a favorite of area law-enforcement officials, had a bar down one side and a collection of mismatched wooden tables down the other. It was paneled to the chair rail in rough-hewn pine stained nearly black. The nearly hidden cream-colored walls were adorned with photos, pennants, soccer jerseys, trophies and hundreds of pieces of memorabilia from the Emerald Isle. At the back of the pub, men and women were laughing, drinking and smoking while the team sporting "Ryan's" T-shirts was running up the score against the dart team from Danny's Pub in the District. The group was boisterous, nearly drowning out the Irish folk music spilling from speakers hidden in the ceiling.

With great trepidation, Patrick O'Hearn eased off one of the stools at the bar and, gripping a half-filled glass of ale, walked over to the troopers eating dinner at the front of the pub. The bartender had related the exploits of the troopers at the table, pointing out the men responsible for a big haul of cocaine. When he reached the table, O'Hearn began with condolences.

"I want you to know how sorry I am to hear about the terrible accident the other night."

"That bomb was no accident," said Trooper Roland Hanks. "Don't believe what you read in the paper."

"Oh?"

The alcohol was loosening the tongues of the men at the table, and enough time had passed since the incident to make them less reticent to discuss what had happened in the hotel parking lot. They took an instant liking to the stranger whose accent was identical to that of the pub's proprietor.

Sergeant Milligan was more cautious than the others and suggested that nothing be said. But several went on talking, and Milligan's resistance faded into boosterism as he recounted not only the explosion but also his discovery of the man on the beltway and his assistance in discovering the cocaine found in the Honda.

"Hell, you didn't find that cocaine," Hanks told Milligan. "If I hadn't pressed to get an order to open that trunk, you wouldn't be a hero today."

O'Hearn said little but laughed a lot. He wanted to drink more, but he controlled his desires. Then he bought another round of beer for his new friends.

"What's it like to make a big drug bust?" he asked the men, pandering to their egos.

"Let me tell you," said Milligan with a smile in his voice. "When I opened that trunk and saw those shiny suitcases, something told me they weren't filled with clothes. And when Hanks opened them and found twenty-four bags of that white powder, I knew I was finally going to get one of those commendations I had never managed to get in all my years on the force."

O'Hearn whistled quietly. Looking across the table to Milligan, he whispered, "Twenty-four bags in each suitcase—that sounds like a lot."

The table erupted in laughter. "Not that much, just twelve in each," one of the officers said. Another added, "But that's enough to give a high to half the county."

"Is that what got blown up?"

"Hell no. You think we're going to let a million dollars of that stuff out of our sight? We figured that whoever came for the car was coming for what was in the trunk, so we set them up," one of the troopers boasted. The others laughed. Then, turning sober, he said, "We didn't know *we* were being set up."

Milligan added, "What I can't figure out is what triggered the explosion."

Another commented, "I think it was a timed thing, set to go off so many seconds after the trunk was opened."

In a whisper, barely audible over the noise of the pub, one of the officers leaned forward and said, "Nobody is stupid enough to blow up a fortune. I think that someone was listening and pressed the button when someone said something he wasn't supposed to."

"Like what?" asked Milligan.

"Reynolds thought he said, 'Murray something.' The others don't remember."

"Now if we can only get Whitehead to talk," Hanks said.

O'Hearn caught the looked of disdain on Milligan's face. Then another officer piped in, "I thought he was dead."

Hanks unconvincingly tried to cover his offhand crack. "He is. We're going to have to have a séance to find out his story!"

O'Hearn could hardly contain himself. He'd gotten the information he'd come for, about how much cocaine was actually discovered—and much more. And it had been far easier to obtain than he'd expected. He could not believe his luck at ending up at a table with the men who'd found Whitehead. He had learned that he could be the only man alive who had heard Segal utter Mary Kennedy's name moments before the car bomb sent two men to their graves. And he'd learned that the newspaper report of twenty-four kilos being found—not the forty-eight that were originally in the case—was correct. He also found out, quite unexpectedly, that Whitehead might have survived the poison that he had injected into the man's intravenous feeding tube on Sunday afternoon.

Deflecting the discussion from Whitehead back to the explosion, Milligan said somberly, "I'd like to meet the man that set that charge. I'd shove his dynamite down his throat and send him on a one-way trip to hell."

O'Hearn listened without speaking. Then Hanks, who had already said too much, added something that intrigued O'Hearn.

"I'd like to meet the man who had the guts to pull a stunt like that. He's got to be one bad dude."

"What would you do with him?" came the question across the table from another policeman.

"I don't know, but it would be a waste to kill him," said the young trooper. "I'd like to figure out how minds like that work."

"Why? So you can track them down better?" a colleague asked.

"Well, there's a lot more action chasing drug dealers than picking up speeders on the beltway."

Milligan shook his head. "Wait till you get to be my age. The last thing you'll want is action."

Hanks laughed, "When I get to be your age, I'll be retired and rich."

The banter went back and forth for a while. After ordering a third round of beers for the policemen, O'Hearn excused himself.

* * *

Lauren Boget sat propped on her bed. A long nightshirt was stretched over the legs that were pulled up to her chest. She was talking to her mother, who sat on the edge of the bed. "Did Mr. Downes say anything else?

Like how the other lady was killed?"

Until now Elizabeth had been circumspect with what she said to her children. She had not mentioned the attempted rape, because she wasn't sure how they would handle it. Now, under direct questioning, she decided to offer more details.

Lauren's eyes got wide when her mother said the "R-word." They stayed wide as Elizabeth, choosing her words carefully, told the story of a possessive woman, a man who looked like Lauren's father and their tragic encounter.

When she was done, Lauren asked timidly, "So where do you suppose Dad is? Do you think Mr. Downes can find him?"

"It's very confusing. Right now nobody knows exactly what happened, and Mrs. Steinbaugh seems to be having some emotional problems, so we don't know exactly what she means by all she has told us." Elizabeth paused for the words to sink in. "We just have to keep praying."

"What if he doesn't come home? Are we going to have to move?"

"Lauren, right now my only concern is today. I'm not planning on moving, but we're going to have to be flexible and trust God."

*   *   *

Mike Downes wiped his mouth with a napkin, signed his bill and walked from the restaurant into the lobby of the Mayan Holiday Resort. Wearing a turquoise shirt, white slacks and boat shoes, Downes looked like a tourist, and his untanned skin suggested that he had just arrived. As he looked around, he tried to imagine the previous Wednesday night and the drama that had unfolded in the lobby. He asked several in the restaurant about the fight, but either because they didn't understand him or they had been instructed not to discuss the matter, the staff would not acknowledge the incident. The clerk at the front desk said only that he had been on duty and had already told his story to the police.

This was very different from the information he had received at the Hyatt, where the clerks readily identified the man in the picture as the man who had stayed at the hotel, even showing Downes the man's bill. The signature on the registration card looked like Peter's—too much like Peter's—and that more than anything else troubled Downes. He had seen Peter's signature on hundreds of notes and memos and vouchers. It was intricate and distinct. What kind of person could learn that signature in a few hours? To Downes, the answer would not come.

After an extensive survey of the Mayan Holiday and its grounds, he headed for the elevator and the third floor. He walked the full length of the hall that passed in front of the room Debbie had occupied and then entered the stairwell three doors away. He skipped down the brightly lit steps and exited to a grassy area on the north side of the hotel. There was nobody in sight. He walked around to the front of the massive hotel complex, entered the lobby and walked to the elevator. Satisfied that the man Debbie claimed to have met could have gotten in and out of the hotel undetected, he returned to the hotel entrance, climbed into a waiting cab and headed to his hotel in the city.

Once there, Mike unwrapped several packs of index cards he had purchased earlier in the day, and began to jot down all the details he could derive from his notes, his observations and his recollections of the previous two weeks. He listened to the tape of his conversation with Debbie Steinbaugh for the third time.

Into the early morning hours, he arranged and rearranged over two hundred cards until they told the story of Peter's disappearance and his own trek to Cancún, as well as all the circumstances surrounding Debbie's incarceration. He arranged the cards chronologically and geographically. Where he felt there were significant gaps in the story he inserted blank cards. When he was satisfied, he numbered the cards, including the blank ones, and then transcribed his findings onto sheets of paper. On each of the numbered blank cards, he wrote down the questions he felt needed to be answered; then he removed those cards from the array on the floor. Finally, he gathered up the other cards and stacked them in a drawer in the room's dresser. Without undressing, he stretched out onto the bed and slept.

17

Thursday, March 29

Patrick O'Hearn had never been in the lobby of New York's Waldorf Astoria Hotel, but he immediately recognized its value as an exchange point. The vaulted central lobby was filled with plants and chairs and dozens of people, mostly businessmen, scurrying to and from the coffee shop, the checkout area and the hotel's various entrances. In seating areas throughout the spacious lobby, women and men sat reading the morning paper. Others, in groups of two and three, were engaged in conversation. The tired Irishman sat in a chair in the hotel's northeast corner.

At eight o'clock in the morning, a tall, thin man with a neatly trimmed beard and wire-rim glasses strode in O'Hearn's direction. The man was wearing a dark suit under an open raincoat and carried a leather attaché case. O'Hearn recognized him immediately from the description Randolph had passed to Mary Kennedy. He watched him intently. What he didn't know was that two New York City narcotics detectives were also watching Murray Ross. The bearded man glanced around until he caught O'Hearn's nod and then walked toward the seated stranger.

O'Hearn said nothing, hiding his accent. Ross sat down in the forest-green overstuffed chair that was positioned at a ninety-degree angle to an identical one in which his contact was sitting. O'Hearn handed the man a stiff cardboard envelope with the flap side up. On top of the envelope was a simple typed note, "Mr. R asked me to deliver this to you."

"Thank you," said the recipient nervously. "I wasn't sure what to expect."

Without responding, O'Hearn took his newspaper, folded it in half and showed the man a second note, written on the back of the paper. It read simply, "Do not move for five minutes." Before the bearded man could respond, O'Hearn disappeared down the short flight of steps to the hotel's Lexington Avenue entrance.

*   *   *

Already at work in his Lower Manhattan office, just three blocks from the New York Stock Exchange, Martin Beale was charting over two hundred of Randolph's and Segal's transactions that seemed to fit a pattern of money laundering.

On page after yellow page in a stack of legal pads, Beale had noted the time, date, nature of each transaction, and origination and destination accounts. Looking over his shoulder, Beale's boss, also an early riser, asked, "If they could trade stock without leaving an audit trail, why didn't they just steal from the accounts of other brokers and pocket their gains?"

"Madaven, their computer man, showed me how that would be impossible. They have a double layer of transaction analysis for all employee accounts. These accounts are looked at by humans once a week. That tends to keep them squeaky clean."

"And," added the man standing at Beale's desk, "oblivious to other types of fraud that could be taking place."

"Exactly." Beale grinned. "That's what Randolph and Segal figured out. By the way, when is that computer whiz going to be ready to try and crack Michaels & Trent's computers?"

"Dawn Early is her name. She'll be—"

Beale interrupted, "Now that's a name!"

"She'll be Michaels & Trent at ten."

"Good, I'm on my way over."

*   *   *

Murray Ross opened the envelope and glanced inside. There were bundles of what looked like hundred-dollar bills, and there was a large Zip-Loc bag partially filled with a white powder. Atop both of them was another typed note. "Next time you talk to MR, tell him to call the office."

Ross slipped the envelope into his attaché and was getting ready to close the latches when a hand clamped down on his right shoulder. Terror gripped him. He reached for the case as it slipped off his knees, but the hand on his shoulder prevented him from moving. The contents of the case spilled across the floor. A second man, burly, black and dressed in a gray suit, stepped forward and picked up the cardboard envelope by its closed end.

"That's mine," Ross said, grabbing for the envelope. Packs of money and the bag containing half a kilogram of cocaine tumbled to the floor. The note floated down with it.

"Oh, please excuse me," said the detective, picking up the packs of money. "Is this yours?"

"Yes . . . I mean, no. I mean, I don't know. Someone just handed me that envelope," Ross babbled as the man holding the money and the envelope displayed a badge affixed to a worn leather holder.

"Detective Hardy, New York Police," the black officer said. Leaning down and picking up the plastic bag, he continued, "Since this isn't yours, do you mind if I inspect it?"

"No. I mean, yes, I mind."

The protest came too late. Melvin Hardy had the bag open and was dipping a pinky finger into the white powder. He placed his fingertip on his tongue as Ross yelled that he had been set up. Ross quickly became the center of attention for the people passing through the hotel lobby. "I want a lawyer!"

The burly detective laughed. "Remember when Chuck Glover said he didn't want his money back, he wanted his coke?"

Ross blanched when he realized that he might have taken money in advance from a policeman.

"Well, we just want to make sure that you didn't skip town with our cash," the detective smiled.

Ross did not respond. Detective Hardy nodded to his partner, who informed the man that he was under arrest for possession of a controlled substance and began reading him his rights.

At the same time, Hardy pulled a portable radio from his pocket, yanked out the antenna and spoke quickly. "Okay, pick him up."

* * *

Scores of people filled each block of Lexington Avenue, most moving northbound from Grand Central Station to coffee shops and offices in the towering buildings that lined the midtown Manhattan thoroughfare. Patrick O'Hearn was walking quickly against the flow of pedestrians toward the station. His sixth sense registered trouble. Then his ears picked up the footfalls of someone following close behind—close enough that O'Hearn heard the buzz of the portable radio.

He was four blocks south of the Waldorf, approaching 45th Street. There, cross-town traffic was intercepting Lexington Avenue's southbound auto traffic and the stream of pedestrians who were bunching along the curb, waiting for the light to change. Despite the noise of the city street, the Irishman was able to hear the words "Okay, pick him up" from somewhere close behind him. He bolted forward, knifed through the cluster of people along the curb and darted into the street. With a simultaneous screech of brakes, horn blast and collective gasp from the onlookers, O'Hearn jumped onto the hood of a taxi that had been racing to make the light. He leaped from the taxi to the roof of the adjacent car and dropped to the street on the other side. He pushed through the crowd on the opposite side and sprinted into the open. His maneuver bought him 150 feet and, more important, gave him a pedestrian shield that he hoped would dissuade his pursuers from using firearms. He never looked back as he raced south, bumping into people as he ran.

Ignoring the shouts to stop, O'Hearn reached 44th Street and was about to cross when a uniformed policeman on the far side of the street blocked his path. Turning right, the Irishman with a marathoner's body and a killer's cunning mind sprinted toward Park Avenue with three pursuers close behind.

He shed his trenchcoat and tossed it into the air near a group of homeless men who were clustered on the sidewalk. As they scrambled for the coat, they got in the way of the policeman, allowing O'Hearn to increase his lead. Rounding the corner at Park Avenue, he dashed across the street and ducked into the railroad station, hoping to evaporate into the sea of commuters pouring from the 80-year-old beaux-arts edifice.

There, other policemen recognized the situation and joined the chase through the cavernous terminal building. They followed O'Hearn through the gates to the platforms, where commuter trains were unloading.

O'Hearn's daily regimen of running five miles was paying off as he widened his lead. He turned down a platform where a train was pulling out of the terminal after leaving behind more than four hundred passengers. To avoid the surging crowd, he jumped down into the drainage channel in the center of the tracks and sprinted to catch the retreating rail cars.

Behind him he heard the demands of policemen ordering him to stop. Then he felt the impact of a lead bullet striking his buttocks just before the report from a nine-millimeter automatic reached his ears. He stumbled forward and grabbed for the coupler on the back of the accelerating train as two more bullets whizzed past him, smashing into the undercarriage of the railroad car.

Clutching tightly to the steel coupling device, he allowed himself to be dragged into the safety of the dark, subterranean tube. Once beyond the view of police, he pulled himself onto the tiny platform on the back of the car and sat down on a very painful rear end.

As the train on which Patrick O'Hearn was sitting hurtled beneath the median on Park Avenue, he pulled out his wallet and inspected the bullet that had pierced six credit cards before being flattened against the bronze badge he carried. His only thoughts were about his escape.

Not knowing where he was, where he was going and who might be there when he arrived, O'Hearn decided to drop off the train at one of the emergency exits that were speeding by.

He lowered himself back onto the coupler and suspended himself so his feet just touched the ground. Then he let go. Curling himself into a ball, he rolled up the tracks behind the disappearing train.

For a moment he lay there, assessing the bruise on his left knee and an abrasion on his scalp that had begun to ooze blood. Realizing he was mostly unhurt, O'Hearn rose slowly to his feet and, carefully stepping over the electrified third rail, walked through the tunnel until he came to an arched passageway in the wall illuminated by a bare incandescent bulb. Stenciled on the door within the arch were the words "Exit to Street."

Eight of New York's finest ascended the stairs of the 125th Street commuter station moments before the train on which O'Hearn had been riding emerged from its tunnel, climbed to its elevated track bed and screeched to a stop. The police surrounded the train and undertook an exhaustive search. They quickly learned that the man they sought was no longer on board.

*   *   *

Monday was usually the day that Elizabeth went grocery shopping. With the wild schedule since Peter's disappearance, and the many meals brought in by members of Lakeside Community Church, however, she had not done major shopping in over two weeks. But one of the older women in the church agreed to come by and baby-sit during the morning, allowing Elizabeth to go out unencumbered. Now, as she walked the aisles of the Ukrops supermarket in Midlothian's Sycamore Square shopping center, she was almost enjoying herself.

The mother of five vowed to make the most of her morning. She had arrived before eight to join other early-morning shoppers in the dash to the back of the store for the marked-down meat trays that were set up each morning at the meat counter. After selecting a few of the cheapest cuts she could find, she had picked up a number of the plastic bags containing past-prime produce and nearly filled her basket with marked-down bread.

Though she had always been a prudent shopper who stretched the family dollars for food and clothing, she was even more so now, knowing that her family was going to be desperately short of funds in the weeks ahead.

In the cereal aisle, Elizabeth bypassed the name brands and picked up a few boxes of the store's brand. As she headed to the checkout, she encountered one of her friends.

"Hi, Elizabeth," Karen Wentworth smiled. "I see you're hitting the markdowns too."

"Yea," Elizabeth smiled back, somewhat embarrassed. "It takes a lot to keep my crew fed."

She didn't want to mention that she was about to write a check that would exceed her checkbook balance on the expectation that Peter's payroll check would arrive at the bank Friday, before the Ukrops check cleared.

*   *   *

Patrick O'Hearn climbed the dirty steel-rung ladder and pushed against the sidewalk grate. Moments later he was standing on Park Avenue at the intersection of 95th Street. Though greasy and torn at the knees and elbows, his suit was intact. It looked terrible close up, but in a cluster of people hailing cabs his appearance was masked. When the first cab stopped to pick up a woman who was waving her arm, O'Hearn pushed her aside, jumped into the taxi and ordered the driver to move. "Pennsylvania Station," he said, slumping onto the vinyl seat. His destination was New York's other railroad station, where he could catch a train to Virginia.

The driver looked back at the tattered and bleeding man in the back seat. "Hey, bud, you get rolled?"

"Yeah, sort of."

"You sure you wouldn't rather have me take you to a hospital?"

For the first time the tough man with the aching behind realized that blood had filled his hair from the abrasion on his scalp. He pulled a handkerchief from his pocket, blotted the wound and said, "I'll be fine. Just get me to Penn Station."

The cab darted through rush-hour traffic and covered half the distance to the railroad terminal before O'Hearn again engaged the driver in conversation.

"Hey, you," he called to the cabbie through the heavy plastic partition. "I need a jacket. Will you sell me yours?"

"You crazy?" asked the man behind the wheel, glancing into his mirror.

"No, I need a jacket, and I'll pay you for yours. I'll give you fifty bucks."

"No way. This is an official Mets jacket," the driver lied. He had bought it from a street vendor for twenty-five bucks, but, after seeing the wad of money, he figured his passenger was good for more.

"Last offer," said O'Hearn, "one hundred dollars, and you give me your cap too."

"The hat will cost you an extra twenty-five."

O'Hearn pulled a gun from the holster under his left armpit and raised it high enough for the cabbie to see. "Okay by me," he said. "One hundred twenty-five and one bullet to cover the tax."

The driver swerved to avoid hitting another taxi and jammed on the brakes, jolting to a stop at the traffic signal at 57th Street. Turning back, he said, "I'm sorry, your first offer was fine. A hundred for both is fine by me."

The Irishman replied, "Hand them back the next time you stop."

Thirty minutes later, wearing the cab driver's jacket and cap, O'Hearn sat reading a newspaper while awaiting the noon train to Virginia.

* * *

Twenty blocks to the north, Dawn Early sat at the computer terminal at Mark Randolph's desk and attempted to execute a transfer of securities between the accounts of two dummy clients set up just for the test. With Martin Beale, Hugh Waters and Singe Madaven looking over her shoulder, the young computer whiz bypassed the data-entry screen, accessed the scripting level of the program's code and discovered a routine written into the software that would allow account transfers to be executed without a transaction record being generated—exactly as Beale had predicted. Early, looking more like a Greenwich Village artist—which she was—than a government worker, also discovered a mechanism by which the routine could be activated from the data-entry screen.

Shortly after noon, Early declared she had found everything she was looking for. "Clever, very clever," said the young woman, describing the embedded code. "I think it'll work."

"What are you talking about?" asked Beale.

"Watch."

Returning to the data-entry screen on Randolph's computer, she executed three trades totaling fifty thousand dollars. Then she turned to Madaven. "Can you check to see if these trades are showing up on your transaction report?"

With some trepidation, the director of information services picked up the phone and called for a trading report. Within two minutes he received confirmation that one account had grown and the other had been reduced by the same amount. He also learned that the trading report contained no mention of the transaction. When he relayed the information to the others huddled around Randolph's desk, emotions were mixed. Madaven himself was dumbfounded. Hugh Waters was shocked. Beale was ecstatic.

A smiling Dawn Early suggested lunch.

* * *

After failing to find a single person at Cancún's airport who could identify Peter from his photo, Mike Downes drove a rented car to the office of the consular agent. He was greeted by Juanita Méndez, who handed him an envelope containing the information he had requested. Back in his car, he reviewed the envelope's contents.

The envelope contained the visitors' schedule for the prison, a letter written in Spanish to officials at the jail requesting their permission to let Downes speak with Debbie at the door, and names, addresses and telephone numbers of lawyers, psychologists and the local prosecutor. Also in the envelope was a handwritten note to Downes from María Escobar, who was out of the office on business. "I have called the jail. They are expecting you before noon. Please call me later in the day and bring me up to date. And, oh, you should know. Jan Stevens died this morning." Downes returned the papers to the envelope and headed west out of the city.

At the Cancún jail, Downes successfully navigated the bureaucratic waters and reached the locked door of bars at the prison. There he waited for Debbie. When she walked up to the fence, she looked only marginally better than she had the day before. But he noticed that she had bathed and washed her hair. She was wearing turquoise shorts and a clean white T-shirt, but neither the clean clothes nor the recent shower had significantly improved her countenance. She responded to Downes's greeting with a faint smile and a question.

"How are my girls? Have you talked to them?"

Downes thought that a little white lie would boost her spirits and began to tell her that he had spoken to them, but something within stopped him. *This woman,* he thought, *needs someone in whom she can place her trust.* He knew she wouldn't be able to do that if she discovered he was untruthful. He responded to her question accordingly.

"No, Debbie, I have not talked to them, though I did ask Liz Clark how they were doing when I spoke with her last night."

Disappointment crossed the woman's face. Then, after a brief pause, she asked, "How is she?" The question was asked with far less intensity than was the first.

"Not well. She and everyone else at home are very worried about you. She's going to fly down here on Saturday to spend Sunday with you."

Those words brightened Debbie's face perceptibly.

Downes explained. "Sunday's really the only day you are allowed visitors, and María has been using up her favors with the police to get me in here."

For fifteen of their allotted thirty minutes, the two strangers engaged in an exchange that began to break down the barriers between them. They discussed their jobs and families, what they liked to eat and what they didn't.

They discussed their respective exercise programs. Without the presence of the consular agent, the conversation flowed more freely and naturally, though Debbie would periodically break down in tears.

During their second fifteen minutes, which the guard graciously extended to twenty, the conversation turned to the events of the past two weeks. Although Debbie had more trouble discussing the events leading up to her arrest, with Downes's help she told the story again. This time Downes carefully followed the flow chart he had constructed the night before, interrupting her each time he thought there was a gap in the story to ask her to elucidate.

With his tape recorder running and his pencil taking notes, he gained a better insight into the circumstances of her attack. But when he pressed for details of the rape incident, she refused to offer them. He wanted to reconstruct Barry's bizarre soliloquy just before he brutalized Debbie, but when he went over his notes with her, she withdrew—not only verbally and emotionally, but physically as well. She turned her back on him, folded her arms and leaned against the bars.

"I'm sorry, Debbie," he said, "I don't want to push you where you don't want to go. I'm just trying to find Peter, and I'm looking for anything this man said or did that would lead me to him."

The woman had closed up. Like a turtle pulling its head and legs back into its shell, Debbie withdrew into her mental shell, effectively ending their discussion.

When she turned to face Downes, her eyes were red and watery, accentuating a gaunt face that was drained of the faint glow of life he had witnessed during the preceding hour. "I'm sorry, I just can't talk about it now."

Downes extended his hand toward the fence to touch hers, but she stepped back and uttered a faint goodby. Then she dropped her head and walked toward the throng of fellow prisoners, male and female, who were milling about the prison's plaza.

Downes's eyes followed Debbie as she walked toward the women's cell block. Though her slow, deliberate walk reflected her heavy heart, some of the men in the prison apparently were only interested in her fair skin, blonde hair and attractive body. They whistled and gestured as she passed them. Downes didn't know Spanish, but it was easy to discern what the men were asking for.

He left the jail with mixed emotions. He was pleased that he had been able to get to know Debbie, because it helped him to better appreciate Peter's interest in her. But he was frustrated with his impotence. He felt he was further away from finding Peter than he had been when he had first decided to go to Denver. He needed a break and was going to have to get help from someone else. But who? He prayed silently as he walked to his car. *God, I need your help. Not for me, but for this pathetic woman who is in prison—and for Peter and Elizabeth. Show me what I should do.*

As he drove onto the boulevard that led back to the center of the city, he decided to call on the lawyer who had visited Debbie in prison. Following the directions María Escobar had included with his address, he headed to the man's office. When he arrived, a sign on the door reminded him that most of Cancún's nonretail business shut down each day for siesta from two o'clock to four. He looked down at his watch and, noting that it was 2:15, turned to go.

Just then the door to the law office opened. Downes glanced back toward the door. Stepping out was a short, dark-complected man with a receding hairline. Downes guessed he was about sixty years old. He was wearing an ornate open-collar shirt that hung jacketlike just below the pockets of his dark brown pants. The buttons on the front of the shirt were hidden by a placket integrating a vertical design that completely covered the front of the shirt. It was the typical attire for businessmen in the tropical climate. Looking at Downes through his bifocals, the man said, "Buenos días, señor."

Extending his hand, Downes replied, "Hello, do you speak English?"

"Yes," the man smiled.

"I'm Mike Downes. I'm a friend of Debbie Steinbaugh, the American who's in jail, and I was looking for a lawyer named Jorge Soto."

The man laughed at Downes's pronunciation of his name while reaching out to accept his hand. "That's me," he said in perfect English. "But it's pronounced 'Hor-hay,' " he explained, sounding out the name. "I was just heading out for lunch. Do you want to join me?"

Downes was surprised at the man's command of English and his speech, which was almost totally devoid of the local accent he had come to expect from the citizens he encountered. "Sure, I guess so."

"Is Kentucky Fried Chicken okay?" the Mexican lawyer asked.

Downes knew he was going to like this man. "Sounds great. Do you want to ride with me?"

Moments later the two men were exchanging personal information during their short drive to the restaurant. Soto described his upbringing in Mérida on the Yucatán Peninsula and his college days at UCLA. "I thought I would try my hand at international law, so I went on to Washington and got my degree from Georgetown. I landed a job with the OAS."

Downes turned and looked at him quizzically.

"Organization of American States," he explained. "After ten years in Washington, I got tired of the rat race and came back to the Yucatán. Cancún was taking off, so I decided to hang out my shingle and get to work." Interrupting his discussion occasionally to give Downes directions, Soto explained how his proficiency in English, his knowledge of the Yucatán and his family's political connections had made him instantly popular with the American hotel developers and professionals who had descended on the city to take advantage of the construction boom.

"Now I just take it easy," he said. "Mostly helping tourists who get into trouble. All the corporate work is handled by my partners at our main office. I like the quiet in this satellite office, so that's where I spend most of my time."

The conversation continued over chicken and cole slaw as the two shared stories of places and events they had in common. When the conversation came back to Debbie Steinbaugh, Soto expressed great concern.

"I'm afraid this woman is in serious trouble," he said somberly. "I have reviewed her case, and I have heard her story. There's no way that I can get her out on bond, even if someone could raise it. Our local law does not allow suspects to go free before trial if they are charged with a crime that has as its minimum punishment incarceration of at least five years." Though he had heard this before from María Escobar, Downes listened intently. "That's why you hear the tales of Americans ending up in Mexican jails for years for possession of just a few grams of cocaine or heroin.

"I talked with the prosecutor," the lawyer continued. "He has a lot of witnesses and over a dozen affidavits from tourists who saw the two women fighting on several occasions. And he has statements from two people swearing that Ms. Steinbaugh said she was going to kill Ms. Stevens. And according to the police, nobody has seen or admitted to seeing anybody resembling the man Ms. Steinbaugh has described as her attacker. Her own version of the story just doesn't hold water."

"What if I found the man she's talking about, and he corroborated her story?"

Soto laughed out loud. "Who would believe him?"

"I don't know."

Soto looked at Downes and continued to smile. "My friend, do you really think they would believe a stranger? Who knows, you could hire an actor. Do you think that if you simply brought someone back here and had him say it was all just an accident, based on that testimony they'd let her walk out of jail?" He answered his own question. "No way." He paused and, staring past Downes, said, "Unless . . ."

Downes waited for the rest, but it didn't come. Finally he asked, "Unless what?"

"I'm thinking. If you could bring this man, this Barry Kennedy or this Peter Boget or whatever his name is. If you could bring him down and he told the exact same story, and described the murder scene to the satisfaction of the prosecutor and the judge, and if he agreed to take Ms. Steinbaugh's place in jail, then . . . maybe then they would let her go."

"That's a tall order."

The lawyer removed his glasses and folded them into his hands. With his elbows propped on the table, he looked Mike Downes in the eye. "No," he said emphatically. "That's impossible."

After letting it sink in, Downes asked, "Then what is the prognosis?"

"Ten years for a reduced charge of manslaughter with parole possible in five."

"She'll never make it."

"An attractive American woman in that jail . . . no, she probably won't. Unless . . ." Soto's voice trailed off, and his face showed he was deep in thought. "Unless she uses her body to buy—"

"Disgusting," Downes said, not waiting for Soto to finish.

"But, unfortunately, reality. I'm sorry."

After lunch, Downes returned the lawyer to his office and agreed to investigate how Soto's fees would be paid. Downes returned to his hotel and placed a call to Washington.

From the moment he prayed at the jail, one name kept coming into his mind. He couldn't explain it, and he didn't want to think what it meant. He checked his watch and calculated that it was nearly six in the nation's capital. It was late, but he guessed the man he wanted to reach would probably be at his desk. Ambitious people, he knew, don't go home with the crowds. He picked up the Mid-Atlantic Bell phone book he had brought with him, located the number and dialed.

Francis Mazzetti answered his phone with a curt "Hello." Downes knew the man needed to go to the company's telephone manners class, but he wasn't about to suggest it.

"Frank, this is Mike Downes. I'm glad I caught you."

It took Mazzetti a moment to reply. "Hello, Mike."

Downes had practiced a dozen different ways he was going to broach the subject with Mazzetti. When it came time to address the man, he decided a straightforward approach would be best. "I need your help."

Mazzetti was quick in his reply. "I know you do, because from what I hear you're running around looking for an employee who should have been fired a year ago. And when you find him, you're going to want me to ignore the fact that he abandoned a company car at an airport, that he left the company without turning in his ID or credit card, and that he's still using company computers for personal business."

Downes wanted to correct him, but bit his tongue and continued. "I'd like to tell you what I know, and why I need your help."

With reluctance in his voice, the vice president for corporate affairs asked Downes to go on. In three minutes Downes brought Mazzetti up to date and put his request on the table.

"I've got Elizabeth and some of Peter's friends tracking down his credit card purchases and his personal telephone bills. I've got Debbie's family checking into any use of her credit cards between the night she was arrested and the day the cards were canceled. They are also trying to get the various credit card companies to flag any attempt to use the cards and notify them immediately of the attempt. So far nothing has turned up.

"The only thing I can't get is usage of her telephone calling card. US West won't release any information, nor will AT&T. And anyway, they may not even have any information because of the time delay between when an international call is placed and when the billing information is passed to the local companies. I'd like you to use your influence to get that information for me."

Surprised that Downes would come straight to him with the request rather than try to get someone to do something under the table, Mazzetti thought for several minutes before he agreed. But not without exacting a concession from Downes. "If I give you information that leads to Peter, and you find that Peter has just run off—for whatever reason—you must agree to fully support my recommendation to fire him and not allow him to resign."

"You're playing hardball," Downes replied. "Do you know what that would do to his family?"

"I'm afraid his family is not my concern. He made his bed, now he's going to have to lie in it."

"Frank, I'm asking for a small favor here, not a million dollars. I can wait till the bill comes in next week and get the information I need for nothing. I just thought you might like to speed the investigation along. You do care about missing employees, don't you? With a little help, you can be a hero when we find him."

"Is that what this is all about? You're running around Mexico so you'll come out looking like a hero? So you can be Mr. Big Shot at the next officers' meeting. Okay, I'll help you. And I won't ask you to support my recommendation to fire Peter, even though I will make the recommendation. Instead, I want you to do something for me. Something personal."

Downes imagined a malicious smirk creeping across his tormentor's face as Mazzetti continued. "If the information I gather for you leads to Peter, you write a memo to the chairman explaining how I made the discovery possible. If he has disappeared involuntarily and you bring him back, we share equally in the accolades."

"I'm not in this for the accolades!"

"I'm not finished," said Mazzetti. "But if you find that Peter has gone AWOL, you agree that you will accept the next early-retirement offer."

"Blackmail!" Downes shot back. "You're talking about corporate blackmail."

Mazzetti laughed, and Downes knew why. Like Downes, Mazzetti was young, bright, aggressive and on the move. More than anything else, he wanted the chance to head up one of Mid-Atlantic Bell's seven operating companies. He had been bypassed at Bell of Pennsylvania when the opening became available. Now, with Earl Hendrick nearing retirement, he had his eye on the office atop the Virginia Bell building in downtown Richmond. With Downes out of the way, the pathway to the Old Dominion would be much easier to navigate.

Mike Downes knew that the next words he would speak could forever change his life. He weighed the alternatives. If Mazzetti put his position and his people behind an investigation, Downes knew the break he was looking for might just happen. On the other hand, if Peter turned up in the wrong place, Downes knew his career would be over. During the long minute while he thought about the consequences of the decision he was about to make, the Bible reading from Sunday's sermon came vividly to mind: "If a man owns a hundred sheep, and one of them wanders away, will he not leave the ninety-nine on the hills and go to look for the one that wandered off?"

Downes took a deep breath. "Agreed. You get me information that leads me to Peter, and if we find him AWOL, I will leave the company with the next offer—even if that means this year."

Mazzetti was more than surprised, he was stunned. He had expected a rejection or an offer of a compromise, not a rival's agreement to step out of the way just to get some information on a no-account employee. Finally he said, "You're one helluva gambler."

Downes couldn't see it, but he knew that the smile on Mazzetti's face would linger for a week.

*　　*　　*

There were few smiles around the Boget dinner table on the second-week anniversary of Peter's disappearance. Even the normally jovial Kristin was unusually sullen, sitting in the high chair between Elizabeth and David. Next to David, Jonathan was complaining about having to eat his vegetables. Across from him, Daniel was picking at his food. Between Daniel and Elizabeth, Lauren sat impassively chewing on a piece of meatloaf. From time to time each of the children would look at the vacant place set for their father, say nothing and resume eating.

*　　*　　*

When Downes returned from dinner, the hotel clerk handed him a message. Mike unfolded it and read: "Cancún to Ephrata, Pa., 1 min, 9:23 pm, 3-21-92, 717-555-0055. Mazzetti."

Downes knew the high-stakes game was on and Mazzetti had rolled the dice first. As he stood staring at the piece of paper, more questions than answers whirled in Downes's mind. He checked his watch. It would be after eleven in Pennsylvania. With so much riding on that call, he decided to sleep on it.

18

fter the children left for school, Elizabeth Boget dropped Kristin in the playpen in the corner of the rec room. She sat down at the kitchen desk to pay her month-end bills and bring her checkbook up to date. She estimated the amount of Peter's check that would be deposited into their account later in the day and began spending it. With the checks she had written on Thursday—one to Ukrops and another to MasterCard—she was already six hundred in the hole, and the water, gas and electric bills were staring her in the face. Besides that, she knew that the fifteen-hundred-dollar mortgage payment would be electronically transferred from her account on Monday, and both the car insurance and life insurance premiums were due. She couldn't even face the prospect of redeeming her car from the transmission shop. She slid the orthodontist bill to the bottom of the pile.

By the time she was done, her checkbook was swimming in red ink. She silently prayed that the check that was being deposited would be more than she calculated. "Another thousand, Lord. Please let there be another thousand."

*   *   *

It was nearly 11:00 a.m. before Patrick O'Hearn arrived at Kennedy and Associates and hobbled down to the basement mail room to check on the status of the day's deliveries. He picked up the phone and alerted his boss to his presence. In a few minutes, the red-headed executive, wearing a fitted, forest-green suit over an ivory-colored silk blouse, made her way downstairs.

"You look terrible," she said when she walked into the mail room.

O'Hearn was sporting a six-inch square bandage taped to his forehead and the left side of his head. Oozing blood had soaked most of the once-white gauze pad. He cradled his right arm in his left hand to relieve the pressure on his swollen shoulder, and he was uncharacteristically bent over.

"Let's sit down and talk about it." She motioned to one of two stools in the room.

"I'd rather not, ma'am," he said with a painful smile. "I've a terrible bruise where my wallet stopped a bullet."

"You didn't tell me about bullets!" she exclaimed.

"Ya didn't ask me."

For the next hour, while employees came and went in the lunchroom across the hall, O'Hearn told his stories of his friendly encounter with the state police in Maryland and his less than friendly encounter with the city police in New York. He also spoke about his meeting with Murray Ross at the Waldorf.

"That was a setup if I ever saw one," he observed. Pulling the badge from his pocket, he showed Kennedy the wide, deep indentation where the bullet was flattened by the piece of bronze. "I never thought the first copper I ever killed would be saving my life."

O'Hearn reminisced, "He dropped me with a billy club to my leg after cornering me in an alley. I don't think he expected an eleven-year-old to have a gun or to shoot it, but I did. And before I ran away, I ripped this off his shirt." O'Hearn grinned and handed the badge to Kennedy. "I've been carrying it around all these years to remind me why we have to win."

"I don't know what Randolph was thinking about when he asked us to keep Ross quiet," Kennedy stated coldly, "but I think we should have provided him with a permanent solution to his wagging tongue problem—not the cash and the coke."

"Randolph is going to have to pay for this," asserted O'Hearn, gently touching his bottom.

"I don't think it's Randolph. He's not that stupid. He has nothing to gain and everything to lose."

Changing the subject, Kennedy had O'Hearn review his findings from his interaction with the state police at the pub in Landover. "So you think Whitehead might still be alive?"

"Yes."

"And you're sure that they only found half the coke?"

"Quite sure."

"Do you think one of the policemen has it?" Kennedy probed the face of her trusted assistant and enforcer.

"Absolutely. It could be Milligan, because he was the first to open the car. But I think it's the young one, the one with the big mouth."

Kennedy smiled like a cat about to leap onto an unsuspecting mouse. "Let's find out," she said.

* * *

With the advent of SS-7, information about every telephone call travels through the nation's vast computerized telephone network and arrives at the local switching center before the voice circuit is established. Part of that information, the telephone number of the person placing the call, can be delivered to anyone who subscribes to the service. Though privacy issues had provoked an outcry by some consumer activists, Mid-Atlantic Bell received permission from state regulatory commissions to implement a wide range of new services dependent on the information passed through SS-7. Of those services, Caller ID was the one Mary Kennedy feared most. She didn't want her phone number showing up on a screen of some of the people she called or being intercepted by call-tracing equipment. She routed her calls through Ireland, so that the electronic fingerprints associated with them were lost in the mechanical switchboard of an "orphanage" she supported in her native land.

The call she was making now was one she wanted to keep anonymous.

"Maryland State Police, Sergeant Johnson speaking."

"Officer Hanks, please."

"I'm sorry," replied the man on the end of the line, "Trooper Hanks will not be in until about 3:30. May I take a message?"

"Please do. Ask him if he found my packages. The dear had been so helpful in getting my trunk open when I lost my key, and he said he would help me locate my lost packages."

"And your name?"

"Don't be silly, he knows my name." Kennedy lowered her voice and in a sensuous voice asked the man on the phone, "Is Trooper Hanks a friend of yours?"

"Sort of. Why?"

"Can you tell me if he's still seeing that girl?"

"Which one? Melissa?"

"I think so," Kennedy purred.

"I don't know. For the past two weeks, since he became a hero, he's got several women tooling around with him in his new Corvette. He thinks he's a god and his red Corvette is his chariot."

"Mmm . . . sounds like the type of chariot I'd like to ride in."

"Me too. But on a cop's salary, I don't know how he can afford it. I couldn't!"

Kennedy pursed her lips and kissed the air, sending a seductive message across the line. "Maybe, sergeant, someday I'll show you how. You've been such a dear."

*   *   *

Mike Downes stared at the phone number for a long time while he sat on the edge of the bed in his hotel room.

He had awakened early and had driven to the beach for a short run. Now he was back to make the call to Ephrata. After two rings he got a recording announcing that he had reached Whitehead's Plumbing and that no one was available to take the call. He hung up and dialed the number again. Again the recording. What was Whitehead's Plumbing, and what did it have to do with Peter Boget?

*   *   *

In Brandermill, the cool drizzle evaporated into warm sunshine by midmorning. After writing her checks, Elizabeth packed a lunch and headed out the door with her two youngest for an hour at the playground in Sunday Park. In the park's sandy playground, Jonathan blew off steam by climbing, sliding, twirling and swinging, while Kristin smiled and laughed during her long ride in one of the yellow plastic swings. Thirty minutes later Elizabeth was at one of the teller windows at the local bank. She was greeted by Jessica Norman, one of her neighbors and a part-time bank employee. "How's it been going?" Jessica asked.

"Okay, I guess. I came by to get some cash, but the money machine outside doesn't seem to be working."

"Let me check it for you. What's your account number?"

Elizabeth handed her the plastic account card she was still holding in her hand. "Oops. Here's the problem," the teller said discreetly. "There isn't any money in there. Looks like you are overdrawn."

"What about the deposit? Peter's check was supposed to be deposited today."

She checked the computer. "I'm sorry, Elizabeth, it's not here. You might want to call his company."

Upset and embarrassed, Elizabeth thanked her friend and, with her two children, quietly left the bank.

*   *   *

The woman who arrived at the vertical steel bars to greet Mike Downes was not the same Debbie Steinbaugh he had talked with twenty hours earlier. This woman had a lilt in her step and a brightness in her eyes that he had previously seen for just a moment or two.

"Good morning, Mike," she sang.

"Well, good morning!"

"Thank you so much for coming. Last night was the best night I've had since this terrible vacation began. After you left, I began thinking and praying. Since I got here, I had only thought about myself. Last night, I began to think about everyone else around me, and I began to see the grief and pain I was causing everyone else. It seems like all of my life I've been nothing but trouble.

"I thought about why you're here," she went on, "and realized that if I hadn't been so secretive back home, Elizabeth and you and God-knows-who-else wouldn't be running around thinking that Peter ran off with another woman. And if I hadn't gotten mixed up with Jan, none of this would have happened, and you wouldn't have to be wasting your time standing here talking to me in prison when you have your own life to lead. And Liz

. . . I can't believe she's coming down here. That's what really touched me. You know, they don't have very much money. This was an enormous sacrifice for them—and I've treated them like dirt. I am such a jerk.

"Something told me that I shouldn't go on this vacation with Jan. I think God was telling me to stay home, but I went anyway."

Debbie paused to catch her breath. "I guess you can tell I need a little stability in my life. That's what I was thinking about last night when I had this peace come over me. I realized that God knows I'm here and he will take care of me. He's already taking care of me! He sent you here to me when I was at my lowest, and now he has made it possible for Liz to come. It's all just too amazing to think about.

"But I did some other thinking last night too," she said, turning serious. "I remembered some things that Barry told me. He said he was a draftsman, I think, and he said something about getting back to Eff-something and . . ."

"Ephrata?" Downes asked excitedly. "Did he say Ephrata?"

"Yes," she paused and checked her memory. "Yes, Ephrata, that was it. How did you know?"

"He used your phone card and made a call to a plumber in Ephrata after he left your hotel room."

"A plumber?"

Downes nodded.

"So you believe what I've been telling everyone? You believe I'm not lying?"

"Yes, Debbie." He looked deep into her blue eyes. "I believe you."

As the words rolled off his tongue, a wave of relief crossed the woman's face. A smile spread across her lips, and tears filled the corners of her eyes. She stretched her fingers through the bars toward him. "Thank you," she said. Downes raised his hand to meet hers, but the guard intervened.

"Ephrata. Ephrata, Pennsylvania," Downes said confidently as he backed away. "That's our way out of this mess."

*   *   *

Elizabeth called Peter's office and reached Marge Conners.

"Let me transfer you to Sharon. The check stub didn't come down on Friday with the rest of them."

When Mike's secretary came on the line, she was deeply apologetic. "Peter's check is sitting on Mike's desk."

"May I come by and pick it up this afternoon?" Elizabeth asked, hoping Sharon Tisdale would offer to deposit it for her, or at least send it out to her by messenger.

There was a hesitancy in the secretary's voice. "I'm afraid that would be a problem. There's a note with the check that says 'Hold for Peter.' There really isn't anything I can do until I hear from Mike."

"Oh, great," said Elizabeth bitterly. "I've got to pay for Peter's house, feed Peter's kids and put gas in Peter's car, but I can't get Peter's check to pay for any of it?"

"Mike should be calling in soon, Elizabeth. I'm sure we can get it all straightened out soon."

*   *   *

When Mike learned that Peter's check had not been deposited directly into the bank, he was angry. He asked his secretary to route his call to Frank Mazzetti and to stay on the line so he would remember to be cordial. While he waited for Mazzetti's secretary to track the man down, Mike updated Sharon on the situation and reviewed the work of the day. He had almost forgotten that the line to Washington was opened when Mazzetti picked up on the other end.

"Mazzetti here."

"Downes here," said Mike mockingly. "Do you know anything about Peter's payroll check?"

"It should be in your office."

"That's the problem—it's in my office and not in Peter's checking account. How did that happen? And before you answer, I should tell you that Sharon Tisdale from my office is on the line with us."

"Hello, Mr. Mazzetti," Tisdale said pleasantly.

"Look," Mazzetti began, "I don't know. I didn't have anything to do with that check."

"Then who did? And why is there a note on the check to hold it for Peter?"

"I don't know."

"Then it probably wouldn't matter if the check were to be deposited into

Peter's account, would it? Can't that be done?"

"With the intent to defraud?"

"What do you mean?"

"I wouldn't give that check to anyone but Peter, if I were you. If someone deposits it into his account while he is AWOL, it could come back to haunt him."

"Why can't payroll just deposit the check like they always do?"

"I guess there was some kind of mistake."

"And you had nothing to do with it?"

"Are you accusing me of something?"

"No, just verifying the facts. Thanks."

When the call ended, Mike asked Sharon to get Elizabeth on the line. The conversation was brief and acrimonious.

"If I didn't need this phone, I'd yank it out of the wall and throw it in the trash!"

"I know how you feel, Elizabeth. I am truly sorry."

"Mike, I know it's not you. It's just that the bureaucracy frustrates me— that, and all the rules."

"I think they frustrated Peter too," acknowledged Mike. "Anyway, I'm coming home tomorrow. The banks are closed now, but let me see what I can do."

When she got off the phone with Downes, Elizabeth called Frank Griffith and told her story. Then she did what came hardest for her. She asked for help.

*　　*　　*

On the telephone message board in the Landover barracks, Roland Hanks read the cryptic message from Kennedy and froze. Somebody had figured out his scheme. He was still standing at the board when he was called to the phone.

"Trooper Hanks here."

"Did you get my message?" said the silky voice.

Almost whispering, he asked, "Who is this?"

"Some would say your worst nightmare. I'd like to think I'm your dream come true."

"What are you talking about?" Hanks squealed into the phone, drawing the stare of a fellow officer. "What do you want?"

"If you didn't find my packages, I don't want anything. If you did, I would like to reward you for your discovery. Don't say anything yet, just listen. I want a phone number and a time to call you to talk business. Don't bother trying to tap the line. You won't find me. Now, can you give me the information I have requested?"

Hanks uttered a tentative yes.

"Go ahead."

When he supplied the requested phone number and time, the phone went dead.

"What was that all about?" asked the officer sitting next to Hanks. "She sounded sexy when I talked with her. She looking for a hot date?"

Hanks responded meekly, his mind trying to figure out what the call was really all about. "I guess so."

"It's that car. I told you, it's like a magnet to women. I don't know how you pulled it off, but I'd like to get one too." He paused and then looking inquisitively at Hanks. "Whadja do, rob a bank?"

Hanks smiled. "Inheritance. My family's letting me spend it now."

* * *

Downes returned to the jail but was granted only five minutes to talk with Debbie. He told her that while he had planned to stay through the weekend to help Liz get around, he felt that he had to get home to straighten out the money mess and to visit Ephrata. He told her that María Escobar had agreed to help Liz Clark get situated and bring her for visitors' day on Sunday.

Downes tried to quickly say his goodbys as the guard hurried him along.

"I'm glad Peter invested his time in you," he said.

"I only wish I was worth it."

"After I find him," he said with a certainty that made Debbie smile, "I'm coming back to get you out of here."

"Thanks, but I'll be okay. I'm glad Liz is coming. Did you ask her to bring pictures of Laura and Jennifer?"

"I did." Downes felt a bit awkward. "Well, I guess I better go."

"I guess so. You know, you've been like an angel to me."

Downes knew that a quick exit would keep him from displaying the emotion that was welling up inside him, but the blonde woman with the soft blue eyes that were filling with tears wouldn't let him go before she had her say. "This week would have been impossible without you. I wish you didn't have to go. I'm . . . I'm really going to miss you."

"I'm going to miss you too." He wanted to reach out and touch her, but the guard was already stepping between them, motioning to his watch. Downes flashed her a warm smile. Then he turned and walked out of the jail.

*   *   *

"I'm told you inherited a fortune that belongs to me," began Mary Kennedy, speaking via telephone to Roland Hanks just after midnight.

The young policeman said nothing.

"You opened the trunk, removed half of the packages, relocked the car and then got a court order to open it again so you would look like a hero."

Hanks remained silent.

"I want the packages back. All forty-eight of them."

"There were only—" Hanks stopped midsentence and tried to retrieve the words that had slipped from his tongue.

"Only what?" demanded Kennedy.

Knowing he was trapped, Hanks began working to protect himself. "Forty-two—twenty-three in each case. Who are you?"

"Either you can't count or you're a liar."

"Who is this?" Hanks demanded.

"You already asked me that," she reminded him. Then softening her voice, she began spinning her web. "Now, you've been a bad policeman, and bad policemen either help bad people or they go to jail."

"Or they capture the bad people and become a hero."

"Ah, Hanks. You've seen too many movies. In real life it doesn't work that way. Long before you catch the crook, you'll be indicted and on your way to prison. Or you might be dead. Now we don't want that to happen, do we?" Before he could respond, she continued. "I suggest we come to an arrangement. You return my merchandise and provide me with some information as payment for the trouble you've caused me, and I'll forget that you were so naughty."

"What kind of information?"

"We'll cross that bridge when we come to it. Now, about the packages. Where are they?"

Things were moving too fast for Hanks. He figured the street value of what he had in his possession was over two million dollars, and if he found the right dealer he could unload each kilo for twenty-five to thirty thousand. If he put that in the bank, the interest would be more than his salary as a cop. But if he could dump the stuff and capture the woman on the other end of the line, he could have two of the things he wanted most—fortune and fame. She could try to nail him, but what judge would believe her story? There would be no evidence. If it came down to it, he could pin the missing coke on Whitehead and come out smelling like a rose.

"The packages, Hanks. Where are they?"

"You don't think I'm foolish enough to keep them anywhere near me, do you? I shipped them out of town to keep them safe for a while."

"All twenty-four?" Kennedy asked casually.

"I only took eighteen."

"And your new Corvette?"

"My aunt died six months ago, and I just received part of the estate. Do you think I'm stupid enough to handle your merchandise? I may be young, but I'm no fool."

"Hanks, don't even think about becoming a hero. If you like action and you want money, I can make that happen for you. But don't cross me." She blew a kiss through the phone line. "I like my men tall, strong, handsome and smart. Let's keep you that way."

The mixed messages had Hanks confused. Then the sensuous voice on the line asked one more question. "By the way, where did they take Mr. Whitehead?"

Roland Hanks's mind clicked into high gear.

She's the one who tried to kill Whitehead, and she's figured out that the attempt failed. But how? It didn't matter. The woman was going after Whitehead, and that meant Hanks could capture an assassin, get back at the woman on the phone and still keep his cocaine. "I don't know," he answered at last. "The FBI arranged it."

"Find out. I will call you at noon."

"I can't find out by noon." Hanks tried to explain.

She ignored his protest. "There's a new Hechinger Home Project Center in Largo. Do you know where it is?"

"Of course."

"At noon tomorrow, stand in the paint aisle reading the directions on the back of a Formby's furniture-refinishing pack. Have directions to White-head in your right hand and give them to the woman who asks you if you have ever refinished a picture frame. She will be wearing jeans and a green sweatshirt."

Mary Kennedy hung up the phone.

19

After a sleepless night, Hanks climbed out of bed, showered and telephoned Ray Harrison, his closest friend on the force. The two had gone through high school and then the police academy together.

"Yo!"

"Hanks here. Whatcha doin' today?"

"I was planning on sleeping a few more hours."

"After that?"

"How should I know?" Harrison mumbled sleepily. "It's only 7:30. Call me back at noon."

"Wait, don't hang up. You interested in some action?"

"No, I'm interested in sleeping."

"What if I said a shoot-out in an old warehouse, a high-speed chase through the District, or a helicopter battle over the beltway?"

"I'd say cut the crap and let me get back to sleep."

"Ray, listen, I'm serious," Hanks said quietly but firmly. "Would you like to be a hero?"

* * *

David and Daniel's soccer games were both to start at ten at the Coalfield Soccer Complex. By 9:45 Elizabeth was on the road to the field with four of her children. Bill McGuire had stopped by earlier to pick up David.

Elizabeth was in good spirits, buoyed by the continued outpouring of support from those around her. Another family in the church had lent her a car. And the head of the deacon board had dropped by the house, just as she was on her way out, with $100 cash and a deposit slip showing that $1,900 had been deposited to her checking account. Even her invalid mother, who had always refused to accept money from Peter and Elizabeth, had sent her a card with a twenty-dollar bill to "treat the kids to a night out."

As she pulled into a spot on the soccer complex's dusty gravel parking lot, she felt great. Daniel dashed off to join his team, while Lauren removed her sister from her car seat and headed to the small field where the younger children played. Jonathan scrambled out after his two sisters, leaving Elizabeth to cart the lawn chairs and the baby bag.

She was greeted warmly by the other parents, but none spoke of her husband's disappearance. When his game ended, a jubilant Daniel gulped down a can of orange soda, and the family hurried to catch the end of David's game. When Elizabeth arrived with kids in tow, a friend who knew her well asked how she was coping with not having a car or money or a husband. Elizabeth pulled a newspaper clipping from her wallet.

"You know, Martha, when I was driving over here today, I remembered this quote that I put in here a long time ago." She unfolded the small piece of paper. "I think this says it best. It's a quote from Helen Keller. 'So much has been given to me, I have no time to ponder that which has been denied.' "

"That's heavy."

"Don't get me wrong, I miss Peter very much and life has been tough these last two weeks. But a lot of people have done so much that I really can't complain. And to top it off," Elizabeth smiled, "Daniel's team just won after two consecutive losses."

"Well, there's more good news: our boys are leading the Flames 3 to 0."

"Really? I wish Peter could see this."

* * *

At ten minutes before noon, Hanks parked his Corvette away from the other cars in Hechinger's parking lot and walked into the store. The huge building housed everything from lumber and lawn mowers to plumbing and electrical supplies. Saturday was the store's busiest day, and hundreds of people wandered the aisles.

Hanks quickly found the paint section. Standing as instructed, he kept an eye out for every woman who approached, but overlooked a girl who walked up to him and said, "Excuse me, sir, have you ever refinished a picture frame?"

The girl barely reached his elbow and looked no more than twelve or thirteen. She was not the woman he expected. But she was wearing a green sweatshirt emblazoned with a print of a rock band. "No, I haven't," he replied as she reached for the paper he was holding in his hand.

Four eyes followed her as she walked quickly to the back of the store and pushed her way through a group of people watching a demonstration of how to erect a deck. She circled the lumberyard information desk, made a complete circle of the garden section, headed to the check-out lanes and walked out of the store.

"Where'd you get that sweatshirt?" asked her mother, who was loading purchases into her car.

"A man came up behind me in the store and made, like, this totally awesome offer to make some quick cash. I mean, he asked me not to turn around, and he slipped fifty bucks in my hand and told me that I was, like, going to help catch a shoplifter. And then he asked me to put on this sweatshirt and walk up to a man in the paint department and get a piece of paper from him and, you know, like, bring it back and he would give me another hundred dollars, and I could even keep the sweatshirt." Grinning from ear to ear, she produced both the fifty and the hundred. "I mean, this is cool! He told me just to be sure I made the exchange without looking at him and without stopping. I mean this was like something in the movies. Like, I'm ready to go shopping!"

The girl was oblivious to her mother's look of incredulity and never noticed the men who were now standing beside her.

Hanks spoke first. Displaying his badge, he said, "I heard your story."

She jumped back in surprise. "You're the man with the note."

"Yes, I am." The girl's frightened mother just stared. Her father walked around the car and asked what was going on.

Harrison responded. "Your daughter was just used to assist us in the apprehension of a criminal, and we want to thank her and you." Turning to the teenager, he said, "You may keep the sweatshirt and the money."

The girl smiled her thanks through a mouthful of braces and a set of expressive eyes. Her parents glowed with pride as they climbed into their car.

"Don't you think we should question her?" Hanks asked Harrison.

"Why? Do you really believe you could get any more of a testimony than what you just heard? We—you've—been had!"

Harrison added, "These are sharp people. We better notify the FBI that someone else knows Whitehead's whereabouts."

"Have you got a screw loose?" Hanks asked. "We tell someone what happened here this morning and we'll be looking for a job on Monday."

Harrison agreed and returned to his car, leaving Hanks to walk alone across the parking lot to his Corvette. The sleek, topless car was resplendent in the early afternoon sunshine. When he got inside, Hanks tried to place his key in the ignition switch. But something was stuck in the keyhole. He pulled out a tiny pice of tightly folded paper. It was a section of the note he had handed to the girl.

"Wake up. You're not dealing with amateurs."

Hanks cursed, then smacked the steering wheel. He rolled the note into a tiny ball and tossed it out of the car before reaching the street.

*   *   *

It was late afternoon before Mike Downes arrived back in Richmond. After stopping at his house for a shower and some fresh clothes, he headed to the Bogets'. He had asked Elizabeth to contact some of the church people so he could share his findings with them as well. From his car phone, he brought his daughter up to date on his travels and told her he wouldn't be at church in the morning.

As he drove across Huguenot Road and swung west on Midlothian Turnpike, Mike thought about all the people he would like to ask to help him locate Barry and Peter. As he thought about it, he realized that every close friend he had was a telephone company employee. Even at church he was more of a pew-sitter than an active participant—and that troubled him. Now, at a time when he needed his friends the most, he couldn't call on them for fear of jeopardizing their careers.

In the center of the village of Midlothian he turned south on Coalfield

Road, aptly named for the first coal mines in America—pit mines from which coal was mined and then transported to the famed Tredegar Iron-works on the banks of the James River. The historical significance of the road was lost on Mike, however, as he covered the six miles to Peter's house.

Jim Parker, Rick Wampler, Josh Sprouse and Bill and Joyce McGuire were all at the house when Mike arrived. Elizabeth, David and Lauren joined them in the dining room. After a quick exchange of greetings, Mike pulled out the charts he had put together from the index cards. He provided a comprehensive picture of what he had discovered and what he believed he would find when he got to Ephrata.

"The man we are looking for knows someone who works for Whitehead Plumbing—maybe the owner. He looks like Peter, and we can presume that he is afraid of capture. I know I would be if I had just tried to rape one woman and left another for dead in a hotel room. Anyway, we need to find him; we need to get him to tell us what he knows about Peter; and somehow we need to talk him into going to Mexico to take Debbie's place in the Cancún jail."

A roomful of eyes stared incredulously at Mike.

Joyce spoke first. "That's impossible," she said, echoing the thoughts of the others.

"I know. That's why I'm here. If this week has taught me anything, it's that I cannot control the outcome of this situation. Just as I sat by helplessly and watched my Susie be consumed with cancer, I am sitting here right now with all this information, knowing that even if I could mobilize all the resources in the world, at best I could find Barry and Peter. Getting Debbie out of prison is going to take a miracle, and I know you people believe in miracles."

Elizabeth spoke up, "Don't you?"

"I wouldn't be here if I didn't. Still, though I thought I had heard God speaking to me the other night, and I did what I thought he was telling me to do, I'm not happy with the way it turned out."

He said nothing more, and no one was prepared to ask what he meant.

"How can we help you?" asked Josh, the state trooper.

"Right now, I need someone to go with me to Ephrata to help me find Barry. After that, who knows? I also need someone to talk with Jorge Soto in Cancún—he's Debbie's lawyer—and find out what can be done to speed her case along and to ensure a fair hearing. I'm not sure her family is in a financial position to offer her much help, and they don't have the expertise that you do," he said, motioning to Jim, sitting at the table.

"Sounds like you could use some prayer too," Jim responded. Then he added, "Let me make some calls. Do you have Soto's number?"

Mike nodded.

"I've got tomorrow off," Josh noted. "I can help you look for this Barry character. When do you want to go?"

"How about now?" Mike said, looking at his watch. "If we leave by five, I figure we can be there by ten. That should give us some time to snoop around tonight and make a visit in the morning."

"Let me call my wife and swing by my house," Josh said. "I think I could be ready to go in fifteen minutes."

While Josh ran home to pack for the trip, Mike offered a few cautionary words. "I'm not sure who we're dealing with here. Barry is a man on the run, and I believe he and Peter crossed paths. As far as we know, he still has Peter's driver's license, credit cards and everything else that was in his wallet—like the address of this house and photos of you," he looked at Elizabeth, "and you," he said, glancing at David and Lauren, "and your brothers and sister. There's no reason I know of for him to come here, but if he gets wind of an investigation, there's no telling what he might do. I don't want you to be overly alarmed, but I think we must proceed with caution."

"What about Peter?" asked Bill McGuire. "Do you think he may be in danger?"

"Who knows? Where did this accident supposedly take place? In Colorado? In Virginia? Maryland? What are the possibilities? I've asked Norwood Clark to see if maybe Peter and Barry ran into each other in the Denver area. He said he and his sons would take Peter's photo to hospitals throughout central Colorado after dropping Liz at the airport this morning. Elizabeth, maybe you can call out there tonight and find out what they've got. Probably another trip through D.C.-area hospitals wouldn't hurt. But first let's see what Josh and I come up with in Ephrata tomorrow."

*   *   *

Mary Kennedy sat at her desk in a pair of jeans, with a T-shirt under her denim jacket. Richard Donovan and Patrick O'Hearn sat in front of her. She held in her hand the torn piece of paper that contained the information on Whitehead's whereabouts. "Good work. Now all we have to do is drop by for a visit."

"Are you kidding?" O'Hearn was quick to reply. "That place will be crawling with coppers. Your friend Hanks brought at least one along today. Now that they know we know where Whitehead is, don't you think they'll be waiting?"

"For us, yes. For Mr. Hanks, no."

"You think he'll work for you?"

"We'll have to see, won't we? But first, we need to know what we're getting into."

"Do you think he's setting us up?" Donovan asked.

"Possibly, but not officially. Not if he's got the goodies." Kennedy paused. "Sunday afternoon is the best time to visit a hospital. Let's leave here in my car at eight."

O'Hearn objected. "But he knows your voice. The moment you open your mouth they'll have you."

"I guess I'll have to let you do the talking, then."

*   *   *

Mike Downes and Josh Sprouse spent four hours in the car getting acquainted. Having stopped only long enough to pick up some burgers, they breezed into Lancaster, Pennsylvania, before nine. After registering at a hotel just north of the city, they drove the last ten miles into Ephrata, stopping at a service station to look up Whitehead Plumbing in the phone book. There were several dozen Whiteheads listed in the book, most with addresses in the surrounding towns. There was no listing for Whitehead Plumbing, but a George Whitehead at 402 E. Main Street in Ephrata had the same number that Downes had called from Cancún.

It was difficult to read house numbers along busy Main Street, except where outside lights illuminated the numerals on doors or walls. Downes decided to park on a side street and locate the house on foot. It took less than five minutes to find the home of George Whitehead. Downes and Sprouse were hoping to maintain a low profile early on, but the house's location was going to make secrecy difficult. Streetlights lit up Whitehead's small front yard. Main Street was busy with Saturday-night drivers cruising up and down the long hill into town, and the bar diagonally across the street from Whitehead's house had a steady stream of customers coming and going.

The duplex was sandwiched between two other buildings, so it could be viewed only from the front and the back. A long set of concrete stairs led up to the building, making an approach rather obvious to any who might be looking. Still, if someone could mount the stairs unnoticed, the dark covered porch would conceal him.

On their second pass by the house, Sprouse casually walked up the stairs and disappeared into the shadows. When Downes walked by again, Sprouse strolled down to join him.

"There's nothing to see. The shades are drawn tight on the front windows. The door's windows are translucent and I couldn't see anything."

"Are you ready to try the back?"

"Let's go."

Walking toward town, the two turned up the hill on which they had parked their car and turned down a gravel access road that ran along the hill above and behind the two-story dwellings that fronted on Main Street. Counting buildings, Sprouse and Downes identified the Whitehead house. They walked down the hill past parked cars and stood at a fence marking the edge of a small yard, twenty-five feet deep. From that vantage point, standing in the shadow of a tree, they could see two men sitting at the kitchen table. From inside his jacket, Sprouse pulled out a small pair of binoculars and focused on the men. "The lighting is bad, but look at the man with the beard," he said, handing the binoculars to his friend.

Downes studied the man through the glass lenses. "Are you thinking what I'm thinking?"

"Dye that hair black, shave the beard and you have Peter Boget. I can't believe it."

*   *   *

Shortly after midnight, Mary Kennedy called the home of Roland Hanks. Hanks was just coming in off his shift and was dead tired.

"Hello." The policeman slurred the word.

"Good evening, Roland."

The voice got his attention. It was soft and sexy and Irish. "It's you! Who are you?"

"I need your help, Roland. I don't want Mr. Whitehead to tell tales on us. Do you understand? Now be a good boy and help relieve the man of his misery."

"But—but—"

"Tomorrow, Roland, tomorrow afternoon at three. I'll be watching."

"But I have to work."

"No you don't, Roland, you're off until Wednesday. Did you forget? Now, why are you lying to me?"

"Why do you keep calling me Roland? My name is Hanks."

"Big boys get to be called Hanks. Little boys like you who play silly games with me are called Roland. Don't you remember that a child took you for a ride today? And you were so stupid to give correct information on Mr. Whitehead. My, my, my. You need some more schooling. Let's begin with Murder 101. I'll be looking to grade your test tomorrow. Please make sure you get an A."

Before Hanks could respond, the phone went dead.

20

Sunday, April 1

A t seven in the morning, Mike Downes and Josh Sprouse rolled slowly down Main Street, observing the Whitehead home and the surrounding area. They proceeded down the hill, past the boarded-up hotel to the shopping area at the center of town. Downes was making a mental note of all the buildings he passed, including the offices of the Denver and Ephrata Telephone Company just up the street from the police station. "That's it," he said pointing out the small building.

"What's it?"

"The phone company. We're not in Bell territory."

"So?"

"So what is a Pennsylvania Bell van doing in the parking lot of the bar across the street from the Whitehead house?"

"Should we check?"

"Maybe we should watch the house and the van for a while."

Downes turned right, looped the block and started back up Main. He drove his gray Buick a block past the parked van and pulled into the parking lot of a convenience store. Dressed in jeans and jackets, and armed with walkie-talkies that Sprouse used for his youth-group outings, the two men parted ways.

Five minutes later, Sprouse's walkie-talkie sprang to life. "Josh, you aren't going to believe this. There is another phone company van up here, and a splice tent has been set up on the cable."

"What's that mean?"

"Somebody could hide all day in a tent fifteen feet off the ground and spy to his heart's content."

"Who's spying?"

"Someone looking for the same thing we're looking for, I bet. Are you in position?"

"Sort of. I'm out of the way, but I don't have the best angle on the house."

"Me either. But if I try to get any closer, I'll be spotted, and I don't want that to happen. At least, not yet. Let me just sit and watch awhile."

* * *

In less than an hour, patience paid off. The other man sitting at the table the evening before—the older man—walked out the back door of his house to a van belonging to Whitehead Plumbing. The man was dressed neatly but casually. He opened the driver's side door, reached inside and retrieved a pair of sunglasses, closed and locked the door, and walked back down the hill into his house. Downes reported the incident to Sprouse. At precisely 8:30, a new white Caprice four-door pulled up in front of the house, and two men in business attire stepped out. Sprouse was on the line to Downes.

"Two men—police, maybe Feds—just walked up the stairs to Whitehead's house."

"What's going down?"

"Beats me."

Downes was twenty feet into thick woods, watching the back of the house, when two cars pulled up on either side of the telephone van that was parked below the splicing tent. He saw four men dressed in suits move quickly from the car with guns drawn. Before they reached the van, the back door opened. To Downes's utter amazement, out stepped Frank Mazzetti. He was ordered by men identifying themselves as FBI agents to spread-eagle on the hood of one of their cars. The man in the splicer's tent was ordered to the ground.

"Josh, what's happening out there?" Downes whispered into his walkie-talkie.

"Looks like FBI making an arrest at the van."

"They just got Mazzetti! I can't believe he pulled something like this."

Mazzetti and the other man were put into one of the FBI cars while one agent walked down to the Whitehead house and knocked on the back door.

Inside, a shaking George Whitehead was sitting in the front living room. Agent Neil Jackson was speaking to him. "I'm glad you noticed the phone company vans and called us. We're taking care of everything right now."

"I guess it was those calls to my answering machine where people were hanging up that made me suspicious. That doesn't happen very often, so five in one day I noticed. Then when those vans were parked out there yesterday—and came back today—I got worried."

"Well, everything is going to be fine," the agent said.

Jackson was called aside by the agent who had come in the back door. Moments later he was back in the living room with Whitehead. "There's nobody else living here, is there?"

Jackson and his partner Cliff Williamson, who was standing at the front door, studied George Whitehead's face. As FBI agents they had expertise in discerning truths from lies. Now they waited for Whitehead's response.

"Yes and no. I do have a nephew who is visiting from Colorado for a while. He's looking for work in the area, and I'm trying to help him find a job. He's probably asleep now. Do you want me to get him?"

"No, that's okay. We can talk to him when we get back this afternoon. Right now we're here to take you to the hospital to see Barry. Are you ready to go?"

Whitehead, slightly dazed, looked around and grunted, "I guess so."

He walked to the back door and let one agent out before locking it. Then he picked up his sunglasses and followed Jackson and Williamson out the front door.

"Can you tell me where we're going to see Barry?"

"I'm afraid we can't tell you specifics, but it's in the Baltimore area. We should be there in two hours."

Sprouse reported the movement of the men to Downes, who asked, "Is he under arrest?"

"No, it looks friendly," said Sprouse. "I can't tell where they're going."

"I wonder if Barry's still inside."

"This is probably not the time to find out."

"Let's stay put for a while."

Thirty minutes later, the car with Mazzetti and two other men returned to the back of Whitehead's house. Mazzetti and one FBI agent walked down the short hill to Whitehead's back door and knocked. Eventually Barry Whitehead, wearing baggy slacks, a wrinkled shirt and a tired face opened the door.

"I'm Jack Morgan with the FBI. I was here earlier, talking with your uncle."

"Yes, sir."

"Can you tell me who you are and where you are from?"

"Sure. I'm Alan Grimes from Fort Collins, Colorado."

"Do you have any identification?"

"A driver's license. Is something wrong?"

"Someone thinks a man named Barry may have come here."

"Barry Whitehead? I heard he was dead."

"May I see your driver's license?"

"Sure, just a minute." Whitehead ran upstairs and returned a few seconds later with wallet in hand. He pulled out the phony license and presented it to the lawman.

The FBI agent scrutinized it and handed it back. "Looks fine, thanks. I'm sorry to have disturbed you."

With Mazzetti by his side, Morgan walked out into the yard behind the house. The splicer's tent was down, and the red safety cones that had been placed around the van were gone. "Mr. Mazzetti, stay by your mobile phone. We will be in contact with you as soon as we get the proper authorizations. In the meantime, I suggest you shut down this surveillance operation."

"Thank you," said the man who hoped to upstage Downes in his bid to find Peter. "And if we discover anything else, we'll let you know."

As the van pulled out, the FBI car followed.

The van that had been in the tavern's parking lot was already gone when Sprouse resumed his conversation with Downes. "I think it's time to rendezvous and plan a new strategy."

"No, now's the time to go in. Barry opened the door for the FBI agent, and he may think we're with them."

"Good idea. Front door or back?"

"Back. I'll stay here. And why don't you bring along our suit jackets and ties?"

Ten minutes later, Barry Whitehead opened the back door to the two men. "What do you need now?" he asked pleasantly, confirming Downes's guess that he would think they were from the FBI.

"Is your name Barry?" Downes asked.

"No. What is this? I just told the other guy that my name is Alan Grimes."

Stepping into the kitchen, Mike Downes gazed into the face of the man who looked so much like his friend. He stared at him for several seconds, making Whitehead very uncomfortable. *Is this the man who left Peter for dead?* Downes asked himself as he stared into dark eyes. *Is this the man who tried to rape Debbie Steinbaugh? Is this the man who killed Jan Stevens? Is this the man who led me on a 5,000-mile trek? His face is too gentle, the eyes too soft, but,* he told himself, *this has to be the man.*

"We're not with the FBI," he said, to Whitehead's surprise. "We're friends of Peter Boget." Downes let the full effect of the statement reach Whitehead's head and heart.

After a detectable flinch, the man said, "Excuse me?"

"We're friends of Peter Boget, and we've come to ask for your help."

"I'm afraid you've made a mistake. I don't know any Peter Boget." Whitehead was nervous and doing a bad job of hiding it.

"Did you see the men who were arrested by the FBI a little while ago?"

"What of it?"

"Those men were coming for you because they know you switched places with Peter." Downes proceeded slowly. The kitchen was cool, but Whitehead was sweating. "And they know you assaulted one woman and killed another in Cancún." Whitehead shifted from one foot to the other, eyeing the door that was blocked by Sprouse. "And when the FBI comes back, they will make life very difficult for you."

"My name is Alan Grimes," he responded belligerently. "I'm just visiting from Colorado. You must have made some mistake."

Downes continued. "No, you made the mistake when you used Debbie's credit card to call this house the night you tried to rape her."

"I didn't rape anyone—you don't know what you're talking about. Now get out of here or I'll call the police."

Downes signaled to Sprouse, who pulled a leather badge holder and ID from his pocket, opened it and showed it to Whitehead. The words *Virginia State Police* froze the draftsman-turned-fugitive in his tracks. Downes continued speaking. "You don't have to call the police, Barry. The police are here. Now do you want to sit down and help us, or do you want to wait until the FBI returns?"

Whitehead slumped into a chair at the kitchen table. "I think I want a lawyer."

Sprouse removed his jacket and sat down. "You don't need a lawyer . . . yet. We're not here to put you in jail."

"Then what do you want?"

"We're looking for Peter Boget. Do you know where he is?"

Placing two elbows on the table, Barry Whitehead buried his face in his hands. "You found me because of a stinking telephone call. Geez, I wonder how she'll find me."

"Who?"

"It doesn't matter."

"What about Peter Boget?"

"That seems ages ago." He looked up into the face of Michael Downes, who had taken the seat directly opposite him. "God, I'm sorry. I'm so sorry."

Within ten minutes Whitehead's story poured out. The pain gave way to relief. Then he told the two men in his kitchen what they came to hear.

"The FBI came by to take my father to see Boget. They tried to kill him last Sunday and—"

"Kill Peter?" Downes interrupted. "Who's 'they'?"

"Probably Kennedy. She's after me," he whimpered. "I know she's after me."

"Who's Kennedy?" Sprouse asked.

"Where'd they take your father?" Downes interjected.

"I don't know."

"So Peter's alive! We've got to call Elizabeth," Downes said as he leaped out of his seat. But Sprouse grabbed his arm.

"They'll all be in church now, anyway. Don't you think we better wait until we actually see him? She doesn't need any more false alarms."

*   *   *

Driving south on Interstate 83 just below York, Pennsylvania, FBI agent Cliff Williamson heard his mobile phone beep. Neil Jackson, sitting next to him, picked it up and began speaking. Sitting in the back seat, George

Whitehead sensed something was wrong. When Jackson concluded his conversation, the agent asked Williamson to pull off at the next interchange.

Once the car was stopped, Jackson turned to Whitehead. "Who did you say the man in your house was?"

"My nephew from Colorado."

"What's his name?"

Whitehead squirmed in the back seat. "Alan Grimes."

"Mr. Whitehead, what if I told you that there is no Alan Grimes licensed in Colorado?"

The plumber did not respond.

"What if I told you that the men staking out your house have reason to believe that your son Barry is in your house, not in a hospital in Baltimore?"

Whitehead still said nothing.

"What if I told you that your son will be arrested for drug trafficking, possibly assault and maybe interstate flight, that he is likely to go to jail for a long, long time, and that you could be indicted for harboring a criminal?"

"I had no idea," a trembling Whitehead said. "I had no idea."

"Then that is Barry at your house?"

Whitehead responded mournfully. "Yes, but he isn't the criminal you think he is."

*   *   *

"Barry, when the FBI comes back, they are going to arrest you, and then they are going to offer you a reduced sentence to testify against your boss," Josh Sprouse explained to the man. "But the moment you're arrested, you're going to become an open target for . . . What did you say her name was?

"Kennedy. Mary Kennedy."

"And if you're lucky, you'll survive your years in prison. And when you come out, you'll be put into a federal witness protection program and will be given a new identity."

"That's what I was planning anyway."

"Well, that's fine, except for one thing," said Downes. "I need you. Every day you're under arrest, every day you're in jail, every day you're tucked away in a witness protection program, an innocent woman will languish in a Mexican prison. Why? Because you are the only person who can save her."

"I'm sorry," Whitehead said offhandedly.

"You've talked to her, you've heard of her difficult life, you've looked into her eyes. What do you think? Should she be confined to a jail cell for the rest of her life because of your actions? God forbid. I need you to go with me to Mexico and tell the officials there your story."

"You're crazy. They'll throw me in jail!"

"For what, an accident?" Downes leaned toward Whitehead. "You can stay here and be in jail tonight, or you can go with us and take your chances."

"What's he going to do?" Whitehead asked, pointing a finger at Sprouse.

The trooper replied, "Just now I have heard a man tell a story that may or may not be true. I have not seen any drugs, and I have no knowledge of this alleged accident except for what you've said. There is no warrant out for your arrest, I'm out of my jurisdiction and I'm off duty."

"What if I say no to you guys and just take off after you leave?"

Downes looked Whitehead in the eye. "You can say no. I will not coerce you. This is your choice to make, and I know that it is a very difficult one. If you go with us, you could end up in jail. They could throw away the key. But at least you'll not have to go through life knowing that you sent two innocent women—Jan Stevens and Debbie Steinbaugh—to their deaths. Barry, I don't know why you tried to rape Debbie, and I don't know why Jan got killed, but I promise you I will support you with the same vigor with which I've pursued Peter Boget. And as far as you just taking off . . . Josh and I are not leaving until the FBI comes and carries you away."

* * *

The car containing Williamson, Jackson and Whitehead came to a stop alongside the Whitehead Plumbing truck behind the Whitehead home. When the three men climbed out of the car, they were greeted by the FBI agent who had been in the house earlier to talk with the man who called himself Alan Grimes.

"He's gone," said the agent.

"Gone?" the three said in unison.

"We got here about ten minutes ago and have searched the entire house. We're checking with neighbors, but so far all we know is that twenty minutes ago an ambulance was called to the bar across the street, but no one there placed the call."

"Oldest trick in the book!" said Jackson angrily. "He gets everybody in the neighborhood out looking to see who's being taken off in the ambulance, and he walks away unnoticed." Turning to the senior Whitehead, he asked, "Does he have a car?"

"No."

"Let's get the local police up here," said Jackson to Williamson. Then, turning to the other agent, he said, "Let's start looking for stolen vehicles and hitchhikers." After the men hurried to their phones, Jackson invited George Whitehead into his own house. "We need to talk."

* * *

From the mobile phone in his car, Downes called the Boget residence to leave a message on the answering machine, but was greeted by an ecstatic Elizabeth.

"Mike, where are you? I got the fantastic news, and we're just walking out the door."

"About Peter?"

"Yes, Frank Mazzetti called about half an hour ago, and David, who stayed home from church today with the flu, took the call and called the church. We rushed home to pick up a few things. We're on our way to Baltimore."

"Mazzetti called you?"

"Yes, when I called him back he said his people had found Peter, and he was on his way to Anne Arundel Community Hospital. We hope to be there before three. Bill and Joyce have offered to take me and the kids."

"Do you have a room number?"

"No. He said something about protective custody. We're meeting in the lobby, but I have the address here."

After getting the address and directions, Downes thanked her.

"You know, Mike, this is the best Palm Sunday ever!"

After he hung up the phone, Downes turned to Sprouse and related what he had heard. "I sure hope this is no April Fool's joke."

* * *

Shortly after ten, at a table in the commons area of the Cancún jail, Liz

Clark was talking to Debbie about Jennifer and Laura.

"It's hard to believe how fast them girls are growin' up. When we was swimmin' in Denver, I really noticed how ladylike they're gettin' to be, 'specially that Laura—I bet she's got all the boys over ta school chasin' after her."

Like so many of Liz's comments, this one only heightened Debbie's despair at being locked up so far from home and the girls she loved.

In contrast to her foster mother's chattering, Debbie was melancholy when she responded. "I hope I can get out of here soon enough to see them before they get so big they forget who I am."

"Come on now, you're gonna get out of here right soon. Mr. Soto said he might be able to get the charge lowered so you can be out in two to three years."

In trying to lift her spirits, Liz was merely reinforcing Debbie's worst fears. "Two years in the prime of my life?" Her eyes filled with tears. "Two years while Jennifer and Laura grow from girls to women? Two years of stinking cells, awful food, and"—she looked past her stepmother at the bleak surroundings and sobbed—"and this?"

Liz reached out and held Debbie's hands in hers. "We won't let that happen."

"And for what? For finding and exposing a criminal? For being attacked and brutalized by an emotionally disturbed man?"

"Debbie, it's Palm Sunday," Liz said softly, trying to redirect the conversation. "Let's remember what that means for us."

"I know what it means. It means that an innocent man is about to be put to death."

"Yeah, but don't you forget it also means that Easter is just around the corner."

"But there won't be any resurrection for me, will there?"

21

Sunday, April 1

Arriving at Anne Arundel Community Hospital just south of Baltimore, Mary Kennedy, Patrick O'Hearn and Richard Donovan made
careful notes of roads in and out of the hospital parking lots and
the location of emergency exits from the building. They secured the
names of three patients in rooms adjacent to the man they believed to be
Whitehead.

On the fourth floor, the three casually walked into the busy family waiting room near the nurses' station. Several children were playing on the
floor, a couple of bored teenagers were watching them, and three older
people were clustered in a corner talking. Kennedy and O'Hearn sat down
across from the television set, while Donovan walked the long corridor
toward Whitehead's room and turned into the room immediately preceding
it.

The only patient in the room was alone and sleeping. After a few minutes, Donovan emerged and walked on past Whitehead's room. Out of the
corner of his eye he could see one man sitting on a chair just inside the
door and another sitting against the distant window. He reported his findings to Kennedy and Donovan.

The three decided to go down to the floor below and plan their strategy.
They were waiting for an elevator when the door opened. Trooper Hanks
stepped out. Even without the silver nameplate on the man's uniform,

O'Hearn knew Hanks's face from dinner earlier in the week. But Hanks didn't notice O'Hearn. He was too absorbed with the striking redhead who stood in front of him.

"Excuse me, ma'am," Hanks said politely, stepping aside to allow Kennedy to enter the elevator.

She smiled and said nothing.

At the entrance to room 430, Hanks knocked and waited to be admitted.

Dwayne Rashad swung open the door to the guest room that adjoined the larger patient room. Rashad was a Maryland State Police sergeant with ten years of service. He hated every minute of protection duty. "What're you doing here?"

"Just visiting," Hanks said as he stepped into the room. "What's Whitehead got to say for himself today?"

"Not much. Every time he becomes alert, he makes noises and starts flailing around. When his hand gets free, even for a second, he grabs at his oxygen mask, so they snow him."

"Snow him?"

"They stick him with a needle and he gets very quiet," Rashad said. "Like snow falling."

The hospital room resembled others on the floor except for its size and its adjoining guest room. It was one of sixteen suites in the hospital set up to accommodate those who wanted or needed to stay around the clock with loved ones. The patient room was kept unusually clean to reduce the risk of infection, but the door to the guest room had been propped open to increase circulation.

Rashad was covered with a yellow paper gown and was wearing a matching paper hat. He pushed the yellow surgical mask under his chin. "We were told that Milligan was coming. You didn't hear?"

"What?"

"This guy's wife is coming for a visit."

"His wife?"

"Yeah, apparently there's been some mistake. This guy may not be Whitehead."

"You're kidding."

Rashad shook his head. "We just got a call to expect a woman and her family to arrive here at three o'clock."

Hanks was more confused than shocked by what he heard, but he tried not to let his emotions show. "You mean this isn't the guy we put on the helicopter down on the beltway?"

"Well, it's the same man, but he may not have been the driver of the car. Anyway, we were told that they'll be escorted by the FBI and someone from the phone company."

Looking nervously at his watch, Hanks asked, "And they're coming at three?"

"You got it," answered Rashad, looking at his own watch. "Just twenty minutes from now."

*   *   *

Sitting in the hospital parking lot, Downes, Sprouse and Whitehead were continuing their two-hour-long discussion of possibilities. Whitehead was convinced that he would be in jail by nightfall unless he did what Downes asked him to do, but he wasn't about to go back to Cancún. That would be worse. Still, he talked about making a mess of his life and wanting to do something right. He just didn't know what that was.

"There they are now." Sprouse spied Bill McGuire's van.

"Okay," said Downes. "Let's go."

"I changed my mind," said Whitehead.

"What do you mean?" Downes asked. "We've been over this a hundred times. If Josh and I don't go in together, someone will think something is fishy, and we're not leaving you out here alone." To help put Whitehead's mind at rest, he said, "There is nothing to worry about. Nobody knows you are with us. Your father is probably home by now and, if anything, the FBI is scouring Ephrata trying to find you."

Whitehead looked very unsure of the situation. Downes reached under his dashboard, retrieved a spare-key holder, opened it and gave the key to Sprouse. "If anything happens—anything at all—here's a key to get Barry out of here." He turned back to Whitehead. "Are you ready?"

*   *   *

After visiting the restroom in the lobby, Hanks returned to the small room adjoining 430. When the no-nonsense sergeant admitted him, Hanks explained why he had come to the hospital. He was sweating as he told of the phone call he had received the evening before, though he left out any mention of the caller's request that he do the killing. "Like I just said, the woman who owned the cocaine we found is coming here at three today to kill Whitehead, and this whole wife-and-family thing may be a charade so she can get close to the guy. I came to nab the person behind the drugs and the murder of the troopers in the explosion last Friday night."

Rashad was flabbergasted. "You what? You wait till five to three to tell me that a murderer is on her way in here?" Reaching for the phone, he said, "I've got to call and get this story confirmed—and get some backup. Dan, did you hear this?"

"Hear what?"

"Turn off the TV, close the hall door and I'll tell you."

Dan Makowski came to the doorway between the two rooms. Given the man's unflattering yellow cap and gown, Hanks could only tell that Makowski was older than Rashad, had pallid skin and gray-green eyes and was overweight. Makowski listened as Rashad related what he had just heard. "Nobody's answering," he said, slamming the phone down. "I'm calling 911 just to be on the safe side."

Makowski quickly grilled Hanks while he helped him put on one of the paper gowns. "Is there anything that might tip us off?"

Hanks replied, "Only her accent. She's foreign."

"Spanish?"

"No, English or Irish. In fact, I would say Irish. If Terry Ryan, the owner of our local pub, is Irish, then the woman who called me is probably Irish. They sound alike, but her accent isn't as pronounced."

"So she may be Irish. Is that all?"

"That's all."

The noise in the corridor and the knock on the door suggested that the time had come. Makowski returned to his position at Boget's side. Hanks and Rashad opened the door.

Stepping forward was Pete Goodrich of the FBI, who presented his credentials. A nurse was standing by his side. She had already been to check on the patient every hour throughout the day, so Rashad tentatively dismissed her as a suspect. Behind them were another man, two women and an assortment of children. Rashad asked for introductions. When he heard the name McGuire, he looked at Joyce. "Oh, so you're Irish."

Bill, not Joyce, spoke first, "Yes sir, we are." Then, looking at the black-skinned man, he asked quizzically, "Are you?"

Everybody laughed, except Elizabeth. "We've come a long way. Can we see him, please?" she asked.

The nurse, conferring with Rashad, suggested that for now the children return to the family room down the hall. Bill McGuire agreed to stay with them.

The FBI agent, the nurse, Elizabeth, Joyce, and Frank Mazzetti were admitted to the anteroom, where the nurse gave them a briefing on Peter's condition while they donned yellow caps, masks and gowns.

"He's doing very well for the condition he's in," the nurse began. "His chest wound is healing well, but he'll be needing bone grafts on his sternum. He's waking up now and then and thrashes around. He can't speak much. And he can't eat on his own. He still needs an oxygen mask."

The nurse passed out latex gloves, but the FBI agent and Mazzetti declined, saying that they did not plan to go into the patient's room.

Elizabeth's heart was beating rapidly, and her breaths were quick and shallow. She was filled with excitement and trepidation. Since the call had come three and a half hours earlier, she had imagined again and again what she might find when she came face to face with her husband. She knew it would not be the same man she had kissed goodby on that fateful Thursday morning. She closed her eyes and prayed before she followed Rashad and the nurse into the patient room. The others remained behind.

*   *   *

After asking at the nurses' station for a mask for a friend who had a cold, Downes, Sprouse and Whitehead walked down the hall to Room 430. Whitehead was wearing a baseball cap to help further conceal his identity.

Hanks greeted the men at the door of the guest room and asked them to wait in the corridor until the others came out. Then, looking over the shoulders of the men he was talking to, Hanks's gaze fell on the woman he had ogled at the elevator. She was pushing a man in a wheelchair.

With his eyes riveted on the woman's red hair and stunning presence, Hanks paid no attention to her companion, who was wearing a long robe and had a blanket covering his legs. The woman wore an apron that identified her as one of the hospital's volunteers. Hanks smiled, deciding that he'd have to visit the hospital more often.

In 430, Rashad kept his eye on the door and strained to hear Joyce McGuire speaking to determine if she had the accent Hanks had been talking about. Elizabeth was standing at Peter's side, with tears streaming into the mask covering her face. "Thank you, Lord, for my Peter."

In this emotional moment Elizabeth recalled the Irish poems her father had often recited to her as a girl. When her father talked of his father's homeland, he would put on the accent that he had left behind when he had entered the business world. Through the years, Elizabeth too had committed to memory meaningful lines of verse and learned to deliver them in the same cultured accent of her father. Her children loved it when she "sounded Irish" and read or recited poetry to them. And Elizabeth would use her accent to lay sweet words on her husband during their most intimate and endearing moments.

Now, as she bent over the bed, she began speaking the lines of a four-hundred-year-old Anne Bradstreet poem that she had tearfully recited to her husband at their wedding reception:

If ever two were one, then surely we.
    If ever man were loved by wife, then thee;
If ever wife was happy in a man,
    Compare with me ye women if you can.

Elizabeth paused and fumbled with the yellow gown she was wearing, trying to reach the pocket of her skirt. Not waiting to see what the woman was reaching for, Rashad, from behind, locked his hands onto Elizabeth's forearms. "Please come with me," he said, turning her toward the guest room.

Trying desperately to twist around so she could see what was happening, a shocked Elizabeth dropped Peter's hand and yelled, "What are you doing?"

Leaving Sprouse, Downes and Whitehead in the hall, Hanks dashed toward the scream. At the same moment, Makowski yanked his gun from beneath his yellow gown in response to the hall door's opening.

Hanks entered the room in time to see Rashad struggling with Elizabeth, and Makowski standing with his gun drawn. Just outside the open door sat the man in a wheelchair. Makowski demanded to know what the man in the wheelchair was doing. The redheaded woman had her hands on the wheelchair's handles.

"Excuse me," Mary Kennedy said, retreating quickly, "I've got the wrong room."

There was little accent this time, but Hanks recognized the voice. So did Barry Whitehead, standing at the next door fifteen feet away. He turned toward the voice and instantly recognized his nemesis. He also recognized one of Kennedy's employees, Richard Donovan, seated in the wheelchair. Not realizing that the dyed hair, beard and baseball cap prevented them from recognizing him, Whitehead turned to Downes and grabbed his jacket. "You set me up!" he said, loud enough for both Kennedy and Donovan to realize that they were looking at Whitehead. "I can't believe you set me up!"

Seeing that the hands of the man in the wheelchair were moving under his blanket, Downes grabbed Whitehead and threw him into room 432. A muffled pop from the vicinity of the man's lap was drowned in a deep-throated grunt of pain from Downes as he felt hot metal rip through his jacket and burn its way into the flesh just below his armpit.

Kennedy screamed in mock fear to help obscure the next pop, which dropped Makowski to one knee. She ran back toward the nurses' station.

Elizabeth's children were already in the hall to see what had happened when Donovan's next shot sailed past Makowski's ear and slammed into Peter Boget's leg. Elizabeth, watching her husband's body lurch in response to the impact, screamed, "Peter, Peter!" and wrenched herself from Rashad's grip. The policeman grabbed for his gun, but a fourth bullet whistled past his ear, tore through the venetian blinds behind him and hit a window mullion. Two panes of glass shattered, raining broken glass onto the windowsill and floor below.

"Stop, David! Wait!" shouted Bill McGuire as David Boget ran toward the sound of his mother's screaming. Lauren and Daniel were close behind. The three were two doors from their father's room when they saw Josh Sprouse dive toward the man in the wheelchair and heard the simultaneous roar from Makowski's gun. The sound froze them in their tracks. The bullet struck the handle of the wheelchair as it was falling to the ground under Sprouse's weight, but Donovan rolled free and raced toward the children, who remained motionless, transfixed by the gun's blast.

With one hand pressed against his chest, Makowski entered the hallway. "Freeze!" he yelled. "Or I'll shoot."

Donovan didn't stop until he was past the transfixed children. Then he spun around and, using Lauren as a shield, fired his gun at the trooper. Lauren's terror-filled scream provided a macabre soundtrack to Makowski's execution. The policeman's head jerked backward as the bullet found its mark. His legs buckled, and he collapsed onto the floor.

Rashad raced into the hall with the FBI agent and pursued Donovan, who was fleeing down the corridor. Pete Goodrich's Beretta exploded in the ears of Daniel Boget, who was only two feet away from the agent's gun. The bullet glanced off Donovan's back, ricocheted off the wall and slammed into the window at the end of the hall. Rashad stopped, aimed and was about to pull the trigger when a patient, hearing the commotion, stepped out of his room—directly in the line of fire as Donovan disappeared into the stairwell.

Sprouse rushed to Downes's side. Downes was struggling to sit up on the floor, as the back of his jacket was turning red in an ever-growing circle around the hole through which the bullet exited his body. "Mike, let me help you."

"Get out of here, and take Barry with you right now. Take my car. Go hide somewhere, and turn on the phone. I'll call you."

"I can't do that."

"You've got to," Downes coughed. "We've got to keep him alive, for Debbie's sake. Now get out of here."

In the confusion in the corridor, it was easy for Sprouse to escort White-head to the elevator. Knowing where to hide him was another story. Sprouse didn't want to go out onto the parking lot until he was sure that the killers were captured or gone. From the lobby he could see county police running toward the side of the building from which Donovan would have exited. He didn't know that Kennedy's assistant had been gunned down in a hail of bullets by these officers, who had responded to Rashad's call to 911. With great caution, Sprouse and Whitehead moved quickly through the parking lot to Downes's car.

*   *   *

Frank Mazzetti waited until he was sure the corridor was clear before emerging from 430A. He knelt beside Downes, where a nurse was already administering first aid. "Well, Mike, it looks like you won." After a pause, he added, "Everybody loves wounded heroes."

Coughing as he spoke, Downes replied, "I haven't won till I bring Debbie home."

"That could take years," Mazzetti reminded him.

"Maybe." He flinched with pain as the nurse touched the wound. "You'd like that, wouldn't you?"

Mazzetti said nothing. He just stood and walked away.

A larger contingent of medical personnel were trying to revive Trooper Makowski. The first bullet had shattered a rib and lodged in his liver. The second had entered his mouth and emerged above his right ear. He was bleeding profusely.

Peter Boget's three older children looked on from the hallway as a young intern examined their father's right leg. Bill McGuire, with Kristin on his left arm and Jonathan holding his hand, walked into the empty guest room and sat down. His wife was comforting Elizabeth, who was sobbing at Peter's bedside. She still didn't understand what had happened. She didn't know why Rashad had pulled her from Peter. She didn't know why people were shooting. She only knew that Peter's breathing had become more labored following the gunshot wound and that his sheet was turning red with blood. When she noticed her older children, she wiped away her tears, walked to the door and told them to go into the guest room and put on gowns. She walked past Hanks and stepped into the corridor.

Downes was sitting in Donovan's wheelchair, waiting for someone to push him to the emergency room. She leaned down and took his hand in hers. Through her mask, she kissed him on the cheek. "I'm so sorry I got you into this mess."

"Go back to the kids—and to Peter. They need you." He squeezed her hand and gritted his teeth to fight off the burning pain under his arm. "I'll be fine."

Taking Kristin in her arms and with her other children by her side, Elizabeth entered Peter's room over the objection of the nurse who was attempting to stop the bleeding from Peter's leg. For her and her children, the reunion with Peter was difficult and bittersweet. Shattered were their hopes and dreams of having their husband and father resume life where he'd left off. They feared he would never be whole again. The three oldest children wiped back tears as little Jonathan clung to his father's good leg and repeated over and over, "My daddy, my daddy, I love my daddy."

They remained at Peter's side until a team of doctors, nurses and aides arrived to wheel Peter to an operating room to remove the bullet from his leg.

As Peter was being transferred to a gurney and his life-support systems were readied for the journey, Hanks studied the nurse's aide standing at the head of the bed. He seemed out of place. Even though Hanks could see only his eyes, there was something frighteningly familiar about the man. Then Hanks observed that the aide was pulling a hose from a bag of intravenous solution that was feeding Boget.

"Just a minute," said Hanks, before the gurney was rolled away. He walked to the head of the bed and placed his hand on the bag of fluid. "Was this supposed to come apart?" he asked the doctor in charge.

"What are you talking about?"

Pointing to the nurse's aide, he said, "This man was taking this apart." All of the members of the team looked at the aide. It was clear to Hanks that they didn't recognize him. "Please remove your mask," Hanks ordered.

The man didn't respond.

"I think you'd better come with me," he said. To the doctor, he said, "I think somebody better check this fluid."

Before anybody could move, Patrick O'Hearn bolted through the door and fled into the busy corridor. There he tripped over Jonathan Boget, who, with his brothers and sister, was waiting in the hall to see his daddy wheeled into surgery.

The .40-caliber Beretta that Hanks whipped out was cold and black. "Freeze!" he yelled at the man on the ground.

With a speed and dexterity that awed the policeman, O'Hearn rolled onto his back as Hanks tightened his finger on the trigger of his automatic. But Hanks couldn't fire. The spinning O'Hearn had scooped up Jonathan and had his left arm wrapped tightly around the youngster as he scrambled to his feet. He held a 9-mm Glock automatic to the child's head. Hanks knew that the Austrian-made plastic gun held fifteen rounds, and he prayed that none would be fired.

"No, *you* freeze," said O'Hearn, his Irish accent reminding Hanks where he had last seen the man. "And drop your gun."

Elizabeth dashed into the hall.

"Mommy, Mommy, Mommy!" her terrified son screamed. He stretched his hands in her direction and struggled to get free. But O'Hearn squeezed the boy tighter and took a step backward.

Reaching deep for a reserve that God had always provided her, Elizabeth began walking toward O'Hearn and her son. "Let my baby go!" Her voice was loud, clear and authoritative. With each step she took toward the retreating O'Hearn, she said it again, "Let my baby go!"

"Shut up," came the forceful reply. "And you, Hanks, drop it. Playing with guns will get you killed!"

Neither Elizabeth nor Hanks followed orders. In fact, each seemed to be strengthened by the other as they walked up the corridor together. Behind them, Bill and Joyce pleaded for them to stop. In front of them, with fear etched deep into his innocent young face, Jonathan pleaded, "Mommy, please help me. Please help me, Mommy . . ."

"Let my baby go!" Elizabeth's demand was not the wailing of a worried mother, it was a command like that of Moses speaking in God's name to a wicked Pharaoh. But O'Hearn's heart was hard and he would not let Jonathan go.

Two dozen eyes peered out of doorways to watch the drama unfold. They saw three people dressed in yellow paper gowns and hats moving in unison through the corridor toward the stairwell at the end of the hall. Only O'Hearn was still wearing a mask.

O'Hearn did not appear nervous. He showed no evidence that he was experiencing pain from the three-day-old wounds and bruises on his shoulders, elbows, knees and buttocks. In fact, he displayed a steely calm. He seemed oblivious to the boy writhing in his arm, pleading for his mother. O'Hearn's cold, dark eyes communicated the message that he could and would shoot the child and anyone else who got in his way. He backed up past the nurses' station. "Drop your weapon, Hanks, and I'll release the boy."

"Go to hell!" Hanks replied.

Elizabeth shouted, "Let my baby go!"

The retreating assassin squeezed the wiggling Jonathan to make it harder for him to scream for his mother. "Your baby's life is in the hands of the copper," he said, his words muffled by the mask. "If he drops the gun, you get the baby."

Elizabeth's eyes were filled with a controlled rage, belying the fear and anxiety that were pumping adrenaline into her system. Her heart was racing, her blood pressure was soaring, yet she walked on toward the faceless man whose right index finger was a muscle spasm away from extinguishing the life of her precious three-year-old son. Hanks was at Elizabeth's side as they closed the gap between themselves and the object of their pursuit. Fifteen feet of supercharged air separated Elizabeth and O'Hearn when the man holding the boy reached the door to the stairwell.

The events of the next three seconds etched a series of images into Elizabeth's memory that would last a lifetime.

The assassin pulled his gun hand down to Jonathan's waist. He pulled his other hand around to the side of the boy, to secure him between both hands at the waist. Then he threw the boy high into the air in the direction of Hanks, leveled his gun and in rapid succession squeezed off two shots at the trooper just before the boy fell into the line of fire.

The first bullet slammed into Hanks's chest as Elizabeth dove to catch her son. The report reverberated down the corridor as the second bullet parted her hair and ripped into Hanks's left thigh, just before Jonathan hit the carpet beyond his mother's outstretched arms and crumpled. Before anyone could react, O'Hearn fled through the door.

For one paralyzing second, a ghostly hush fell on the corridor as the acrid smell of cordite hung in the air. Then a cacophony of outrage and anguish filled the hall, traumatizing the two dozen patients and family members who stood trembling behind the large wooden doors, hoping for protection against whatever was happening in the corridor. But over the wailing of Elizabeth and Jonathan, and agonizing screams from Jonathan's three older siblings as they raced toward their fallen mother, another noise—louder and even more horrifying—filled the hall.

From beyond the stairwell door, blasts from exploding bullets shook the entire hospital wing for six seconds. Moments later, Sergeant Dwayne Rashad of the Maryland State Police crawled through the stairwell door and collapsed. Blood oozed from two holes in his chest and another in his abdomen. The thick red fluid ran down through his jet-black hair from another wound high above his left ear.

Instinctively, Elizabeth crawled to help the dying man. David scooped the screaming Jonathan into his arms, and Bill McGuire knelt by his side.

Nurses had already reached Hanks, who was lying on his back gasping for air. His Kevlar vest had stopped the first bullet, but the direct hit to his sternum had knocked the wind out of him.

*   *   *

When Mike Downes returned to the fourth floor with his right arm in a sling, he slipped into 430A, where the Bogets and the McGuires were praying. Kristin and Jonathan—who had survived the fall with little more than a bump on his head—were asleep on the bed in the room. Elizabeth sat on the sofa with her arms around Lauren and Daniel. David sat on the floor against the wall at the foot of the bed, facing Bill and Joyce. All were very happy to see Mike.

"What did they say?" Elizabeth asked.

"They said I was lucky, but I don't believe it. God was watching out for me. From what I was told downstairs, he was watching out for you too."

Elizabeth's response lacked the power of her challenge to O'Hearn. "I want to take Peter and my children and get as far away from this place as I can."

Then Elizabeth retold the story of the horrifying three seconds when she was sure her boy would be killed. Mike told them the good news that the bullet had entered beneath his arm and sailed out his back, tearing some muscle but missing the bone. Then all focused their attention on Peter.

Police were waiting to interview the family about the events of the afternoon. Mike had already given his story to the police, so he excused himself. "Josh is downstairs waiting for me," he said. "He's got to go back home in time for his late-night tour of duty."

Mike didn't have the heart to tell them that the man who had tossed Jonathan into the air and shot Hanks had escaped.

*   *   *

Mary Kennedy kept her eye on the speedometer as she drove south on Interstate 95 through Virginia. She didn't want to get stopped when she had a man sitting next to her with two bullets in his body. O'Hearn was in agony, but Kennedy couldn't stop. She knew that every hospital in the area would be on the lookout for a man filled with lead. No doubt a description of her would be circulated as well. She had to get O'Hearn back to Norfolk, where she could call on a doctor sympathetic to the cause.

*   *   *

With Whitehead lying under a blanket on the back seat of the car, Josh Sprouse drove to the front entrance of the hospital, picked up Mike Downes and headed for the interstate back to Richmond. Downes told the story of the action that had unfolded after Sprouse and Whitehead left the hospital. Then he spoke heart to heart with the man who sat up in the back seat.

"Your options are changing, Barry. Now they know who they're after— an assassin and police killers. They probably don't need your testimony now to put Kennedy behind bars. That means when you tell your story, you'll end up in jail. And if you go to prison before they do, you will never be able to close your eyes. You will never be able to go anywhere without wondering who around you may be a paid killer. A conviction on drug charges could get you lots of years behind bars. Only time will tell if you actually live that long." Downes paused.

The break gave Whitehead a chance to point out where he had had the flat tire that had triggered the whole terrible chain of events.

"It'll be a lot easier for you to testify in Mexico if you come of your own free will," Downes went on, "and if you are not under arrest in the U.S. Once you land in jail here, anything you do to help someone else will look like you're trying to help yourself. The courts here won't buy it, and neither will the judge in Mexico. Anyway, it will probably be too late to save Debbie."

Whitehead listened quietly as Downes spoke.

"I told you I will do everything I can to support you. I'm not going to take you down there and drop you into prison. In fact, the only way you can end up in jail is by convincing the authorities that you're a bad man. That is your choice, and that will always be your choice. You can tell your story and take your chances. I think you know by now that we didn't set you up today; we didn't know anymore than you did what was going to happen. And you're still alive and you're not in jail."

"I know," said Whitehead, offering a reluctant thank-you. "But what guarantees do I have?"

"None. Sometimes in life you have to go by faith."

Nearing the last exit before the Woodrow Wilson Memorial Bridge, which carries the Capitol Beltway across the Potomac River from Maryland to Virginia, Sprouse eased the car onto the shoulder and stopped.

"Mike, with what I know, I have to arrest Barry once we cross into Virginia."

Downes looked at Whitehead. The scared, pensive draftsman waited a long time to respond. "Let me call my father first, please."

"Okay, here." He handed the mobile phone to Whitehead.

"Pop, this is Barry."

"Where are you?"

"Should I go and tell my story to the police?"

"The police are right here. Why don't you come home?"

"That won't be possible."

"Where are you?"

"I'll let you know what happens." Whitehead handed the phone back to Downes. "What next?"

Downes looked at the man beside him. "Josh, take us to Union Station."

* * *

Forty-five minutes after Mike Downes left the hospital, and while the Bogets were being interviewed by both a state policeman and an FBI agent, a doctor walked into the room where the shell-shocked family was huddled with the McGuires.

"He's out of surgery and doing well," the doctor announced. "We're going to put him into intensive care for a day or two so we can observe him better, but he handled the operation well."

"Thank you, doctor," said Elizabeth, "but Peter won't be staying."

The doctor sidestepped Elizabeth's comment. "His lung function is getting better every day. He still drifts in and out of sleep, primarily from his pain medication now, but he's not had any measurable brain damage from the accident. Except for that brief period of cardiac arrest two weeks ago, before he was transferred here, his heart has been performing admirably, given the overload it experienced from his burns."

"Cardiac arrest?" the McGuires and Bogets asked.

"What else are we going to find out about Peter's stay here?" Elizabeth added.

The doctor again chose not to answer the question directly. "Mrs. Boget, you may want to come down and see him briefly, then go get something to eat. We'll be moving him out of post-op later this evening." He thought a moment and then added, "Oh, yes, a Pastor Griffith and his wife are downstairs with him now."

Elizabeth was shaking when she walked through the double doors into the recovery room to see Peter. She asked the Griffiths and McGuires to wait outside with her children.

As the doors closed, Elizabeth looked around the high-tech, antiseptic sanctuary. The sound of her husband's labored breathing was broken up by the slow, rhythmical electronic *ping* that echoed the beat of life. She was alone with Peter for the first time after the longest separation of their marriage.

In the solitude of the recovery room Elizabeth closed her eyes and reflected on an adult life devoted to her family, her home and her husband. Despite all the trials, all the disappointments, all the setbacks, hers was a wonderful life that had been spent with a wonderful man. Yes, it had been fragile in its infancy, strained by tight finances, unexpected children and communication problems. But she and Peter had found common ground in God and used that foundation to build a better life for each other. In her mind, Elizabeth relived her wedding day. Only the handsome athlete with the wavy hair, square chin and expressive eyes was not standing by her side—he was lying on a bed with tubes and wires attached to every orifice, and a plastic oxygen mask fitted over his mouth and nose.

Fighting back the tears that had become an all-too-regular part of her life since her husband's disappearance, she leaned down amd kissed her lover and her friend. Then she completed the recitation of the poem she had begun four hours—and what seemed like a lifetime—earlier.

> I prize thy love more than whole mines of gold,
>   Or all the riches that the East doth hold.
> My love is such that rivers cannot quench,
>   Nor aught but love from thee give recompense.
> Thy love is such I can no way repay;
>   The heavens reward thee manifold, I pray.
> Then while we live, in love let's so persever,
>   That when we live no more we may live forever.

Elizabeth reached under her paper gown and pulled out Peter's wedding ring, the ring that had adorned his dresser for the three weeks, three days and twenty hours since he had removed it to play basketball with David.

In a slow, measured rhythm, emoting a conviction far deeper than when she had first said them, Elizabeth restated her wedding vows. "I commit myself to love you," she said, choking up just as she had done on her wedding day. "To cherish you and to serve you, so long as God gives me the strength to do so—for richer or poorer, in sickness and in health, until death do us part."

She slipped the ring on Peter's finger and, holding his hand firmly in hers, leaned forward to kiss him. Unexpectedly, his hand tightened around hers. His eyelids parted, and with eyes that could communicate love and tenderness and commitment, he conveyed all three. With a smile, he tried to push his oxygen mask out of the way, but to no avail. Her tears fell into his hair as he closed his eyes and slowly released his grip on her hand.

*   *   *

Twenty minutes south of the hospital, Elizabeth, sitting in the back seat of the McGuires' van, shouted to Bill. "Stop the car. I'm going back." She turned to Joyce, who was sitting next to her. "I've got to take him home."

"Elizabeth, we talked that all through at the hospital. We just can't take Peter home in the shape he's in."

"Mom," said David, who was riding shotgun, "I'm with you. We can't leave Dad in that hospital."

"Bill, will you please go back?"

"Elizabeth, you and your kids are exhausted. It's been an emotion-filled day. Let's get everyone home, get a good night's sleep and I'll bring you back in the morning."

Turning to look out of the back window, Elizabeth asked, "Are the Griffiths behind us?"

"I think so."

"Bill, Joyce, I know you're thinking about what's best for our family. But so am I, and I think what's best is bringing Peter back to Richmond with us. Would you be willing to let me use your van to go back to the hospital? You two can go on home with Frank and Jennifer." Elizabeth wasn't pleading. She was forceful. "I never want to have to come back to the memories of this day. Please take me back, or . . . or at least let me use your car."

Bill exited from the Baltimore-Washington Parkway and pulled over. The Griffiths eased to a stop behind him. Bill walked back to their car.

"We're going back for Peter," he told them. "Do you want to come?"

22

Monday, April 2

Frank Mazzetti knew his moment in the sun might be short-lived. But until his rival from Richmond took center stage, he was ready to bask in the news stories that chronicled his discovery of a missing employee. He was quoted extensively in the *Baltimore Sun* as an eyewitness to the tragic events at Anne Arundel Community Hospital. The story was picked up by the wire services, landing on the front pages of newspapers throughout the nation.

By nine in the morning, accolades were pouring into his office. Not once did he mention the source of his leads, or the ill-fated stakeout in Ephrata. To hear him tell the story, Mazzetti had personally taken charge of the investigation when it dragged into the second week and other investigators were being led on wild-goose chases to foreign countries. Although he praised Downes's dedication to Boget, in the same breath he wondered aloud why Downes had spent so much time with an accused murderer in a Cancún prison.

*   *   *

The carpet and passenger seat were still wet from the water that Mary Kennedy had used to clean blood from her car at two in the morning, but nothing else contradicted her comments to several employees about the quiet Sunday she had spent at home. She also told them that Richard

Donovan had gone home to Ireland to attend the funeral of the man who'd raised him after he was orphaned. No one questioned the story, and life proceeded smoothly until two FBI agents arrived at Kennedy and Associates and asked for the woman in charge.

Kennedy made her usual grand entrance and escorted the men to her office, where she was questioned again about her knowledge of Segal and Randolph, their clients and her growing stock portfolio.

"We believe that stocks were inadvertently credited to your account," one agent explained for the second time. "So, just to be sure that everything is okay, we would like to review your records of stock purchases for the past three months or so. Any documentation at all would be fine," he said, scratching his head and looking away. "You know, canceled checks . . . receipts from Michaels & Trent. Maybe your records will show when the trades were made."

Kennedy's response was disarming. All weekend long the agents had studied the case presented to them by the SEC and correlated it with the information passed on to them by the New York City police who had arrested Murray Ross. A dozen other interviews were being conducted simultaneously in New York, in an operation that the FBI expected to net a large number of drug dealers. Available evidence showed that there would not be any documentation to prove that the stock sales or the stock purchases were made. The FBI agents were certain they would have Kennedy in custody by the day's end.

Kennedy agreed to provide whatever records they needed. "It's a bit slow this morning," she said, "so I'd be happy to dig out the records." She opened the center drawer in her polished mahogany desk and pulled out a set of keys. "I don't like the whole world looking at my papers, so I keep them locked up in a private file cabinet."

In less than a minute, Kennedy produced folders containing transaction records for the current year and each of the previous two years. The agents were not sure exactly what they were looking for, but the paperwork in front of them looked like what they'd been told they would not find. Stacks of trade-confirmation notices on Michaels & Trent letterhead looked legitimate.

"May we take these?" asked the lead agent.

"No, they are my only copies. But I'll be glad to make copies of any particular trades in question." She noted the look of surprise on their faces and then asked, "You do have a list of the ones in question, don't you?"

"Yes, yes, we do," mumbled one of the agents, pulling a paper from his pocket. "Thanks for your cooperation."

*   *   *

By the time Elizabeth and her children arrived home and tumbled into bed, morning had arrived. When Josh Sprouse knocked on the front door at ten o'clock, only Kristin and her mother were awake. He was still in uniform from his overnight duty. He looked very official, though very tired.

"Mike asked me to drop by and tell you how sorry he was about what happened yesterday. He wanted to tell you himself, but he had some important personal business he has to attend to today."

"In Mexico, I bet," a sleepy Elizabeth said, motioning Josh to come in and sit down. "I don't know how he has the energy. I'm still trying to figure out what happened yesterday." She paused to stifle a yawn. "You want a cup of coffee or something?"

"No, I won't be staying."

Standing up with her baby cradled in her left arm, Elizabeth said, "Do you mind if I start some water for myself?" She didn't wait for her guest's response. "Why's Mike sorry? He didn't do anything . . . did he?"

"I don't think so. I guess he just wanted to say something."

"Well, if he tried to call, he wouldn't have gotten me. I've taken both lines off the hook so we could get some sleep. And I turned off the front doorbell."

"So I noticed. I didn't know you could."

"That was one of Peter's inventions." Elizabeth filled the tea kettle with water, lit a fire under it and, after transferring Kristin to her other arm, returned to the table where Josh had sat down. "The only problem is that I sometimes forget to turn it back on. So do you think Mike went to Mexico?"

"I'd be surprised if he wasn't already in Cancún. The last thing he said to me is that he would get Debbie out of jail if it was the last thing he ever did."

"He's quite a guy. He sure helped me these past two weeks. That's why I was so surprised when Frank Mazzetti called yesterday morning. I thought for sure Mike would find Peter. I didn't know that the company security people were doing anything to help."

Josh picked up his hat off the table and took a step toward the door. "We didn't either. I'll let Mike tell you the story when he gets back. I need to run and get to bed, but if there is anything at all that I can do for you, please call me."

"You aren't leaving already?" Elizabeth asked. "But what happened in Ephrata?"

"You wouldn't believe it if I told you. And, from the looks of things, we're both too tired to think about it now." Walking toward the door, the man in the crisp gray uniform said over his shoulder, "I'll call you later on— if you plug your phone back in."

*　　*　　*

Getting calls through to the Public Relations department at Virginia Bell was next to impossible. The news of Peter's discovery spread like wildfire, and everyone in the company was calling to Richmond for additional details. In Virginia's capital city, news media outlets were looking for the local slant on the national story. Reporters who were unable to reach Elizabeth Boget by phone searched for the names of family friends who could help them arrange an exclusive interview with Peter's wife.

For Janice Bland, doing double duty as News Media Relations manager and acting director of public relations, this had already been the most exhausting day of her career. She had been in the office since ten the previous evening and had been joined by two of her employees at midnight for a strategy meeting to plan for dealing with the news media.

At 10:30, she called all members of the staff into the library conference room and gave them an update on Peter's condition. Then she allowed them to describe the nature of the calls they were receiving and noted the questions for which there were no answers.

Of course, Megan Churchill had a few answers that nobody was interested in. "Well, it looks like we know who the next president is going to be. Mazzetti has wrapped it up," she offered.

Glaring at Megan, Janice said sternly, "We've got a lot more important things to worry about now. If everyone is straight, then let's get back to work." As the staff moved out to the ringing phones, Janice called to Lucy

Williams. "Do you have an update on the newsline?" she asked, referring to the company's dial-a-recording news service for employees.

"Updated at ten. And I've got bulletin copy in my computer waiting for a call from Mike Downes. We just need a quote and an okay from him."

"That's great." Then the woman who was serving in Peter's place signaled Lucy to come closer and, in a lower voice, asked, "What do you really think's going to happen to Peter?"

"I don't know. It's great to hear that's he's back in Richmond, But, you know, he's gotten some bad press over the past two weeks. But even so, if Mike moves up, Peter may get the nod too. They're good friends." The newsletter editor stopped speaking and closed her eyes momentarily. "Wait a minute. I'll leave the fortunetelling to Megan . . . even though I like my version of the future better."

"Well, I hope he gets back here fast. Another day like today—another week like the past two—and they'll have to commit me to an asylum."

*   *   *

The newspaper account of Trooper Hanks's successful defense of the assassins' target, and his work in getting a child hostage released by a fleeing assailant, was more therapeutic than anything the hospital could offer. Lying in a hospital bed one floor down from where the action had taken place, Hanks read the article over and over. The facts were wrong, but Hanks loved it anyway, especially the quote from an alleged eyewitness who said, "Even after he was shot and bleeding all over the floor, he kept after the man, finally forcing the guy to give the little boy up." Another person said that from behind her door she saw "the policeman diving into the air and catching the baby."

But Hanks's supervisor wasn't reading the paper. He was reading the police reports of actual eyewitnesses. Like Elizabeth Boget, Bill McGuire and members of the medical staff who were caring for Peter Boget. He also had in his hand the transcript of Rashad's call to 911 for help. But it was the anonymous report of Hanks's encounter at the Hechinger Home Center that led him to the conclusion that Hanks was not a hero, but a lone ranger whose actions had cost the lives of two good men, jeopardized the life of the man they were guarding, traumatized an entire family and placed the lives of many others in grave danger.

When Hanks's supervisor entered the trooper's room, the young man was all smiles.

"I guess you saw this in the paper," Hanks said, holding up the article for his boss to see.

His boss wasn't smiling. "Hanks, I have some bad news, and it can't wait until you're feeling better." Hanks blanched as the captain continued. "You tried to arrange an arrest at Hechinger's on Saturday, didn't you?"

"Who told you that?"

"And then you came here to play hero, didn't you? You've twice been warned that you have to stop playing supercop. But you don't stop. You keep placing lives in danger—including your own. Effective immediately, you're suspended pending a termination hearing. I'm recommending that you resign before the hearing. Or it's going to get ugly."

"You can't be serious."

"I'm sorry, Hanks, but I have no choice."

Hanks's displeasure was vented in a string of obscenities. Then he vowed, "You'll never get away with this. You can't fire a hero!"

*   *   *

"Cancún!" Earl Hendrick bellowed. "What are you doing in Cancún?"

"You told me to take a few days off to fish and swim and get some rest, and I decided you were right. I plan to stay the week, and—"

The Virginia Bell president cut Downes off. "What are you talking about? Don't you know that Peter's been found and that Mazzetti is strutting around Headquarters telling the world he found him?"

"I'm not surprised. He's probably just trying to make the most of his situation. How'd he find Peter, anyway?"

Hendrick was agitated, and the calm in Downes's voice was only making it worse. "What do you mean, 'how did he find him'? He is telling the world his security people tracked him down and . . ." Hendrick's voice abruptly dropped in volume and in intensity and the statement became a question. "Did you hear about what happened yesterday?"

"Where?" Downes wanted to know how much others were saying about the incident.

"It's all over the news. We are being inundated with calls. There was a shoot-out at the hospital and two men are dead."

"Is that all?"

"Isn't that enough for you?"

"I guess Mazzetti hasn't been telling the whole story. Ask him if he remembers talking to me after I was shot in the hall outside Peter's room."

The president couldn't believe what he was hearing. "You? Shot? Nobody told me you were there! How could you be there and in Cancún at the same time?"

"Earl, I know you've put your reputation behind me. I know that you have stood by me through some tough times. And I know that you don't like the thought that Mazzetti may be angling for your chair. But you have to trust me. First, Mazzetti did find Peter. I called for his help last week, and he cashed in on the information he located for me."

"He—"

"The next thing is that the man who shot Peter in the leg also shot me under my arm. I wish I could have gotten to him before he started shooting, but I didn't, because Mazzetti was right: I'm no detective. And speaking of Mazzetti, that man did a cruel thing. He blocked Peter's paycheck from getting to Elizabeth and caused almost as much emotional anguish as everything that went on yesterday. I'd like you to see what you can do to get Elizabeth some money so she can pay her mortgage and not have to be embarrassed that her checks are going to bounce."

"Mike—"

"And I didn't just come back to Cancún for the sun. Remember I told you last week about Debbie Steinbaugh? I'm here to help her get out of jail." Downes abruptly stopped his monologue, leaving a crackling silence on the long-distance line.

Eventually Mike's boss asked, "That is it?"

"No, I'd like you to transfer me to Sharon, please."

* * *

Martin Beale was dumbfounded when the calls from the FBI started coming to notify him that the agents had transaction receipts from the suspects he had identified. To the agent who had visited Mary Kennedy and reported that he had copies in his hand of dozens of the receipts, Beale simply said, "That's not possible. She can't have receipts, because the transactions never went through the trading system."

"Maybe not," the casual response came through the phone, "but you sent us a list of transactions, and we gave them to the woman and she pulled out receipts on Michaels & Trent letterhead for every one of them. She was cooperative, and there is no evidence that she runs anything but a legitimate business."

"No way."

"The reports will be on the fax in ten minutes. If you've got any questions, give us a call."

*   *   *

By midafternoon the entire Boget family was at the burn-trauma unit at the Medical College of Virginia, where the doctors and staff were giving Peter a lot of attention.

The unit's new young director had already mapped out a strategy to accelerate Peter's needed bone transplants and to get him home as quickly as possible. The doctor met Elizabeth and her family in the conference room.

"Mrs. Boget, I'm Clinton Moore." He extended his hand. "And this is Justin Spencer. He's our head nurse, who will be responsible for your husband's day-to-day care." Moore and Spencer sat down, and the director began speaking. "Your husband"—he looked at the children sitting at the table—"and your father is stable. He's had a rough night, but he's asked for you and that's a good sign.

"He's inhaled a lot of smoke and his lungs are still sensitive, but his sternum blocked the phosphorus from burning through to his organs. His bone is charred pretty badly, but his internal organs are all doing well."

"What about his heart?"

"Any severe burn places great stress on the heart. Smoke inhalation aggravates the situation, since more blood has to be pumped through the lungs to be oxygenated properly. The worst is clearly over, so his heart should be fine. His mental state is really more of a concern to me now than his heart."

Elizabeth waited for an explanation while her children fidgeted.

"He's probably been awake a fair amount during the past two weeks, but the medication keeps him from communicating. He's heard conversations, he's experienced pain, and he has probably been aware of the daily nursing ritual of having burnt flesh tweezed from his chest. It's not pleasant, and he may be having bad dreams. That's a lot of what the thrashing is all about.

"We have eased up on his pain medication so you could speak to him. If you're ready, we'll go." Dr. Moore smiled at the children. "Are you all ready to see your father?"

A roomful of bright eyes answered the question.

*   *   *

The flight to Miami, the overnight stay in a hotel near the airport and the morning flight to Cancún with Mike Downes gave Barry Whitehead a lot of time to think. He knew the bullet that had ripped through Downes was meant for him. He knew that his silence was enormously important to Mary Kennedy, or she would never have gone to the hospital. He knew that jail loomed as a strong possibility, yet what troubled him most was the thought that, if he went to jail, he might never get to see his children again.

He had figured they didn't want to see him, yet he couldn't get them out of his mind. With his world caving in around him, they represented the only good thing he had ever done. He realized that they would carry his seed to successive generations, and he wanted to see them face to face and tell them he was sorry—sorry for the way he had treated their mother, sorry for the way he had ignored them, sorry for failing to be a real father to them.

Whitehead didn't know where all these feelings were coming from, but they had become much stronger since he had encountered Sprouse and Downes—especially after he had come eye to eye with a killer and dodged a bullet that had his name written on it.

By the time Whitehead and Downes entered the office of Jorge Soto and exchanged introductions, neither of them was interested in small talk. "Jorge," Downes began, "I want you to listen to this man's story and then tell me what you can do with it to get Debbie Steinbaugh out of jail." Then he leaned back and motioned for the draftsman to begin.

In painful, choppy sentences interspersed with long pauses, Whitehead told his story. Neither Downes nor the balding lawyer interrupted.

Finally Whitehead concluded, "I guess that's about all."

Soto looked at Downes. "Either you're one great acting coach, or he's the real thing."

Downes smiled. "I told you I'd find him. What do you think?"

Soto turned his attention to Whitehead, peering through the top half of his bifocals. "If I told you that your testimony could get you five years in prison, maybe three suspended and nine months off for good behavior, would you tell it to our local prosecutor?"

"I didn't come to get myself locked up." Whitehead pointed a thumb at Downes. "I came because he told me that my testimony might help get an innocent woman out of jail. Can't you just tell them what I said?"

"What do you think?"

Whitehead looked down into his lap and didn't respond.

"Barry, my friend, I don't know why you're really here, but if you want to help get an innocent woman out of jail, it's going to take some sacrifice from all of us." Motioning to Downes's arm, which was cradled by a sling, he said, "I don't know if Mike's arm has anything to do with this, but he has already given a lot to help a woman he didn't even know before last week. You know, he's not some paid private eye. He's an ordinary citizen with an extraordinary sense of duty."

Downes tried to interrupt, but Soto waved him off.

"I don't see too many people like him in my work around here. Everybody seems to be doing their thing for themselves. It's always 'get me out of trouble' or 'help me get the guy who's done me in' or 'how can I be sure that I get my money even if the others go broke?' But Mike came in here wanting to know what he could do to help get Debbie out of jail. And I'm not talking about some fashion model here. I'm talking about a woman who the first day I talked to her was incoherent, dirty, smelly and obviously depressed. She also had been booked on charges that guaranteed her a long prison stay. But this man took the time to listen, test the story and then go looking for you. And, like he told me on the phone, he also found the person he started out looking for in the first place. That's quite a man. But now, he can't help Debbie unless you tell your story to the prosecutor. What do you think?"

Whitehead sat motionless and speechless for nearly a minute. Soto and Downes waited. The latter observed that the Peter Boget look-alike was looking less and less like Peter with each day of new growth in his beard and with his new sandy-colored hair. Finally Whitehead spoke. "I'm not ready to go to jail."

A disappointed Downes responded first. "I understand, Barry. We will not coerce you. You have done everything I've asked you to do. Anything else must be your choice."

"My friend," the lawyer said in earnest, "I have only one chance of using your testimony. I've got to show the police that you are who you say you are before you ever meet Miss Steinbaugh, before you ever talk to her. I've got to establish that you left the country when you said you did and that you returned today. But if I can promise you that you will not be arrested if you tell your story, will you tell it one more time?"

"I thought you said if I tell it, I'll go to jail."

"I have one angle. It's a long shot, but I can try."

Whitehead shrugged his shoulders in a way that Soto took for a yes. He picked up his phone and dialed. For nearly ten minutes the lawyer yelled, whispered, argued and cajoled. Finally, he triumphantly lowered the phone to its cradle.

"It's all worked out. We go to the courthouse now and meet with my uncle, who is one of the judges. One of the local prosecutors will join us. They are sending for Miss Steinbaugh." Looking at Whitehead, he said, "Now, after you tell your story, you will be asked to produce some evidence that what you are telling us is true. Until you produce the evidence, you will not be charged with any crime. The meeting is set up for siesta time, which is highly unusual, but I have many friends in the court, and I don't ask for many favors these days. The few I ask for are usually granted, especially since I told him that we would pay for his dinner tonight."

"You go to dinner with the judge?" Downes asked.

"Not exactly. He goes by himself, but he decided he would have about five thousand dollars' worth of dinner tonight."

"Five thousand dollars?"

"Yes, he gets very hungry when he's working on special cases."

After sharing in the laughter, Downes leaned forward. "Thank you, Jorge."

"I should be thanking you! Without your work, there would be very little I could do for Debbie Steinbaugh."

23

Amatron in the jail handed Debbie a dress and indicated that she was to change clothes because she was going before a judge.

"Vas a ver al juez."

"What are you saying?" asked Debbie.

In hard-to-understand English, the matron replied, "See judge!"

"But Mr. Soto said my case wasn't coming up for weeks. Why am I going downtown?"

"Cállate y ponte la ropa!" the matron shouted, pushing her hands through the air.

Debbie didn't understand, but the comment wasn't friendly and it seemed obvious that the woman wanted her to hurry.

*   *   *

From his hideaway in Brighton, England, Mark Randolph placed a call to Mary Kennedy. Unlike half the people in America, he had no knowledge of the incident in Baltimore. The call was short, Randolph wanting to know what had happened to Murray Ross, and Kennedy wanting to know where he was.

"For the time being, I'm where no one can find me."

"What I need to know is how your transaction receipts will stand up under scrutiny."

"Who's looking?"

"The FBI, maybe the SEC."

"That's not good."

"Why?"

"They could ruin Michaels & Trent."

"What?"

"I've attached a few lines of code to my program so when it's discovered it will look like the trades were made by the partners to cover some illegal activities . . . I needed some insurance."

"So the receipts will stand up?"

"They should. They're the real thing, printed on real Michaels & Trent paper."

Kennedy smiled. "I like your style, Randolph."

"Too bad I don't like yours. Life is short enough as it is. We don't need to be blowing people away. It's a lot easier to let the computer do your dirty work for you. You want to move money around in checking accounts? That's not easy, but possible. Bypass the phone company's measured service? Steal long-distance service? Real tough, but we do it every day." He paused. "Destroy all of the files in an architectural firm's computers? Piece of cake."

"Are you threatening me?"

"I don't need to get into your computers to destroy you. But I can. No," Randolph said, "I just need to call the FBI and help them with their investigation."

"You bas—"

The phone went dead before Kennedy completed her sentence.

*　　*　　*

At Peter's bedside, the Boget children effervesced with excitement. One by one their father called them close enough to whisper a few words. "David, you're the man of the house for now. Take good care of your mother and your brothers and sisters. I'll be home on Sunday. I love you, son." He signaled to his oldest daughter. "I love you, Lauren." Peter's smile was aborted with a wince of pain. "Daniel, how's your soccer coming?"

"Good, Dad, real good."

"I want to be out there to see you next week."

"You know we're not playing on Saturday because of Easter, but you can come and see us the next week."

Peter struggled with a whispered "I will."

Jonathan climbed onto a chair so he could see his father, but said nothing. "Hey, boy, I missed you," Peter said. He tried to reach out to Jonathan, but the straps on his arms limited his movement. "I think we have a fishing date. Don't let me forget."

By the time Elizabeth stepped forward with Kristin, Peter was experiencing excruciating pain in his chest. Without medication, the fiery pain in his leg was also distracting him. Tears were in his eyes as he whispered to his wife, "It hurts, Elizabeth. It really hurts." Then he began to cry, and nurse Spencer twisted a knob on an intravenous feeding tube and allowed relief to enter his bloodstream. He slid Peter's oxygen mask back into place.

"He just needs a little rest," Spencer said. "If you'd like, you can stay with him here for a while."

*   *   *

The office of Judge Héctor Cabrillo embraced the Mayan theme that the government fostered with paintings of ruins, prints of Mayan art, and nearly a dozen simulated artifacts stretching across the front of a richly carved desk. The office made a statement about the power of the Mexican judiciary—a statement that was not lost on Mike Downes or Barry Whitehead as they were led into the room by their lawyer and newfound friend Jorge Soto. An English-speaking prosecutor joined the four men in the room.

After a lengthy exchange of greetings, Judge Cabrillo set his agenda for the meeting and made it perfectly clear what he would and would not do. Though heavily accented, his English was understandable, and in deference to his visitors, that was the language he spoke.

"Mr. Whitehead, please begin. Speak slowly and clearly. Do you understand?"

Whitehead nodded and began telling his story, beginning with the flat tire on the Capitol Beltway and ending with his return to Cancún. He was interrupted frequently by both the prosecutor and the judge, who sought clarification and tried to trap the man into saying something that would suggest he was lying. But Whitehead's story held. The two officials discussed in Spanish what they had just heard and correlated it with the testimony already given by Debbie Steinbaugh. The two accounts were surprisingly consistent, with just enough difference to suggest that Whitehead and Steinbaugh each brought a differing perspective and had not collaborated to tell the same story.

Judge Cabrillo dismissed Downes and Whitehead to an adjoining room and summoned the prisoner, who had been brought to a holding cell in the building. Debbie's hands were cuffed, her hair was matted, and her face was fearful as two guards ushered her into the judge's chambers. She was buoyed by the sight of her lawyer sitting near the judge's desk.

"I want to ask you a few questions," the judge began.

Debbie looked at Soto, who nodded that she should answer.

The grilling lasted for thirty minutes, with all three men asking questions. Debbie faltered at times but answered to the best of her ability. She had the greatest difficulty describing the physical attack, but the men were more interested in what Barry had said than what he had done, until the point when he shook Jan Stevens from his back.

They also probed her description and analysis of how and why he took her wallet, what it looked like and what was in it, as well as her description of chair placements and the appearance of the room when she and Whitehead entered.

Then the judge asked a question that Debbie was totally unprepared to answer. "If I could bring this Barry in here, would you identify him for me?"

Debbie was suddenly swept into a flood of questions: *Where was Mike Downes when she really needed him? Where was Liz? What did the judge really want?*

The judge rephrased the question, thinking she might not have understood. "If Mr. Soto found this man you call Barry, and could bring him to Cancún, would you be willing to meet him and identify him?"

"Would he have to see me?"

"Yes."

"I don't know," she began to sob. "I'm afraid."

Judge Cabrillo pulled a box of tissues from behind his desk and pushed them toward the woman. Then he spoke in Spanish to Soto, who quickly left the room. Moments later, Soto returned with Mike Downes. He wanted to comfort the weeping woman with an embrace, but felt awkward. Debbie was not aware of his presence until he spoke from behind her chair.

"Debbie," he said.

She spun her head around in response to his voice. "You're back!" She excitedly lifted her cuffed hands. He extended a hand briefly and then withdrew it.

"I've brought Barry with me." Her jaw dropped as a wave of disbelief oscillated through her body. "Señor Soto says that Judge Cabrillo would like you to meet him and identify him."

She tensed her body and seemed to want to draw herself into a shell. Her voice quivered, "I know . . . Will you be here?" Downes looked at the judge, who looked for the assent of the prosecutor and the lawyer. The judge nodded and so did Mike.

*   *   *

An angry Roland Hanks was talking to his mother, who dropped by Anne Arundel Community Hospital to spend some time with her hero son. Only he wasn't acting much like a hero.

"You know, Mom, they don't know just how good I am. They're always putting me down."

"That's probably because they feel inferior," comforted his mother. "You're so smart that they're worried you're going to take away their jobs." Puffing up her chest, she added, "You should be proud. I am!"

Hanks's response was interrupted by the ring of the phone at his bedside. He picked it up before his mother reacted. He was still sullen, and his sharp greeting reflected his mood. He immediately recognized the voice on the other end of the line.

"You don't sound too chipper, Roland. I thought all those nice articles would have cheered you up. I'm sorry I couldn't be with you yesterday, but my schedule kept me here. I believe you met some of my employees though, and unfortunately, one did not come home. Can you tell me why?" Hanks just listened. "I'm afraid you failed your test, and now we will have to deal with you in a more personal way."

Hanks waved his mother out of the room and whispered into the phone. "I don't know who you are, but I'm going to find you and destroy you."

"I'm afraid you have that backwards." Kennedy's voice was as smooth as silk. "It is you who will be destroyed. You apparently did not have the opportunity to drive your car last evening."

"What about my car?" he shot back.

"We left a present for you in the glove compartment. Our way of saying thank-you for a job well done. But that was before you decided not to play with us, and we were unable to pick up the bag of cocaine we left for you. I hope you don't mind, but we'll be calling your supervisor this afternoon and asking him to pick it up and hold it for you. I'm sure he would be more than happy to do that."

Hanks's anger bubbled over in invective. But when the swearing stopped and his mind cleared, he asked, "What do you want?"

From the tone of his voice, Mary Kennedy knew she held another man in her web.

*   *   *

The faint steady swish of cool air pushing through louvered vents in the ceiling of Judge Cabrillo's office was the only sound that could be heard in the room. The usually busy hallways were quiet during the afternoon siesta, and no one said anything while awaiting Barry Whitehead's arrival.

The room's warm glow could not diminish the tension in the air as Downes escorted Barry to his chair in front of the judge's desk. The two men sat down. Neither Barry nor Debbie looked at the other.

Judge Cabrillo turned his attention to Debbie. "Is this the man you met at the Hyatt?" He dipped his head toward Barry.

Debbie's heart was thumping beneath the sundress that the matron had brought for her to wear. Perspiration was dripping down her arms. Trying to get the butterflies in her stomach to fly in formation, she slowly turned. Both the prosecutor and the judge studied her intently, looking for a clue that this was all a charade. When her eyes fell on Barry, Debbie gasped. The hair color and the beard surprised her, but there was no mistaking the man sitting six feet from her. She began trembling, pushing herself back into the leather chair. She wanted to disappear, and the judge could see it. She opened her mouth to say "Yes." But it wouldn't come.

The next five seconds of silence seemed like an eternity. Then Judge Cabrillo spoke to Barry Whitehead. "I promised Señor Soto that I will take no action against you unless you can prove that you participated in the action that led to the death of Señorita Stevens." He spoke slowly so that Barry would understand. "I also tell him that I will not consider releasing

Señora Steinbaugh on bail unless I have a witness who testifies she did not kill the woman in her room. I believe you have done something to this woman," he said, pointing to Debbie, "but for now I only have stories. What evidence do you have? Will you present it? But remember, if you do, Señor Alvarez will want to arrest you."

Barry sat motionless. Debbie had pulled herself into a ball on the chair, her knees wrapped by her cuffed hands. She was crying softly. Soto had pulled his chair close to hers and rested his hand on her forearm.

"Please look at that woman," the judge said.

Barry obeyed, instantly recognizing the woman he had left sitting on the bed when he fled into the night. She had the same look of terror, revulsion and helplessness that he had seen on her face. The memories of that night came flooding back—his pleading, then his ordering and then the physical abuse—like a motion picture in his mind that rolled by one frame at a time. He squeezed his eyes to block the images, and he cupped his ears to shut out the sound, but the movie wouldn't stop. Finally it came to an end, and the last words he'd spoken on that night echoed in his brain. He opened his eyes. To the woman whose future now depended on him, he said, "I'm sorry. I'm so, so sorry."

The sound of his voice hit Debbie like a blast. She lurched back violently. Despite Soto's quick reaction, she tipped over her chair and fell to the floor. Pulling her hands up to protect herself from her fall, she snagged her leg on the edge of the handcuffs and ripped a long gash in her left shin. By the time Soto and Downes could react, she was on her knees. No one noticed the injury until she stood up, revealing the blood on the rug. The judge rang for assistance. Two police officers ran into the room but didn't know what to do. The prosecutor jumped to his feet and, speaking rapidly, ordered one of them to get a first-aid kit.

Barry moved to Debbie's aid, but Downes pushed him back toward his chair. Soto righted the woman's chair. While Downes pressed a wad of the judge's tissues against her leg, Debbie apologized to the judge, who had not yet seen the bloodstain on his carpet.

The policeman returned with the first-aid kit, poured some peroxide on the wound and wrapped it in gauze. Judge Cabrillo suggested that they quit, but Soto and Downes pleaded for five more minutes to allow Barry to respond.

But the spell was broken. Barry had had time to think, and he'd decided he didn't want to go to jail.

Downes knew that the door to Debbie's freedom was swinging shut. He had to do something, say something. "Lord," he prayed to himself, "you've brought me this far. You aren't going to leave me hanging, are you?" And then, while the judge waited for something to happen, Downes revised his prayer. "I'm sorry, Lord. Forgive my arrogance. Thank you for giving me this opportunity to be here with this judge. Grant him wisdom."

Cabrillo eyed the two parties. He spoke twice in Spanish to the prosecutor and once to Soto. Then he asked Debbie, "Why do you want to go free?"

Without hesitation she said, "My girls. I have two daughters, Jennifer and Laura. I lost them when I was young and foolish. They live with my former husband. I can never be the mother to them that I should have been, but for the past two years I've been trying to put my life back together. I'm trying to be their mother again." Tears streamed down her face as she spoke, each phrase filled with compassion. "If only to see them once more, if only to ask for their forgiveness for not being there when they needed me, if only to tell them I love them—that's . . . that's why I want to go free."

Downes knew that her words had struck a responsive chord within the prosecutor and the judge. Then he noticed that Barry was crying.

Her story sounded too much like Barry's own story, but he knew he would never be a father to his children. He wanted to see them again, but he could not think how that might be possible. Now he realized that by helping reunite someone else with her children, he could vicariously live out his own dream.

He looked at Judge Cabrillo. In voice that was just audible above the sound of the air conditioning, he breathed, "I have her driver's license."

The revelation took Downes and Soto by surprise. They had been hoping Barry would be able to tell the police something about the scene or the incident that only the police would know, or name a witness that he hadn't mentioned before. They'd never considered the driver's license. Early on, when Debbie had mentioned the wallet, Downes assumed that nobody would walk around with evidence that could put him in jail. But Barry Whitehead did.

Five sets of eyes turned toward the man who had not had a moment of relief from the pressures of a failed life since he had left Norfolk on that fateful Thursday afternoon. He followed his revelation with a plea. "I don't want to go to jail. I have been in captivity all of my life." He dropped his head into his hands to cover his tears, yet he spoke clearly. "I don't know, maybe I can find some freedom by helping another go free. Maybe I can find out what it means to do something for someone else, like Peter did for me when he stopped to help me on the highway. Maybe I will learn what makes a man set aside everything to go looking for a friend." Barry paused to wipe his eyes. "I don't want to go to jail, but . . . but this woman needs to see her children. I hope she gets to do that."

Judge Cabrillo talked briefly with Soto and Alvarez, then dismissed the people assembled in his office. Soto explained to Downes and Whitehead, "The judge asked Alvarez and me to prepare for a hearing by the end of the week. He wants Barry to turn over the driver's license to police in front of the prosecutor as soon as we leave here. With the evidence in hand, he will charge Barry with petty larceny and assault and arrest him. Until the hearing, Debbie will remain in jail."

Soto continued his explanation. "Now I must warn you, prosecutors like murder convictions on their records. No matter how good you feel right now, this will be a long week. Not only will we have to go over everything that was said today, but we must turn up every shred of evidence we can." Looking up at Barry, Soto said, "You've done a noble act, my friend, but now I'm going to need your help to remember everything you said or saw or did from the moment you arrived in Cancún until the moment you left. What happens in the courtroom will depend on your testimony and whatever Mike here can help me with."

Barry nodded.

"I'll do whatever it takes," Downes volunteered.

*   *   *

After dinner in the hospital cafeteria, Elizabeth and her children returned to Peter's side. Three bouquets of flowers had arrived during their absence. Bill and Joyce McGuire were in the hallway, as were three members of the Virginia Bell public relations staff.

A burn-unit attendant with a blooming plant in her hands walked into Peter's room. "Mrs. Boget, this is from a Mr. Hendrick." She turned to go and then looked back at Elizabeth. "You sure have a lot of caring friends.

My goodness, our telephone has never been this busy!"

Elizabeth smiled and turned her attention to Peter, who, though only half awake, smiled his joy at being in the presence of his family. Not knowing whether he would understand what she was saying, Elizabeth nonetheless began recounting the story of the previous two and a half weeks. She asked questions for which she expected no answers, but was surprised to see Peter's left hand moving back and forth as if he were writing on an invisible sheet of paper. She pulled back his oxygen mask and listened for a response to why he was on the east side of the beltway on the night of the accident.

"The Bulls and Bullets . . . Who won?"

David laughed when he heard his dad speak. "Were you going to the basketball game?"

Peter nodded gently. "I guess I should have gone straight to the hotel. Everything would have been fine today."

"Maybe," Elizabeth responded, not wanting to tell her husband about the horrible disaster he could have been in. "We'll never know."

24

Standing by Peter's bed while Dr. Moore examined his chest wound, Elizabeth listened as the doctor marveled at her husband's progress. "I'm not a religious man, but someone is looking out for him. If the flare had burned another minute, it would have burned through his diaphragm and he probably wouldn't have survived. If he hadn't been taken by helicopter to one of the best burn-trauma units in the nation, he probably wouldn't have survived his first forty-eight hours. And if he didn't have someone pulling for him, he wouldn't be where he is today."

"Someone *is* pulling for him," Elizabeth said, smiling. "When will we be able to take him home?"

"By the end of the month, maybe sooner. After that he'll be able to check back in for his bone and skin grafts. They'll take six months or longer. The bullet wound will be completely healed in a week or so."

No longer on oxygen, the partially awake Peter added his own commentary. "I want to go home for Easter."

The doctor responded. "You're in good shape, but not that good. You can't imagine what the pain will be like when we take you completely off the medication, but I can tell you it will be unbearable."

"Doc, they beat Jesus till his back was raw. Will it hurt that badly?" Peter asked.

"I don't know."

"If he could survive a beating, a crown of thorns pressed on his head and death by crucifixion, I think I can endure a little pain for my family. Please let me go home for Easter."

* * *

For four days Jorge Soto and Mike Downes, working with three assistants, turned Cancún and half of North America upside-down looking for witnesses and evidence. In the end, a deposition from a woman in Raleigh, North Carolina, and the testimony of a housekeeper at the Mayan Holiday convinced Judge Cabrillo that the testimonies of Barry Whitehead and Debbie Steinbaugh were essentially accurate.

Through hotel records, a travel agent and a lawyer, Mike reached the woman who had occupied the room directly across from the one in which Debbie and Jan had stayed. The woman had been leaving her room when she heard the door across the hall opening. Through her peephole, she observed a man and a woman entering the room. She returned to the lobby and with her husband headed out for a night on the town. She had never been questioned, because the police believed she was not in during the incident. The housekeeper had been questioned earlier, but her testimony had been ignored by police since it was inconsistent with the conclusion they had already drawn.

During the week, by special arrangements made by Judge Cabrillo, Mike spent ten minutes each day in separate sessions with Debbie and Barry at the Cancún jail, learning more about them and discussing details of the incident. Mike couldn't figure out why Barry was insisting that much more cocaine was in the Honda when he abandoned it on the beltway than the police reported. If the trunk was locked and Barry didn't have the key, who could have gotten into the trunk before the police . . . unless it *was* the police? But such thoughts weren't germane to the hearing on Friday, so Mike dismissed them from his mind.

Debbie's last night was spent in the holding cell at the police station while her papers were processed. Mike stayed with her at the station throughout the night. Then he made one last visit to the jail to thank Barry for his noble and courageous act, and to reaffirm his promise to help get him out.

Finally the papers were complete, the prisoner was released and Jorge Soto, Michael Downes and Deborah Steinbaugh stepped through the door of the police station, into the warm morning sun.

"I can't believe it's over," sang Debbie as she jumped and threw her hands into the air. "I'm going home, I'm going home!"

Before either of the men knew what was going on, Debbie grabbed each and planted kisses on their cheeks. Then she danced to the parking lot.

At the airport, Mike and Debbie said their goodbys to Señor Soto and Señorita Escobar, who joined them for the farewell. "I can never thank you enough for all you've done for me," Debbie said, embracing the consular agent. "I'll never forget you."

*   *   *

With too many government agents looking for too many things in too many places, Mary Kennedy sent a patched-up Patrick O'Hearn back to Ireland. He and Mark Randolph did not recognize each other when they passed in the crowded US Air terminal at New York's Kennedy Airport. O'Hearn hurt too much to notice much of anything. Randolph had a singular objective in mind: accessing the computer at the offices of Kennedy and Associates.

*   *   *

"Peter, how are you? You're looking a lot better than when I found you last week." Frank Mazzetti was friendly, too friendly, but Peter, his comprehension clouded by the effects of his sedative, didn't recognize the subterfuge.

"What brings you here on the Easter weekend?" Peter responded in a hoarse whisper.

"Just thought I'd drop in and see how you are doing."

The two exchanged pleasantries, though Peter was nowhere near as talkative as he had been before the accident. Then Frank subtly shifted gears and started talking about computers. Taking advantage of Peter's dulled senses, he zeroed in on the real reason for his visit. "What's your strategy for correlating your desk files with those on your laptop?"

"Aside from the personal files on the laptop, I download the files I'm working with every evening. Why'd you ask?"

"It's nothing. We just noticed that you had some parallel files, but we couldn't recognize any pattern. We went through both of them when we were looking for clues to what happened to you."

"I guess that's how Debbie got involved," Peter offered.

After a few additional exchanges on nothing in particular, Frank stood up and began to excuse himself. "I'm sure glad you're feeling better," he said."I want to wish you the best of luck. Get back to work soon. We need you here in Virginia." Then he walked toward the door, paused and turned back. "Oh, Peter, one last thing. My boys are trying to wrap up their reports on your disappearance, and Piper asked me to ask you the password to the encrypted file on your desk computer so he can say he scanned it and didn't find anything that could help with his investigation. It's just routine." Frank's tone was deeply apologetic. Before Peter could answer, he added, "Oh, forget it. Our investigation can wait till you get back."

Peter took the bait. "No, that's fine. I was about ready to share it with them anyway. It's just some research I've been doing. The password is HACKATTACK—one word, no punctuation, just like it sounds."

"I'll try to remember that," said Frank, backing out the door. "Now you take it easy. I'll try to get by again in a week or so."

"Thanks, thanks for all your help." Peter watched as Frank disappeared out the door. He started to press the button that would release a painkiller into his intravenous fluid. But he changed his mind, pulled up his blanket and closed his eyes.

*   *   *

When Debbie and Mike arrived at the home of Liz and Norwood Clark, a joyous celebration began. Friends and family took turns hugging, kissing and speaking their greetings to the woman whose release from prison had been as unexpected as her incarceration.

Well into the celebration, John Clark approached the foster sister from whom he had distanced himself for over two decades. "Debbie, I'm glad you're back," he said quietly. Then he hugged her for the first time in his life. "I'm sorry. We're all sorry you had to go through such a terrible experience."

Debbie backed out of the embrace and looked up into John's face. "I'm the one who should be sorry—and I am. Sorry that I never gave you or Mom and Dad or any of you guys any reason to want to be part of my life. My days in that jail gave me plenty of time to think. Can you ever forgive me?"

His smile said yes. "You're home; that's what really matters."

Shirley and Liz joined them, nodding their heads in agreement.

Despite Debbie's weariness, her countenance said more about her release than any words could. The woman was stunning. Yet when Mike Downes looked at her, he saw much more. He saw the inner beauty he had discovered, piece by piece, during the minutes and hours he had spent with her at the barred door in the Cancún jail.

But despite his attraction to this woman and to the family that hailed him as a hero, Mike knew the time had come to return to Virginia. The corporation man who had tasted another side of life for three unforgettable weeks finally pulled himself away from the festivities. To Liz and Norwood's insistence that he stay—and twelve-year-old Jennifer's asking if he was going to marry her mom—Mike responded that he had booked an overnight flight from Colorado Springs to Richmond.

*   *   *

Sitting in the chair beside his bed, Peter Boget gingerly pulled a pair of green cotton pants over the bandage covering the bullet wound on his right leg. The inability to use his bandaged right hand made the task doubly difficult. A matching hospital shirt was already covering his upper torso. Once the pants were in place, he slid a pair of paper booties over his sock-covered feet. He was aware of his injuries, but for the time being his nerve endings were not able to send their messages to his brain. He calculated that the pain would kick in in about thirty minutes and would become nearly unbearable in an hour.

He stepped into the quiet hall. To his right, the trauma room was abuzz with activity, but the corridor to his left was empty. He limped quickly to the double doors and stepped through into the tiny vestibule. The woman behind the sliding glass window to his left looked up with great surprise.

"Mr. Boget? What are you doing?"

Peter hesitated. Then, holding his bandaged finger to his lips, he said, "Shhh. I'm on a secret mission. It's something I've got to do. Please don't tell a soul." Then he slipped through the second set of double doors and turned left. By the time the woman ran around the reception desk to follow him, Peter Boget had disappeared.

*   *   *

After the last of her children went to bed, Elizabeth Boget tiptoed to the attic and pulled four Easter baskets out of a large box. She brought them down to her bedroom and filled them with jelly beans, pink and yellow marshmallow bunnies, a popcorn bunny and an assortment of chocolate bunnies and eggs. Even though the funds were tight, she had spent the few dollars she had on the children. She and Peter used traditions to communicate a connectedness with their past and to help provide common threads to tie their children and, someday, their grandchildren together through succeeding generations. The greatest Easter tradition was celebrating the resurrection of Jesus at the dawn service beside the lake in Brandermill. But finding hidden Easter baskets was also part of the annual celebration.

Her work was interrupted by the ring of the telephone.

"Elizabeth." The voice was a hoarse whisper. "It's me, Peter. I need your help."

"What's wrong? Where are you?"

"I just figured it all out. Mazzetti's out to destroy us. You've got to help."

"Mazzetti? Peter, are you all right?"

"I gave him a password to my computer. He's going to find some information I forgot I put in there. I've got to get it out."

Elizabeth was alarmed more by the desperation in Peter's voice than by what he was saying. "Peter, it's after eleven. We'll be over right after church tomorrow. We can talk about it then."

"Tomorrow may be too late. I've got to fix it tonight."

Elizabeth didn't like what she was hearing. "Is there a nurse there that I can talk to, Peter? You don't sound like yourself."

"Elizabeth, I am myself for the first time in three weeks. I cut down on the medication to see how bad this pain really is, and as my head became clear, I realized that Mazzetti tricked the password out of me while I was under. He may have already been over there . . . He might be there now. If he reads the file, I'll probably lose my job."

"Peter, just relax," Elizabeth said calmly. "I'll call Bill and come on down tonight, if you really think I should."

"Don't bother Bill, just get down here as fast as you can. Meet me in the parking garage under the Bell building, on the green level. I'll be there in twenty minutes. Oh, and bring my extra electronic key."

"Peter," Elizabeth said sharply, "You can't get out of that hospital. The doctor said—"

"I'm already out. This is about my job and our future, Elizabeth. Please come quickly."

*   *   *

Ten blocks from the hospital, Frank Mazzetti was totally engrossed in the information that scrolled up on Peter Boget's computer screen.

The DBS file, "Destroying Basic Service: How Computer Hackers Can Shut Down the Network," was filled with anecdotes about attempts to gain control of local and long-distance electronic switching systems. It was a compendium of innovative schemes, with actual computer code interspersed with text. After each story, Peter had listed the name of the person alleged to have used the scheme, the switching machine or control center on which the attempt was made and the computer bulletin board from which the information was retrieved. He also listed a confidence rating from A to E on the reliability of the information.

Mazzetti intently read each item, such as the scheme of "Mark the Shark" of Connecticut to trick the phone company's SS-7 into adding a factor of two to each digit of the calling number to prevent the called party from getting an accurate readout on who was doing the calling. The explanation told how the hacker used the scheme to keep his employer from discovering who was accessing the M & T computer at night.

Mazzetti couldn't believe it. Peter Boget's document contained more data on more ways to steal phone service or disrupt the network than Mazzetti had ever heard. And he had heard a lot.

*   *   *

Peter Boget limped toward the quiet, vacant streets of Richmond's business district, looking decidedly out of place in his hospital garb. As he hobbled around the corner at Cary Street, the imposing Virginia Bell building came into view. He stepped into a darkened entryway to get out of the cold air and catch his breath. His bare arms were not used to 50-degree temperatures.

Peter stood trembling for a full minute and then dashed to the garage under the telephone company building. An uneasy Elizabeth was waiting for him in a locked and running car. When she saw her husband, she said, "Peter, are you okay? You look terrible. What are you doing? What are *we* doing?"

"I'm fine," he said unconvincingly, "I really am. Did you bring the key?"

"Yes, but Peter—"

"Let's go."

*   *   *

Rain fell on the car as Debbie drove through the streets of Colorado Springs. Mike asked if she had ever been to Virginia.

"For the past year, that's been high on my list of places to visit," she said, staring at the wet road ahead of her. "I'd love to see Peter and Elizabeth and meet their children. And now that I know you're there, I'd very much like to visit."

Mike watched the wipers slapping back and forth as the car pulled up to a red light. He said nothing while the car idled in the rain, leaving Debbie to wonder what he was thinking. At the next intersection, he finally said, "I'd like to have you visit too."

Debbie's response was tinged with remorse. "I'm afraid that after Cancún and all the legal bills, I won't be doing any traveling for quite a while."

"I see."

Debbie had a hundred things she wanted to tell Mike, but the words would not form in her mouth. Mike, too, was unable to articulate the feelings that he was having trouble understanding and acknowledging.

The silence lasted as they reached the airport and ran from the rain-soaked parking lot to the terminal. It lasted through the ride up the escalator and the walk through the security checkpoint. At the gate, Mike seemed incapable of initiating the goodby, and Debbie was unwilling to. In the nearly vacant terminal, a few family members and friends milled around the thirty-eight passengers lined up to board the late-night flight to the East Coast.

Mike stood at the end of the line with a ticket jacket in one hand and his suitcase in the other. Standing beside him, Debbie fought back the emotions that were welling up inside her, but her head soon lost the battle with her heart. Tears filled her eyes. Still, she could say nothing.

Mike turned and looked at her. The woman standing before him bore little resemblance to the person he had encountered at the Cancún jail. For the first time since his wife died, he gazed into the eyes of a woman for whom he felt passion as well as compassion.

He transferred the airline ticket jacket into the hand that held his suitcase and reached his still-sore arm out to Debbie the way he had at the door of steel bars. This time there was no guard to stop him. Leaning close to her, in an unsteady voice Mike whispered the lines of a Robert Frost poem. "But I have promises to keep . . . and miles to go before I sleep." Then he disappeared down the long tunnel that connected the terminal to the Boeing 727 that would transport him out of her life.

*   *   *

Eleven floors above the garage, only the lamp on Peter's desk and the glow of his computer monitor illuminated the office. Frank Mazzetti reset the calendar and clock on Peter's computer. The disk containing a copy of Peter's original document nestled in his pocket. He checked one last time to be sure the computer would show that the last change to the DBS file took place before March 15. Then he shut down the machine. He had more information than he needed. Not only would Peter be gone, but Mike Downes and Earl Hendrick would be so disgraced they would have no choice but to step aside.

When he looked up, he was startled by the two people standing in the shadow of the doorway. "Peter? Is that you?" he asked. Mazzetti masked his surprise with the smoothness of a politician working a crowd. "Mrs. Boget." He nodded a greeting. "Are you okay? What are you doing here on a Saturday night?"

"I was going to ask you the same question."

Mazzetti answered in a compassionate voice. "Before any of my boys came by to check out your computer, I thought I'd—" He stood, walked around the desk and then stopped. "You look awful, Peter." Looking at Elizabeth, he said, "I don't know why you're here, but don't you think that Peter should be in the hospital?"

"I don't know why I'm here either, but maybe you can tell me. Why on earth is a vice president from Washington prowling around my husband's office at midnight on a Saturday night—on Easter weekend, no less? Don't you think people will think this is pretty strange?"

"We don't need to talk about it," Mazzetti said smoothly. "I just wanted to be sure that there was nothing embarassing or incriminating in the computer. After all you've been through, I didn't want one of my zealous people—who had mentioned that they thought that some personal letters were in the machine—to create a stir. But, now that you're here, you may want to take care of that yourself . . . That is why you're here, isn't it?"

"You've seen it, haven't you?" Peter asked.

"Why, no," Mazzetti responded. "I just arrived."

The adrenaline pumping through his system helped to squelch the pain knifing through Peter's chest. He limped to the desk and put his hand on the computer. "You're a liar, Frank. It's still warm."

The pain in his chest caused Peter to flinch as he walked around the desk and sat down. Through his thin cotton hospital pants he could feel the warm seat.

Mazzetti stepped forward. "That's the last time you will ever sit in that seat, so enjoy it." Mazzetti smiled and strode out the door. Elizabeth moved to her husband's side.

"Frank, wait!" called Peter.

The man returned to the doorway. "It's 'Mr. Mazzetti' to you."

Elizabeth had heard enough. "I don't know what's going on here, but I don't like it. How dare you talk to my husband like that!"

"Your husband has been assembling information and maybe selling it to steal telephone service—big time. I knew we should have let him go, but Downes and Hendrick pleaded for clemency and this is what he does to them. He makes them look like fools! Ask him to show you," he added, looking in Peter's direction.

"He's a liar," grunted Peter, fighting back tears of pain as he accessed the private file. "He wants to destroy us so he can become president."

"I wouldn't stoop so low. Right now I'm golden up in D.C."

"But you won't be for long, because you have been intercepting E-mail messages from Earl and Mike and half a dozen others. I know, because I intercepted you. I have the phone logs to prove it."

"Not anymore you don't."

Peter ignored the comment. "That's why I came tonight. I knew that if security got this information, you'd go down. But if you got it first, we'd all go down. I may not like the way you do things, Frank, but I wasn't planning to use this against you. It was just some insurance."

"Well," Mazzetti smiled, pulling a computer disk from his pocket, "your policy's just been canceled. You're right about going down, though."

Elizabeth intervened, walking around the desk to approach Mazzetti. "Haven't you hurt us enough? Just go away and leave us alone. Peter's done nothing to you. Please go," she pleaded.

"Wait!" Peter gasped as he scrolled through the file. "You erased my intro. You took out my explanation of why I was gathering this information."

"It doesn't matter what's on there now. When security checks the printout on Monday, they'll see that you accessed the building tonight. Your key will be recorded once for the elevator and once for this office. Will anybody believe you didn't come to erase your love letters?"

"But Frank, how will you explain *your* access?"

Mazzetti pulled an electronic key from his pocket and grinned. "I won't have to. This is your key from Whitehead's father. You came here twice today. I was never here." He laughed aloud, slipped the key into the same pocket where he had deposited the disk, bowed gently and departed.

Elizabeth sprang like a cat and reached Mazzetti at the entrance to the public relations office. She grabbed the back of his jacket and, catching him by surprise, jerked him to the floor. Before he could respond, she plunged her hand into his jacket pocket and retrieved the key and computer disk. "*Everyone* will know we're here by the time I'm finished with you!" she yelled as he rolled her over onto the floor.

"The hell you will," he snarled, grabbing her wrist and yanking the key and disk from her hands. But then three fingernails dug into his face at his cheekbone and plowed channels to his chin. He screeched in pain and brought his right hand hard across Elizabeth's face. He leaped to his feet just as Peter limped to her side.

Mazzetti pushed open the glass doors and disappeared into a stairwell before anyone could reach him. Elizabeth was on her knees. Her cheek was bright red from the blow she had received.

Peter dropped to the floor next to her.

"I forgot I married a tiger," he said. Then, as the reality of their situation began to sink in, he started to weep. Tense with pain, he looked deep into his wife's face. "I'm sorry, Elizabeth. I thought I was doing something special, something that would let them see I care about this company. Something to maybe get a bonus to replace what I had lost . . . something for you and the kids."

She crawled to the man she loved. "You've already given us all we could have ever asked for." She put her arm around Peter and pulled him to her. "We thought you were dead, but God brought you back. He won't let us down," she said compassionately. "Not now, not ever."

"Take me home, Elizabeth," Peter said in a near whisper.

"No, I'd better take you back to the hospital."

"I know I should go back to the hospital," he said in earnest. "And yes, it hurts. But I want to go home."

Gritting his teeth against the pain, Peter stood up and limped back into his office. Elizabeth came to him and wrapped her arm around his waist.

"I liked this office," Peter said as he walked over to turn off the computer. His cracking voice triggered tears in Elizabeth's eyes. He slowly scanned the room, turned off the light and headed for the door. "I'm going to miss it."

"Maybe you won't have to," whispered Elizabeth, reaching out and taking her husband's hand.

*   *   *

Far from Virginia Bell's public relations office, far from the long loop of concrete that carries countless vehicles on a seemingly endless journey around the nation's capital, far from the stench, humiliation and despair of the Cancún jail, Debbie Steinbaugh was lost in her private world of pain. She began her trek across the nearly deserted airport toward the terminal exit. Two gates away from the one where the plane to Atlanta was loading its final passengers, she turned and walked past a vacant check-in counter, past rows of vacant seats, to the rain-streaked windows that overlooked the vast airfield. She stood with a fresh tissue to her eyes, waiting for the plane to taxi to the end of the runway and climb into the blackness of night.

Pulling her damp raincoat around her and wiping the tears from her eyes, Debbie was able to see the lights of the airfield clearly. White and blue and red, they sparkled on the wet tarmac like jewels on a black evening gown.

"Beautiful, isn't it?"

The voice was familiar, but she couldn't—wouldn't—look back, because she was sure that no one was there. Then the voice spoke again. "I do have promises to keep, but they tell me there will be another plane tomorrow."

When she turned around, Mike Downes allowed a weary smile to creep across his face. His suitcase was on the carpet by his side. He opened his arms. In the embrace that followed, their fatigue was forgotten.

Then, side by side, they walked past the idle guards at the security checkpoint, down the escalator, through the airport lobby and into the cold rain.

"Looks like a pretty dreary Easter," said Mike, breaking the silence.

"Dreary?" asked Debbie, stopping beneath a light in the parking lot. She looked up into Mike's face. "Not this Easter." Rain and tears had already made a mess of her makeup, and her wet hair hung in strings. She blinked away the water droplets that were collecting on her eyelashes. "You went looking for one lost sheep and found two." The rain could not wash away her radiance. "And for me, at least, you have made this the best Easter ever."

*   *   *

It was well past midnight when Peter and Elizabeth pulled into their driveway. Peter climbed out and hobbled up the walk, with his wife close behind.

Suddenly, the door swung open and the glow of five happy faces illuminated the night. Lauren burst into tears and reached out to hug her father. Remembering his injury, she stopped. But Peter, whose pain had miraculously subsided during the twenty-five-minute trip home, drew his daughter to him and let her lay her head on his arm.

"Daddy—oh, Daddy!" she cried.

Jonathan echoed her cry as he latched onto his father's leg. Peter leaned forward and drew Daniel's head toward him and kissed the shy boy's cheek.

Beyond Daniel stood David with Kristin in his arms. The teenager shifted the baby to his shoulder to free his right arm. Tears filled his eyes as he extended his hand to the man he longed to emulate someday.

"Welcome home, Dad," he said through trembling lips. "Welcome home."